The Martyrs, The Lovers

Catherine Gammon

55 FATHOMS PUBLISHING LLC
GIG HARBOR WA

Printed in the United States of America
10 9 8 7 6 5 4 3 2 1

First Edition, March, 2023

ISBN-10: 1-942797-33-3
ISBN-13: 978-1-942797-33-3

Cover design: Jess LaGreca, http://jesslagreca.com/

55 Fathoms Publishing LLC
6516 112th Street Ct
Gig Harbor WA 98332
55fathomspublishing@gmail.com

Also by Catherine Gammon

China Blue

Sorrow

Beauty and the Beast: Stories from the 1970s

Isabel Out of the Rain

For Jim and V

It is the innocence which constitutes the crime.

—James Baldwin, *The Fire Next Time*

The Martyrs, The Lovers

1. Like medieval lovers

Abba Poemen said of Abba John that he had prayed to God to take his passions away from him so that he might become free from care. In fact, Abba John went and told one of the elders this: "I find myself in peace, without an enemy," he said. And the elder said to him, "Then go and beseech God to stir up warfare within you so that you may regain the affliction and humility that you used to have, for it is by warfare that the soul makes progress." So he besought God and when warfare came, he no longer prayed that it might be taken away, but said, "Lord, give me the strength for the fight."

—from *The Sayings of the Desert Fathers*

Like medieval lovers, they ended up dead, side by side, their corpses rotting, undiscovered.

I understood it as a suicide, a shared action, shared despair—"ego despair," I said at first and several times throughout the day. I elaborated: not despair at the state of the world they had struggled so long and so hard to remake; if that had been the motive, they would have killed themselves in public, their deaths a statement, immolations. This suicide was private, secret, hidden—ashamed—it left not even a note.

This image I made of their deaths, their bodies, was wrong, but I didn't know it yet. The first news was too slight, too incomplete. In the early hours, a day, a night, this was how I saw them, decomposing lovers, Esmeralda and the hunchback, bones entwined. Her soulmate, she had called him—this man old enough to have been her father, this man who until the year he met her had lived his life in service to militaries she all her public life opposed. "My soulmate," she had written to me. "He is key to my political and personal reality for eleven years." This is the man who shot her, or so they said, still say, and then himself.

Like medieval lovers, they ended up dead, side by side, undiscovered. That was how I pictured them when J., on hearing the news, telephoned from New York. They had been dead three weeks, shot, their bodies decomposing.

Independently, on hearing that first, undetailed report, we had the same thought: they had committed suicide, had done it together; and in the separate moments before our thoughts found words, we each experienced a bodily shock, a muffled but palpable blow to the flesh.

She and I had not been friends. In our brief acquaintance the year before, we had disappointed one another—failed one another. But even in that brief acquaintance, she and the General with her had touched depths in J. and me that brought their decomposing bodies, an ocean and miles of land away, home to us both with physical force.

For the world she was a hero, even a saint.

She was a woman who attracted people, both as friends and as followers; she had many distant friends, of the kind who follow, and followers of the kind who love. She had other, more intimate friends, though none as intimate as the man who died with her, unless it was her grandmother, who cursed him at her grave. And she had enemies. She had spoken to me of enemies, of death threats. She no longer traveled alone, had not traveled alone for many years, always kept the General, her deathmate, at her side. I was with her in his absence only once, in the ladies room of a hotel restaurant in Washington DC, and in those few minutes, she, who at table had spoken without interruption for three hours, had nothing to say. He was more than her protector. Some of their friends refuse to believe that he could have killed her. I do not always believe it. Nor do I disbelieve. It is possible to imagine the truth of every explanation. All roads lead to that room, to their bodies, alone, undiscovered.

Still, the shootings did not take place as I first envisioned them; the bodies were not entwined, nor even lying chastely side by side: she (her body) alone on the bed, dressed, as if she had been asleep but only napping when shot in the head at close range; he (his body) in the hallway, outside the bedroom door.

I have read these facts, the official, public facts, but cannot picture the distances involved, cannot picture the positions of the bodies, the exact gestures caught in death. Or can, but cannot know. A room does come to mind: a distance, a bed, her body on it, curled on its side, her back to the door. (Is the door open or closed? I don't seem to know. Closed, I imagine. He shoots her, leaves her, closes the door. It is one explanation. The official explanation.) She is lying on top of the covers, the door closed and he outside it, just outside, fallen, crumpled to the floor.

Is this image accurate? Unlikely. I see an austere little bed: a blue and green and purple woven blanket, a plain white—or pale yellow?—pillowcase and sheet. The room is empty except for the bed, the walls pale yellow, off-white, cream, like the sheets; dark woodwork at the windows and doors, the floor dark wood, in the bedroom and outside it, where he has fallen. No carpet. In the room, perhaps, two pale, nubby woven rugs. A reading chair: wicker, with cushions? an overstuffed armchair? a Boston rocker? Maybe a table, a little table, for cups of tea and piles of papers and books, more piles of papers and books on the floor. (But what does this tell us, this inventory of the imagined contents of an imagined room?) Most of her books and papers are in her office overlooking the garden, and more in the living room, the dining room, even the kitchen, more in the basement, where they are archived, some indexed, too many still in boxes almost two years after her departure from the Bundestag.

Perhaps the reader knows who she is, was. Recognize her. It won't help. The real woman died. This isn't biography. The woman here is fiction, invention orbiting fact.

Like medieval lovers, they ended up dead, their corpses rotting. They lay there, alone, for three weeks. They were known internationally, had friends all over the world. Her grandmother was closer to her than a sister. His wife, his grown children (yes, they are part of her story), had never gone out of his life. Was it three weeks before they were missed? Or were they missed earlier, sooner, their colleagues and friends and relatives anxious, finally desperate to reach them, until at last the police opened the modest house where they had lived together for so many years— a modest house protected by a security system so reliable it stood as evidence that no third party could have reached them, no forced entry could have occurred, no murder from outside. They were sealed in before they died, untouchable, the modest little house impenetrable as a tomb.

Had the neighbors noticed? Not at all. The neighbors knew

the couple to be reclusive, unfriendly, maybe arrogant, even cold. It was a quiet residential neighborhood, lower-middle and working class, full of grandmothers and young families with children, *gemütlich* and conservative, uncomfortable with the aristocratic manners of the tall stoop-shouldered old gentleman, the intensity and passion of the woman—which even though you heard nothing you could see when you watched from your kitchen window as she walked with him into their little back garden from the car that only he drove, could see because you saw her hands, always in motion, her mouth, how fast she talked, her eyes, sunken and lined with dark circles that until you got used to them led you to worry that she couldn't be well; all the years she lived here beside you, you had never seen her without those dark circles, and because you had heard it on television and read it in magazines, and because when each of your children was a baby and you were awake with them in the night you had seen the upstairs lights on and her shadow against the curtains, you knew she was tireless, worked herself to exhaustion and kept on working. It was odd living next door to them, knowing they were famous. Maybe you wouldn't have expected them to be more outgoing, maybe if they had been famous for something other than what they were famous for, if they had been movie stars or athletes (and what would movie stars or famous athletes be doing living here next door to you?), but these two were famous for working for justice and peace, famous for their active compassion, you had heard her speak on TV. You would have thought people like that would be friendlier, would respond when you invited them in to see your new baby, the woman at least would listen if you wanted to tell her about your child's talent for painting or your mother's funeral or the latest problems on your husband's job. You'd have thought these two would care about the people around them. But they didn't, they kept to themselves. They came and went, and often they traveled, and if they were gone for weeks or longer nobody on the cul-de-sac missed them, no one knew or expected to know anything about them. And then they were dead, their corpses rotting.

Like medieval lovers, they had broken taboos. He was married, and old enough to have been her father. He lived in two cities, with his wife in Munich, with her in Bonn. Their relationship was a public fact. They didn't marry, he didn't divorce his wife, although as time went on his wife was left more and more behind. At first the tabloids treated their love as a scandal but soon enough it was old news. The papers liked to photograph them, especially her: she was beautiful, most of all back then, in the heat of battle and victory, in her prime. The international press liked her too: she was fluent in English, eloquent in either language, an inspirational speaker, all fire and zeal. It was NATO's projected deployment of Pershing II and cruise missiles in West Germany that brought the two of them together and established her international fame. He, a senior general in the Bundeswehr, left the army over these missiles: resigned in protest, retired, or forced out for objecting—I have read all versions and don't know the truth. Assume the most noble: he resigned in protest, refused his pension. But as soon as I write this I doubt. Let him have the pension. Therese, his wife, will need it. (I am changing a name here. Soon I will rename them also, the famous dead.) With his pension in hand, resigned, retired, forced out all come to the same thing. Pension in hand, he joins with other retired and pensioned senior NATO officers to protest the Pershing II deployment. These are his peace credentials when he meets her in 1980. His background is conventional. Like most German men of his generation he had served in Hitler's army: a young lieutenant home from the Russian front when he marries Therese at the end of the war. For a decade or so he works in publishing before returning to the army—the new army of the new reformed, democratic, de-Nazified West Germany. For almost a decade more he is a member of a right-wing Christian political party, until he resigns in protest over the extremity of its leader. Does he leave the right then—for the center perhaps, or for a studied political neutrality, good for an ascending military career? I don't know. Either way, his later break with the army when it comes is for him a radical move, and his meetings and working encounters with the young, beautiful Joan of Arc of the antinuclear movement—she needs a name now: call her Jutta Carroll—awaken and arouse him to a courageous activism that goes beyond the theorizing, educating, speech-making, and letter-writing that already consume so much of his time. Together they lead peace marches and sit-ins, get arrested, sit in and march again. In 1983, with twenty-five other members of the alternative political party she has helped to found, they are elected to the Bundestag: Jutta Carroll and General Lukas Grimm. When they arrive to take their seats, they and their twenty-five comrades in peace demonstrate the transformational significance of their election by carrying flowering tree branches into the stuffy parliamentary chamber.

Nine years later they are dead, she forty-four, he sixty-nine, their bodies undiscovered for nineteen days. They had still been living in Bonn, in the house they had shared since coming to parliament. The winter before they died they had installed a security system. For years she had traveled only with him. She had been threatened. He kept a gun, a model that held only two bullets, the gun that killed them. It is not true that they were sealed in. The upstairs balcony door was found unlocked. But because the Bonn police also found gunshot residue on the General's hands, and no signs of struggle, they drew their conclusions quickly and perhaps too quickly closed the case. When news stories appeared, then obituaries, then longer, more thoughtful tributes to Jutta Carroll's life and work, the accounts were contradictory, in small details and large. None of those stories reaches the truth, not of her death, not of her life.

This writing, too, will fail.

Here is her father, Gerd: a young soldier returned from Hitler's army, dark-haired, handsome. Jutta Carroll will have his sharp features, his intensely focused, charismatic eyes. The war over, he marries Johanna, who will be Jutta's mother, and becomes a journalist for a left-wing newspaper, two dangers Johanna (who after the alarms and deprivations of war craves safety, security, order) fails to notice, young and swept away. At first, probably, they are happy. We don't know for how long. Even in the photographs we can see that he is restless, a wanderer; Jutta, in her way, will not be unlike him. He has grown up a soldier, in a wartime state. He has passions now, ideals: shame and, to transcend it, rage. He marries Johanna. In 1947 the child is born. He wants to name her Rosa, after Rosa Luxemburg, but Johanna prevails: the Blessed Jutta of Diessenberg was a gatherer of holy women, the teacher of Saint Hildegard, who wrote on the Blessed Jutta's death, "This woman overflowed with the grace of God like a river fed by many streams." Johanna envisions her daughter a teacher, a delicate flower, but hardy, like the wild-flowers that grew everywhere from the rubble, in Köln and Berlin, in her husband's bombed-out Dresden, in her mother's Nürnberg and nearby Würzburg, where two months before surrender the bombs fell for twenty minutes destroying half of everything, and even here, in this sleepy southern market town. She permits Rosa for her Jutta's middle name, but only because Frieda, her mother, also admires Rosa Luxemburg, not as a Red but as a pacifist and a woman brave enough to have challenged the men who made war, the men who held power but also the men of her own party. Perhaps it is the sole occasion when Johanna's mother and Gerd see eye to eye. Frieda is forty-one when Jutta is born. The family is poor—most Germans are poor in these years—and together they are fortunate to share Frieda's tiny inherited house.

For Gerd the maddening irritations grow with Johanna's pregnancy and after the child is born: the lack of quiet for concentration, the lack of privacy for love, but he also must suffer Frieda herself, who speaks forthrightly, challenges him, does not allow him to be the man and master: alone since 1944, she has been running her little two-woman family too long to yield authority to him. And if that were all, but there's more: as Johanna's young body swells, as her face puffs out with pregnancy, as she tires and draws away from his touch, in the next room it is Frieda's body he sees. She is only forty-one, a widow, and alone too long. She is not an old woman. She is his mother-in-law, but not an old woman; in the Ukraine he made love to women older, and at night, beside a Johanna collapsed in fatigue, he lies awake sucking cigarettes, picturing Frieda's breasts in the swirling smoke.

When Jutta is born the pain increases. Johanna's breasts belong to the baby, and the baby never leaves their room. The women make a world that has no place for him. He drinks with other men, journalists and party men, stays out late, and in the morning when the baby cries he hits it. The first time he is ashamed—Johanna shocked, Jutta howling. Frieda stares at him without a word. He takes his hat and coat and leaves them. Days later he returns. Johanna forgives him. She offers Jutta to him to hold, tries to gentle him with his daughter as a plaything: *Feel her golden hair, how soft, how fine, see how sweet she is, how sweetly she smiles*. He surrenders. He desires her, Johanna, his wife. Frieda takes Jutta out for a walk in the winter air. She speaks to her son-in-law even less than before, in functional sentences only: *Pass the potatoes. Hang up your coat*. This home life is hell for him, and by the time summer comes it is only Jutta who smiles when he walks in the door. He hides in her, plays with her, and when he is out, with men, watches other women, looks for other women, a woman who will smile at him as Jutta smiles, a woman who will love him as his little Jutta loves, until the night comes when he finds her, that woman, and on arriving home hits Jutta again. Now he feels no shame, justifies himself: Jutta has been defiant, Jutta has disobeyed. When the women turn on him he takes his hat and walks out, goes to his lover, stays with her days, until he misses his daughter, wants a clean shirt. And so on.

This is the shape Jutta's father gives to her earliest childhood, but the details of his presence, the rhythms of his coming and going, are not what she will remember. Instead she remembers walks with her Oma, bouncing baby carriage walks and later, wild running walks in the cemetery forest and the town park woods— the walks, and days, weeks, of illness, nurses in white, antiseptic smells, hospital walls. For Jutta is frail. She lies in her bed and dreams. She knows stories, poems, visions of Nürnberg spun and woven by her Oma, who stays home with her during her illnesses while Johanna goes out to work. Gerd stays home with her, too, plays the piano for her and sings, sits with her on her bed in the evenings, her reward for pain, dependency, complaint: her father at her side, reading to her from science books and newspapers and telling her stories from the larger world. Her eyes grow big as she listens, her heart beats fast at the sound of his voice, the touch of his hand on her cheek and her hair. Get well, he tells her, get well for Papa, and when she's better he'll take her somewhere, on a boat up the river, to the movies or the zoo, or on the train all the way to Omi's Nürnberg to see the great rebuilding, how about that? And so she recovers and Papa begins to disappear again, not without keeping at least one promise, sometimes two, and then turning on her his rage, the back of his hand, the buckle of his belt. And is gone. Again and again.

In his absence the women mutter, secretly at first, as if Jutta asleep in her bed can't hear them, until she learns from them what she already knows: that her father, Gerd, is the enemy, that the anger he turns on her is not justified by her own behavior, that she is not a bad little girl, she has done nothing wrong, that they, her mother, her Oma, blame him, not Jutta, for the distress of their lives. Jutta lets them know she has understood, at five years

old gets up from her bed in the night to say *My Papa's a bad man.
Not Jutta is bad? Her Papa?* and after that they include her in their
conversations, stop whispering. Now Jutta has a new secret: she
loves her Papa anyway, loves it when he comes to her and reads
to her from the big world, loves it when he holds her hand, when
he sings for her, when he makes promises and she can't guess
which one will come true. Her illnesses linger, the lists of promises
grow, fill her body, her blood, bring heat back to her pale cheeks,
until she can stand it no longer, the dam breaks (she knows what
a dam is, Papa has shown her, and that's what she feels in her
heart, a raging river, a force against a wall, until the wall cracks
open and the water floods through), she gets well, recovers, awaits
her punishment and her reward. She is silent now when he beats
her. She has learned to be silent.

All this changes when Gerd suddenly leaves, for Hamburg he
says, leaves them totally and for good. Jutta is six years old.
Johanna cries, Omi is glad. Jutta knows herself triumphant: she
has driven him off, her will against his. When her sickness took
her into the hospital, when her body was alone in a room with
machines, when the doctors filled her stomach and head with a
leaden sleep unlike any sleep she had ever slept before, when
they cut into her flesh and left it stitched and scarred, these
tortures were the acts of magic her secret will submitted to in
order to invoke for herself the power to run her angry, unreliable
father away. She looks at her mother's tears without comprehension. She takes Omi's hand. Now Omi reads her the newspaper.
Now Omi teaches her dinosaurs and stars. With Papa gone she
will no longer feel the river raging in her body, the pressure under
the heart, will no longer have to guess the truth of anyone's
promises, pretend to be contrite for a badness she does not feel,
suffer the pain of beatings or the excitement that takes her all
out of her body, out of her life, that makes her bigger than
anyone or anything else she knows. With Papa gone her days are
calm, ordered: Mama goes out to work now, riding her bicycle to
the American base and back, while Jutta goes to the convent
school, and on Sundays they all stay home. After the bustling,
whispered mornings at school, lunch at home with Omi is
lingering and cheerful, and later Omi reads the news magazines

and helps her with her lessons, her Latin, her catechism, her lives of the saints.

She studies her Latin, her catechism, her lives of the saints. She lives in a world of women: later, she will make much of this, how living in a family without a patriarch nurtured her feminist spirit; others will see her father's absence as accounting for the series of stubbornly enduring sexual relationships she enters into with older, married men. At the time of her father's departure, she keeps both her sense of victory and her grief to herself. She becomes a model convent girl, gentle and shyly friendly with the other girls, obedient and serious in her studies. Her voice rings out in choral prayer and although the sisters instruct her to sing more softly, behind her back they remark the haunting beauty of her voice. She excels in all her studies, secular as well as sacred, but in her heart gives herself to the convent, tells herself she is a nun already. It is most of all the female saints who attract her, and not the sacrificed martyrs either: her heroine is Hildegard of Bingen, whose holy visions transformed her from an obscure cloistered nun into a writer of theology, medical lore, poetry, and music, and made her a prominent public figure in the religious politics of her day. Hildegard at seven or eight was taken from her family to live in a holy cell with the Blessed Jutta of Diessenberg, there to begin her studies and practice of cloistered faith; Jutta, already eight when she hears this story, selects and commits to memory fragments of Hildegard's songs, and begins to observe the holy hours, waking herself through the night for silent prayer. Secretly she reads from Hildegard's writings, making of them what she can, and at nine discovers that sadness is a vice, that among the purifying practices for its cure are fasting and flagellation. She experiments on herself; at home, alone in her room after dinner, getting ready for bed, to the sounds from downstairs of the radio and Mama's and Omi's voices, uses her bookstraps on her bare back, and in this act of self-punishment discovers her crime, deeper than sadness, the consequence of sadness: her wickedness in forcing her Papa out of the house. He was never the enemy. All along it was herself, she is—after all—

a bad little girl, a sickly, unhappy child, a dark cloud in her Papa's eye. She hits her body harder, her naked legs, her naked arms. She scratches her skin with her fingernails, careful to scratch only where nightgowns and convent blouses will cover the marks her nails leave: her stomach, her chest, her ribcage. Then she scrubs herself, her hands, dresses herself to say goodnight to Mama and Omi. Other nights, under the covers, awash in the sighing breath of the sleeping house, she gouges at the tender skin where her legs join the rest of her body, stopping only when she feels herself bleed. No one will see her damaged body. She bathes and dresses carefully, alone. She eats little at table, pretends to have no appetite, slips food from her plate to the napkin in her lap, to her pockets, so her plate will empty as if she has been eating. Her will is strong but her frailty undoes her: taken sick, she confesses to Omi what she has been thinking, doing, but not what it means in her heart. Omi is tender with her, tells her she is overzealous, calls on Jutta's favorite sisters to give her counsel; but when two by two they visit her in the hospital and read to her again and again from Saint Hildegard the same passage condemning excess mortification, which leads to bodily illness, thereby leaving unfinished the holy task of repentance, Jutta only pretends to listen, concentrates instead on creating for herself another penance, one they will not discover and steal from her with their gentleness and compassion.

All this self-imposed austerity will not later be discussed, or even willingly remembered. The public Jutta Carroll is a heroine of hope and affirmation, of resurrection for the planet and peace among all peoples: yes, she will speak of having felt called to the convent, of her early and powerful Catholic training and faith as the ground for her later, more expansive sense of the spiritual; but the heroic Jutta Carroll will never have harmed herself, and the nun this Jutta Carroll might have become cannot be medieval, self-absorbed, or self-abusing, can be envisioned and invoked only as overflowing with love and service to humanity, a Mother Teresa of a nun, because this nun, after all, this vision of herself from childhood, must live within her still, must be part of the Jutta Carroll the world imagines it knows. The child flagellant and penitent will have to be put behind, forgotten.

But not yet. For now, she goes only underground, and the energy and will it took to create her Jutta applies more fervently to her studies, theology and natural science, history and Latin, rhetoric and poetry, racing ahead of the other girls and lying awake extra hours mentally composing poems in a soaring Romantic style. She still means to become a nun, dreams of renouncing men and taking the son of God as husband and consoler, embraces Hildegard's sweetest lover, and dreaming of that sweet embrace, sings to herself Hildegard's antiphons for the Virgin Mary:

> *What a great miracle / that into woman's low body / the lord came. / God did this / and raised her humility above the world. / And what great happiness / that in this body now, evil / which flowed from woman, / woman now drives away, / and sweetens the air with virtue / and ornaments heaven, / she that before / rained confusion and shame / on the green earth.*

Her secret self-denials: she refuses liquids, hides her thirst; limits sleep, denies exhaustion. Later, she will claim that she developed her nocturnal working habits in high school, when, having come with her mother and her mother's new husband to the United States, each night after doing her daily homework, while her mother and stepfather and little American sister and brother slept, she studied another four hours to perfect her English. She will have forgotten that her insomnia goes farther back, back farther even than the convent, to the time when her Papa was still sometimes with her and she lay awake in bed listening for his turning of the door, his footsteps on the stairs—listened for him, and crawled out of the bed in her tiny closet of a room and met him before he disappeared into the room and bed he shared with her mother. She waited for him, she caught him, she whispered in his ear and put her arms around his neck and breathed in his smoke and whiskey smells. She kissed him and asked him to kiss her. Then she went back to bed and listened to him in the next room, listened to him taking off his shoes, listened to him sometimes waking her mother, listened sometimes to her mother's whispering, her anger or happiness, sometimes to her tears, listened to them breathing, listened until she heard her Papa snore. Only then did she fall asleep, and on the nights when he never came she seemed to lie awake forever watching the darkness change slowly to day, until she had come to love a certain hour of the night, the hour when everything went lit as if from inside, etched and silent and gray. This was the hour she sought when she woke herself for prayers, the hour she sought, during penances and fasting, for enumerating her vices and inventing new ways to deny her hunger secretly and secretly to torment her flesh, the hour she sought during illnesses when she stared at the ceiling and counted the shadows and held her eyes open without blinking until they burned, the hour of silence, the hour of emptiness and devastation, the hour when she was alone and all things including her body were one and flattened, lifeless, the living, the dead, the absent and present, her father, her mother, her Oma, herself: the universe erased, a chalkboard at the end of the school day, when all the children have gone.

Here she is at eleven: she lives in a world of women. She excels in school. Her uncertain health excludes her from sports. She doesn't mind not playing sports, but feels in her body a strength, a wild and restless energy that won't be channeled into quiet games or choral singing or mental work. Secretly she recites Hildegard's Song of the Virgins—*We are in the world and you in our minds, and as if you stood beside us, we embrace you in our hearts . . . oh sweetest husband, who saved us from the jaws of the devil, our first mother's seducer*—and more and more, on holidays and weekends, she walks, leaves the town park for the cemetery forest, where she is freer to turn herself loose, to run, even to cry out, to test her lungs: to shout, in Latin, prayers or speeches, to invest the words with magic, invocation, to project into her voice a power greater than that of her tiny flesh. She runs, full of the sweet heat of the clover growing in the rolling grass. Her mother is seeing the American now, soon will marry him: Bob Carroll. He wears a uniform, a lieutenant-colonel. Jutta runs, enters the forest, runs deeper in, the path narrowing, the dappled light darkening. She knows this path, runs it every day she spends at home, her feet know it, her eyes know it, her body. She is safer here than anywhere, here she is always alone, here is where she raises her voice, cries words for the noise they make only. But today she shouts and no sound comes, the breath dies in her throat, her chest knots. She stops running. She listens, hears only the rapid beating of her heart, then, again, the songs and cries of birds, underbrush and leaves rustling with skittering voles and squirrels. She tries her voice once more. Her heart beats fast, in fear now. Her palms sweat, in fear. Her arms go cold, her chest. The darkness encloses her, the birds' cries, the raucous trees and weeds. She digs her nails into her palms. She forces breath into her chest, sound into her throat. But no sound comes. Only tears, streaming. Tears! She's angry, outraged. Tears from her eyes and no sound, no words. She looks at the palms of her hands where her nails have been digging, stretches her fingers, rubs her raw hands together, making them sting. She turns back toward the light, back the way she's come. A snake crosses her path, black and winding slowly over the earth. She stops, it stops. They eye one another as she edges her way around it, and before she runs again she catches sight of little darting redbirds high in the trees, at her feet a pale wildflower-winged tiny purple butterfly, up ahead half-hiding in the sunlight-dappled leaves a fat man. She knows this fat man. She runs, is already running, in his direction, past him, runs, keeps running. This fat man is not an ordinary fat man, he is a very fat man, and a mean fat man, a man so fat and mean he seems never to move, sits on his step all day in summer leering, wearing an undershirt and suspenders, looking whiskery and unwashed, talking familiarly to all the people who walk past, no matter what their age or station, whether he knows them or not. In winter he disappears, but each year when the first warm days come Jutta dreads him, dreads passing him around the corner from her Oma's where he sits on his stoop as if waiting for her, where he watches, his whiskery toad-face drooling as she passes him by. Now she runs, passes him without looking, tells herself he can't be here, in the forest, knows he's a vision, an ogre, a troll. The Elf King, a demon, made up in her mind. She runs, keeps running, no longer afraid, something other eating her heart.

By the time she gets home, by the time this afternoon has become a story, a memory, she will have seen the snake, then the Elf King, as she entered the forest; her panic will follow from seeing him, her ugly fat man, hiding there among the leaves. She will no longer remember that this is not the sequence of events, will no longer remember that the fear that assailed her came from inside, not from the world, will no longer remember the silence and darkness that rose from her own body, or what she saw in that silence and darkness, or what she felt. She will have put a face on those feelings, that silence, the face of the whiskery man. She will suddenly no longer be shy in the presence of Bob Carroll. She will suddenly no longer refuse to think about life with him as her father, life in a family with a father in it. She has turned away from her fear and given it a nameable face: a face she will be happy to leave behind now, a face Bob Carroll will help her leave behind when he marries her mother and moves his bride and her daughter to a large apartment near the American base, where her mother will no longer have to work, taking them away from Omi's little house after so many years—lonely, luxurious for one, Omi will say, already planning to leave it, to return at last to Nürnberg—and Jutta will ask Bob Carroll to tell her what life will be like in America, where sooner or later she knows they will go. She will embrace Bob Carroll now, for taking her away from the little house on the backside of the marketplace of her dead and unknown grandfather's little town, away from the fat man on his stoop, from the sudden cold darkness in the summer forest and the memory of her father that almost caught up with her there, his belt buckle hard on her naked skin.

Here she is at twelve, arriving in America: Jutta, her mother, Bob Carroll, and Emma, her new baby sister. Jutta calls Bob Carroll Dad now, and when speaking of him "the Colonel," an expression she learned back in Bavaria when the young American soldiers came by the apartment or called on the phone. Jutta liked the young soldiers, liked how they spoke to her and helped her with her English and told her she was a pretty girl. She began to see that they were boys themselves, not very much older than she was. She had never known boys before these soldiers and the boys in her sixth grade class at the American dependents school, where the Colonel had enrolled her to work on her English. She was timid and shy in the school, but forced herself to practice with the soldier boys until she almost enjoyed it, smiling and speaking in English, because the Colonel had already told her that in America she would live in a house on an army base with him and her mother and Emma and from now on she would go to school with boys as well as with girls. So Jutta practiced, with the young soldiers back at the apartment and with strangers on the ship, and asked the young men to tell her about going to school in America, about what it would be like always to be in school with boys, asked them what she would study and how she could write poetry when she still could hardly speak English, and every one of them said the same things: Smile, your English is cute, you're smart, too, but don't scare the boys, you'll be a popular girl for sure, go out for cheerleading and you'll have the best dates in the world.

Jutta laughs when they say all this. She doesn't plan to go on any dates, the boys at the school were rough and silly, and besides she plans to become a nun. But the first soldier boy she said this to told her to keep it to herself. Why? she asked him. That kind of talk will scare people, he told her. Why? she asked. In America, he said, girls don't become nuns. There are no nuns in America? she asked. He shrugged. Sure, he said, but they're old. Girls want to play and have fun.

Jutta thought about this and for a while kept her calling a secret, and when she spoke of it again, the response came back the same. Even her mother and the Colonel seemed to think she should let her vocation go: That was your childhood, honey, the Colonel said. You don't want to decide anything so soon.

She leans hard against the metal rail, watching the gray ocean and the clouds. The baby has been cranky since the ship's departure, and the Colonel stays in the cabin close to her mother, holding her shoulders while Jutta roams. She stops and talks with strangers, and sometimes she thinks they talk about her too: watch her striding up and down the decks on her short skinny legs and say things to one another they don't mean for her to hear. She smiles at them and they smile at her, and then, she thinks, they exchange their secret words.

Soon, she will understand these glances, these secrets. She is aiming her face at the wind, watching the sky. She already knows she must become braver. She is not a little girl anymore. Her Omi can't protect her. She is arriving in America.

A possible death: she has agreed to die. She has thought every-thing through. Lukas is writing his letters. He has no idea what she is thinking at this moment. But when she gets up from the chair where she's brooding and walks over and interrupts him to say, "Stop now, it's time," he will stand and hold her and know her meaning. He will obey. She will leave his arms and climb the stairs. She will lie down and wait. She will grow impatient, waiting, the time stretching as if forever, her thoughts uncontrolled and unfo-cused, ranging, until she forgets that he is putting the two bullets into the gun, that he is climbing the stairs, that he will enter the bedroom quietly and put the gun to her head. They will have discussed this. They will have discussed it for months, maybe years. Secretly, somewhere, they will have known this always. Only recently will they have spoken of details, only recently made their plan, their vow. The time is coming. The time is now. But still she doesn't hear him, doesn't feel his body enter the room. She waits in the semidarkness. She strokes her hand across the soft nubby surface of the bedcover. She looks at her hand, tiny and pale, almost blue. She asks what she has given her life for, not this life she is lying here waiting to leave, but the life of her living years. She has thought everything through but her mind goes on thinking, repeating. She finds herself in a hospital, again and again. She is five, six, nine, eleven, thirteen, twenty, twenty-seven, thirty-two. The hospitals never end, they grow and darken, they thicken, they choke her. Emma dies. Jutta is in and out of hospitals always, but it's Emma who dies and takes with her the world. Why? The world is a hospital, run by poisons and rules. There is no escape. The pain in Jutta's body drives her back in. This pain the doctors can't cure. She fights it with every weapon she knows, but light fades, the world grows darker, her vision dims, the circles under her eyes deepen: outside it is night. Where is Lukas? He should be here with the gun. Has he not heard me? Not understood? We have agreed to this. We have already agreed. We offer no explanations. We die from love and grief. Any single explanation will erase all others. The world is its own explanation, the far and the near. Every detail contributes. Let everyone know this guilt. Let no one off. No one is innocent. Everybody knew.

No one in Germany had taught her this—not even her Papa, not even her Oma. In her hands she is holding a magazine, full of pictures: piles of fleshless naked bodies, piles of shoes and hair; standing behind barbed wire, human skeletons hung with skin, maybe men, maybe women, looking out through living eyes. In Germany no one had spoken of this. Railroad tracks, railroad cars packed with men and women and children, piles of dead babies, the sign over the gateway: ARBEIT MACHT FREI. No one had told her this about her people, about her Mama, her Papa, her Oma. No one had spoken.

The American boy, Jimmy Wolf, stands beside her, watching her face. He is a handsome, dark-haired boy, with very dark eyes. "Don't say you didn't know," he says.

"I didn't know," she says.

He laughs, as if he would cry. "Nobody in Germany knows," he said. "Nobody in Germany ever knew." He takes the magazine from her, as if to walk away.

"Wait," she says.

"For what? More lies?"

"Please," she says.

She takes the magazine home to her mother. Her mother sighs. "We didn't know," she says. "Not really."

"But a little," says Jutta, and walks away.

In America, fat white men in uniforms arrest black college students, boys and girls, men and women, for sitting at lunch counters to eat. Jutta lives in Georgia on an army base with the Colonel her stepfather and Emma her sister and their enormous, pregnant mother. She has seen black Americans on the army base. They work as mechanics and nurses, maids and janitors and gardeners and cooks. All the students in her school are white. All the teachers are white. All the officers and wives who come to the Colonel's house as guests are white. In town many people are black. On the base many of the soldiers are black. They have always been black, but back in Germany she never thought about their blackness. She had not seen fat white Americans in uniform arrest them for the color of their skin. She had not understood that blackness in America was different from whiteness. She asks the Colonel to explain this and when he does she shows him the pictures in Jimmy Wolf's magazine, Europe's murdered Jews. She asks, "Is this what it means?" Of course not, the Colonel says, and talks to her about American democracy, which she is studying now in school. But her school is white and her teachers are white and when the Colonel finishes she asks him again, "Like this? Not like this?"

A silence surrounds her then, and her life is newly divided: the new life as divided as the old. What she least understands is why no one told her, and still won't tell. Adolf Eichmann has been arrested to stand trial in Jerusalem, and she has to read the truth in books and magazines she borrows from Jimmy Wolf. She reads the newspaper too every day now, not the Fort Benning newspaper, not the Columbus or the Macon or the Atlanta newspaper either, but *The New York Times*, which comes days late in the mail to Jimmy Wolf's house and which he gives her after everyone there has read it. He tells her that his parents are Russians, Russian Jews. They were born in New York. "Then they're Americans," Jutta says. "I am also an American now. I am not a German anymore. I will never be German again."

Everybody knew. This thought is hard to hold on to. At night, to study her English, she reads *The New York Times* and books and articles in magazines about the German effort to annihilate Europe's Jews. Everybody knew. Jews had been rounded up in Nürnberg, where Omi lived, and even in Jutta's little hometown. In 1942 rumors of death camps were so widespread that the government issued an explanation: the permanent security of the German people called for ruthless severity; therefore Germany's Jews were being sent to labor camps in the East. But death camp rumors persisted, and German Nazis and Germans who worked for Nazis and obeyed Nazis continued killing German Jews: shot them in Kaunas, Riga, and Minsk, slaved and starved them to death or gassed them in Poland, at Auschwitz, Kulmhof, Sobibor, Treblinka, Lublin/Majdanek, and Belzec.

It is impossible to grasp. In one year, in 1942, 2,700,000 Jews from all over Europe killed. Hundreds from Jutta's own town: from the town where the sisters who had educated her prayed to God every day and night. How was this possible? From her own town: and suddenly, briefly, she sees the face of the fat man. She shakes her head. The fat man is not the truth. She sees the photograph of her father in his uniform, the photograph her mother used to keep beside her bed. She sees young black Americans marching in the streets. She writes a letter to her Oma, begs her to tell, writes through the night, her letter long and passionate, calls on God and Saint Hildegard, calls on her Oma's love, begs on behalf of her baby sister and the brother her mother has just given birth to, on behalf of the black Americans getting arrested for their rights, begs in the name of Martin Luther King, Jr., their spiritual leader, and John F. Kennedy, the young candidate for president, whose photograph she encloses, insists in memory of sixty-nine black South Africans shot dead in Sharpeville, insists in memory of six million murdered Jews.

Her Oma replies: Yes. We knew. We knew by rumor but we couldn't prove it. We knew but we could not stop it. It had gone too far. We had no voice. We were powerless. I can tell you the story of one brave priest. In Berlin he prayed openly for the Jews and was denounced. He begged to go to the Jews in the East, but a special court sentenced him to two years in prison. After he had served his time the Gestapo arrested him. He died on the way to Dachau. Gerd, your father, was ten years old when Hitler came to power. He was not a Nazi, just a soldier in the war. He fought on the Russian front. He was young. A little older than your mother, but still very young. The children grew up under Hitler, fed on hatred and lies. There was no possibility of resistance of the kind you describe. One supported the regime or one kept quiet. One could not speak freely even at one's own table. Children denounced their parents. No one could be trusted. No one. It is impossible to organize resistance in such a climate. These will sound like excuses to you, dear Jutta. And maybe they are. Every act of resistance I ever heard of failed: individual, romantic, doomed. Sometimes there were rumors. Your mother was a child when Hitler marched into Poland, younger than you are today, and I was not brave. Very few of us were brave. In Nürnberg the Nazis were very strong. My in-laws all supported the party. Fritz, your grandfather, worked with the railroad managing the movement of war materiel. He was drafted only toward the end, and eight months later he died. The Allied bombs devastated the city, and every day I went out with the other women to clear the streets of rubble, brick by brick. By then I had sent Johanna away to live in the safety of a country school, but when our building was bombed to nothing I left the city to get her and we moved into the little old house where Fritz had grown up in your own familiar town. And once or twice, my little Jutta, the bombs fell even there. What men have done to this green earth! My dear, my little love, let go of this brooding over a past that you were never part of, involve yourself in your new life, in your good new home, in your darling sister and new baby brother. You are too young to let these old-world demons swallow you up.

But Jutta could never deny the demons, not then, not now. She wrote back to her Oma, using English here and there when she lacked the German word:

In my school, they make nicknames for two boys whose names are Bill: Bill Adams and Bill Bowers. We call them A-bomb and B-bomb. I didn't understand these nicknames until we had an air raid drill. All over the United States, in every city and town, everyone practices for surprise attack. I understand those boys' names now. We practice bomb drills. We file into hallways and get down on the floor, our eyes shut tight and our faces buried in one arm to protect ourselves from blindness, the other arm wrapped around the backs of our heads. We were shown a movie of atomic clouds and atomic destruction and how to build a bomb shelter and stock it and protect it from assaults by our neighbors, the same way we are shown movies about menstruation and marijuana. We are shown movies about everything the grownups don't know how to talk to us about, and we understand these movies in exactly that way, as representations of taboos, although most of my classmates don't know how to say this, and for me, my English isn't yet good enough. To one another we indicate by secrecy and giggling our understanding that these are the terrors of the adult world, terrors not even the adults can face or name. These terrors and taboos are far removed from our experience. The one taboo these children, my friends, know in their flesh forbids them to mix with blacks. For me, this taboo has no meaning or force, but the other taboo lives, is alive, this silence about bombs and war. What I remember is images of rubble, and the feel of the fear inside peace. I know those bomb clouds are beautiful, I know men must desire them, the same way the Germans desired the elimination of the Jews. I don't need the adults to tell me. But I believe, my dear, dear Omi, in spite of everything, that it is possible to make a change. Here I see it. It is possible to gather together, in spite of fears and taboos, to resist together. No more Hitlers, dear Omi, no more Nazis, no more lynchings, no more daily obedience, no more quiet standing by. Here I see heroes—living heroes, not medieval dead ones, heroes every one of us can be.

This possible death: she lies, she waits. Time has come full circle. She has resisted all she can resist. She has had her victories. Her words have been spoken unsilenced. Her words have been heard. She has inspired millions. All for nothing now: the demons have returned to Germany. She has prepared herself to fight them, to do further battle. With her one kidney and fragile health, she has always feared an early death. She can't afford to slow down. But she is tired, and worse than tired (she has been tired before), without hope. Lukas and she together have become hopeless, an inch at a time. Attacks on Turks and Arabs and Africans and Asians are increasing all over Germany. When Sonam Pasang was beaten in an alley, his pain assailed her body as if she herself had taken the blows. Handsome Sonam Pasang, her Tibetan brother. She had found hope in him for a while. But his hope could not sustain her. The erotic had no more hold on her, no longer came to life in her body. Lukas was fading, and she was fading with him. Without him, she knows, she cannot go on. So many years later, she knows at last why sadness is a sin. She has suffered sadness all her life without understanding. But in these moments, waiting for Lukas to climb the stairs, she sees her own paralysis, the paralysis she struggled against even in childhood. In these last moments, she surrenders that struggle as a mistake: if she had given in to paralysis, let it have its way with her, allowed the demons to win...what warm, luxurious life then, what a bath of sleepy tears, what gentle sorrow—hopelessness, how familiar!— it was home, it was sweet hot bread and fresh ground coffee and Omi's lap and breasts and warm arms wrapped around her tiny body.

Outside now the demons are quiet, the doors locked against them. She invites them in: gets up, walks to the back of the house, to her office, opens the balcony, whispers *Come* to the darkness, the night. She despairs of Lukas. He has changed his mind, lost heart, will not climb the stairs to kill her. If she broods any longer she too risks changing her mind. She goes back to bed, pulls the covers up over her shoulder, turns her face to the wall, instructing herself: No energy and no desire. Nothing left but to sleep.

Her Oma's reply:
During that terrible time I did perhaps one brave thing. For many years the SA and SS had been harassing the German Jews, forcing them through violence and economic pressures to emigrate. When the war came and as it deepened they hardened the policy and deported the Jews from Germany to camps, as they had deported the Jews from the annexed and conquered lands. Publicly they said they were merely labor camps, for state security—as if this were not injustice enough. The roundups began in every town. Perhaps then I did a brave thing. Early one morning,

as soon as Fritz had left for work, a woman came to my door, a neighbor I knew only slightly, by sight, to nod hello to for many years. She begged me to take her in, just for that day, and I did. They were coming for her that day, a friend had warned her. We drank tea together and told one another about our husbands, our children. Everyone in her family had already gone or been taken. She was missed only by accident. I watched from behind the curtain as the SS van drove up and stopped outside her building. She refused to look, preferred to sit at the table, her back to me. When night fell, just before Fritz would return, I gave this woman a little money and food and she disappeared. I don't know why she risked coming to me. But then, I think, she had nothing to lose. Maybe I was the only one on the street who had continued greeting her after her family disappeared. Or maybe she chose me because she knew I was alone. Still, I think how many times she must have seen your mother in her black neckerchief, marching in the youth parades and singing Nazi songs. Maybe she knew the Hitler girls were all away in the mountains that week, knapsacking for the Führer. Do not blame your mother, Jutta—she was thirteen, fourteen—so many of the children belonged, what did they know? At first I tried to stop it, but Fritz prevented me, out of worry for his war job. Maybe I was braver than he was. Later I sent her to the country. We had to get through it, any way we could. Do not underestimate the power of daily life. You admire and sympathize with the leaders of this movement for black civil rights in America, and so you should. But remember where you live, who your friends are, who goes to your school, to your church. Everyone you know is white, and you are white too. Do you think your moral sympathy makes you innocent? What?— you say you are powerless? Have you joined the marches? Your mother, your stepfather wouldn't allow it if you asked? You are too young? And the blacks who march—are they not as young as you? I do not write this to criticize or shame you, Jutta, certainly not to weaken your enthusiasm for great ideals. I ask you only to face more squarely the realities you imagine you are resolved to challenge and to ask yourself how serious you really are—for now and for the future. And even then I caution you to wait (reminding myself, as I remind you, that you are still a child) and not to judge the rest of us for our weakness. You have not yet earned the right.

Here she is at thirteen: the convent behind her, Germany behind her, an American girl now, who sits up half the night writing poems and working to improve her English. Pinned to her bedroom bulletin boards, photographs from newspapers and *Life* and *Time*: John Kennedy before his election, campaigning in West Virginia, squatting on the ground, surrounded by coal-blackened miners, grinning in his suit and tie. Martin Luther King, arm in arm with students demonstrating in Atlanta. Eichmann on trial in Jerusalem behind his bullet-proof wall of glass. The first Freedom Rider bus, on fire outside Anniston, Alabama. Kennedy addressing a crowd that reaches to the horizon, alone against a stormy sky. Also, huge closeups of brilliant flowers and quotations from her new heroes, lettered carefully in heavy black ink.

In school she twirls baton and sings in the chorus, joins Future Nurses of America, and learns to dance with her left hand on her partner's shoulder, her right hand in his hand. She flirts with Bill Adams and Bill Bowers, but with Jimmy Wolf her friendship is too serious for flirtation, too full of grownup shadows. He is the handsomest boy in school and always has a girlfriend, but never a girl he talks to or cares about the way he talks to and cares about her. Jutta's girlfriends from baton team and Future Nurses and honors English all admire her, and she's a popular girl, with busy weekends, at the heart of a popular crowd, but at home, when she lies in the grass out behind the house with Emma climbing all over her and stares up at breezy silver beech leaves and clouds and the sky, Jimmy Wolf's is the name she daydreams and his the face she sees. She daydreams in English now, a groping English made of movies and television and newspapers and popular love songs and greeting cards and school talk and classroom talk and dictionary translations from German and the great works of American and English literature. She lies in the grass bouncing Emma on her raised-up knees, Emma laughing and clutching her fingers, Jutta imagining the touch of Jim Wolf's hand in her hand. She sees his eyes inside her eyes, his face in the sky. She feels his lips on her lips, on her cheek, on her neck. Blushing when these sensations come over her, she invents contexts, tells herself heroic stories in which such gestures might occur: they are riding a freedom bus, stopped on the highway, surrounded by an angry mob and guarded by troops who are not on their side, when Jim Wolf touches her face and together they whisper a prayer for victory. Policemen come to arrest them for sitting with their black brothers and sisters in a segregated Greyhound waiting room when Jim Wolf breaks free of their grip to kiss her good-bye. Camped out in a bus depot, uncertainly waiting for violence, safe passage, or arrest, they lie together stretched out close, body to body through the night. Sometimes the setting changes, the cause, the enemy: in Berlin working against the communists, Jim Wolf is captured, she helps him escape. Sometimes she dreams pure romance: on a stormy beach, when he begs her to marry him, she declines, committed to the convent, but on the eve of taking her vows, leaves it for service in the world, yearning to find him, until at last he arrives at her door. The theme from the movie *A Summer Place*, the number one hit song from the year before, repeats relentlessly in her ears. Her dreaminess annoys her. It steals over her when she plays with Emma. Otherwise she's moving too fast, doing too much, to have time or space for sentimental fantasy. She is studying American government, American history, American law. She is studying biology, plant life. She is painting, writing poetry, singing in glee club and chorus, translating a song of Saint Hildegard's into English to share with her Sunday school class, still a good Catholic girl. When she thinks of Jim Wolf in church she blushes. She imagines him sitting beside her, taking her hand. She imagines him whispering in her ear, tempting her with alien knowledge. On the lawn in back of the house she watches clouds drift across the sky and wills herself to see the silver beech as moving, the clouds as fixed, until she feels in her body the sensation of motion, as if she and the silver beech and Emma were on a ship, crossing the ocean, sailing away.

Then in Berlin the communists stop traffic at the Brandenburg Gate and under cover of night barricade open streets, lock elevated train and subway gates, post guards in U-bahn tunnels, and begin to construct a wall that cuts through the heart of the city. Kennedy sends more troops and Lyndon Johnson with them as East German soldiers erect concrete block and barbed wire and all along the boundary board-over and brick-in doors and windows that open on the West. The wall rises higher. Kennedy and Khrushchev trade threats.

Jutta cuts out a new picture from *Life*: a little blond girl knocking at the door of the house where her friend lives, a house that is now, on its West Berlin side, bricked up, sealed closed. This picture pains her. For the rest of her life this picture will pain her, whenever it comes to her mind: this child, no more than four, knocking at a house that for her stays empty forever. Twenty-eight years later, when the Wall falls, Jutta will wonder about that little girl: where she spends those days, those nights, how she is celebrating, what her hopes are, her dreams, whether she even remembers that door, that fruitless knocking, the friend who lived on the other side.

In 1989 the Wall fell. In 1990 the two Germanys were reunited. Jutta Carroll opposed this. Her party opposed it. But the Germans voted overwhelmingly to reunify and Jutta Carroll and her party were voted out of office.

Jutta had feared this reunification. She had opposed it on principle, and she had also feared it. The East Germans had made their own revolution and their own peace. Over the forty-five years of separation they had developed their own history, their own aspirations for a new society. Jutta had worked with the dissidents of the eastern regime. They had been her very close friends, her colleagues. With Lukas she had helped them in many things, large and small. This reunification, this acquisition of the new free East Germany by the old West, betrayed them—those who had worked under desperate conditions for a third way, a free society not based on the capitalist market and war state, or on the communist war state either, but on principles of peace and justice and ecological sanity for all.

And beyond these issues of principle, Jutta had simply been afraid—afraid of the Germans unrestrained by external forces, unlimited by duality, reborn into chilling nationhood. *Wir sind wieder da!* had been the celebratory cry. And who, exactly, did the celebrants mean? In 1991 neo-Nazis observed the first anniversary of reunification by setting fire to asylum homes and stabbing and beating guestworkers and refugees, foreign students and tourists, and as the second anniversary approached, every day one read of new assaults. In Frankfurt on the Oder, when the German-Polish border was first opened for travel, gangs of neo-Nazi youth stoned visiting Poles. In Dresden skinheads threw a Mozambican off a moving streetcar and when he died armed themselves with knives, pellet guns, and baseball bats to confront his memorial march with shouts of *Foreigners out!* and *Sieg Heil.* In Schwerin right-wing gangs threatened Vietnamese street peddlers. In Berlin they beat up Turks in back alleys, and gay blond Germans and gay black American men. In Hoyerswerda they teargassed a group of leftist rock musicians. Also in Hoyerswerda, for six days and nights, as crowds of law-abiding Germans stood by cheering, they (and who are this "they," these rowdy boys, doing what the rest can only applaud?) threw stones and Molotov cocktails into shelters housing guestworkers and refugees from Mozambique and Vietnam, and when the government brought in a convoy of buses to transport the foreign workers and asylum seekers to safety, the gangs attacked the buses while the crowd cheered them on. In Wittenberge neo-Nazis broke into a hostel for Namibians and threw two men out the windows. In Rostock they firebombed refugee housing. In Hannover they beat up Sonam Pasang.

All these events proved that she had been right to fear the Germans, and still was right.

And the violence was not all. As bad as the violence, and for the future more chilling, was the political support that fed it and kept it alive. Lukas, too, was afraid. He remembered the old Germany, the Germany in which Hitler had risen to power. He had been a child, then a student, a member of the Hitler Youth, a soldier. He too had been shamed by the revelations at the end of the war: shamed as a German and as a man, he told her. Together they had dedicated themselves to resist the contemporary return of the forces of hatred. But they were tired. She understood why Lukas was tired: he was not young, he knew the past, had lived through it all before, had given so much already, only to find now, as they awakened to this historical moment—which should have been the true celebration, a moment begun as an astonishing victory for forces they themselves for many years, not only in Germany but throughout the eastern bloc, had helped to nourish by raising their voices in criticism of both the capitalist West and the communist East, at painful personal cost (for they, who had defied NATO, camped out at US military bases and missile sites, and been arrested in the West countless times, had also, in supporting the dissidents of the East, and for their open criticism of the communist states, been called pawns of the US, agents of NATO and the CIA), theirs the leading West German voices to call for a third way, neither capitalist nor communist, neither right nor left, neither West nor East—at times even, at odds with the party which Jutta herself had helped to found, the only voices, insisting on maintaining a position of high principle—and in acting on principle they had been correct: this collapse of the East, this peaceful revolution from below, had proved them correct, this was what they had worked for in their own Germany and everywhere, what they continued to work for, only to find now, as they come into the dawn of this new world, that they are again, or still, trapped in the old nightmare. To resist the nightmare had to be their highest priority. But Lukas was tired. This victory was not a victory. Half their colleagues in the East turned out to have been agents of the Stasi, two of them Jutta's close friends. Lukas was tired. And so was she.

This possible death: skinheads had beaten Sonam Pasang, in an alley not far from his home. When she heard of the beating, she felt the blows. With Lukas she rushed to Hannover, to the hospital, where Sonam was recovering. He took their hands and spoke to them bravely. He made an effort to be cheerful. But a light had gone out of his eyes. Not for good, Jutta told herself, but in that moment, and in that moment, the light gone from his deep black eyes, she seemed to know just what each of them was. Exhaustion welled up in her, sorrow, and shame. Sonam must have known this emptiness also. Not long after, he broke everything off with her, and she collapsed and recovered and never stopped working, and even now, a year later, cries until her head explodes. She sleeps so deeply that when Lukas wakes her she is still asleep and doesn't know him, his face in her face, his face coming out of a dream, his face someone else's face and suddenly his, so close to hers, alarmed. She cries out his name and grips his hand. Her head explodes.

This possible death.

Or this:

When John Kennedy was shot in Dallas she felt a chill. Not on hearing the news, not on watching the images played and replayed on television. Before that. The instant the gun was fired, the instant the bullet hit home. She felt a chill. It ran up her spine into her shoulders and up her neck into her hair. She looked at the clock. She was five days shy of sixteen, her parents had planned an early birthday party for Saturday night, and suddenly, sitting in class, before anyone in school had word of the Dallas gunshots, she knew her party would be a wake. Only an instant passed before she brought her attention back to the teacher, but her body was trembling and she raised her hand and asked to be excused. It would be an hour or more before the news came over the school's public address system, an hour before she understood what was shaking her. During the waiting time she held herself in suspense, her thoughts empty of everything but the chill that had crawled up her spine and through her flesh. She sat on a toilet in the girls' bathroom and pressed each trembling hand against a cold beige wall. She told herself to go to the nurse, to ask to be sent home, she was probably sick, but she knew sick, was used to sick, and this wasn't it. Someone was dead or dying and she was hiding and she was ashamed. This was what she knew, though not yet with words. What she knew was without words: was darkness in her vision and chill in her flesh. This death would be hers. This bullet would be hers. She would shed tears later, mourning, one among millions at last, her earlier ungrieved innocence lost, now theirs, everyone's, made American finally in common grief and shock.

And underneath that shared grieving she will hide this secret knowledge of her own secret fate.

Alone, on her knees on the floor of the toilet stall, pressing her head against the seat, her weight into her hands on cold tile, with closed eyes she sees angels, tiny rings of golden light; demons, swastikas, red, black on white; green—a great green ball exploding out of darkness, shooting green stars. Darkness falls, the chill returns, the familiar pain in her body, and the unfamiliar knowledge: this death is hers. The word *death* is missing still, but not for long. Out in the world beyond, the bell rings. The halls will be full, girls will come banging into the bathroom. She should go to the nurse. She grips the toilet seat, pulls herself up off the floor, her body heavy, dense inside the light of her will. She knows her pain now, the familiar pain, knows what she has to say to the nurse, to her mother, to her doctor. But now there is something more, something she will carry in secret for the twenty-nine years that remain of her life, something she knows but can't yet articulate, missing the essential piece of information that will reach her in the infirmary when the announcement of the President's death comes over the P.A.

She will know this chill again, four and a half years later, in April, when James Earl Ray (if it was Ray) shoots Martin Luther King, and in June, when Sirhan Sirhan (if it was Sirhan) shoots Bobby. By then she will have met Robert Kennedy, first as a foreign student, then as a volunteer for his presidential campaign. She will be in the campaign office when news of King's death comes in: chill, darkness, angels, swastikas, green shooting stars— the whole thing replays, trembling, headache, nausea, and the new pain, her phantom kidney, a knife in her scars. *This death will be mine.* This time she knows the words, no other prescience, grips the cold chrome back of a chair. Two months later, at three in the morning, awake with a crowd of campaign workers, watching returns, the candidate's victory in California, his victory speech, his retreat through the hotel kitchen and sudden chaos, the gunshot, Jutta stares at the images until they disappear and the familiar vastness opens inside.

By now she knows her fate: not only her end, but the path she will take to reach it, or at least that part of the path she is already walking; knows her calling if not yet her cause. Sooner than most, she will be willing to work for the election of Hubert Humphrey. She is twenty years old. At forty-four she will be shot dead. From the age of fifteen she has known this, uneasily and inexactly, never the date or the place or the circumstance, only the fact: someday a bullet would enter her body, an assassin's bullet, a political bullet—she would die a martyr's death, a red martyr, not white; she has given up white martyrdom, the martyrdom of the convent, the flagellant and penitent, the contemplative and ascetic, in order to enter the world, where martyrs shed blood, where her blood will be shed. The first distant chill had told her: in tiny golden lights, black and red geometries, green shooting stars. On her knees in the high school bathroom, she had known. Gripping the chrome-backed chair, she knew. Alone in the crowd of campaign workers, she knows.

She will not dwell in this knowledge. Most of the time she will keep it hidden even from herself.

In the summer of 1963, when Martin Luther King led 250,000 mostly black freedom marchers to Washington, Jutta watched the event on television and cried for the hope she saw and heard. Hope was her greatest passion, she wrote to Jimmy Wolf, whose father had been rotated to Spain. She sent him a newspaper clipping of King's speech and in her letter copied out two of King's sentences: *"Let us not seek to satisfy our thirst for freedom by drinking from the cup of bitterness and hatred. . . . We must rise to the majestic heights of meeting physical force with soul force."* When Dr. King spoke these words, an airy tearful laughter had trembled up from her belly until she gasped and gasped again. As if the words had sprung something deep inside her, she wrote to Jimmy Wolf, some knowledge long since buried. Even the light in the room had seemed to sharpen, the sunlight shimmering and haloes rimming Emma's black hair. There was pain in all that laughter, in that brightness, a pain so clear and hollow, pressing under her ribcage like a blowing-up balloon, it made her giddy and itself impossible to name. By the end of King's speech the tears were streaming down her face. Writing the words to Jimmy Wolf brought the tears on again, and they plomped to the page and made the blue ink puddle and run before she could stop writing long enough to wipe them well away.

Jimmy Wolf wrote back asking whether after such a dose of inspiration she meant to continue her rah-rah activities, cheerleading, twirling batons for the pep club, writing love poems to the President, prepping for the ROTC. Then he apologized, said he had been drinking the wine of Spain, it made him bitter and sad. Still, he said, he felt called to warn her against luxuriating in her coddled sentimentality. *Hope can be your greatest passion*, he wrote, *only if it is also your most elusive object of desire.*

Jutta laughed when she read Jim Wolf's letters, no matter what they said, and it was only when she read them again, alone, at night, months and years later, that she felt their anger and grief. Then she would write to him, a new response, *To your letter of September 1, 1963*, defending her adolescent activities as political practice, and even her dreams: *I am preparing myself. I know who I am.*

The first death threat came in 1982 when she was aggressively and violently heckled during a speech against the deployment of Pershing II and cruise missiles; the last, we may not know; the last known (from hearsay, not evidence): a letter signed with swastikas and blood, a letter she had spoken of, shown to no one, although Lukas must have seen it, a letter never found. Among her enemies were a small LaRouchite party whose members had been threatening her since 1982, dogging her footsteps and public appearances so zealously that she traveled only with the General or her Oma at her side; also, the government of China, inconvenienced in Germany by her strong personal support for a free Tibet and her unrelenting condemnation of the massacre in Tiananmen Square; all skinheads and neo-Nazis and the right-wing parties that encouraged them, especially the

German People's Union and the xenophobic Republikaner party, led by a former SS man, which had been growing rapidly in her home state of Bavaria; along with various environmentally damaging economic interests and leaders of her own party, former agents of the Stasi and other secret police apparats of former eastern bloc nations, and the resentful adult children of General Lukas Grimm.

Who among them had both the will and the means to kill her?—who capable, for example, of faking the gunshot residue on the General's hands? Why, after almost a decade of caution and slowly growing terror, did she and the General, only nine months before their deaths, install an expensive household security system—a security system that may have failed? The balcony door was found open—the balcony door overlooking the garden at the back of the house. It opened from her office, piled high with papers and books. It is here, perhaps, that the threatening letters might have been found—may be found still: in all that paper, what clues may not lie hidden, neatly or carelessly filed? Could an assassin have taken the time to go through all that chaos of paper to find the anonymous letter or letters that might lead investigators to him? No more time than the police themselves took maybe. Or maybe she got rid of those letters in the first place—couldn't bear their presence under her roof, felt their hatred calling, chilling her, passed each one back to Lukas as it arrived, saying: *Destroy this.*

And did he then, this orderly, obedient man?

Is that what he was? She shook in his arms, he held her as he had once held his own frightened children when they woke in the night from bad dreams. She was the royal, he her consort. Or not: increasingly isolated, she hides from the world behind him, he screens her letters, her calls. They have no secrets from one another: or she has no secrets—but what do we know about him? They go out to the world together, out to colleagues and friends, together they plan for the future, together write appeals condemning the rise of racism in Germany, together drive to Hannover where Jutta will spend days and nights with her lover Sonam Pasang, while the General waits, or flies to Munich to visit Therese and three days later returns to drive Jutta back to Bonn.

The death threats come, from beginning to end. They never surprise her, only their form.

In the summer of '63, on her brother Peter's third birthday, Jutta writes to her Oma: I once asked my Papa for a doll. I was Emma's age. He listened to me without speaking, then got up from his chair at the table. He went to the cupboards and found a piece of corrugated cardboard and some string. I watched him with great interest. He wrote on the cardboard and tied the string through holes he had poked in its corners and having thus made a sign he tied it around my neck. He took my hand and walked me out to the market square. It was not a long walk, but it was long for me, and we nodded to our neighbors on the way. In the square my Papa told me to stand still and wait and he told me what the sign said: "This child for sale." Where were you, I wonder, and where was my mother, when he wrote this sign, when he took me to the square to abandon me, to leave me looking at the feet and knees and faces of the strangers walking past? Working probably, or shopping for groceries or the other necessities that were still so scarce when I was small. He sat in a cafe drinking beer and watched me from a window. He saw that I stood there firmly and refused to cry, that first I looked down, at the stones of the ground, but then straightened myself and raised my head and my eyes. Maybe in my heart I knew that for him it was a terrible joke of fate—that his firstborn and so far only child should be a girl! Maybe I knew that he was trying to teach me not to be one. I had heard him talk to the men and yell at my mother what a disappointment it was not to have got a big healthy, red-faced son—instead to have pale sickly female little me. My request for a doll was the last straw. (And of course it was not the last—but just for that day.) And on top of all that, a doll cost money that my Papa didn't have.

Now, so many years later, my mother has her big three-year-old son and I have all the dolls any girl could desire, although of course, dear Omi, I am too old for dolls and my dolls belong to Emma now. But sometimes with her I play with them. Sometimes I hold a doll and imagine myself a mother, the mother of a son, the mother of a daughter. Sometimes I imagine myself a little girl in Germany whose father loved her, a little girl in a Germany which did not kill Jews, or Russians, or Poles, or Serbs, or Roma, or communists, or anarchists, or homosexuals, or people institutionalized with physical or mental anomalies, a Germany which did not kill anyone at all. Sometimes I hold Emma to myself and pretend that she's mine and no one can have her, I am her mother, she is me, no man will beat her with his belt, no man will lead her into the street and hang a sign around her neck, no man will lie to her about his life or the life of her country. Every night I work on my English until I cry.

Something to observe, although Jutta herself finds chronologies hard to assemble: within days of John Kennedy's death, her stepfather leaves for Korea on a posting of indefinite duration. When Martin Luther King dies, toward the end of Jutta's sophomore year of college, Emma's cancer will have been diagnosed and declared fatal more than a year before; the family will be back in Germany, living in Würzburg, not far from Omi, and Jutta will be left in Washington alone. When Robert Kennedy dies two months later, she will already have packed to join them for the summer, to drive with them for Emma's papal audience in Rome.

The death threats and hate letters come: *NATO whore. Jew lover. Nigger lover. Green cunts bleed Red.* From the left, from the right, sometimes long letters, diatribes against actions she's taken, positions she's held, rages against her personal life, sometimes literate, sometimes crude, always anonymous, sometimes handwritten, sometimes typed, often brief, sometimes words and letters pasted up from magazines, accompanied by photographs, obscene, pornographic, violent: *This is what we're going to do to you, home wrecker, gook lover, slut.*

She gets other letters, too, and they come in greater number —letters of admiration, of courage inspired, from women and men everywhere on earth, but most of all from Germans who share her pain at the German past, her longing for a saner future for the human world, if not her passion to achieve it. These are the letters that keep her going, the letters that keep her working late into the night, writing replies, and exhortations to her colleagues and fellow activists, to institutions and governments, to men and women in power, to the public, to anyone, everyone, bearing endless moral and political witness. She dares not rest. She remembers the story told of Gandhi, that one morning he asked for his important letters, saying, "I must reply to them today, for tomorrow I may not be," and wrote his letters and went outside to conduct his daily prayer meeting and in the heart of the loving crowd fell to his assassin's bullet.

Hildegard, too, had answered all the letters written to her, and Jutta, in spite of her eventual break with the Catholic church, or maybe because of it, still holds Hildegard close to her heart. Like her, Hildegard bore witness against the powerful men of her time. Like her, Hildegard made disputatious enemies and devoted friends. Like her, Hildegard was sickly. Like her, Hildegard, with inspiration and eloquence, triumphed over sickliness, transforming it into a tool and a strength. How often Jutta turns to her for guidance and comfort, not in prayer—Jutta long since gave up prayer—but in reflection (and perhaps they are the same thing), as if Hildegard stands with her in spirit, like Emma's ghost, or her Omi when they're apart. Hildegard, too, had been envied and libeled, charged with pride for daring to speak and to lead; she too had been loved, widely received in her world as she journeyed out from the cloister and traveled through the German kingdoms, preaching even in the cathedral at Würzburg, the great medieval city where Emma now is buried. Hildegard, a twelfth-century woman, all rules bending before her, enemies surrendering to her moral will.

From Hildegard's example Jutta has learned to use the letter as a weapon: to write personally, profoundly, passionately to the men who hold power, to invoke the God they claim to believe in, the heroes they claim to emulate, the principles they claim to hold dear, and her own young girl's then woman's heart, her certainty of righteous purpose, her faith in the heart and essential goodness of the man she addresses, his courage, his moral fiber:

flattery might get her a moment's notice, but the case she makes is more potent than flattery, its argument earnest, truthful, seductive; secretly it holds out promises, says in its silences I love you, I want to love you, we all of us want to love you—knowing, because it is one with him, that underneath everything this love from the stranger is what the great man craves; it identifies with the hungers of his neglected heart and intuits what offerings to make to them, what insinuations of desire to be satisfied, and then, as swiftly, turns, reminds, goads, demands, reprimands, names its price.

When Jutta's American father the Colonel returns from Korea, in the summer of 1964, the family moves to Virginia to another base—they are still in the army; Jutta's new friends, like her old, are other army children; in Virginia, as in Georgia, she aspires to study nursing and sometimes teaching and plans to join the ROTC. She still works hard at being American, and the following summer, when she goes back to Germany for the first time, except in Omi's kitchen with her family, she feels herself a stranger there too.

Omi lives in Nürnberg now, working as a nursing supervisor in a big modern hospital where everything shines and gleams. When Jutta visits her there, she shivers at something she can't identify, the hospital so new, yet still somehow familiar. The muted voices seem to roar in her ears, and the known and strange come at her in the smells, in the shiny, antiseptic chill. The roar is silence. There was a silence there, in Germany, even at her Omi's table, full of her mother's chatter and Emma's and Peter's games. Being there was like stepping into a fairy tale, spending time in a kingdom trapped in a spell. *There is a silence here*, she wrote to Jim Wolf in Spain. *Silence is everywhere*, he wrote back, and, *Come eat olives with me. Run away, come see Granada, come to Barcelona, come to Seville.*

Jutta first encounters the teachings of Gandhi at the beginning of her sophomore year in college when she takes a course in theories of violence and nonviolence and their role in social change. The class will read, on the one side, Lenin, Mao, Frantz Fanon, and Regis Debray, and, on the other, Thoreau, Tolstoy, Gandhi, and Martin Luther King. The professor, a Nicaraguan, clearly takes Gandhi's position, and Jutta's own strong response to Gandhi's teachings and example will lead her into lifelong friendship with Dr. Daniel García Guzmán. From the first class discussion he recognizes in her a passionate nonviolent spirit and takes her aside and suggests she begin reading Gandhi at once, even though it will be November before he comes up on the syllabus. Dr. García Guzmán, later Daniel, encourages her to participate in the nonviolent actions planned in civil disobedience at the Pentagon the following month. To Jim Wolf, a sophomore too, at Berkeley, she writes: In America I have discovered remarkable heroes, inspired leaders whose example counterbalances the evil-inspired leadership of the Germany whose rubble I came out of. In America I have learned that not all leadership is evil, not all heroes must be killers. Also in America I have begun to see the evil side, the racism, which does not go away, the willingness to carry on this terrible war, the cold calculation that supports the bombing of civilians, the petty jealousies and naive and childish anger of the young people who oppose it, the hedonism that wants to pass for rebellion, when what is called for is a true revolution of the spirit. I long to speak of these things with you more deeply and cannot wait a minute for your arrival in Washington. Yours in the struggle, my first true teacher— Love, Jutta C.

Nine months later she will send him a final postcard: In America I learned to worship heroes and aspired to become one. In America I have seen how heroes die.

They die like this:

After a day of work, she lies down to rest before dinner. They never cook at home, always go out to a cheap little restaurant or cafe. Her daily routine: she rises late, takes tea and bread with Lukas, works through the afternoon, rests briefly, goes out with him to dinner, and works again through the night. Her workday so far: she read the news and her correspondence; wrote a fax reiterating the substance of last night's long telephone conversation to the editor in San Francisco with whom she has been negotiating over several years for the development and publication of an American biography; studied a report on Serbian violence in Bosnia-Herzegovina; on the phone with Hilmar Knapp, one of her original party colleagues, discussed her plans to run in 1994 for a seat in the European Parliament, as well as her concerns for Lukas's health and spirits in the wake of his injuries of six months past; put together a package for Lukas to mail to her Oma, including small souvenirs and copies of the agendas from the conferences she and Lukas had recently attended in Salzburg and Berlin; drafted an open letter to members of the Bundestag and the Kohl government strenuously objecting to the foreign minister's planned visit to Beijing; wrote to the Tibetan daughter she sponsors in the refugee community at Dharamsala; wrote to the Dalai Lama, despairing of her countrymen and challenging herself to rise above despair in cheerfulness and love, as the example of His Holiness always teaches; made preparatory notes for the speech she is to deliver at the University of California at Berkeley in early November; and took a call from New York from Eva Schulz, who is working to secure for her the $100,000 foundation prize with which she and Lukas plan to open a German human rights office to combat neo-Nazi violence and racial hatred. After the phone call, she lies down to rest.

For his part, Lukas rises early, while Jutta sleeps. His first work of the morning is to tend to the notes and instructions she's left him the night before; drafts to be read and typed and revised together, often for joint signature; calls to be made on her behalf, letters and clippings and drafts to be photocopied, letters to be posted; suggestions, ideas, and brainstorms. He sorts these through, makes notes on whatever action or research they require, then goes out on his morning errands—post office, copy shop, newsstand, library—and returns with bread and fruit for Jutta's breakfast. He switches off the telephone while he's out so that Jutta can sleep undisturbed, and at home again screens her calls. He is following with detailed care the upsurge in Germany of right-wing violence, reading newspapers from each of the German *Länder* and compiling precise accounts of incidents, victims, perpetrators. He pays special attention to the progress of events in Bavaria, his and Jutta's home *Land*, where membership in Franz Schönhuber's Republikaner party is steadily growing. In the late afternoon he goes up to Jutta to collect her letters and photo-copying, then goes out on his second round of errands. When he returns he sorts and screens her mail and attends to his own corre-spondence. When she gets up from her evening nap they will go out to dinner, tonight to a little workers' cafe where she will prob-ably eat an omelette and bread and salad and he grilled fish and boiled potatoes. Sitting at the typewriter, set up on the table in the living room where he generally works, he is writing a letter to Therese. It is a letter of no particular consequence, although in it he briefly mentions his increasing fatigue and political despair. He seems not to want to dwell on this note of complaint with his wife, perhaps in recognition that had he not left the army for his principles, or Therese for Jutta, he would now be sharing with her the comfortable retirement they had often imagined for them-selves, living together in the small family house in Munich, puttering with her in the garden neither has touched now for a dozen years, taking short trips in the fall to Vienna and Paris, trav-eling in the summers to Italy and Greece. Whatever the reason, abruptly the tone of his letter changes, becomes chatty and almost cheerful, full of questions and comments about their sons and grandsons, the autumn weather in Bonn, his recent trip with Jutta to Salzburg and Berlin.

This letter finished, signed, folded into its envelope, he will write one more, then go up to get Jutta for dinner. He puts a clean sheet into the typewriter, and begins a note to his attorney concerning a minor matter that he has left too long unattended. Mid-sentence, he hears an inexplicable sound he knows to be a gunshot but refuses to identify, a sudden impossible silence. He gets up from his chair, listens, hears only the strange loud beating of his pulse. He moves cautiously toward the stairway. "Jutta?" he calls, and gets no response. He looks at his watch. It is time to wake her. With peculiar alertness and unusual caution he climbs the stairs, his knee still giving him pain, six months after the acci-dent. He clutches the bannister as he climbs. Time slows down and opens. In the shadows just above, he makes out a figure, dressed in black, and in the figure's black-gloved hand a gun—in the slow and open time that now surrounds him, sees also that the gun is his own derringer, which holds only two bullets. He understands: Jutta is dead. He is walking straight for the assassin, straight for the gun only inches from his eyes, hard on his forehead, straight for the bullet that kills him.

Jutta became a dissident first within her own family. Here she is at seventeen: studying politics, in the classroom and out of it, struggling to understand herself, as a girl, not yet a woman. She has many friends at school and church and on the army base but her closest friends are her correspondents, her Oma and Jim Wolf. She sees her Oma only for a month every summer, and Jim Wolf not since he left Fort Benning, but she sends them each the annual school photo of herself, and from Spain Jim Wolf sends a photo back. He grows more handsome every year, and Jutta more beautiful, although she is indifferent to her own beauty, discounts its importance, reads her undeniable effect on people as a result entirely of her intellect and will. In the mirror she sees a pointy chin and pointy nose, bony cheeks, sometimes almost a witch face. Already the flesh under her eyes is darkly shadowed, and because in the mirror her face is at rest, she never sees its joyful animation, only its pain. She lives with pain, manages pain, for her tendency to kidney stones takes medication that she believes gives her eyes their sunken shadows. She hasn't slept more than five hours any night since she was thirteen. She still writes poems: political poems, love poems, romantic rhapsodies to nature. She also writes speeches, has begun to master English prose, and in history class this year finds a voice and talent for debate. Sometimes she goes out on dates, usually in groups, and although she's been friendly with the boys who took her out, even curious about them, she's never been interested enough to want to go out with them again. A year older than most of her classmates, and still a good Catholic girl, she believes in chastity before marriage, as she has been taught, but the more she sees of marriage, the less in it appeals to her—only the children, Emma and Peter, but especially Emma. It's not that her mother isn't happy—she is, or seems to be, and the Colonel, too, but the life that makes them happy looks less and less to Jutta like a life she will ever choose to lead. She knows she wants more, is more, without quite knowing what that more might be, and can't see how marriage or children will fit. Whenever she feels this, she seeks Emma out, holds her tighter, takes her for a walk or to the beach or to eat ice cream. She sometimes still has fantasies about Jim Wolf, but they involve heroics, not marriage. On dates she has let a boy hold her hand and found it clammy, let a boy kiss her and found it cold. She knew something in her body then that wanted to respond to the touch, to the contact, but not to the touch of *these* boys, not to *this* contact. She wants to feel about a boy what she feels when she opens a letter from Jim Wolf and he's signed it "With love"—something dangerous and uncertain, something that points to the immensity and mystery of the world.

She is still trying hard to be like the others: American, seventeen, a girl; serves on the junior prom committee, goes to dances and out on dates, listens to popular music, Joan Baez, Bob Dylan, the Beatles, but even her response to this music tells her, more clearly every day, that she's different from her friends: they listen to this music and dream and dance and hold hands and kiss their boyfriends, while Jutta feels this music drive her ever deeper into knowledge of reality. When summer comes she cares more for books than the beach or boys. She is studying the human order, every facet of it, and everything she learns awakens her hunger for more knowing. I eat newspapers, she writes to Jim Wolf. I have to know what's happening every minute, I have to know it whole, all inside me. I find books to study the background for every story and every important event everywhere on earth. I know I ought to narrow my field, I ought to choose. But I don't want to. There's time for everything, but never enough time. I'm reading college catalogs.

This is warrior culture Jutta lives in. Don't forget it. A world of discipline and perfection, always in readiness, always on alert. One feared mistakes here, one feared defiance, deviance, departure from the official but inaccessible script. One lived with secrecy and stoicism. One became a good little soldier. Pain was denied until one had no pain. One lived at the heart of a drama that was always outside, manifested in the interaction of daily ritual and the news. And Jutta is oddly at home here, where the personal self and personal history have no valued place, perhaps because the convent also had been a ritual world.

Here everything is scrubbed, polished, shined. Jutta's mother has become a perfect army wife, strong and resourceful, also obedient. She likes commanding, and being commanded, likes knowing her place in the ordered chain. She has taken to life in the military, she doesn't mind saying, because it establishes clear lines of authority. It's the nearest thing to the—she hesitates—to the good aspects, of course, she says, of the Germany of her youth. She blushes when she evokes Germany, and shines and polishes harder, and everything in her house is as clean and precise as the creases in the Colonel's khaki pants.

Jutta carries this warrior culture with her, into the future, into the rest of her life. (Jeanne d'Arc, after all, led armies.) She wills herself onward, lives in the consciousness of history unfolding moment by moment, the personal permeated with the political, the fate of the world always at stake. Only her physical pain expresses rebellion against this internalized economy of readiness and alert.

With reunification, Stasi files began to appear. Jutta Carroll liked to describe a surveillance photograph she had been shown of herself and Lukas Grimm crossing a bridge just after they'd entered East Berlin. Other pedestrians crossed ahead and behind them or passed them by on the intersecting street. On the photograph six faces in the crowd had been circled: six faces of six apparently ordinary people identified now as Stasi agents. Six Stasi, Jutta would laugh, just for Lukas and me!

She identified the location shown in the photograph. She remembered that on that day in East Berlin they had gone to the home of a dissident friend who was ill. They had gone to meet with her and her husband, to draw up a shopping list of necessities from the West—books, office supplies, typewriters, fax and copy machines—and to help her in her illness. On more than one occasion Jutta had brought antibiotics for her and administered her insulin shots and made her tea, and when the Stasi files were opened it turned out that this woman had been reporting on her husband and the others for years.

Nor was she the only one among their dissident friends to have reported to the Stasi.

Jutta felt used, damaged, defiled by these people, and by none so greatly as by the musician and poet she had long desired and one morning almost made love to after an all-night discussion in Anna Albert's kitchen, a man whose poor little hovel of a rat-infested room had moved her to tears, a man she now knew had kept another room, a luxurious room in a luxurious apartment in an elite neighborhood of East Berlin.

Who were they, these Stasi observers, these agents, these traitors to their loved ones and friends?

Ordinary people.

Jutta understood that.

They were, most of them, ordinary people.

People who just wanted to get along in life.

Like the average citizens of the Nazi Reich, like the military parents of the children she grew up with, like her neighbors in Tannenbusch, who cared only for their families and their jobs, who failed to see the larger dimensions of everyday realities, even the ordinary people who went on the march against NATO's Euromissiles and then one day just had enough, just went home.

She could not understand these people.

She had never been one of them.

She had always had a mission, or a sense of mission, even before her mission was revealed.

As if all her life up to that moment she had been waiting for orders—until one day in falling snow, a morning so distant now but always present to her, her orders had appeared.

And they remained her orders.

The end of the cold war had not brought an end to the nuclear peril. To think that it had was illusion, a shell game, sleight of hand. If anything the peril was greater than ever. In Germany reunification had heightened the danger, not of nuclear war, but of nuclear peace.

She had always spoken against this, from the beginning until the end. One could not oppose the bomb and embrace the reactor. The two were inseparable. The so-called peaceful uses of nuclear power shared a common boundary with military uses, functioned on the visible side of the nuclear skin. Nuclear research for peace nourished nuclear options for war, and vice versa, and together laid the foundation for the worldwide nuclear state. (New world order, indeed!—an appellation that sent shivers up the spine of Germans like Lukas old enough to remember the new order of the Nazis.)

Jutta's objections had once been ascendant. They were no longer. Reunification had swept over everything she and Lukas had built, threatened to sweep it all away. Still, Jutta had a mission. Even tired, she was tireless. Even hopeless, she found hope. The struggle continued. She had been raised to be a warrior, and before that a saint. One did not surrender. One did not admit defeat. She considered herself a permanent dissident within the corporate nuclear state.

In the spring of her junior year of high school she did a history research project on the war in Vietnam and volunteered to take the antiwar position in a class debate. When the Colonel heard about it he told her she would have to withdraw, that taking an antiwar position during wartime would be a damaging mark on her record, and by extension on his.

"My record?" she repeated.

"These things are noticed," he said, and reminded her of her desire to join the ROTC.

She argued with him—read him passages from the books she was studying, read how in 1956 Eisenhower had admitted— "Right there in *Life* magazine," she said, "without pretense or apology"—*admitted* that the US was violating the agreements signed in Geneva when the French withdrew, was denying the Vietnamese the elections they had been guaranteed because an open election as scheduled would have put the communist Ho Chi Minh into power by a projected 80 percent of the vote.

Unmoved by her appeal to law and history, the Colonel spoke of Korea and China, brainwashing and communist godlessness, anti-Western and anti-Catholic terror, Viet Cong and Viet Minh atrocities, the danger that all of Asia would fall. Jutta countered with the global collapse of colonial empires, the principle of democratic self-determination, the fact that in the 1920s Ho Chi Minh had sought help from the western democracies, turning to the Soviet Union only after the democracies refused him.

The Colonel rejected history and principle. He spoke of national security, *Realpolitik*, the need to hold the line against world domination, first by the Nazis, now by the Reds.

"But these are not Nazis!" Jutta cried. "This is not an invasion, it is an internal war, a civil war, one that would not have come into being if the US had allowed the elections, one that would have been lost and won years ago if the US had not involved itself— there is one Vietnam, not two," and argued still more passionately in the name of Vietnam's whole people, whose right to decide their fate as a nation the US had stolen after they defeated the French, the first thieves—and so on, until the Colonel threw up his hands and laughed a false surrender: "You oversimplify but you're gifted, you're relentless. You should be a lawyer," and she quit trying to reason with him, but just for that hour, that day. She had practiced with him every turn of the argument and was primed for the class debate, in that debate felt an exhilaration she could not remember knowing, felt the righteousness of her argu-ment, the confidence of her command of the facts, and something more: the shock of her passion, its effect on her listeners, their awareness of the broken taboo, that fear and their rapt attention, their eyes, their ears, their minds attentive only to her: she was emptying her heart to them, pouring herself out, and they drank, and she drank from their drinking; she was not drained after her performance, but full of energy, ready to act, unclear what action might mean: went home to her desk, wrote a letter, letters, wrote to congressmen and generals, wrote to senators and the President, to newspapers and magazines, to Joan Baez and Bob Dylan, wrote her heart and mind out and looked at the pile of paper when she was done and shook her head. She picked up her pen and wrote again, in German, to her Oma: In writing all these letters I discover why it is so personal, so urgent for me: I was a German and the Germans did nothing to stop the killing, and now that I am an American, I can do something to stop it: *As an American I can, therefore I must.* But then I ask myself what can I do?—I, a high school girl who lives on an army base with a lieutenant colonel who tells me it is dangerous to object and who when pushed to the wall abdicates debate by asserting the necessity of trusting our leaders—to me, a German! I have written letters, a big pile of letters, but then what? I don't know, but I will find out. I will read and study and learn until I find out.

Dictionaries define a dissident as one who disagrees, in opinion or belief, one who refuses to recognize or submit to a formal authority, as of a church or state. But these general definitions leave out the most common contemporary usage, in which a dissident is a citizen of a communist country who stands, or stood, in active opposition to the communist state system. In capitalist and western countries, critics of the system are not called dissidents: Jutta Carroll, as thoroughly opposed as any of her eastern counterparts had been to the ideology and system within which she worked and lived, was never called a dissident. To have called her a dissident would have been to call attention to the global reach of her critique.

Focus instead on the particular action, the particular issue of the moment, or even the particular scandal—her love affair with Lukas Grimm, his daughter's death by anorexia, their murder-suicide, the bodies rotting. Focus on the particular act of courage, the particular act of heroism or generosity. Get good photos—the band of twenty-seven new members marching into the Bundestag waving flowering tree branches; Lukas Grimm, the General, squatting cheerfully in the arms of police as they carry him from a protest at a US base. Focus on the personality. Recognize her glamour and, at her side, his. Elaborate their glamour, create it. Use them. Seduce them. Dazzle them with the illusion that their personal fame strengthens their cause (which in the short term, of course, it does).

And for whom is this recipe written? To whom have these instructions been given? Explicitly, no doubt, to no one. Yet read their press coverage, then read what Jutta and Lukas wrote themselves. Compare.

What vanishes between the one and the other is the totality of the system under critique. Invisible in its utter visibility. Therefore the word dissident need not apply. To protest this or that policy is one thing. To challenge the whole at its foundations is something else again.

In whose interest, then, is her death? In what economic and political interests closer to home?

It is too easy to say that she and Lukas were powerless, had become mere private citizens, failed politicians struggling to find a forum, a space for themselves, a base. She never left her party, although in every way it had failed her. She was planning to run in the 1994 European parliamentary elections (elections her party will place well in, reestablishing its role as Germany's true third force with close to 11 percent of the vote). The failure of 1990 then, with hindsight, will be seen as temporary, tactical. But in 1992, who knows this? Jutta Carroll herself, in her brighter moments. And who else?

When better to destroy a tenacious opponent than in her hour of defeat and weakness, especially if the method of destruction will mimic murder-suicide? And who better to execute such a false murder-suicide than the newly unemployed professionals of the Stasi? Don't Nazis and other political terrorists claim their victims, take pride in their acts of violence and assassination? Who hides such acts?

What opportunities for development, extension of power and wealth, does the collapse of the communist East make possible? (There are facts here, specific facts, available but hard to come by.) Who profits from this collapse, which she has helped to bring about? (Has she outlived her accidental usefulness?) Who profits from this unification, the absorption and erasure of the East, which she resisted? (What has been her central mission?) Who have been her greatest enemies? Who profits from her death?

If not the nuclear industry, to which she so long and so actively stood opposed, who?

It was a theory, one rumor among a thousand.

She dreams a phalanx of missiles, advancing across the sky. Emma runs up the beach. In the distance, a mushroom cloud. A silence falls. Jutta wakes. The silence is palpable, as if it has touched her, deep in her sleep.

She sits upright in bed listening to the silence of the sleeping house and waiting for her vision to settle. The dream images run through the darkness like a movie, the missiles advancing, Emma running, the cloud mushrooming into the sky. The silence that follows is a sickness in her stomach, a weight in her head. Her hands are shaking. She can't sit still. She gets up, turns her desk light on, can't resist the need to make sure Emma is all right.

She goes quietly out to the hall and nearly jumps in her skin. The Colonel is there in the dark, at the top of the stairs. They look at each other.

"I heard something," she says. "Well, or I had a dream."

"I was just coming up to bed."

But she can see that he has already been to bed and is suddenly up. He's wearing only his pajamas. He rarely leaves his bedroom in pajamas at all, and when he does, even in the heat of summer, always covers them with a robe.

"Is something wrong?" she asks.

"Of course not," he says. "What could be wrong?"

"I had a dream," she says.

"Well, go on back to bed," he says. "Close your windows if they're open."

"My windows?"

"There's a storm coming," he says.

But no storm came.

Later, years later, she will come to believe that about this time (on this very night), a minor breakdown at a nearby nuclear power plant led to the release of radioactive steam. It will have been a small breakdown, a small release, almost within safety limits, and unrecorded—one, she is sure, among several during the family's three years in Hampton. She will be tracking this kind of data by then, digging deep to establish a link between radiation exposure and Emma's death from cancer. Elsewhere she will have succeeded in establishing statistical patterns of radiation exposure and high cancer incidence. But Emma's case resists proof:

Georgia's reactors are far from Fort Benning, and in 1964, when the family left the area, they had not yet come online; nearby Alabama had no nuclear plants; and Surry 1 and 2, the Virginia plants near their home in Hampton, came online only after the family left for Germany. Perhaps that night or another there was a construction accident, or a research accident, or maybe a weapons emergency at Langley Air Force Base next door. Jutta won't know, but not knowing won't matter. Despite her inability to confirm the reality of such an exposure, she will continue to blame Emma's long sickness and ultimate death on these phantom breakdowns (accidents happened at other sites, they killed other children), as well as on the radiation treatments for the cancer in progress, and on the Colonel's own exposure when, as a young lieutenant, part of the occupation force, he arrived in Hiroshima just weeks after the bomb.

Her body made pain. She lived with pain as a constant, at times more acute, at others less. She assigned her pain no meaning. Not as a child or an adolescent, not as a young woman or a woman matured. Her body made pain. She lived with it. Sometimes it forced her to stop, to rest. But she rarely gave in. In the form of pain, her body was enemy, allied with the enemy, the forces of destruction that threatened all life on earth. To deal with her pain was a burden, time spent with doctors, in hospitals, undergoing tests a distraction from causes more urgent than her own comfort or ease.

Still, pain frightened her, being in pain—indecipherable, inexplicable, irreducible pain, pain that seized her head and stomach and sent her reeling, inward and irrational, pain that took over her lower back, at times in the exact place where she often said she had no kidney left. (In fact, she had had four operations, three as a young child and the last in 1967, when a third of her right kidney was cut away.) When the terror of her own fragility overcame her, she retreated to the dark, and even in retreat kept working, willing the work of her political reason into the world by means of the technologies that kept her going, the telephone, the fax machine.

She defied the pain, refused it access. It was brute, it was physical. She allowed it no voice. She declared for her pain its own *Berufsverbot*—no social vocation, no active forum, no context for making meaning. (The *Berufsverbot*: a 1972 decree of the governing Social Democrats denying employment in education or the higher grades of civil service to anyone politically affiliated to the Social Democrats' left.)

A martyr is defined as one who chooses death rather than renounce religious principles, or by extension one who sacrifices or suffers in order to advance a cause, belief, or principle. But the word has another meaning, obscured by the torments and tortures meted out over centuries to early Christians later made saints, and revealed in its Greek root, *martus, martur-*, meaning witness.

Martireo: I bear witness.

It is this sense of the word martyr that inhabits Jutta's aspirations. She is preparing to be a Christian soldier bearing witness in a dangerous world. It is true that she has lately aspired to study nursing and join the ROTC, but already she suspects her calling will be something less predictable, more intellectual and international. Her politics are an uneven, if at the time not uncommon, mix of anticommunism, economic liberalism, and pure democratic principle. She sees her difference from the world around her (from the Colonel's world) in the priority she gives to enacting democratic integrity. Thus her defense of Ho Chi Minh. She believes in the spiritual need to bear witness in the face of injustice. She believes progress and justice are possible in the human world. She remembers Martin Luther King's demand that physical force be met with soul force, and, however inchoately, her awareness of the power of this demand begins to grow.

As time passes and practice catches up with theory, these early beliefs, although expanded, deepened, and sophisticated, will change fundamentally in one way only: they will lose their underpinnings, their context, their grounding in the as-yet-unexamined and thus still implicitly assumed corporate capitalist economic, social, and military state.

Martireo: I bear witness.

First as a nun, then as a soldier, then in a world and a death all her own.

She chose American University in Washington, DC, for its program in international relations and for its location, its proximity to power and to home. Jim Wolf went to Berkeley to get as far from his parents as he could and to study philosophy and grow his hair long and experience at first hand the youth rebellion made famous by Berkeley's Free Speech Movement two years before. He and Jutta still hadn't seen each other since parting at fifteen and still exchanged passionate letters full of secrets they shared with no one else. At the beginning of their first year of college he wrote to her of his loneliness, she of her excitement to be on her own and her sadness at missing her sister and her family in general, he that his loneliness could not be filled by his family, that his loneliness went deeper than any filling, that even writing letters to her, receiving hers, could not fill it, could not answer it or shake it or wash it away. The world is big, she wrote back, enormous, open your eyes, open your heart: the world is full of sadness but the sadness isn't inside me, but everywhere suffering people cry out for love and justice. All you need is love, she wrote (a sentence soon to be singable). Then Emma's cancer was diagnosed and Jim Wolf wrote back: I have love—it drives me crazy with loneliness, the more love I get, the more I need, I'm a master of love and a sponge. I'm dying to see you. I'm raging. I carry your picture close to my heart and when one of my girlfriends looks at it I spit in her face.

Jutta didn't know how to answer that letter and left it unanswered until months later another arrived, in another voice altogether, raging, yes, but not about himself or his loneliness or his girlfriends either, but about the world at large, the world you seem so to care for, he wrote, the world is eating itself alive, our fathers are killers, they kill their own children, and the children of the world—my father, your father—in the name of the rich, the inhuman, the corporate machines, and there is nothing new in it, it goes back hundreds of years, millennia, Rome never died, we are Rome, justice is evil and mercy is dead. Love can't answer it, Jutta. Nothing can answer it. I went to a teach-in about the war, I saw photographs, I heard stories. I went to the demonstration in L.A., I saw people get their heads bashed in. Love's not enough. Love's never been enough. Love always loses. Here you read the truth sprayed on the stucco walls: *Storm troopers don't love back.*

She waited for him in her dorm room, watching out her window, hanging over the stairwell, pacing the lobby, and ran back upstairs, where Karen, her roommate, slept undisturbed. Late the night before he'd called to say they'd made it as far as Pittsburgh, were driving through, would sleep in the car somewhere outside the District, and he would look for her in the morning as soon as he dropped his passengers off—he would see her soon.

He had bought the car, a 1953 Dodge that needed oil every hundred miles, with money he'd saved from his summer job stocking supermarket shelves and a cash refund on his meal plan. His passengers were paying for the oil and gas and helped with the driving. On the phone from Pittsburgh he told her they'd seen a lot of people on the road, talked to them in filling stations and truck stops, people like themselves, young and long-haired, heading for Washington to protest the war.

She was watching out the window when he strolled up, wearing dark granny glasses and carrying a big bunch of flowers. She ran out her door and down the stairs and hung back at the edge of the lobby. She watched him speak to the girl at the desk, watched him take off his glasses while the girl rang upstairs and Karen slept through the call, watched him until he met her eyes across the big empty room. He gave her a little smile, a smile she recognized but had forgotten until that moment, and suddenly she ran to him, calling his name, bubbling over with laughter, arms outflung, and stopped short. For a moment she lost recognition of him, his face gone wolfish, thin, his black eyes bright with an animal luster. "Jimmy?" she said. She had never thought about his name, had never thought that he might someday resemble it, become wolfen, animal. She felt the animal in him, and in herself. She laughed, nervous, and began to talk, saying anything, nothing—the sleeping arrangements she had made for him, did he want to get breakfast, where had he parked?

He held out the flowers, daisies and snapdragons and crysanthemums, a sunflower and roses. "From California," he said, his voice slow and deep, and she saw that the flowers were wilted and bruised. "I kept them in a bucket of ice," he said, "but the car was crowded." He shrugged, and the little smile returned. She had planned for his arrival but now couldn't think what to do. "I'll take them to my room," she said, and raised herself on tiptoe and still couldn't reach him, he had grown so tall. He bent down for the kiss she pressed to his cheek. Alarmed and almost wild, she turned and ran upstairs.

She dropped the flowers onto her bed. Karen was still sleeping. Jutta looked at her own hands—trembling. She had felt this before, she didn't know when. She sat down on Karen's bed. "Wake up," she said, shaking her shoulder. "Karen, quickly, wake up, wake up. He's here. He brought flowers, from California, they died on the road, I don't know what to do, everything's gone out of my head, my heart beats too fast, you can't imagine his eyes, I want to throw up."

Karen yawned and asked what time it was and whether Jutta had slept at all, but Jutta wasn't listening, was frowning at herself in the closet-door mirror, next to the photo of herself and Emma in the dappled sunlight of the Würzburg woods. "I'm still a nun," she said, thinking how conservative she looked, even in her blue jeans and embroidered peasant blouse, suede jacket and dark leather boots, "I will always be a nun," and almost cried in rage at herself, and left the room to run back downstairs, to go with Jim Wolf into town for coffee and breakfast, to get him away from her schoolgirl dormitory and into the historic world, where she would be confident again and free.

The day was clear and bright, would soon be almost warm, and as they stepped out into the sun he put his dark-lensed glasses back on. Walking, she felt his body beside hers, behind hers, ahead, as if they were constantly in contact, the air, the empty space between them palpable as flesh. She felt the heat of his body, heard the movement of his arms against his clothes, his cowboy boots on the sidewalk, saw again without turning how long his black hair was growing, falling down his cheeks, soft on her skin where it had brushed her as she kissed him hello, saw his black glittering gaze again, heard his low voice almost whisper her name. She was breathless in his presence; words failed her, disappeared.

Briefly the car saved her, gave her a simple task to perform, navigating, directing him down Massachusetts Avenue. Otherwise she was silent, watching the traffic and streets and resisting her body, yielding, then resisting again. Beside her Jim Wolf was talking, telling stories from the drive across country, and she listened as best she could, but his voice, which she could feel in her skin, took his words back. They slid away from her, withdrew. She lost them somewhere in his flesh, as if they had reeled her in to his body, a place where sound was physical only, where spoken words carried no sense.

At breakfast she had no appetite, but the plates and forks and knives and food and cups of tea and coffee served as props, helped her to escape her body's alien excitements and direct her energy into rescuing and reclaiming words, the only words she could master, words of principle and analysis, spinning out of her into the air between them, until he reached across the table and touched her hand. She stopped. He looked at her through his dark lenses. "Stop a minute," he said. "One minute. I'm counting." They sat there in silence, his hand on her hand.

"Jimmy—" she began.

"Shh," he said. "Now I have to start at *one* again."

She couldn't do it. One minute was too long. She laughed, bubbled over, kept talking, shook his hand off, then grabbed it back and laughed, "I'm hopeless," and gave up trying, ignored his game, went on talking. She knew she could win this way, talking, had always won with words—in high school debates, in silly army-brat schoolgirl conversations, in family disputes, and here in Washington, too, more seriously at last, where after only a year she already drew attention in her class, noticed by professors and fellow students, and most of all by her favorite, Daniel García Guzmán, who had singled her out for special instruction and about whom she was talking now: Professor García Guzmán and Mahatma Gandhi, whose writings she had been reading intensely for six or seven weeks, ahead of the class, beyond what would be assigned altogether—she was as a drought-ridden plain drinking Gandhi in, did he understand? Nonviolence wasn't passivity. Active nonviolence required nonattachment, courage and love. She knew she wasn't fearless yet. But she was ready to make a start. The demonstrations of the weekend would be her first opportunity—to bear witness with her physical presence, not only with written words, to know for herself the feel of a crowd composed of so many tendencies and extremes, to confront her own fears in the face of armed policemen. Nothing could make her happier than his presence here to share this. They would begin this afternoon with the draft resistance march. Her professor and other pacifists and students and draft resisters from all over the country would gather at a church on Capitol Street and walk quietly to the Justice Department, where draft cards would be collected, along with letters and affidavits from young men who had already turned in or burned their cards, until, the many statements and speeches done, William Sloane Coffin, the chaplain from Yale, would take the draft cards and letters inside and present them to the Attorney General. They all risked being jailed, Coffin and the linguist Noam Chomsky and the poets Denise Levertov and Robert Lowell, and all those who made a public point of aiding, abetting, and counseling young men to resist and refuse the draft. She wished that she too had a draft card to submit in rejection of the law.

Jim Wolf had taken a pen from his pocket and written something on a napkin. Now he pushed it across the table to her: "If you fall forever you fall into the sky."

She didn't understand. He smiled and shrugged, watching her

warmly. Suddenly he laughed and said, "I remember when you wanted to join the ROTC."

Through quiet residential neighborhoods, in a column two-by-two and flanked by police, four or five hundred people walk to the Justice Department. Among them is Jutta's professor, Daniel García Guzmán, who shook Jim Wolf's hand at the church and welcomed him to their group. "I could be deported for this action," he told them—it was the first Jutta knew of this. "It is hell in my country but nothing to compare with the hell this country makes in Vietnam."

Now Jutta is mostly silent, walking side by side with Jim Wolf, feeling the presence of his body again as she felt it at first and thinking he is too old for her to call him Jimmy anymore—he feels old in a way that she knows she is old herself, the way they have always shared, and also in some other, alien way—but she can't think of him as Jim without adding his last name, as she has done for years on envelopes, and especially now, with his lean wolfish jaw and long mouth and loose, long-legged walking that won't keep stride but pushes ahead and falls behind, restless in the confines of the polite double-file, police-flanked column making its way through the peaceful streets.

"In Berkeley we do this differently," he says.

He says maybe he should have stayed out there for the demonstrations at the Oakland draft board; people there battled police, overturned cars to make barricades, got arrested, beaten, gassed. It had gone on all week, was probably still going on; he'd heard about it early in the morning when he dropped his passengers off; a guy at the house had flown in overnight; in the weird blue darkness he was wearing bandages on his eyes after being sprayed with a new teargas called mace. "This little march is too polite," he says. "But I wanted to see you," and there is something in his voice as he says this that thrills her, as if his hands are touching her skin. She blushes, remembers her childhood fantasies. "Jim," she says, and he turns and walks backward, facing her. The sun is high and almost hot now in the early afternoon and they are carrying their jackets and his shirt is buttoned low. She looks for his eyes behind the dark glasses. For an instant she is speechless.

But the word-ridden rarely stay speechless for long.

Gandhi knew that the end was to be found in the means: there was no end, is no end, the means themselves are the end, the only end: the present, the ongoing present. Thus peace would not be brought about by violence, by war, but only by peace—by consciously chosen and deliberate acts of peace, by living in active love.

"Jim," she says, "listen to this." She digs her notebook out of her shoulder bag and reads: "All fear is the baseless fabric of our own vision. Fear has no place in our hearts, when we have shaken off the attachment for wealth, for family and for the body.… Wealth, family and body will be there, just the same; we have only to change our attitude towards them. All these are not ours, but God's. Nothing whatever in this world is ours. Even we ourselves are His."

Jim Wolf leans down close to her, a hand on her shoulder, enfolding her, drawing her in. He says nothing, but smiles. Sunlight flashes off his dark glasses. He nudges her, plays with her hair, taking possession, silencing her—she feels it, resists, reads: "As the means so the end. There is no wall of separation between means and end. Indeed, the Creator has given us control (and that too very limited) over means, none over the end. Realization of the goal is in exact proportion to that of the means. This is a proposition that admits of no exception."

Beside her Jim Wolf sighs. He drops his hand from her shoulder, falls behind, then comes back pointing, angrily asking, "What about them?"

Jutta looks up for the first time. While she read, the line of march had moved from residential streets into the busy downtown, and now, as the marchers arrive at the Justice Department, there to greet them, held at bay by police, are five young men wearing swastikas, yelling, holding high the red, white, and black Nazi flag. Jutta stops walking, and Jim Wolf takes her notebook. "I don't want an answer from the book," he says. "I want your answer."

The march continues around them, past them, and the young men in Nazi armbands shout insults and slogans. *What about them?*

is a question Jutta has been trying to answer, a question Gandhi himself tried to answer many times, but until this moment the question for her has remained abstract: no live bodies filled the uniforms, no swastika flew in the streets. In the first moments the sight of those young men drives her farther from speech than her body's response to Jim Wolf did, until shaking in her hips and forcing the words to come, with tears in her eyes, she turns on him and demands: "Do you point them out because you think I'm wrong, Gandhi is wrong? Do you think we should fall on them, beat them with their flagpole, rip up their flag, overturn cars, storm the White House, burn the city? You want to do how it's done in Berkeley?"—and she has more to say, to insist on, but before she can continue or Jim Wolf respond, a policeman orders them to keep moving or step off the line.

At the shallow Justice Department steps, the marchers are assembling: Coffin and the other leaders in front, news photographers and TV and movie news cameramen below, the crowd spreading out on the sidewalk and into the street. Soon the speeches will begin, and Jutta would like to listen to them freely, with a clear heart and untroubled mind, but something is choking her now, Jim Wolf, whom she so loved and so wanted to see, who excited her, she can admit it now, unlike any other boy she's known, can admit it because it's over, he's killed it—

"Jutta, Jutta," he says, their bodies pressed closer in the crowd, "please, Jutta," and she bursts into tears, sobs, rests her head on his shoulder, lets him hold and comfort her and feels the agitation in her hips, in her bones, the fear and the heat of him, her cheek against his chest where his shirt is still unbuttoned, until she raises her face to his for the kiss she knows is coming, and suddenly laughs, hops up onto the curb, raising her height just right for his, so that he kisses her at last, and she kisses him, a real kiss now, a kiss she can feel in all her skin, a kiss that won't stop, not even when she turns away to listen to the speeches.

She reads from her notebook, quoting: "The means may be likened to a seed, the end to a tree; and there is just the same inviolable connection between the means and the end as there is between the seed and the tree." The evening light is fading. They are sitting alone on the back porch of the house where Jim Wolf's friends are staying. Jutta had planned for him to stay in a boys' dorm with one of her classmates, but at the Justice Department he rejected her plan, said he wanted to be where she could be with him, stay with him, somewhere without parietal rules. The demonstration was winding down then, the major speeches and statements over. Coffin and a small delegation, including Professor García Guzmán, had carried 994 draft cards and affidavits into the building, while outside, entertained by music and more speeches, the rest of the demonstrators waited for news. Coffin and his group were engaging in an act of conscience, a deliberate violation of the law, and anticipated—hoped for— arrest. The five Nazis were still present and shouting, still restrained by police. The air was cooling, the sun lost behind clouds, and every minute of the waiting Jutta felt electric, couldn't separate her body's alien energy from the risk to Daniel García Guzmán or the touch of Jim Wolf's hands, which never stopped holding her—her hands, her wrists, her shoulders, her neck, her hair. She could feel his restlessness behind her. He kissed her neck, her ear, and she shivered, "Oh wait, wait, please wait," and knew she didn't want to wait any more than he did, was craving his touch and impatient for the demonstration to end, the music to end, the speeches to end, Coffin and García Guzmán and the others to emerge from the building, or a message from them, or from the law. She took Jimmy's hand and held it, kissed it, squeezed it tighter. She prayed—for patience, for news, for Coffin and García Guzmán, for the government to stop the bombing, for the war to end, for Emma to get well, for Jimmy to love her. He talked in her ear. He told her he wanted her to stay with him, to come with him to his friends for the night, he didn't mean make love (she had suddenly tensed), she didn't have to, just to stay with him, not to leave.

"I'm afraid," she said, "to stay out all night," and all at once she was going on again about Gandhi, his call to detachment as the source of courage, his commitment to chastity, his indifference to the flesh, until Jimmy Wolf interrupted her to say, "Gandhi was a puritan," and out of nowhere out of her mouth came the words, "Oh teach me. Teach me everything."

He held her then, his body warm and close behind her, an arm draped loosely around her shoulder, across her chest, his other hand pressing her hand to her belly, his cheek caressing her hair, until at last Coffin, García Guzmán and the others came out and announced that nothing had happened, the Attorney General (a man who, many years in the future, after his own profound political conversion, will be among the German Jutta Carroll's friends in the US peace movement)—the Attorney General wasn't in his office, his assistant had refused to receive the draft cards and affidavits, the government had sidestepped the challenge, trying to turn their whole endeavor into an empty rite. More people from the delegation spoke, Dr. Benjamin Spock and Daniel García Guzmán and many others, until at last the demonstration broke up.

Jutta didn't want to admit that she was disappointed, and as they walked back to the church where the car was parked, Jim Wolf also was silent, although hours later, after she had signed out from her dorm for the rest of the weekend and he had driven her to the house where his friends were staying, after they had sat around awhile with the others and then found a room to lie down in alone, their clothes all on and their bodies pressing together as urgently as if they were naked, fingers and hands and tongues and kisses penetrating the barriers of fabric until Jutta's heart beat so fast it scared her and her body rippled and terrified her with joy beyond her control, after Jimmy had released her and pulled her hand to himself and with closed eyes she let him fold her hand around his penis, bigger and harder and hotter to the touch than she could ever have imagined, and let him hold her hand around it and rub it up and down until she felt his pulse in her skin and he breathed in her hair and held her forehead and held the hand that held his penis while it pulsed up her palm and shot hot liquid onto her wrist, after they had lain there in the gathering darkness, after they laughed and kissed, and kissed again, after they got up and looked for food and found the house deserted, everyone gone, out drinking probably, or looking for dinner, after those many hours had passed, and when they sat on the back porch steps, waiting for a pizza to be delivered, he finally told her what he thought: "The problem with nonviolence is it's too easy for them to ignore. Look what happened today. All those good intentions, all that courage. But for what?"—so that now she is reading again from her notebook, rebuilding her wall of words.

What she wants, she knows, is someone she won't have to debate with, someone who sees life as she sees life, someone who shares her commitments, her passions. What she wants is the Jim Wolf of her imagination, the Jimmy she has loved all these years. It is the Jimmy of her imagination that she lay down with, the Jimmy of her imagination whose fingers touched her where she had never touched herself, the Jimmy of her imagination whose erect hard flesh she had held until it was satisfied and went soft in her hand. Not this Jim Wolf (although she won't see this yet, refuses to know it): this ordinary, contradictory Jim Wolf, tender and lost, full of loneliness and lust and anger, cynicism and reined-in violence, this Jim Wolf whose desire is not spiritual, whose love for her might be from the heart but is not of the soul. She reads:

"He is the devotee who is jealous of none, who is a fount of mercy, who is without egotism, who is selfless, who treats alike cold and heat, happiness and misery, who is ever forgiving, who is always contented, whose resolutions are firm, who is dedicated mind and soul to God, who causes no dread, who is not afraid of others, who is free from exultation, sorrow and fear, who is pure, who is versed in action and yet remains unaffected by it . . . who treats friend and foe alike, who is untouched by respect or disrespect, who is not puffed up by praise, who does not go under when people speak ill of him, who loves silence and solitude, who has a disciplined reason. Such devotion is inconsistent with the existence at the same time of strong attachments." She stops suddenly.

"You don't believe that yourself," he says.

"I aspire to it."

"It isn't true," he says. "Look at your letters. You're all attachment, nothing but attachment."

Tears come into her eyes. "You don't understand," she says, and doesn't know whether his lack of understanding is the reason she's crying, or whether it's the note of anger in his voice or the challenge itself that upsets her.

But he is agreeing, sighing, says, "You're right. I don't."

She tries to explain, while he sits silently beside her, tearing leaves from the bush that grows up next to the stairway, not listening she thinks, until she pauses for breath and he says, still tearing leaves and not looking up, "When we were children, when I left you in Fort Benning, I was more alone than I've ever been. At first I hated you for being beautiful and German. But you were the only one in that place anything like me. We were both outsiders, no matter how hard we tried to fit in. You made me love you, and after that I hated the way you tried to be like all the rest. I hated all my girlfriends too. I wanted you, at night in my bed I dreamed about you, but you were too good for fucking, Jutta. I was afraid of you. I'm still afraid. I want you the way you give yourself to me in your letters, the way upstairs just now you gave me your body, but with no more limits, no more rules. If you don't want me that way, I can look for somebody else."

Which is why, thirty-odd hours later, with darkness fallen on the Pentagon and bonfires lighting up the night, Professor Daniel García Guzmán finds his sophomore student Jutta Carroll weeping in his arms.

Alone of Jutta's early heroes, Hildegard of Bingen lived out her years to their natural end, dying at eighty-one without intervention of human violence. From Hildegard's example Jutta learned to turn physical weakness to moral strength, learned both the tactical use of prophecy and prophecy's deeper value as the source of righteousness and courage, learned the necessity of binding to oneself and one's cause a spiritual companion and faithful friend. For what will seem to her many years, Jutta will regard Jim Wolf's kiss outside the Justice Department as a doorway into delusion and terror, into violation of herself and beliefs she had thought were her own most basic principles, into chaos and ecstasy, pleasure and shame, until finally, older and more knowing, more understanding of her own erotic nature, her emotional and spiritual hungers, having encountered the spiritual sexuality of Tantric teachings, and with their help and the help of Alexandra Kollontai's socialist feminist critique of sexual property rights, having resolved and redefined for herself the apparent conflict between sensual desire and the ethical intellect, she will come to understand this weekend's encounter with Jim Wolf as the first step on a journey in search of her own Volmar of Disibodenberg, Hildegard's faithful companion and spiritual friend. In Lukas Grimm, she will believe she has found him. And perhaps she will be right. But on the evening of the day she and

Jim Wolf first kiss, her own desires still confuse her, and Jim Wolf's demands disorient and dull her mind.

She ignored his cruel remark, understood it as a threat, a kind of blackmail, an act of violence. She drew away from him, walked down the stairs, paced a circle around the small back yard. He sat on the steps watching her, and after a while went in. As the darkness deepened she let herself cry, until suddenly the porch light came on and he stood there smiling, holding the pizza box and a bottle of beer.

"I can't drink beer," she said, "my bad kidneys, remember?" but she went up the stairs to him and for a while they called a truce, ate pizza and went to a movie and laughed over memories of Fort Benning as they walked back. They found the house crowded, beer cans everywhere and pot circulating, the living room floor piled with sleeping bags and full of long-haired students making posters and banners for the next day's march. Jutta joined a group of girls at a spot by an open window and worked with them painting slogans, flowers, rainbows, stars, pushing out of her mind the question that kept returning: what would happen with Jim Wolf? Now and then she caught his eye across the room, saw him talking easily with one group or another, saw him drink, smoke, shake his hips to the music playing on the stereo, until at last he came to sit with her, looking at her so tenderly that the other girls teased him and got up and walked away. He laughed at himself and took the paintbrush out of Jutta's hand. "Will you sleep with me?" he asked, and her body said yes and her mind said no. "As much as you want. No more," he said.

"No more?"

He shook his head.

"With all these people?"

"Out in back," he said, "in my sleeping bag, in the dark, alone. Like camping."

She had to smile. They had gone on an overnight camping trip once, he and she and a gang of their friends, two mothers for chaperones, and while the others clung close to the fire, she and Jim Wolf had drawn away, whispering through the night.

"All right," she said, and from that moment surrendered, gave herself exactly as he wanted her to, without words, without questions, without caution: her thinking mind gone out of her, up on the roof somewhere, watching her with the owls, with the airplanes and satellites passing overhead, with the stars. He came into her like a knife, and when the pain faded he was still there and she was dizzy, and weak with joy and wanting. She lay in the dark, Jim Wolf sleeping beside her, and couldn't bring her thinking mind back to her body and couldn't sleep either, waiting for the gray light, the morning dimly glowing. The longer she lay there, wide awake and unsated, the more she desired him, again and again.

Her articulate mind stands outside herself, disapproving. It has lost its voice, its connection to her body. Up on the roof with the owls and crows it knows the truth about Jim Wolf and about herself, but cannot reach her, can't stop or save her. She has yet to achieve that fusion of will and idea that later enables her to make rational every action and desire—that demands that she make them rational, that she rationalize. She is still a girl: lying awake in a back yard in Washington, DC, the city from which every day orders are given for bombs to be dropped on innocent men, women, and children half the globe away. She has just surrendered her virginity to a boy who will treat it carelessly. Up on the roof her mind knows. Up on the roof her mind thinks of Berlin: imagines itself decades back, three decades, say, before she was born, imagines herself there in that city, awake on a rooftop, under stars, awaiting an action to oppose, to resist; thinks of tomorrow, the march on the Pentagon, with tens of thousands, maybe hundreds of thousands, to protest the bombing, to stop the war. She and the Pentagon lie exposed tonight to the same satellites, the same stars, and her mind casts into the future, abandons the issue of her sexual purity, understands that it must be lost sooner or later, that this is not an age of chastity, that this moment is not the issue, not this boy, not her body, but something other that calls to her from the future, something unnamed yet, but always with her, if not in her body then up here on the roof, a vision, a crowd, a crowd like the crowds that surrounded John Kennedy, spread out to the horizon as far as the camera could see, but a crowd of the future, a crowd raising banners not written in English, a crowd of Germans, new Germans, and she among them, above them, speaking, lifting them up, leading the Germans ahead of all nations on the road to a higher peace: expiating the millions of murders, the war dead, the guilt of her father, her mother, her Oma, the guilt even of the fat man, paying the debt in service to humankind, finding the way to a better world. Up on the roof the crows are cawing. The Pentagon is quiet, fatter with troops, more heavily guarded than usual, and armed. The day begins to rise. The German crowd spread out before her vanishes under a mass of swastikas, black on white on red, black shiny boots. The soldier boys raise their arms to her, shouting *Sieg heil;* their hands pumping air become fists, draw close to her body, her flesh; her mind leaves the roof and she wakens to Jim Wolf caressing her body in the dawn. She yields, she kisses, desires. Her mind flees. Its dreams burn off like mist.

Night is falling, the crowd thinning out. On the lawn, fires are lit, placards and signs and banner posts burning, dark figures huddling around them; on the periphery, crows shriek from tree to tree. The Pentagon hugs the earth, the evil machine: up close two masses of warriors, rows of theirs, pools of ours, and down here the people, long haired and beaded, bearded, flowered, making music and fire and love. Moments come back from the day. On the carnival lawn around the reflecting pool, she and Jim Wolf listened to music and speeches, held hands, picnicked on bread and cheese and pears. She was outrageously in love, on fire body and spirit, in her body for this boy become a man at her side, in spirit for the festival spread out around them, for what she was part of, for the first time, the rush and chaos of history, the seduction of action, the illusion of power in the mass and beauty of the bodies, the smiles, the October sunshine, the colors, the banners, the hope, the innocence—even the rage, because it was the moral rage of the righteous. The fine sweet metallic taste in her mouth, the taste of Jim Wolf and the pears and fear: she had never seen so many people, never been among so many bodies, never felt her pulse so fill her flesh, never heard in her mind the wordless voice of unreason—she had lost all her guard and never until now knew she was beautiful, or the value of her beauty, its meaning, but felt it today in her body, not only in her love for Jim Wolf, with Jim Wolf, but in the circle of her friends and in the multitude they were part of, in the wild heart of the whole. Packed tight, then, crossing the bridge from the Lincoln Memorial to Arlington and the Pentagon, the crowd pressed forward, stopped, expanded, contracted, helicopters hanging overhead, almost close enough to touch. She was sex. She was fear. She was reason. The fragments stood apart and looked at one another. She took Jim Wolf's hand—cold, clammy—glanced up, frightened, found his eyes, hidden behind their dark glass. The crowd made slow progress, then suddenly breathed as the pressure released, and moved faster at last, along a road and off it, onto grass, the Pentagon briefly visible, low on its rise in the distance, then lost again. At the first sight of it fear left her: she knew military people, had lived among them half her life: they were not a machine, did not constitute a machine; they were moral men, but misguided; wrong, but not evil; she had been overwhelmed by the day's rhetoric, by the rhetoric of her own imagination; they were no more Nazis than the Viet Cong and Viet Minh were; they were her father the Colonel and his friends and fellow soldiers, men doing work, men trusting their bosses, the elected leaders of the nation—trusting them just as the Colonel trusted them: because he had to, because if he couldn't trust them he couldn't do his job. "The Pentagon isn't the enemy," she said, and took it back: "Or maybe it is?" Jim Wolf looked at her. She began to talk—her old voice returning. She remembered Gandhi: "Democracy dreads to spill blood," he had written while struggling with the question of how to resist Mussolini and Hitler. Again and again the best he had come up with was a nonviolent army willing and ready to confront armed soldiers and innocently, courageously, die. But the US was not a dictatorship, LBJ and Humphrey and McNamara were not dictators. There was nothing to fear. Jutta smiled at her friends, caught Professor Daniel García Guzmán's eye. Fear was an illusion, an error of understanding.

Hours later the night is falling. Up on the Pentagon plaza several thousand demonstrators are sitting at the feet of armed soldiers. From the lawn it has been possible to reach them only by climbing ropes fifteen feet up the embankment wall or by dashing behind lines of MPs guarding the ramps. The crowd around the base of the wall has been so thick, so densely packed, that from where Jutta and her friends and Jim Wolf have been standing it hasn't seemed possible to reach the ropes and ramps at all. But now night is falling. The crowds on the mall are thinning as out-of-town demonstrators leave for their buses, and others for home. Jim Wolf paces, prowls. They had marched with Jutta's friends, with her handsome professor the Nicaraguan, and now as the temperature drops and Jutta and her friends gather around a pile of burning posters and placards and the wooden sticks they had been stapled to, Jim Wolf is sure his own friends must be in the vanguard up on the plaza and the steps. He's been sure of it since reaching the vast north parking lot and waiting again through endless speeches and rumors of demonstrators already arrived, ahead, at the Pentagon, eye to eye with bayonets. He had begun to grow restless then, and still is—impatient with Jutta and her insistent questioning and her tendency to pacifism and her moral concern for the human face of the enemy, impatient with her friends, who prefer sitting beside a fire, hugging their knees and talking, to putting their bodies where the action is, impatient with her handsome professor, the advocate of Gandhi, and the decorous gray-haired Quaker ladies who marched with them and are passing out fruit and sandwiches now and counseling everyone to reflect and prepare themselves to bear witness through the long night. This is not his revolution. He stares at Jutta, radiant in the cold air and firelight, and wanders away, toward the front, but can't leave her for long. At one campfire he smokes hash, at another trades his Quaker sandwich for a can of beer, at another to the music of the Rolling Stones playing loud from a portable radio dances with a topless pale-skinned girl gone orange in the glow of the fire. She kisses him, tongues his ear, says, "Stay. I'll give you acid." But he goes back, returns to Jutta.

In the cold and darkness, in Jim Wolf's absence, Jutta's thinking mind has returned, all the way now, taking hold: this is not her revolution either. She doesn't believe as most of these people believe: in the liberating power of drugs, random sex, revolutionary violence; doesn't want revolution at all, only an end to the injustice that is this war, and the making of peace, a new peace, in which war-wasted resources will be turned to the good of human lives and the extension of liberty at home, where too many people still live in ignorance and poverty, closed out of a system that willfully forgets them. She believes a Vietnamese peace can still be made if the US withdraws, at least will have a chance, a peace that will guarantee justice without destroying a nation and its people. She never forgets that Ho Chi Minh was inspired by the American Declaration of Independence. Unlike this ragtag army here—unlike Jim Wolf—she does not admire communism, neither its rhetoric nor its reality. She has lived too close to it, she thinks, and even though she was a child and ignorant then, she remembers the atmosphere of its proximity, and remembers the images that came from it, and later from across the sea, to America, in *Life* magazine, the little blond girl knocking at the sealed-up door; she still believes in God, in the Pope, in the virtue of the nuns at her convent school, is still confused at the new liberties she has taken in her body with Jim Wolf, at the rules she has broken, baffled at herself for breaking them. Since Emma's illness, she has renewed her dedication to prayer. But with Jim Wolf's arrival her vigilant recollection of Emma seems to have disappeared. She is safe here by the fire, with Professor García Guzmán and the Quaker women and this group of students committed, as she is, to seriousness and nonviolence. But beyond this familiar circle, out in the night, in the darkness, a wildness has taken hold, shouts rise up, and sometimes music, and sometimes the shrieks of the crows. Sometimes news from the plaza comes down from the young men with bullhorns keeping watch up on the wall. The Pentagon on its rise regains its aura of evil, its sulfur orange glow: Nazis maybe not, but killers evenso, killers for hire and for honor—but what was the difference?

Jutta shivers. Her sweater and thin leather jacket do little to keep out the cold. Her friends circle closer, tighter around the fire of cardboard and one-by-twos. Jim Wolf returns with an armload of posters and sticks to burn. He kisses her and her cheeks flush under the gaze of Professor García Guzmán. She tastes beer on Jim Wolf's breath, and her hips and legs want to pull away from the fire with him, into the darkness, where she knows the darkest shadows are couples making love. She despises them for it and her body desires it and desires him to fill the space between her legs, his weight on her breasts, and the fire rises as he tosses in cardboard and wood.

The night goes on. The flames die and rise. He leads her out of the circle to forage for wood and paper. From out there the Pentagon looks under seige, surrounded by enemies and flame. He tells her there are two things he wants: to make love to her out in the darkness and to get up on the plaza, the steps, where the soldiers are, where danger is. Jutta resists him with more talk. He cuts her off: What she wants out of nonviolence, he says, is to have her cake and eat it too—to make a revolution and still be a good girl for Daddy. There are two things he's going to do here tonight and if he has to he'll do them without her: he's getting laid and he's facing the guns.

Jutta walks in a raging silence, the words of her rage accumulating in German, accelerating, the words and her walking, running, up over the lawn toward the base of the Pentagon wall, until he catches her, grabs her, and she turns on him, yelling: "You want to go up the ramp and face the guns? I'll go up the ramp with you. I'll face the guns. You think I'm afraid? You are so American, so American and sick, you are just what the nuns always said boys would be, all desire until you have me and then you have me and you push me out, you run away and replace me, you don't want me anymore."

"Oh I want you, Jutta, but you're too good to want. You'd rather talk than fuck."

She slaps him. Slaps him hard and runs again, back the other direction, into the firelit darkness, away from the demons and her own violence, toward the safety of her friends, her friends who don't know her, who can never know her as Jimmy Wolf has known her, her friends who will always leave her lonely, her friends so American like Jimmy Wolf, so far from knowing the pain that riddles the world, the pain she carries in her body and spirit. Only Professor García Guzmán knows, seems to know. She looks for him: arrives in the darkness, hangs back from the group at her fire, searches from face to face, and stares until his eyes meet hers, unsure of her in the darkness. She draws farther back, still staring, and waits. The voices on the bullhorns call to the crowd for reinforcements. The government troops have been rotated throughout the evening, but suddenly something new is beginning: she and everyone listening can hear it, an alarm is being sounded, and shadows rise from the fires and move into the night, disappearing and reappearing across the flames of the next fire up the mall. Professor García Guzmán also rises from the lawn. He speaks to the students around him and the Quaker ladies, Jutta too far from him to hear his words. One by one, they stand, turn away from the fire, toward Jutta, toward the wall. Professor García Guzmán lingers at the fire and at last she knows he has seen her in the darkness. In her mind she sees Jim Wolf naked with a stranger in the grass. Slowly she walks to Professor García Guzmán, and as she steps into the light of the fire she sobs, sobs again, puts her hand out for him and is suddenly weeping, half fallen into his arms.

The rest is well known, or was at the time, even though the violent drive against the demonstrators coincided with the last press briefing, held inside the Pentagon, the journalists sheltered from the beatings and blood, as if someone had hoped the reporters and photographers and cameramen would pass over this part of the story and because they had not witnessed it themselves, deny it altogether. Jutta and Professor García Guzmán moved up the ramps, no longer defended, behind their friends, her fellow students and the Quaker women, and, with others who had been on the mall, joined the demonstrators sitting on the plaza in front of the main Pentagon doors. They were far to the back, but as they arrived they could see the soldiers up ahead swinging long black clubs and beating and dragging people away. Reinforcements from the mall kept arriving. Everyone sat, clasped arms, drew close, inched forward, packing the plaza with their bodies and waiting to find themselves at the front of the line, waiting for blows. In the noise of it Jutta heard a strange silence: the muffled thwunk as wood and hard rubber struck flesh, struck bone, almost the breath of the beaten girls and boys, women and men, almost the silence of the held-in cries, always the whisper of the crowd's attention: they were waiting, everyone was waiting, each to offer his and her own flesh to the clubs, to the blows, as if they believed that in this voluntary suffering and punishment they could balance the deaths in Asia, as if they believed that by these small immolations they could cleanse the perception of the bureaucrats and politicians, redirect their understanding, and purify the nation. Somewhere nearby someone was crying, loudly, screaming—the cries and screams somehow muffled and far away. Who were these people? Jutta wondered, and saw that other than the bands of solemn churchpeople and the small groups of students and professors like her own, most of the crowd were the same pot-deluded, hedonistic long-haired bearded children she was in the habit of condemning as unserious. Was she wrong then, or were they, or were they all? She shivered and pulled herself closer to Professor García Guzmán, who had not left her side since she sobbed so heavily against him. He knew what was wrong with her, he knew it was that boy who had come to visit her from California. For this reason he had hesitated to point him out when, as they crossed the mall, he saw him off in the darkness, holding on to a bare-breasted girl with long black hair, and before he could make up his mind, Jutta had seen the boy herself and stared at him until he stared back at her, as if without recognition, and raised a bottle of wine to his lips and pulled the half-naked girl to his body. At García Guzmán's side, Jutta had stiffened her step and held his arm more resolutely. Now she pulled herself closer to him, in reaction to the chill of the violence ahead, he thought, and suddenly he wanted to protect her, wanted more than all the world to protect her, more than peace in Asia or freedom in his own country, wanted safety for this little girl, for that was what she had become in his arms, a child, no longer the brilliant student (yes, she was brilliant, outstanding, only a soph-omore but far ahead of any student he had known since the student he had been himself, and maybe not even then, though it was hard to admit), but suddenly fragile, breaking. He did not want her to be one of this army of the suffering, did not want to sit beside her and watch the clubs come down on her shoulders, her back, her head, didn't want to see her blood flow, or face her the next day, when released from jail, disillusioned because the war would go on as usual and the bombs still fall, she would question the meaning of the blows her flesh had taken, the value of her passive reception of pain. He didn't want this, utterly refused it, would fight the men with the clubs, would seize the clubs from their hands, would rouse the crowd to violent resistance, casting off all his principles, would kick those soldier boys in the balls, would pull them down, scrape their skin, tear their hair, would do anything, would steal their guns and shoot them back—and understood again (the girl almost in his arms, in his lap, he could feel her in his flesh) the meaning of Gandhi's statements on attachment, and also understood again why Gandhi would declare violence preferable to cowardice, violent resistance better than no resistance, active nonviolence possible only in faith that it is stronger than violence, only knowing that nonviolence alone can prevail. Again, Daniel García Guzmán was face to face with his own unbelief, made visible to him in the tears of this girl. He held her harder, gripped her shoulder, was about to say to her *We must leave here at once*, as others were leaving, pulling out to the periphery and slipping off into the night, while the line of soldiers moved solemnly, slowly, blow by blow, body by body, driving a wedge through the dazed and waiting demonstrators pressed in tight formation at their feet, was about to say *This is a mistake. We must give up. We must go home. We have understood incorrectly*, when up ahead again something changed. The advancing solders stopped, stayed their clubs. The protesters waited. The soldiers pulled back, withdrew. Slowly, rumors traveled through the crowd. McNamara had arrived. The Secretary hadn't authorized this assault. He had arrived and called it off. The demonstration permit allowed the demonstrators to occupy the plaza at this hour—in fact allowed them to occupy the plaza throughout the next day. There would be no more violence, no more arrests.

More than the violence, perhaps, this change confused the crowd: was this victory, or not? What merit now in staying through the night, putting the body on the line for chill and darkness, transgressing nothing, challenging nothing, facing no risk but the cold? One might as well be warm. One might as well go find a drink somewhere, a bed. It was a long way home, a long way back to wherever one had parked the car, a long wait for bus or taxi. People who had nowhere to go stayed where they were, or went back to the fires, replenished now with wood brought in from outside, along with sandwiches for the hungry, more wine and beer.

Jutta stayed with García Guzmán the rest of that night. He did not take her to his apartment, a duplex near DuPont circle where he lived with his wife and two children; he took her to a hotel. She was not shy with him, and she was not afraid: she was already fallen, her mind was gone, she had no belief, no distance from herself, no sense of sin, no remorse, no shame; she touched him everywhere, took him into herself, dropped tears on all his skin, tears she had no name for, no feeling for, knew only their saltiness, their heat, the trace they left as chill. He knew her and took her and she would never need to be known or taken again. She would burn through this, get past it, drive the flesh out of her flesh in his flesh. She would be free of this desire, this violence. After this night she would not offer her body up again for blows, certain that an army of victims dying would never bring peace. She felt those blows that had not reached her on the Pentagon plaza in the blows of their flesh against flesh, until her tears became blood and she drank her tears and pressed them into his mouth and into his eyes, and she yielded herself to this man as she never had and was sure she never would yield herself to any man or to any man's blows again.

In the morning he telephoned his wife and Jutta listened to him lie in Spanish. She could not understand the Spanish but she knew he was lying, and she didn't care. She was the truth, here in this bed with him: this was the truth, their bodies together, and they stayed in bed all day and tuned in the television for reports on the demonstration until they got restless with the news and with each other, with the four walls of the hotel room and the dull room service food, and he called his wife again and spoke in Spanish again and this time, whatever he was saying, he was no longer lying and Jutta was no longer the truth; so that a few minutes later when he put her into a cab to send her back to the university, she could not guess what it would feel like the next morning to walk into his classroom and told herself it didn't matter, she didn't care, still repeating these words to herself in sleepless stupefaction when she stepped into her empty dorm room and found Jim Wolf's California flowers still fanned out dead on her bed.

And then again maybe Lukas killed her for reasons of his own.

The winter before, he had suffered an accident, crossing a busy street in the midst of traffic, rushing to get to a market to buy her some fruit, bananas he was thinking—she had been working all day in their hotel room and suddenly realized she had not eaten, gone pale, weak, hotel food wouldn't do, he knew exactly what she could eat, should eat, and was criticizing himself brutally for failing to provide sooner the light meal he knew she must have in the early afternoon and now here it was nearly dark and the traffic thick and the grocers all crowded and wanting to close. They were in Munich at the time, and he was distracted by complaints brought to him by his younger son, complaints of neglect of the children, his grandsons, complaints against his loyalty to Bonn and Jutta, even now, when neither they nor their party held seats in the Bundestag, when the pace of work they kept up was no longer justified by salaries, authority, public power. It was an old argument, modified for the newer circum-stances, already old in this form too, and Lukas was tired of his almost forty-year-old son's infantile whining and mentally raged at him as he zigzagged through the hostile traffic, paying little attention to the rush-hour automobiles, when from nowhere one of them, red and shiny and slow enough moving, spun him off his

feet, time going limp all around him as against the black hood of
a braking sportscar he took the momentum and weight of his fall
up the right arm, wrist to elbow to shoulder, and stood back,
pleased with himself that he wasn't sprawling, but righting
himself instead, nodding to those beginning to gather, and already
proceeding on his way, yes, he was fine, of course, fine, and fell to
the sidewalk, dazed, the sky gone pale above.

Jutta followed him into the hospital, collapsed at the stress of
his pain. For the first time, Lukas, immobilized and brooding,
worried what would become of her once he was gone. He had not
fully felt his age before this. He talked about it carefully when he
telephoned Heike Bauer to ask her to come out from Karlsruhe
to keep Jutta company while he waited for the operation on his
crushed knee and then to drive them to the Black Forest where
he would recover at Jutta's favorite convalescence hotel. "You
know she must have assistance," he said. "I won't be able to
continue it all." Therese came by the hospital and begged him to
stay in Munich until he was well. He sat helpless in his wheel-
chair—leg propped out straight, knee studded with steel—and
refused. In the next room, Jutta's grandmother insisted that she
come home to her. "You need rest. Exhaustion throws you into
bed, how will you manage? How will you even get your laundry
done? Who will take care of you?"

As much as Jutta loved her Oma, these questions enraged her.
She hated any reminder of her weakness and dependence. She
wanted to take care of Lukas herself, even though she knew she
had no capacity for it. She cooked from boxes and cans, couldn't
walk a street without him, let alone drive. On the way to the
Black Forest with Heike Bauer while Lukas slept she complained
of all her failings.

When finally they got back to Bonn, Lukas took taxis to do
her errands and to get to the physical therapist for work on his
shoulder and knee. He let the laundry pile up, the house get dirty,
and even as his strength and range of motion slowly returned, and
eventually his ability to drive, his mind seemed frequently to
escape him, to wander and trail off. He slept less and brooded
more, waking even earlier in the morning, sitting up in the dark
over coffee, listening to conversations unrolling in his memory and

dreams. He willed himself through his duties, item by item down his daily list. Something dead inside had hold of him: everything dead he had ever seen—soldiers in winter, blood and ashes in Russia, corpses piled up in films he had been shown again and again at the end of the war—that red and black and white flag like a weight in his body, collapsing his sullen knee, clenching his weakened shoulder, filling his stomach, his bowels—that flag, that sign he had grown up under, fearing, shouting for, wearing, unintentionally loved: that sign, which like the Christian cross would not be erased from his body and bones.

Now Nazis were rising again in Germany, and Lukas kept detailed files. Too much was the same as in the days of his childhood, when the original Nazis had begun to rise. Time was repeating itself: as the beginning of his life, so the end. Eternal recurrence. His heart laughed bitterly at the recognition that a thing so terrible and mundane might have been what Nietzsche meant.

With each new violent racist incident Lukas had grown more silent, more desperate. With Jutta he made plans for the human rights project, the institutional resistance that together they would make possible. Together they wrote letters, organized meetings, sought funds. But for him the work had gone hollow. He had no hope of stopping these new young Nazis, and the hopelessness at the core of him grew. He felt it in his painful knee and shoulder, felt it every morning in the stiffness in his back and bones. For Jutta's sake, he kept up an appearance of optimism, or tried to. But she saw through him. After so many years together, she knew him too well. Her own depressions had always run deeper than his; all along she had relied on his certitude and steadfast faith. These were gone now. Of course she would know. Despair ate them out from inside. But they kept working. More relentlessly than ever, if that were possible. If hope was dying, they had nothing to go on but will. In the early hours of the morning, when he rose just shortly after she came to bed to sleep, Lukas was troubled as never before by the specter of her fate without him. He was afraid for her future and even in the present bore the weight of their practical problems alone. Their resources for daily living had diminished. The occasional lecture fee, the larger ones

Jutta's, provided their only income. During their years in the Bundestag they had been required to donate half their salaries to the party, a rule designed to prevent the development of economic distinctions and cooptation, designed like other mostly misguided party rules to prevent the aggrandizement of leadership. The personal consequence for Lukas and Jutta—for there had been other, more serious consequences, political consequences, the loss of vision in ideological bickering and factional disputes—was that they were left short on savings and now depended financially on Therese's willingness to share his military pension with them and the investment income which until the lost election he had assigned all to her. At times they had even turned to the generosity of Jutta's Oma, or their friends, Hilmar Knapp or Heike Bauer, and until last year Sonam Pasang. They had tried several ventures since their electoral displacement— Jutta's failed television show, her repeated attempts to contract for an American biography, now the human rights office they were campaigning to create. If it all came to nothing she would have to return to Brussels and complete her term of service with the European Community, from which she had officially been on leave since 1983. A mere six months was needed to secure her modest pension, a technicality, and nobody there really wanted her back—she had been a free agent too long for her own comfort or any bureaucrat's—but they held the technicality out against her just the same.

With these worries bearing down on him, Lukas took less pleasure than before in daily life. His view narrowed. Old memories came back to him in troubled dreams. He saw Jutta everywhere, in street scenes from his childhood, in Russia during the war. She wore a military uniform with NATO insignia. She shouted *Sieg Heil*. He saw her small pale breasts in Sonam Pasang's dark hands. He hated himself for such images: for what they revealed about himself, his buried hatreds, his atavistic soul. He pushed himself harder in compiling his accounts of new brutalities, sent for daily papers from ever more numerous German cities and towns. His weakened arm grew tired, his shoulder ached through the night. His knee awakened him with pain—phantom pain, he told himself, like the pains in Jutta's phantom kidney—but real enough. And every waking brought to consciousness another dreadful dream.

Again, so badly.
Again? she asks.
But where are her eyes?
I have dreamed, Jutta—
But he is still sleeping. The bed is empty beside him. From her office down the hall, he hears the rustling of her papers, the scratching of her pen, her voice—she sometimes composes out loud or talks for hours on the phone, calling New York or California or waking friends from sleep, Heike or Hilmar or Frieda, her Omi, to detail her woes. "Lukas!" But this voice belongs to Therese. She is young. Her breasts are in his mouth. His mouth is enormous. He devours her, swallows her down. She kicks inside his chest, in his belly. From his bowels her voice cries: "Lukas! Lukas!" He pisses into a ditch and out she flows. She cries his name, she takes his penis into her mouth. He is afraid, naked in Russian snow. And suddenly the flags: red field, white circle, black broken cross. He comes without ejaculation. Therese is gone. He falls to his knees.

I am living in the old times.
There is too much to do, now, in the present—
To do.
The Sakharov Prize, the work—
They waited with Therese in Munich. They waited in Hamburg and Hannover and Hoyerswerda. In Berlin and in Bonn. They waited in the stones, in the ghosts of the rubble. In my sleep I hear his voice.

Gravel under his bare feet. He stands on the parade ground, surrounded by boys. The dawn comes up. The flag rises. Over loudspeakers, the voice of God, the god of his youth. A naked man appears before him: a dark-skinned, handsome, naked man, his black hair long, his eyes blindfolded: Sonam Pasang. Hitler's voice grows louder. Lukas can't make out the words. In his hand he holds a gun with two bullets, one for Jutta, one for Sonam. A crowd surrounds him. He can see nothing but flags, red silk filling the sky. But the sky darkens, rain falls, and flags fall clinging to his head, the gun still in his hand tangled in wet silk. He loses Sonam Pasang behind tall blue-eyed Germans, long-haired hippie Germans, blond Germans wearing Birkenstocks and Levis, bearded Germans, braless Germans, peace-seeking Germans, Green Germans, Red Germans, Social Democrat Germans opposed to war, feminist Germans, gay Germans, Turkish Germans, guest-worker Germans, Asian Germans, African Germans—a carnival of Germans, all marching toward the voice, which hasn't stopped in all this time but which gradually has changed, is Jutta's voice now, and Lukas is standing beside her on the speakers' platform and on her other side Sonam Pasang. Everything is normal, so exactly like reality that his consciousness of dreaming fades, he stands and smiles and holds an umbrella to protect her from the rain, until suddenly the gun comes alive in his hand: stands at attention, aims itself down into the crowd, finds its target there, oblivious, Leni, his daughter, and fires. The rain stops, the gun drops. Lukas falls to his knees.

     I was not a Nazi. I had no sympathy for Nazis. I refused to join the party, so they drafted me to the Russian front.
     Of course I know—
     Where do these images come from, this nostalgia, this sentimental yearning?
     You are doing all you—
     Leni keeps returning to me. She wears your face.
     Leni is dead.
     But not her brothers.
     You work every hour to put an end—
     She wears your face. She speaks with your voice. She makes love to Sonam.
     You knew long ago, from the start—
     It isn't jealousy. I fire a gun. Or you do.

The voice comes over the radio, Lukas at the family table with his mother and sister, listening and still. The speech goes on for hours. At the end they stand and join in the singing: *Deutschland, Deutschland über alles.* The doorbell rings. Lukas hides under the table, his mother raging somewhere above. He hears the voice of a neighbor: *Take our daughter, please take our daughter.* Terrified, his father slams the door. The air raid sirens sound. His mother looms in the doorway and Lukas walks with her into the night. The sky is full of explosions and light. His mother says: *You must be physically tough, morally firm, mentally supple.* The shelling stops. They are standing in Russian snow, lined up with Lukas's men and fellow officers. The announcement comes: *Hitler is dead.* Lukas cries. His tears freeze his eyes closed. His father canes his bare bottom, shouting at him not to cry, German boys never cry, and canes him harder, across his back and up his spine, bad shoulder groaning under the blows.

With you it seemed everything was possible. You were my teacher. I found hope in you. Release.
From the silence, the secrets.
But so many secrets remained.
Unspoken.
Now there is nowhere to turn.
It is not too late. It can never be too—
I don't understand you—
It never crossed your mind—
That you could love him. Him.

Leni stands before him in her summer shorts, twelve years old, the dry skin of her sunburned legs scratched with swastikas, swearing at him the forbidden names: Hitler, Goering, Goebbels. *What did you do in the war, Daddy?* He wants to answer her, *Nothing, nothing, I was a student and then a soldier,* but before he can speak she offers him her hand and leads him to the parade ground where he lines up with the other boys to march under the red, white and black flag, under the burden of his Hitler Jugend knapsack, the skin beneath the straps raw, bad shoulder in spasms under the weight.

I thought you couldn't love him.

Because I loved you.

Because you loved me. Because I am who I am and he is who he is—

Our friend.

Our dark friend.

How could this—

Matter? How could I have cried under the blossoming trees when Hitler died? How can it repel me from your flesh to have seen it in our friend's dark hands, inhabited by our friend's dark skin?

You permitted—

I permitted it and then I abhorred it.

You agreed from the start—

I had no idea.

But he—

You compelled me to beg him. To go down on my knees. On your behalf.

He refused—

It never crossed my mind. That you could love him—

Enough to survive—

Without me. You could. You would have—

But who is speaking here? Which voice is which?

We have lived together too long.

Leni in her hospital bed. Gray skinned. Dying. Fleshless as a camp corpse. Killing herself. Only her eyes alive, and those but barely. She grins at me. She shows me her teeth. *Your whore*, she says. *Is your whore happy now?* She throws off her covers, she raises her thin cotton hospital gown, she opens her legs. I have seen such legs—the legs of the refugees, the camp women, the dead. In the Ukraine sometimes it was warm and the women still had flesh on them, they were Cossack women and Tartar women, they liked us, they shared their flesh and showed off their bodies in bikinis at the beach. We could forget sometimes for a minute or longer what we were doing there, why our lives had become so bleak. We were happy when the war was over but we were afraid and the closer we got to home the more frightened we became. It was then that Therese took me in. Leni was our first child, our oldest. And here she is, lying again in her hospital bed, starving herself, beyond saving—dead but still talking. *You thought you could make up for it*, she says. *Your whore thought you could fix everything. Well, not for me.* She salutes me as a general of the Bundeswehr. She laughs at me, at us, at our pretensions, until beside her bed the window breaks, glass falling, birds and yellow butterflies swarming into the room. I can't breathe. The birds beat at my shoulders. I fall to my knees.

I am an old man. All this is nothing. Phantoms. History. The dead lie dead. Jutta gave me the future, a new future. When we met she was so beautiful, and Leni was still alive. In fact it was Leni who called her to my attention, Leni with her hatred of my general's uniform and her passion for justice and peace. She was fierce. Best loved of my three children, the best of everything in my life before Jutta. At first she blessed us. She was proud of me for quitting the army and maybe it even pleased her notion of her new resistant father that he should throw over his conservative Catholic wife for such a radical heroine as the beautiful Jutta Carroll. But Leni's enthusiasm staled as my love for Jutta grew. She saw me vanishing. She was the first to call me what everyone came to call me in the end: *Kofferträger*—baggage carrier, Jutta's gofer—the rationalization for Leni's complaints, but not the source of her rage. It was so pathetically clear what she wanted, what she could never have. She grew closer to her mother, her mother who had until then been the object of her greatest scorn. Meanwhile, all across Germany, the crowds grew larger, until we marched into parliament bearing our potted plants.

To tell the truth, the potted plants embarrassed me. The pine boughs, the forsythia blossoms and acacia. They were Jutta's idea. She loved flowers, the way she loved all things sentimental and harmless, and in that season of our victory they symbolized everything she hoped for. I was swept away by her too. Everyone was, even her enemies, in and outside the party. So on we marched and took our seats, our flowering branches rising like so many golden scepters from our little parliamentary desks.

That was a small show. We made bigger ones. We got ourselves arrested in the East, on the Alexanderplatz, protesting the nuclear arsenals of both alliances. Nor did we allow our parliamentary status to inhibit our participation in antinuclear actions in civil disobedience at home, still gave our bodies to be carried from US missile bases, going limp in the grip of soldiers and police. Over time, of course, the parliamentary work did slow us down. We got involved in legislation, took our responsibilities seriously, evaluating government proposals, offering objection and alternative plans. It is because of us, our initial shocking victory, our first little band of twenty-seven flower-carriers, that Germany now has the strongest environmental protection laws of any industrial nation. It was we, Jutta and I, who brought the Dalai Lama's movement for a free Tibet out of the narrow world of right-wing anticommunism into a wider hearing throughout the liberal West; we who on principle and in all practicality encouraged the dissidents of East Germany and Hungary and Czechoslovakia when Social Democrats and Communists and even members of our own party continued to defend their corrupt oppressor states. We could direct our attention anywhere, locally, globally, and raise our voices and make them heard; we had a public forum, and public resources always at our fingertips—information, staff assistants, copiers, postage, telephones, fax. And still, scarcely a week went by that Jutta wasn't ejected from the chamber for some little parliamentary demonstration or other.

When we were forced finally to leave all that, to carry on alone in our little rented house, Jutta upstairs in her office, me down below, once she got over the defeat and the grief of failure, the greatest shock was the loss of material support for our daily labors. From then on she did all her correspondence by hand. She had never typed—had always had typists. Now the typing was left to me. Typing for her was no great change. We reserved it for the big things, the speeches, the public letters, the funding proposals—the work we had always gone over together, in any case, drafting, redrafting. Yet every task was now more time-consuming. We had no one to file for us. We lost hours searching for missing papers, and in the daily errands, the xeroxing and posting, the banking, in raising money and screening phone calls and faxes and mail. We could no longer afford the housekeeper who had come in once a month to clean. Once a month! Now I became the housekeeper, too. But we kept going.

Leni was dead by then, had killed herself by starvation years before, a protest, she said, against us. *You tell her all your secrets*, she had accused me. *You tell her the truth about the war.* It wasn't so. Jutta and I never talked about the past, not then. That came only much later, as we counted our losses. But Leni was obsessed, fixated. I never knew what she imagined I was withholding. It was as if she needed to hear that I had been a sadist, a monster, a vicious torturer, Nazi butcher of millions. But it wasn't true. Not even her grandparents had been Nazis really, although my mother was a sympathizer and my father did join the party in the later years. My sister was a Hitler girl, we boys were Hitler boys. Like everyone. Did that make us Nazis? Not at all. I am exempt from political charges, like all of us born after 1918, by virtue of the youth amnesty. Our innocence has been legislated. Our educations, our minds, were marred by all that, scratched you could say. But for me and my brother and sister, at least, not the will. Even our father, who joined the party to protect us and because our mother insisted, kept his private will intact. We participated but withheld our approval. We thought that was enough—the most we could do.

Of course it was not enough, nor altogether true.

That is why I keep my records now, why I make a new accounting. I am preparing for a new future.

Beyond that, I write letters. I warn the Germans, I warn the world. The old men and women of this nation were educated as I was, under the Nazi flag. Thanks to those scratches, those mars, that legislated innocence, we are adept at blindness, adept at sleep. I work to awaken them, to open their dreaming frozen-shut inward-turned eyes. Jutta has made this possible for me. She learned it in America. All of our years together lead to this. We started in hope and end in despair but we continue the struggle to speak the truth.

And beyond that?

What troubles me then …

We survived Leni—

Survived Leni's death—

But this minor accident, this shoulder, this knee—

We are not surviving it.

Have not survived it.

She is too young to age with me, to die with me.

She has Sonam Pasang.

Had. It isn't possible. He isn't possible. He's left her already. Gone back to his wife.

I imagine—

Don't.

I see—

Don't.

She couldn't go on without me. She said it. I heard her say it. Hilmar heard her.

Yes but of course she's said many things.

Last week, last month. More than once.

Last year. She was making love to Sonam Pasang. She was taking his—

Penis into her mouth, into her anus, into her opening heart.

Sometimes she called you Papa.

Never.

With your penis up her ass, she cried out—

Papa. Papa.

Now, like Leni, she's dead.

Sleeping.

Dead. The gun holds two bullets. The bullets have been fired. One into her, one into you. You fired that gun.

I love her. We have work to do. Even in the crippling and the weakness of my shoulder and my knee, even in doubt for the future, even in shame at my jealousy and loathing of Sonam Pasang, and in my rage at him for leaving her, we laugh, we dine with friends and laugh and make hope for ourselves and for Germany and for the world. Jutta has the power to do that. She has the power to do that for us all.

Did have. Go upstairs. She's waiting.

I want to see her one more time.

The gun is empty. Go up again and look.

I want to touch her. I want to hold her. I won't give her away, not to Sonam Pasang or to anyone. I want her with me only.

Go on, keep going. You'll find the bodies. Her body there on the bed more peaceful than sleeping. You out here in the hall. You didn't have the courage—

To lie down with her, beside her, to take her in my arms—

To caress her last dead flesh.

I didn't do this. It wasn't me.

Emma. These few things we know about her. Jutta Carroll's little American sister. So far we have seen her only as a baby, a kind of doll. Later, she will be a child made sign. A dead child: an ordinary child, a gifted child (all children are gifted), made extraordinary by disease. Her particularity before her illness erased, lost. (This too perhaps a sign for Jutta Carroll—her own erased particularity, a private self before the public, a subject before the subject.)

Years later, when Jutta Carroll writes about Emma, she writes perhaps more eloquently than about anyone or anything else. Yet closely examined, what she writes reveals only more of Jutta Carroll, her own self-awareness unfolding, the original Emma lost and outside.

Original Emma. Dark hair and freckles, pale skin, green eyes. She plays with other children as if they are figures in stories who will always do her will. Resistance rolls right off her. She laughs and shrugs and walks away from any child who doesn't take her word for law. Because she is pleased to be alone, other children flock to her, compelled as if for reasons they will never understand. In their presence she becomes melancholy. Her stories and games grow sadder, until at last she tells her mother to send the others home.

She starts kindergarten a good little teacher-pleaser, shooting her hand up in response to any question, staying late to erase blackboards and talk to classroom animals and put away story-books and toys. By second grade, something is wrong. Jutta has gone off to college and maybe that's it. When the teacher doesn't call on her, her heart breaks. When the other children don't obey her, tears well up in her eyes. Out on the playground, she hides in the shade of a sycamore tree and watches them at their games. She is missing from their circle, but watching them to learn. For the first time she wants to be like the others, and only in that desire discovers that she is different, has been different all along. From across the playground she tries to study their faces, their gestures, but she's too far away, and they are tiny in her sight. She can feel their pull from the distance, knows that soon she will go to them and beg to be let in. The teacher will be surprised, alarmed that she hasn't noticed her absence, until Emma reassures her, confesses to breaking ranks in the urgent need to go to the bathroom. She already knows how to pretend; will use this knowledge differently now, and joining them, forgiven (but just this one time), will imitate the children at her right, her left, and across the circle. They all seem to know something she doesn't; something is lacking in her which they seem to share. In class she no longer shoots her hand up in answer to questions. She is silent unless spoken to. She runs home right after school.

Resist the temptation now to imagine her a dream child (how form alters truth). Neither melancholy nor out of this world, she knows practicality in her games and passions, in all things remains the Colonel's daughter. Ever since she could babble, fling out her arms and run, Jutta has been her favorite after her father. But her father is too often absent, and Emma abandons her sister for that uniform every time. Now Jutta's desertion to college Emma takes as her own fault, no matter what Jutta or her mother tells her, and it is this more than her isolation from the other children that awakens her need to be among them. Since she was two she has watched her mother with Peter and dimly known she was seeing her own baby body in her mother's tentative hands. What frightens her still is her mother's silence, and out of nowhere her startled glance, the way it rests on her face, or on Peter's, immobile, too many seconds passing before she smiles and begins her stream of talk.

Now, with Jutta gone, Emma has only children her own age to turn to, and, even when Jutta comes home for a weekend, Emma pretends to play happily with these others—at Monopoly and trading cards, bike riding and roller skating, television shows and parade ground and war, until sometimes she believes this happiness herself.

At night, though, when Peter is sleeping and all her own bedroom lights are out, she tells herself she must be a very old soul. She was even once a dinosaur. She envisions jungle, birds in the air. She lifts her towering body, swings her enormous tail. The earth rumbles beneath her and her skin grows hot. She clutches her sheets, and sweats in the night. The dinosaur inside her falls and crumbles. A yellow butterfly crawls out. She must at some time have been all things, *all things bright and beautiful, all creatures great and small*—

The song trails away from her. In the day her vision is clouding, but the nights grow ever more vivid, until at last she sleeps.

Jutta's little American sister. Her little American self.

Emma's illness begins with headaches and blurring vision, early in the winter of Jutta's first year at college. Jutta gets the news just after returning to school from Christmas holidays at home. It's Emma herself who calls to tell her, against their mother's expressed wishes, gambling that under the circumstances the disobedience will be ignored. Jutta's first impulse is to rush to her sister's side. On the phone her mother tells her again not to be hysterical—Emma is still quite well, surgery is scheduled and the doctors hopeful. On the phone Emma herself sounds cheerful. It is not enough, and Jutta disobeys her mother, leaves school for Emma's surgery, and when it's over throws herself all the harder into her studies and campus activities, organizing the university's first International Week—a festival of films, food, music, and talks by politicians and diplomats around the theme of world understanding—and later wins election as secretary of the student union board.

Jutta's little American sister. Her little American self. The Colonel's daughter, vanquished (but undefeated) by disease. "My little Cyclops," Jutta said when she saw her, and Emma roared and shook her shaved little one-eyed head. "Jutta," she said, and gripped her sister's hand. "Don't let them whisper about me. Make them say every word out loud. Promise." Jutta did. She stared into her sister's one green eye—more gray than green, ringed in brown, edged in yellow, enormous suddenly, the white fine-lined with red—and softly pressed her hand to Emma's unbandaged cheek and down the side of her naked head.

"Can you see it yet?" Emma asked. "Will it still be black when it grows in?"

"Of course," Jutta said.

But Emma said not necessarily, a boy here was growing in white. Only six years old, younger than she was, and already a funny old man. "He says he really is an old man, because old men know they're going to die. His grandfather told him. We colored together. They let us so we wouldn't be lonely. We made doctors' faces, like this," and she squinted her one eye and puffed out her cheeks, and her expression went blank and stern. "Then we laughed so loud playing barracks inspection they took me back to my room. Today they won't let me see him."

"Today you have to rest."

"No." She shook her head. "While I was in surgery he got sicker. Nurse Sestili told me. The doctors never tell."

Jutta went to the hospital every day for a week and sat with Emma and read to her and watched her hair grow. In that hospital room while Emma slept, she remembered sensations—nausea, the clammy sickly sweetness, the jelly her body was, gone languid, unable to move. That green so pale and chemical, so unlike the color of anything living. That muffled hum, the distant whispers, the whish and swoosh of nuns' skirts, the clicks of rosary beads. Her head tormenting her, bright colored lights in the swelling darkness. The tiny crucifix on the opposite wall, the little red candle perpetually burning. An inability to speak, mouth agape, tongue moving, no voice coming out. Her Omi's hand in her own cold hand. They had cut her body open. More than once. It had become familiar. The quiet death of anesthesia. The unbearable coming awake. Tubes torn out of her mouth. Thirst unsatisfiable. Cries and whispers and hammerings as if from deep inside her head. The pain like axe blows from her belly. She had seen an axe, a man's big red hands, with every spasm. As if her little body had been a tree, young and full of sap and jelly, still green in its vegetal flesh, the blows taking it down. As if that little body had been a different body from the one she inhabited now, as if that little shadow body, that little subject of torment, occupied this bigger, sometimes happier body, that little indwelling body alive inside her taking the blows.

As soon as Emma was able to travel, Johanna took her to Heidelberg for radiation treatments and more surgery, and two months later the Colonel secured a transfer back to West Germany. For the summer holiday the whole family spent a month at a rented house in the country, where every day Jutta and Emma took long slow walks in cow pastures and woods, and late at night out under the stars Jutta rested and sometimes cried in her Omi's arms. It was here, not in Washington or Virginia, that she knew the names of flowers, the wild yellow *Hahnenfüsse* that grew across the meadows, the *Margaritte* and *Veilchen*, the *Mohn-blume* and *Pflingstrose* and tall standing *Rittersporn* in myriad shades of blue. In the daytime a small herd of a dozen brown cows wandered over the rolling hills and in among the trees, and walking alone at night Jutta sometimes came upon their big slumbering bodies risen like boulders from the earth, double their daytime size. When they were close enough to the fence and the road, she sometimes stopped and spoke to them, but if she stayed more than a moment, they rejected her human company, the nearest pushing awkwardly to her feet, lowing at Jutta in protest, or at the others to rouse them, until slowly, one by one, they got up and lumbered away. Jutta waited there sometimes, watching them vanish, and one night, in the darkness, as she stood there just after a rain, under the stars and moon, with fireflies hovering on the empty hillside, when the air was warm and fresh and faintly carried the scent of wild roses, with thunder still in the distance and lightning green in the distant sky, a strange scream rose in her chest, as if from an alien force inside her. Long and loud and full of outrage and unholy joy at being alive, it tore out of her body, and when at last it ended, its echo still dying in her ears, she hunched herself over and threw up.

At home she would have kept this visitation to herself, would have known no one to speak it to, no words even to describe it. But here, with Omi beside her, she was bold. The words came more easily in German (hated, loved, cruel, damaged, forever discredited German), soft and southern in accent, not yet analytically educated, above all young, the German of her childhood. It had been a kind of seizure, a possession, as if a ghost, a spirit, had passed through her body, then poured itself out. It was something *unheimlich*—in English, uncanny, but the undertones of *uncanny* (unknown or unknowable?—in German *unbekannt*) were less resonant than those that arose with *unheimlich* (unhomelike? unhomely? or the not-made-homelike? the never-homed? the nowhere-at-home?). In German *Heimlichkeit* was secrecy, what was secret was *geheim*, maybe kept at home, held at home. In English one had to work hard to find in these words their shiver, their shudder of threat. But on the farmhouse porch sobbing in her Oma's arms, Jutta knew all this already, could say all this in her childhood's German, her Oma's German, the German of her intentionally forgotten convent nuns, and discovered that she herself was the unhomed, the never- and nowhere-at-home, that this *unheimlich* presence of herself had been with her in her body, as her body, all her life.

In the daytime she walked on the hillsides with Emma and watched her tromp bare-armed and barelegged through the wild grass, her hair growing in long enough almost to fly out a little behind her, flashing like a blackbird's wing when she ran through the sun and shadows of the rich green summer leaves. Sometimes they sat quite still, hiding in a clump of bushes and waiting to see what birds came, counting their bright and sometimes secret colors, blue and black and orange, yellow, red and even green. In the distance sometimes they heard rifle fire, and knew it was the Colonel or some other man hunting, and were silent for a moment, and made the sign of the cross. Sometimes Jutta sensed their mother and Peter watching them, as if from far away.

"There are no green birds in Bavaria," the Colonel said when Emma reported their sighting, and she winked her one eye at Jutta and laughed.

After the Pentagon march, Jutta collapsed. It was irrational, she knew, to take her sister's cancer on herself, to blame herself in any way. Still, that's what she did. The pain in her own body wore Emma's name. It was emergency pain, an attack in her kidneys like none she had known. She keeled over, they wheeled her away. She woke up with one-third of a kidney gone and a lost sense of time.

By Christmas, Emma was back in the hospital, and despite her cheerful telephoned greetings and the dinosaur and cyclops and pirate and cow she had painted as presents, the atmosphere in Würzburg was grim.

As if driven to self-parody by the catastrophe of his daughters (the one a pacifist, the other dying), the Colonel, uncharacteristically military, barked orders to Johanna as to the lowest of enlisted men and stopped Peter's whining over his lima beans with a shout and a flip of his hand. Down at her end of the table, Johanna, pale and red-eyed, stiffened her posture and sucked in her lower lip. When into this fortified silence Jutta tried to express her pain at Emma's deteriorating condition, the three of them briefly closed ranks against her, called the discovery of new tumors a little setback, said the treatments would be difficult, "but our Emma's a trooper," and Peter: "She gets ice cream every night." They came to sudden, almost cheerful life only when Jutta, with keen if not yet fully conscious political instinct, stifled her own fear and sorrow to mobilize them around the mission of making Emma well. Anger, a sharper tool than sadness, nearly broke through the fortress wall, and up in her bed that night, in a fit of brilliant outrage, she poured forth her afflictions, heart, and despairing spirit in a letter to her Omi, so nearby in Nürnberg (a letter she would later copy out, expand, revise, and mail to the Pope).

Emma came home for the new year, determined to live. Radiation therapy and the spreading cancer had left her looking sicker than Jutta had yet seen her, her body pale and bony, her one eye bigger than ever in her oddly shrinking face. Her head was nearly bald again, her hair growing back fine and thin. A thought made Jutta smile, and she said it out loud: "I have one kidney and you have one eye." But her own two eyes filled up with tears.

"If we keep losing parts of ourselves like this," Emma said solemnly, then laughed, "it will take two of us to make one whole girl."

"We'd better save your nose, then," Jutta said. "This one of mine's too pointy."

"Your skin. She won't want my freckles."

"Your mouth."

"Your voice. I can't carry a tune. And your hair."

"No, definitely, yours. Once it grows in."

Then Emma held her hand up next to Jutta's small hand and said matter-of-factly, "Mine will never grow so big." At once Jutta protested, but Emma went on talking: "They say I'll be like the Little Prince now, tiny forever, even when I get well."

In fact the doctors offered little hope, even while proposing more intensive, experimental therapies that might, however briefly, prolong her fragile life. They didn't want Emma to know how slim her chances were, but Jutta kept her original promise and secretly repeated all she learned. Together they conspired against the doctors' refusal to tell a child the truth, against their parents' unacknowledged acceptance of the prognosis, against Peter's now open pretending that Emma had already died. Only Jutta seemed to know what could be going on in that living little body, and only she and Emma seemed to believe every day, whatever the body's shifting declines and rallies, that Emma could fight for her life and win.

Jutta prays every morning and every night, fasting and doing penance and lighting candles at shrines of Madonnas and saints. She prays for Emma's full recovery, prays for her Omi, and the soul of every German, prays for Jim Wolf and Daniel and his wife and for peace for the people of Vietnam. The candles she lights flicker all night in her consciousness, and nowhere in her memory does she encounter her own body's stupefaction or its corruption or its pain. It is 1968 and the war goes on. It is a long war, an old war, a war that can't be won. Men come home from it shattered, young people rage in the streets against it, and the bombing still goes on. These realities come together in her nightmares: a one-eyed Vietnamese man grows tumors like potatoes in lumps just below his skin; urine and frothy feces from Emma's hospital bedpan seep through the Colonel's khaki, the pus and suppurations of a hidden, wasting wound; Emma's phlegm and sometimes bloody vomit run down a gutter where in a mass of demonstrators Daniel's body cracks under policemen's blows. Jutta's eyes open in darkness any night she dreams. She talks suddenly, compulsively, to Karen, who sleeps through everything. Sometimes then she gets up and writes—maybe a letter to Emma, or one to Omi, maybe notes for an essay, never a poem anymore, or almost never, instead a letter to an editor or politician. She is busy with several campaigns, the organization of a second, bigger International Week, her own run for student senate, and Bobby Kennedy's new candidacy for the Democratic nomination, when Dr. Martin Luther King, Jr., is assassinated in Memphis.

Shocked and grieving, vaguely intuiting her own uncanny intimacy with such a bullet, but living in a whiter, more sheltered part of the District, Jutta learns that vigils and demonstrations have mutated into uprising and fire only when the President calls in thousands of federal troops. Curfew is imposed; marines with machine guns guard the Capitol, army infantry the White House; the National Guard patrols the streets; and Jutta adds this massive military occupation to her grief. Within the few days it takes to restore what is commonly called order, more than seven thousand people are arrested, over a thousand injured, and thirteen killed.

Two months later, in California, after victory in the Democratic primary, Bobby Kennedy is shot and dying.

She is making it all too personal, Jutta knows this, but she can't forget the day she met him, how—when everyone said he was awkward and arrogant and even sometimes shy—he held her hand seconds longer than was called for and looked with deep recognition into her eyes. She had counted on him to win the presidency, the war to end; and once she had finished college, or even while still in school, she would have taken a job in his administration, the best and brightest all over again, and together with his new young army would have made a sane, a just, a more peaceful world.

When they heard the news, she cried in the arms of campaign coworkers and resisted the desire to call Daniel. It was three o'clock in the morning, already nearly four. She resisted the image of Daniel's body, naked in the sheets with his wife. After the Pentagon she had meant never to sleep with him again, in fact had slept with him only twice more. She had never intended to fall in love with a married man.

Now as the dawn comes up she sits alone outside her dorm and tries to imagine the city as it was in October, for a few hours a carnival of hope and rallying cries and chants and banners and balloons. For the first time in months she thinks of Jimmy Wolf, and the next day, drained of tears, in the airport waiting for her plane to Germany, will write him her last card. She looks at the glossy photo of the big white statue of Lincoln and remembers her first sight of it, the Colonel and her mother and Peter behind her and Emma's hand in her hand. She remembers, suddenly, hospitals, damp green walls and the sweet sick antiseptic smell, remembers hearing her name, called from an enormous distance, her eyes opening from a dead sleep to see and feel a doctor and nurses pulling a tube as thick as a garden hose out of her throat. She remembers heavy machinery and cold metal tables, year-long days in bed, nuns and nurses under winged hats floating through shaded rooms. She remembers pain and narcotic oblivion, remembers the shouts and coughs and cries of other patients, doctors who smiled at her and played with her hair, whispers blowing in from the corridors, sudden breathing silences, and everywhere strangers' eyes.

Before the assassination—when Kennedy, still watching cautiously from the sidelines, had not yet declared his intention to run—late in February of 1968, in the wake of the Tet Offensive, when Vice President Hubert Humphrey appeared on campus, Jutta had worn a black armband and with Daniel García Guzmán and a hundred others walked out on his talk to stand in silent witness and mourning for the dead in Vietnam. Jutta had been writing to Humphrey since the previous spring when she was organizing the first International Week. This protest, she explained in a new letter, wasn't personal. She admired his record on civil rights and economic justice. She understood his loyalty to his office, although, as a German, of course, she was obliged to question loyalty of that kind. Three and a half months later, on the death of Bobby Kennedy, while waiting to leave for Germany, in despair she wrote to Humphrey again. He answered with an invitation to join his campaign, and by the end of summer, with Kennedy dead, and despite the lies and violence of the Chicago convention, Jutta saw Humphrey as America's last best hope. Back at school in September she canvassed and stuffed envelopes and strategized daily and answered phones. With other young campaigners she flew to Minneapolis for election night and as the returns came in told a *Tribune* reporter that although she had brought her citizenship papers with her and had planned to file them immediately on Humphrey's victory, his defeat had crushed for good her desire to become an American.

Bobby Kennedy was dead, Martin Luther King was dead, Humphrey was defeated, and every day in Vietnam women and children and soldiers and old men perished. This world was no different from the world of her mother, the world that had starved and imprisoned and gassed its Jews. All difference was illusion. Logic was illusion. Sin in the heart made sin in the world.

From the beginning of Emma's sickness Jutta had helped her keep up with her schoolwork, and that summer in Germany, they read *The Little Prince* together (that first summer in English, later in German and French) and secretly laughed at the others for acting like grownups. "Children should always show great forbearance toward grownup people," Emma would say, quoting Saint-Exupéry, and on days when the progress of her illness provoked the falsest medical and parental behavior, spoke to Jutta in a language coded from the book. When the Colonel was angry she whispered, "He has never smelled a flower. He has never looked at a star." On the eve of new surgery and another round of radiation, she wrote to Jutta in Washington that her tumors were like the Little Prince's baobabs: they had to be rooted out every morning or they would cover her whole tiny planet. "Sometimes," Emma wrote, quoting the Prince, "there is no harm in putting off a piece of work until another day. But when it is a matter of baobabs, that always means catastrophe." And once the dreadful work on her body was done, when she woke strapped into a metal-framed hospital bed, weak and with tubes in her arms, and found Jutta in the chair beside her, she laughed a little and whispered: "I must endure the presence of two or three caterpillars if I wish to become acquainted with the butterflies."

Or at least these moments are how Jutta has remembered Emma's dying over the years: her love for the Little Prince, her fondness for his sayings, and the sayings of the Fox and the Snake and the Rose, the language the story gave her to express her hope and humor, and finally her love and her tears. Maybe it was all too precious, Jutta can think in her coldest, most critical hours, but how else was this fierce and powerful child to fight through her dying to live? She had grown up among people who had no language for love or dying, not even Jutta—Jutta had hidden that language away from herself, taken it, buried it, left it behind with her Omi, spoken it in German, not English, written it in poems that nobody read. It was a language she has had to struggle to relearn, to bring back to the body of speech, to say these simple things: *I love you. Don't leave me. I'll miss you when you go.* To risk embarrassment, sentimentality, to reach the helpless truth of her heart.

"You become responsible, forever, for what you have tamed," the Fox tells the Prince, and sometimes lately Jutta has wondered whether she may have constructed her entire politics on the fragile foundation of Saint-Exupéry's little book. "When you've finished your own toilet in the morning," the Prince says, "then it is time to attend to the toilet of your planet, just so, with the greatest care." Had this not been her daily principle? If you want to change the world, first change yourself? Think globally, act locally? Love what is given you to love? And every day weed out the baobabs that threaten to strangle your planet: the nuclear industry and nuclear missiles, chemical pollution, racism, poverty, political violence, war?

"If you tame me, then we shall need each other," the Fox says to the Little Prince, and more than any other she has tamed Lukas, and maybe over the years he has tamed her too.

"One runs the risk of weeping a little, if one lets himself be tamed . . ."

Nationality: none. It began with Humphrey's election defeat, with the words she spoke to that reporter, and even though what she said was printed in the next day's newspaper, she might have abandoned the decision of that moment if it hadn't been for the grilling she got coming home from Prague three months before. Or maybe Humphrey's defeat would have been less defining if back in February American University hadn't refused to let Dick Gregory stage a mock presidential inauguration on campus, or maybe the following year (anyhow, too late by then) if protesters hadn't been shot in Berkeley, or the year after, if students hadn't died at Jackson State in Mississippi and at Kent State in Ohio, or maybe if she had really believed that Emma would live.

Now she stands alone at Emma's gravesite, snow falling fat across the headstones, a West German citizen, a resident of Amsterdam, a woman without a home, and expects a miracle.

All along she has wanted a miracle. In 1968 at Emma's request she had written to the Pope, and the family was granted an audience. Jutta had flown to Germany in mourning for Bobby Kennedy and drove with the Colonel and her mother and Peter and Emma to Rome with Emma clutching her hand. At the Vatican they waited in a receiving room with thirty or forty other visitors who had also come for the Pope's blessing, all English-speaking sufferers from illness and their families, some wearing hospital clothes, sitting in wheelchairs, attended by nurses, even tubed with IVs. When the Pope came in, those standing dropped to their knees, and he raised his hand and prayed over them in Latin, then signaled for all who could do so to rise. He spoke informally then in Italian, a priest translating beside him.

When the Pope reached Emma, Jutta kissed his ring and told him, who heard it from the translator, that she and Emma loved God and loved the Church, that Emma was a girl of tremendous faith, that Jutta was sure God had chosen her to live, that she, Jutta, was prepared to do anything, make any sacrifice possible, if only it could be given her to save her sister from dying. The Pope nodded while he listened to her words, repeated by the translator, and murmured, "No one is saved from dying, my child," and, as Jutta continued, saying yes, of course, Eminence, but Emma was so young, only nine years old, and still had so much to do, to give, to live for, he bent down and took Emma's hand and made a blessing over her wigged and lace-draped head.

The photograph was taken at that moment, the Pope's hand raised in benediction, Emma's hand in his other hand. She held him a moment longer. She whispered, "She loves me so much, she just doesn't want to let me go," and when the translator asked Emma whether she had more she wanted to say to him, or questions, she shook her head no. The Pope asked her a few little questions himself then, which she answered with an air that suggested she knew they weren't what was important—only his lingering with her and the song of their voices. "Whatever the material outcome," he said, "you will pass from pain to joy, my child. I can see that you are a very brave and beautiful girl. God is good," he said. "He purifies the body through suffering and prepares it for eternal life. And sometimes though it grieves us," he added *sotto voce* to Jutta, and the translator after him, "He calls His little angels home."

A miracle.

Now, after the memorial on the first anniversary of Emma's death, the snow is still falling. Their mother and the Colonel and Peter are driving Omi back to Nürnberg, and only Jutta remains to watch the fat flakes cover Emma's grave. It will be her own grave, too. She has arranged that when she dies she will be buried here beside her sister, under a common headstone, and she finds it strangely soothing to stand in the cold air and falling snow looking at this stone she knows will someday bear her name.

After the papal visit, toward the end of Jutta's summer, she and Omi took a little vacation in Prague. In Prague that year a miracle was in progress. Jutta had seen the cartoon, a tiny leaf and flower growing from the stump of a huge felled tree. She was looking for that flower.

Explain this to the US immigration officials when you attempt to return to Washington, to that country which you will soon abandon. They have taken your West German passport, your US resident visa, your military family member ID. They want to know what you did in Prague, who you saw there, why you went. They want the names of your Czech connections. They know you have been involved in protesting the war, in sit-ins and a building takeover at American University, they know your sister is dying of cancer, they know your stepfather is an army colonel and your grandmother a nurse, that your professors consider you outstanding in your class, all your professors, not only the one you are sleeping with. They know you have never been arrested and remind you that should you be arrested you will be at risk of deportation. They know everything about you, except what they want to know and you can't answer: the chain of contact between officials in Czechoslovakia and Americans advising draft resistance in this country (they know you sympathize), and worse than resistance, defection. There is a line of command here, a line of communication, and that is what they're looking for. So who did you see in Prague, who gave you names, who sent you, what did you do?

Answer them. Tell them about your sister, who is dying, whose death-to-come they already know, whose medical records they have in their files. They will say Prague has nothing to do with your sister. But you know that it does. Tell them what the Little Prince says, that the thing that is important is the thing that is not seen. Sure, go ahead, try it. Say a prayer for them. Tell them you took Emma to meet the Pope. But they already know that. Tell them again what you did in Prague, how you danced in

Wenceslas Square with free Czech people and overnight saw the tanks roll in. Tell them you were there just a day and a night, barely twenty-four hours, before you and your Omi were confined to your hotel room by the invading Soviet army. Tell them that if they hold you much longer, you will have spent more time in this interrogation room than you did at large in that city.

Don't bother to tell them that your dancing in Wenceslas Square was part of a festive demonstration of international solidarity with the people of Czechoslovakia. Don't imagine they care that in your dancing you stood implicitly opposed to the Soviets—they are obsessed with the Soviets. You know already that these men can't be trusted, that admitting to having done anything political at all in Prague would be a mistake. As it is, these men are treating you like a criminal, you with your dying sister and your colonel for a stepfather. They circle the table where they've sat you down, repeat the same questions again and again, refuse to let you leave the room to use the bathroom or make a phone call. You think you have the right to a phone call. But they say, *Why? You're not under arrest.* They ask if it isn't true that you're a communist, that you support a victory for North Vietnam, that you have been recruiting American servicemen in Washington and Hampton and Würzburg to go AWOL to Czechoslovakia. You tell them you are a pacifist, nothing more, you oppose the draft system because all war is immoral and self-defeating, but you have never talked to servicemen about going AWOL or deserting or defecting to the East. They talk to you about national security and the good of your country, as if forgetting that because of the way they are treating you, you might yet choose to be a German, and they ask how you feel about the American boys out there in Southeast Asia, fighting and dying so that you can enjoy your jet-setting way of life.

They held her for seven hours before they let her go.

All along she has been looking for a miracle, has wanted through faith and resistance to bring the war to an end. At rallies, she tended to stand in the crowd, not at the podium, and even when more active, kept a clear distance from the SDS and other militant groups. She saw them as magnets for middle-class kids more committed to looking revolutionary than to revolution itself. The only freedom most of these students seemed to her to care about was freedom to indulge in drugs and sex and rock and roll. They had no patience or discipline. They didn't want to combat poverty or work for human rights. They hated themselves and the world of their fathers, but they were no different from their fathers, or from the politicians down the other end of Massachusetts Avenue—all playing with guns to escape their own helplessness and emptiness and despair. Even now, with snow falling on the graves, Jutta cannot forget the voices of two young girls at a rally, raising their fists high in the air and chanting over and over, "Women fight in Southeast Asia—we'll fight too." She had wanted to go up to them and shake them by the shoulders, had wanted to shout in their faces, *Do you know what it is to* be *a woman? Do you think you are women because you lie down with your boyfriends? You silly girls, do you know what it is to live in a city where buildings fall down all around you under a terror of bombs? To be alive and watch your child dying? To be driven to kill for your land and your people because you have no other choice?*

Even after breaking things off with Daniel, she had continued to work with the pacifists, but lately she has been thinking that they too had been merely children playing, since Emma's illness maybe, or since moving back to Europe, or maybe since the failed election—the inability of those idealists to make a distinction between pure action and practical possibility in order to support a candidate who, for all his flaws and in the absence of a true alternative, had offered at least a little hope. As a Nicaraguan, Daniel was different, but she had often found herself annoyed by the lack of fire in the others, their hesitation in the face of risk, their reluctance to commit themselves to lead. Some core of engagement had been missing in all those young Americans— either they raged and fizzled out like fireworks, all illusion, too quickly spent, or they plodded safely on in some pale imitation of a misread Christ.

Only one political incident during her college years had satisfied her desire for direct nonviolent action. When the university refused to permit Dick Gregory's mock presidential inauguration in protest of the war, a coalition of students organized an occupation of the administration building and the president's office, and held them through the day and half the night. Despite what she would later regard as an overcautious concern for legality—a care not to risk criminal charges, expulsion, or even curfew violation—five hundred students had discussed every decision collectively, voted democratically, and successfully avoided doing material damage or through their conduct embarrassing Gregory in any way. They lost the issue—Gregory did not perform on campus—but won press coverage of the protest. Jutta herself had argued for holding the building all night. On the first vote the majority agreed with her, but later the question was reopened and at 2:30 a.m. she voted with the others to vacate. For the first time she experienced the power of a small but well organized action, and felt again as she had at the Pentagon the exhilaration of erasing abstraction by putting her body into the fight. She understood why the radicals behaved as they did, breaking windows, making bombs, going on the run, and although she believed, after Gandhi, that active nonviolence was the only effective response to injustice, in this action she had discovered that she too felt more affinity with violent resistance than with no resistance at all. This knowledge underscored for her the importance of principle—because in the rush and danger of the unfolding moment, without discipline adrenaline would always take charge. That night in her own body she was reminded why self-command was essential, why *satyagraha* was a discipline one had to practice inwardly—why it was necessary to change oneself before one could change the world. She had almost called Daniel that night from the president's office, had longed to kiss him and hold him again, and with the same intensity wanted to paint *Be practical—do the impossible!* and other borrowed slogans on the president's office walls.

Over time, Jutta lost faith in the doctors. When chemotherapy and radiation seemed only to make Emma sicker, the medical response was to up her dosages. By then Emma was suffering from malaise, irritability, and clumsiness. Her mind began to wander for ever lengthening periods and a thick yellow phlegm accumulated in her throat; she carried a plastic cup with her everywhere to collect the spittle, and sometimes faded out in the middle of a conversation, in the middle of a sentence she herself was speaking. She lost teeth and was constantly thirsty and some days wore socks on her hands to prevent herself from scratching away her itching skin.

In search of a miracle, Jutta questioned and bullied the doctors and spent enough time in the various hospitals to observe that although toward her and her mother and her Omi they were bland, evasive and comforting, to the Colonel they spoke the medical truth. It took her only a little longer to see that what made the difference was not only her stepfather's rank. It was because he was a man that the doctors—men themselves—trusted and respected him and answered his questions fully. They neither trusted nor respected the women, not even her white-haired Oma, who still worked as a nurse.

Before Emma's illness, Jutta had been oblivious to these distinctions, had been so rewarded in her own world for her independence, intelligence, and tenacity that she had not been fully conscious of the rarity of her position, had neither encountered nor questioned the contempt for women common in the larger world. If anything, she shared it. Women's liberation was new on the radical scene, and she tended to dismiss it as the creation of privileged white girls who didn't know what real oppression was. Karen and some of her friends had started a consciousness-raising group, but Jutta steered clear of it, thinking it suitable for girls brought up to be wives and mothers, girls who needed to liberate themselves from the expectation of finding identity through dependence on a man. *Brides Magazine*, she thought, was the enemy, and Max Factor, but thanks to Omi and the Colonel, she had grown up knowing she had other choices than that between madonna and whore. The medical establishment's condescension toward her took her by surprise. She had staffed the offices of presidential candidates and kissed the ring of the Pope, but in this world on which Emma's life depended she was nothing: hysterical, childish, uninformed. One day in Heidelberg she cried in rage for three hours—down the hospital corridors, outside the complex, in the taxi back to her parents' hotel, alone in the room—after an encounter with an American doctor (dear God, barely older than she was!) who had brushed aside her questions about Emma's treatment by saying he could hardly be expected to give her a complete course in anatomy and physiology during one brief chat in the hall.

Here is Jutta in Amsterdam, studying economics and reading Rosa Luxemburg, preparing to campaign for an internship with the European Economic Community for the following year. By the time she starts her work there, she will have found her own mission, although she doesn't know it yet, her politics at the moment still searching and wide-ranging, not yet driven by the singleness of purpose that will launch her public career.

She is doing a year of graduate study, writing a thesis on European economic integration, and discovering a new heroine. She sleeps four hours a night. Emma's death and the return to Europe have brought about a revolution in the foundations of her thinking, and half her studies now are efforts to catch up with her new conviction that capitalism is an economic and social system doomed to fail.

Here she is one Saturday morning late in autumn, walking along a canal, alone and deep in thought. Emma is on her mind, but also Rosa Luxemburg, another hero martyred by assassins. Jutta has been reading Luxemburg's letters and the more she reads the more confident she is that at last she has found a woman on whose example she can model her own life. In Rosa's presence, through her letters, Jutta feels less alone with herself and with Emma's loss, and as she reflects on this new sisterhood, her step along the canal picks up, her boot heels ringing on the stones.

The morning is crisp and cold, though not as cold as it might have been so late in the season, and when the gray sky suddenly opens, the radiance rising off the water fills the barges and houseboats and buildings and the faces of the people she passes along the street with light.

Here is the miracle, not quite out loud. *Here*, the voice Emma's maybe, or Rosa's, not quite yet Jutta's own. But she follows the thought:

Here, in the street—here is where hope will be found, among people going about their daily human business. Give people a chance, and they embrace the truth. Seek the truth, clarify it, articulate it passionately, and they will not reject you. Bobby Kennedy, Martin Luther King, Rosa Luxemburg, Gandhi—despite the variety of their ambitions, in action they achieved the same thing: they mobilized ordinary people with a passion and clarity of purpose that frightened the bosses and policemen in their closed corporate offices, union headquarters, and stuffy party rooms. Kennedy's enemies criticized his ruthlessness and ambition; King's said he was a communist and womanizer; Gandhi was perverse, taking little girls to bed to test his celibacy; Luxemburg lived sexually outside of marriage: Jutta can find no flaw anywhere in them, only inspiration.

That morning what had set her heart racing and her body out to the street was this passage in one of Rosa's letters to her confidant and lover: "I will not play the role of an obedient donkey who works for others . . . I want to strive, and I will strive, for the most influential place in the movement, and that does not in the least contradict my idealism since I will not employ methods other than the use of my own 'talent'—insofar as I possess it."

Here was a permission Jutta had not known she was seeking. This was the spirit she missed among her American pacifists, with their artificial self-effacement and their unwillingness to lead. Since the shootings at Jackson State and Kent State, the whole American movement seemed to have fractured into sectarian debate, terrorist adventurism, and drop-out silence, and in Amsterdam, where, even in November, international hippie young people panhandle and live outdoors in the park, she believes she has seen the consequences of rebellion without responsibility: hedonistic withdrawal from the encounter with all that must be done.

And these young people, too, she knows suddenly, now, as she walks along the canal, can be reached. Symptom and expression of fundamental social collapse, in their lives and with their bodies they reject the bankrupt world system of both sides, East and West, left and right. What they need is an alternative, and Jutta's heart's desire suddenly is to create it, to grow it for them, with them. The American new leftists had this goal but lost it, mired in guilt at US destruction of Vietnam and the naively new discovery of their country's bloody past. Jutta has sympathy for the pain of that discovery, but unlike her American friends, she has already endured it—ten years earlier, when Jim Wolf showed her photographs of the Germans' work at Auschwitz. For her, loss of illusion about national virtue is familiar, a repetition of earlier loss.

As if from a great distance, a few months later, she will recall that morning in Amsterdam, as she stands at Emma's grave in falling snow. Since her childhood in America she had been a leader in whatever world she entered. It wasn't permission to lead that Rosa's words gave her that morning, but something else: the forthrightness, the arrogance, the declaration of will. She felt Emma in those words, felt Emma in the gray light rising off the canals, felt Emma driving her legs forward, taking her hand, leading her, pulling her on, heard Emma under Rosa's words repeating *Live, live.* She came back to life that morning—maybe it was that morning. Since Emma's death, until that morning, she had felt only dead. She had gone through the motions of living, finishing school, graduating, packing, starting again in Amsterdam, and it had all been vaguely unreal. In her heart she was near to dying and only Emma's spirit had kept her moving dutifully on.

At her last Christmas Emma was ten and weighed hardly forty pounds. Her skin had not yet healed from the last round of radiation treatments, and already new swellings had set in. She was sick with flu when Jutta arrived, but eager to see her, and Jutta went directly to her bedside and kissed her gray little face.

"I must look as if I'm dying," she said.

"I won't leave you," Jutta said and took her hand and kissed her tiny fingers.

"They won't let you stay," Emma said and stopped. "We're going," she said and pulled in a breath, "on this holiday. " She had to stop for breath between each sentence and again inside them. "And then when I survive it—Mother will send you—back to school. She won't—want you here," she said, "waiting around. And anyhow—I'll look dead. Don't stay—to see it."

Jutta squeezed her hand and Emma squeezed back. "Once I go—to the hospital," she said, interrupting herself to breathe, "they won't—let anyone—sit with me—for long, and anyhow— in the hospital—most of the time—I can barely—stay awake—from the drugs. They want—to make things—easier for me. They don't know—that easiest—will be to have you—with me—long enough—to get used to it—that I'm going. Even Mother and Omi—won't let me—talk about it. Going away—on holiday—isn't—going to help." She stopped and breathed and whispered, all in a rush, "In the hospital they bring everyone in and throw everyone out and every time you come back you have to get used to me dying all over again."

Jutta said, "I won't let them throw me out."

Emma said, "No," and shook her head. "I can't die until you let me go."

They sat, holding hands and looking at each other, and after a time Emma said, "It's very far away, where I'm going. I can feel it."

"Yes," Jutta said, "I feel it too."

"Someday you'll come and find me."

"I will," Jutta said. "I know I will," and stroked Emma's cheek and couldn't stop stroking, even after she seemed to have fallen asleep.

She woke hours later, sullen and demanding, wanting water, unable to drink it, wanting music, unable to stand it, wanting soli- tude, crying for company, wanting company, sending Jutta and Omi away. Then she cried again, an altogether different cry, and turned to Jutta very gravely, reaching out her arms to her until Jutta bent close enough to be held. They sat like that a long while, Jutta feeling Emma's fluttering heartbeat, her desire to speak. But no words came.

After the family holiday, Emma went into the hospital, and although much of that time she was foggy from drugs, on one lucid morning she cried for an hour in despair at her moods. "They give me drugs so I won't annoy them," she said, "and then when the drugs wear off, I annoy them even more terribly. It isn't me," she said. "Jutta, I love you, don't let me send you away. It isn't me who's cranky and disobedient and pulling out my IVs," and then she cried again and shouted at the nurse who came in to monitor her drugs. One afternoon, when she had seemed not to know at all that Jutta was with her, she suddenly grabbed her hand and reminded her not to let her grownup concern for matters of consequence weaken her love for the roses and stars. One night she was awake long enough to talk about other dying children she had known, and after saying she wished they were with her, added, "Grownups don't know how to comfort dying children. But it's better now that you're letting me go."

They had moved her to a private room so that Jutta and Omi could stay with her longer hours. The Colonel came every evening and sat in the chair with his eyes closed, holding Emma's hand in his hands, or stood behind Johanna while she wept, or made an effort not to weep. Under hospital rules Peter was too young to come to the room. An exception was made for the last rites, so that he could say good-bye to his sister, but as far as Peter was concerned Emma was already two years gone.

Finally, she died. No one was in the room with her. A nurse showed Jutta the body, still so recently dead it had not yet been moved. The one-eyed face looked exhausted and startled and absent and caught in a moment of peace. Jutta placed her hand on the cool forehead, and rage shook her so violently that the nurse had to hold her to keep her from throwing herself against the walls and onto Emma's dead shell. But the strength of her anger was too great for the nurse, and before the woman could call in the orderlies to subdue her, Jutta had swept water glasses and flower vases and spittle cups and tissue boxes and Emma's disconnected IV stand to the floor. Her hand was bleeding and the rage poured out of her in sharp, animal cries, even after the big arms of the men closed around her and dragged her away.

But this scene Jutta made over the body is fantasy. In fact, Emma died holding her mother's hand, after Jutta, against her will, went back to school. She got the news by telephone, and wept in the faith that God had called Emma home. Did she still expect miracles? Yes, she did. She believed she was a virgin again.

She believed in the power of love to stop armies. She believed in the Pope's blessing and had believed in the power of love and will and faith to keep Emma alive. Miracles. In the falling snow a year later she is still waiting. Something is taking shape here, some knowledge, some vision, out of her anger and Emma's dying, out of the language of belief and failed belief, out of hope and loss, ambition, disgust. She speaks herself to herself here, empties herself, stands alone in her new emptiness under the falling snow. Religious faith has collapsed in her—no more Pope, no more Jesus, no more God, no more prayers to Madonnas and saints. Emma's death erased all that was old and received in her. Some other faith remains, some pure structure of knowing, still unclaimed. She is waiting. Vigilant as the heron poised for a sign of prey. Something is on the verge of encounter, capture. She can sense it, out beyond the gravestones, in the woods. She calls it to her, feels the tension across the snow. Every word is metaphor. She knows this, and also knows that what she's waiting for will not reach her from outside, not from inside either. She has given up the adolescent drive toward the heroic for its own sake. She stands at Emma's gravesite, emptied of will and idea, a pre-crystalline solution at the instant before it turns. A sea change waiting to happen here in the snow. Pure anticipation as she listens into the silence and the occasional cry of a bird, the rustlings of twigs and underbrush off in the forest. As if from out there, in the distance, approaches a knowledge that has been slowly growing on her for a too-long time—a knowledge she has been unable to admit into consciousness, and even now cannot name, can only await. Until in her mind's eye an image begins to shape itself: on a disc of golden yellow, three black triangles, radiating outward from a central point, sigil and death mandala of the nuclear age— radiating.

And from here on, the skin of her public self begins to form.

2. Is that it then?

Never share my dying, don't lay claim to what
you never touched. My death will be enough.

—Antigone to Ismene

Is that it then, the *Bildungsroman* of the public woman? The unsolved mystery of her death? After this, the public record?

Never share my dying—

In the mornings the light comes up before I sleep. Every night I work until the light comes up and I wait for the moment of the slow rising of the radiant, sunless sky. I do not sleep when others are sleeping. I have been tireless for this reason also, this bodily, neurotic reason: I am unable to sleep in the night.

Now: I lie in the dark. I listen to my pain. I invite it to name itself. It refuses, denies me, escapes. I have silenced it too long. It has forgotten how to speak. Words are beyond it. It eats words, grows bigger, emptier. Tears fill its hollows. It presses on all that is knowable, becomes heavy, opaque. The mind shrinks, flees. Doubt lines the interface. Pain on one side, thought on the other. The will is gone. The flood is coming. This isn't life. This isn't my life.

The nuns hid the infamous Dr. Mengele in the convent where I went to school. Maybe that's where my/self is? My missing so-called self.

In 1957, on October 9, at Windscale, the site of plutonium-producing reactors and a plutonium separation plant in Cumbria, England, on the Irish Sea, a burst fuel element started a uranium fire that drove high levels of radiation into the atmosphere. Fallout from the accident was measured as far away as Frankfurt, as well as in London, 300 miles to the southeast, and in Ireland and Belgium. As part of the cleanup, contaminated milk collected from a 200-square-mile area downwind of the plant was dumped into the sea. I sometimes imagine that milk, swirling and fading into the deep. In reality, no doubt, the cleanup crews delivered it in containers, barrels and tanks, to swirl out among seaweed and bottomfish only when wood rots and metal corrodes. I have asked myself whether by then that milk could still swirl, or whether it will just curdle, fall like pebbles, dribble, dissolve into the skin of the earth, radiant and cancer-making.

I am a stranger in my body, in my hair. My fingers move my mind moves my mouth moves and it is all somebody else. A child knocks at the door of a house that stands empty forever. Storm troopers don't love back.

Storm troopers don't love back. Jimmy Wolf sent those words in a letter a hundred years ago. They feel like a hundred years. Every one of them. I don't know how long it was. I was still a child, pretending to be an adult, a child who was not a child and never would be but was no adult yet either. In the end, this end, now, what can the words mean? I was who I was, a youngish being full of pretense, protected from life, pretending to live, and for all I've done and seen I don't know that this has ever changed.

I was a river fed by many streams.

It is said of Mengele, doctor and SS captain at Auschwitz, head doctor at Birkenau, that on those occasions when a prisoner gave birth, although he would shortly—within minutes —order mother and infant to their deaths, sometimes even killing them by his own hand, he would first perform the delivery with utmost scrupulosity, following standard medical procedures exactly as he would in an elite metropolitan hospital. It is said that he was kind to those children he kept alive as experimental subjects, that he joked with them, gave them sweets, ruffled their hair, and when it was time for them to die invited them for a ride in his car and drove them personally to the hospital or crematorium or to the gas. He is remembered by various associates as friendly, and even surviving prisoners have described him as playful, gentle and cultured, a man who gave the appearance of having nothing whatever to do with murder, although others have claimed the evil was visible in his eyes, variously described as wild, cruel, nice, indifferent, fishlike, evasive, dead.

The light comes like this: so faint you almost don't see it. The darkness thins, radiance saturates as through a scrim. This is the moment of beauty, the turning of night. Most people miss it, insomnia's gift. In German, *Gift*: poison.

For example: outside it is raining. I hear the sound of cars out somewhere in the wet streets, the water splashing. The light falls gray through my study window. My head hurts. My back is stiff. My fingers resist the pen. Words stare at me from the page like bricks in a wall.

Dread of decomposition. Anticipation of decay. Violation of the body. We have seen these things. We have seen everything. As by Creon's decree the body of Polynices becomes carrion for birds and dogs, so our living selves and sisters and children for the nuclear chemical spectacle that dominates life on earth.

Martireo: I bear witness.

I will die as I planned before—the words of a Japanese suicide, a Hiroshima survivor, *hibakusha*, an explosion-affected person, on the day of the bomb a fetus still in her mother's womb. At nineteen she took her own life. As a certified atomic-bomb victim, eligible for medical benefits for treatment of her radiation-related eye and liver damage—but the family's economic circumstances left her no time to seek such care. She lived with her grandmother and sisters, one older, one younger. Three years after the bomb the mother died and the father abandoned his daughters. They went to work instead of high school. The middle daughter, the suicide, blamed herself for the family's problems, for its poverty, perhaps for her own pain: *I caused you too much trouble so I will die as I planned before.*

You understand this girl. You could be this girl. You are fatal twins. You will die as you already planned. But first we will make it difficult for them, our killers. We make it as difficult as we can, until exhausted by pain and if not poverty (I am forced to admit the privilege of class and geography) then by its nearest manifestation, this freefall, this collapse to abjection. We slip through the cracks. We disappear. Measure this: we lie dead almost three weeks before our bodies are discovered, before anyone comes knocking.

You elude me. You rack my head. You darken the skin under my eyes. These shadows are your only voice. You ache my muscles and creak my bones. You knot up the pain in my back, in my phantom kidney, you tie my stomach, you sear my loins, my vagina at anyone's touch, you burn at the flow of semen into my flesh: this is you, this is all you, here, inside me, hollering, I know it is you. But your language is impossible to read, to listen to: speechless, opaque, beyond translation.

The voice of the body, my body. Not the dead body. The body that lived. The so-often abandoned body. The body for which (for whom?) physical pain became rebellion. The body the true fighter.

Windscale was originally developed, along with a uranium processing plant at Springfields, Lancashire, and a uranium enrichment plant at Capenhurst, Cheshire, as part of Britain's post–World War II program for the production of weapons-grade plutonium. On the occasion of the 1957 fire, government officials sought to allay the fears of the British public by claiming that all harmful radiation had blown out to sea. How reassuring this claim must have been across that sea on the Irish coast. For example: six students then living at an Irish boarding school across from Windscale will later, at an average age of 26.8 years, give birth to Down's Syndrome children, an unusually high number for women so young. In England, meanwhile, at Maryport, sixteen miles from the plant, eight Down's Syndrome children will be born to young women alive or *in utero* at the time of the fire—a rate nearly ten times the norm.

Every time I fell in love I wanted a child. I fell in love seriously. I wanted a child seriously. Even today, so many years after knowing that I would never become a mother, sometimes in the summer evenings I look down from my window to watch the children play.

It's you who keep me awake at night, answering letters, talking endlessly on the phone. It's you who sit up in the darkness brooding. You who can't sleep, who never could, you who used to lie awake the night, gray and still as bone, refusing to breathe: you who became a statue, sought yourself as a statue, a photo in black and white, polished on glossy paper, the gloss that comes off on the fingers, the damp sticky fingers, the smudges of Georgia summer heat.

I envision the face of my father. My first father, my German father. In strange separate moments I see it. It comes, it goes. At first, when I came back to live in Europe, I thought I might meet him, find him. When I traveled from German town to German town to work with local resistance to reactors and waste sites, I told myself maybe here, maybe here. In Grohnde, in Gorleben, in Brokdorf, Kalkar, and Wyhl, I thought: Here I will face him, my father. When we founded the party, when I campaigned in Bavaria and all over West Germany, when I spoke to millions against NATO's Euromissiles, when I discovered that I had become famous, the thought of my father came to me again and again: the man with only shadows of a face, dark eyes, a dark moustache, whiskers, a grizzly voice and hands that loved me, a belt that caused me pain.

Christa Wolf: "What is past is not dead; it is not even past. We cut ourselves off from it; we pretend to be strangers."

Outside, the child keeps knocking. From where she stands the house seems empty. On the other side, inside, life continues: nobody hears the little girl knocking, or if they hear, they know her knocking is futile, they are powerless to answer, they use another door now, other windows, streets that will never lead to the street where the knocking girl stands. *Storm troopers don't love back.* Jimmy Wolf took the words from graffiti painted on Berkeley walls. But before that somebody wrote them down.

Sometimes in the early morning before I go to bed I go out to the garden, wild and overgrown with flowers and weeds. I love this wild garden, although Lukas has always tended it more faithfully than I, and I love our weeds equally with the flowers. It is an honest garden. In the light before sunrise I squat down close to the earth and watch the bugs crawl and feel between my fingers the silk and whiskers of green leaves. Sometimes I look at these plants and insects, these pure colors more abundant than their names, these creatures I think more alive than I am, and ask myself what other life I might have had, what life a child desires before the failures of adults awaken it to this world of sorrows. The insects, the plants, the desiring child—these have been my nourishment, my sleep. Now, mostly, they are lost to me, left too far behind. Hope is gone out of me, the hope that gave them meaning. I see bugs, I see weeds, I see killers. The garden ugly, the world decayed.

And then one day a kiss that takes me briefly into delusion and terror, into violation of myself and the beliefs I thought were my own most basic principles, into chaos and ecstasy, pleasure and shame, a kiss that opens the door on all my desires, known and unknown, the conflict of will and idea, the door maybe even that leads to my death.

Mengele served at Auschwitz from May 1943 to January 1945, about twenty months, one of many doctors practicing research and genocide there, medical director only at Birkenau. The camp's killing systems were well established before he arrived, yet while the names of the others remain obscure, around Mengele's an aura has risen, the anti-halo that concentrates on him the Nazi evil and the immeasurable evil of the camps. The reasons? Perhaps simply that he is young (thirty-two when he arrives), handsome, elegant, charismatic. When like the other doctors he takes his turn at the selection ramp to order newly delivered prisoners to life or death, he performs the duty with an actor's grace and attention to spectacle and detail. Wearing high black boots and impeccable black SS uniform, riding crop tapping against his thigh, across his palm, he flaunts his medals, most proudly the Iron Cross earned during three years with the Waffen SS in the East, where he served, brilliantly according to his commendation, until a wound (camp rumor says to his head) took him from the front. No longer fit for combat, he requested immediately to be stationed at Auschwitz, where for the sake of his research with twins he appears on the selection ramp even when it isn't his turn, lest an oversight of the doctor on duty lose him new specimens for his collection. Sometimes he does the killing himself: in laboratory or hospital directly injects phenol or chloroform into the hearts of his subjects, in order that he and his prisoner pathologist can examine the bodies in careful detail; after deliveries is said to throw newborn babies into the open fires with his own hands; on the selection line, if met with disobedience, draws his gun and shoots, enjoys the killing, and occasionally makes a whimsical decision to let a frail but beautiful young person live.

Goethe's Iphegenia says the gods speak only through our hearts. Iphigenia is sacrificed by her father Agamemnon on the altar of war. *Martireo*. And Emma too.

The dead: singular, irreplaceable.

In 1964, at Windscale, British Nuclear Fuel Limited began reprocessing uranium metals from domestic and foreign power plants, routinely discharging plutonium waste into the Irish Sea. These practices and their consequences were opened to public scrutiny when in December 1976 the Labour government agreed to hold a public inquiry into BNFL's proposal to build a new thermal oxide reprocessing plant at Windscale, known as THORP. "Waste management," "reprocessing," "treatment of spent fuel": the words make the project sound environmentally responsible, benign. No need to worry that the technology aggravates the waste problem it pretends to contain, or that it provides the link between so-called peaceful nuclear power and nuclear weapons of war. But these facts did worry me. They worried Patrick Curran. They worried thousands of British and Irish opponents of British Nuclear Fuel's Windscale expansion. We fought it for years. In May 1978, despite cautionary studies, opposition testimony, and popular protest, the House of Commons approved the special order authorizing THORP's construction. We continued our protests.

I wanted a child. I never stopped wanting a child.

It is only when my father, my American stepfather the Colonel, retired from the army that I learned he had been in Hiroshima not long after the bomb destroyed it. There was nothing secret about his assignment there; he played a small part in the occupation force. Still, it was a fact he had never chosen to share. Even my mother learned of it later than I. He took me aside in response to my conviction that radiation exposure had caused Emma's death. He told me about it in private and asked me not to discuss it with my mother. He blamed himself for Emma's cancer, his own bomb-damaged genes. He hadn't known any better. He had held things in his hands. He had taken souvenirs. It never occurred to him to blame the bomb itself, or the military that delivered it, or the government that ordered it made. Instead, he lived there, inside himself, alone with this self-blame, and until that day when he spoke to me, he had told no one what Emma's death really made him feel.

Inertia. My body gone sluggish, weighed to the ground. I have fought this all my life. With what weapons? The heart. The cry from the anguished heart. Drama. By abstract power of imagination and will. What does this mean to anyone? Nothing. Who sees this struggle? No one. Only the fireworks. The nonstop explosions, the rattatattat of uninterruptible speech.

The 1957 fire was the largest and most visible accident at Windscale, but the Windscale plants had experienced other, less dramatic "incidents," "criticalities," and "accidental releases," a record that came out during the 1977 inquiry. The emergence of these facts, combined with the prolonged public opposition, account for the management decision to rename the Windscale works Sellafield, as if with the change of a name the ground and sea and air around it, the health of the fish in the sea and the people in the towns nearby and on the other side could be saved.

But *no one* isn't true. Lukas knows. Lukas sits with me in the silence.

We make no secret of our problems, do not pretend to be better than we are. Our friends know the contradiction in which I live: to the world I embody the movement for peace and ecology, but in the ecology of the self I run myself ragged, waste my resources, allow my body no rest. My only defense, my excuse: I have too little time. Because of the frequency and intensity of threats to my life, the Bonn police have declared me an endangered person, and in any case my health has never been good. I have lived forty-four years with a sense of crisis. Crisis is my air, my breath. I admit my friends are right. Sometimes I know. Sometimes I wish I could be more like them. It is satisfying to sit together over dinner for hours, laughing, relaxing, but even this, a simple dinner with friends, becomes for me an occasion for work, for plans, for driving the need home, the point, for digging in deeper, into my will and the conscience of the world, even this little world at the table of people who love me, Lukas and Heike and Hilmar and Gisela, his wife.

From among the arriving prisoners Mengele collected doctors, as well as dwarfs, giants, twins, also Romani with heterochromia—unmatched eyes, one brown, one blue. From the giants and dwarfs he gathered the bones; from the heterochromic Romani the eyes;

from Romani victims of noma, a skin disease that eats away facial flesh, their heads; along with, in general, aborted fetuses and crystalline gallstones. These specimens were taken (except perhaps the beautiful gallstones) in the name of ambition and science—preserved in glass jars, shipped to Berlin.

When Lukas spoke I listened. He adored me and his eyes were the universe, the eyes of God. Even angry, impatient, frustrated, to me he gave way in all things. He opened a space around me which no one else could enter. He emptied himself and offered the empty container of himself to me to fill. He was the lover of my soul. He knew that place of silence I went to. For others I rallied words, ranks and files of words, arsenals and stockpiles of words, blasted them out of the silence, drove them into action. But for myself—back here, farther back—there was no one, nothing, until Lukas. Forever after, only he could know me. Not even Sonam found me so deeply or could join me in this place of stillness, before life, without life.

In 1972, when Willy Brandt led the Social Democrats to victory, I stood outside the chancellor's office with tears in my eyes and a lighted torch in my hands, shouting "Willy! Willy! Willy!" with the crowd. But the SPD and Willy Brandt and after him Helmut Schmidt betrayed our expectations, until fed up with all of them we created an alternative. We rejected the established parties. We would never allow ourselves to become a party of business-as-usual, a party seeking power for its own sake. We rejected alliances and coalitions. We had not come into being to resuscitate any failing old political entity. Our purpose would always be to serve the citizens' initiatives for peace and ecology, the citizens' action groups, the grassroots. No matter our electoral success, we would remain the anti-party party.

At my funeral one of our friends will describe us as *pure, blameless, holy children of the universe*, but Lukas and I know, if our friends forget, that these words can be true of the two of us only if they are true of us all. If we have lived by a public ideal, privately we have failed it. Some will sanctify us for the attempt. Others will vilify us for the failure. Either way, they will debate about us, two frail and fallible human beings, while the ideal vanishes in the obfuscating dust. We will be blamed for this loss also. Our friends alone will grieve. Our enemies will say, *Who cares how they died? They had become irrelevant.* Others will be more polite, will regret, at last, now, when they can safely do so, with no obligation to improve their behavior, the cruelty with which they treated us. And then they will go on making deals.

In the vicinity of Sellafield, flowers that once grew white with red at the tips now bloom completely red.

When I was a child I was alone. Then I had a sister. Then I was alone, a child no longer. As a child I pretended not to be a child. I let my sister be the child, and when she died I stopped pretending. I had never been a child, not in my whole life long.

Sometimes, there is no harm in putting off a piece of work until another day. But when it is a matter of baobabs, that always means catastrophe.

A story:
She was walking in New York with her friend Susan Strasburg. She was wearing a scarf on her head, everyday clothing, nothing glamorous—her plain self. Nobody recognized her. Then she said to Susan, "Shall I do *her* for you?" Maybe they were talking about acting. This was during that time in her life when she was trying to educate herself, studying her craft with master teachers, Susan's parents. She went quiet for a moment, until out of that brief silence Marilyn emerged. Suddenly, right there in the street, strangers noticed, flocked to her, surrounded her. (Suddenly

you know her too.) There was all at once a radiance about her, Strasburg says. Even her skin changed.

This child for sale.

Wittgenstein: "The human body is the best picture of the human soul."

In his work with twins Mengele took endless, overdetailed measurements of every aspect of each twin's body and ran experiments intended to prove that heredity, not environment, determined an organism's development and systems of response. Among his experiments were occasionally fatal surgeries and carefully executed twin murders that made possible the pathological comparison of twin bodies at simultaneous moments of death. Most of his twins, though, Mengele kept alive. For reasons of eugenic ideology, he had been interested in twin research long before the war, and the river of human beings passing through Auschwitz seems to have motivated his request to be stationed there. He is reported to have remarked that failure to take advantage of the unique conditions at Auschwitz for the conduct of twin research "would be a sin, a crime." There was nothing aberrant about this conviction: he sent all his careful measurements and test results to the sponsoring research institute in Berlin. An example of his practice: he follows the progress of syphilis in a girl he soon loses to diphtheria. Distressed at her loss, he gives special personal and medical attention to her twin, and once the girl recovers under his care from the diphtheria that took her sister, in order to determine by autopsy whether like her sister she was infected with syphilis, he has her killed. He had become very fond of this girl. They say this later: *He became fond.* And I ask myself, in such a sequence of events, what can it mean to have become *fond*, or, in such a place, that the children were *fond* of him? He made pets of them. He kept them alive. They called him uncle and believed that he liked them. Most child survivors of Auschwitz were Mengele twins.

Before Emma's death I was potential. After Emma's death I was action. I peformed a morality. Yes, it was a performance. Not false: enacted. Because morality must be performed. Ideas require bodies. Reality speaks in physical voice.

We planted saplings at Gorleben, where in the name of death the bulldozers waited to plow up the earth. We plowed up the earth in the name of life. We said no to the bulldozers, no to the nuclear burial ground they were preparing to construct. We were not armed and we were easy targets. I spoke to the crowd that day. I said these things. I spoke of nonviolence, I laid out its program, its possibilities, its stages of escalation, from letter writing and information campaigns to symbolic actions to noncooperation to civil disobedience. I quoted the conviction of Cesar Chavez that nonviolence is more powerful than violence when one's cause is moral and just. I spoke about members of Greenpeace who risked their lives defending hunted whales and blocking nuclear testing and nuclear dumping at sea.

There at Emma's bedside you were with me. You held my hand. You held Emma's hand. You have always been with me. As if you were a film, between my hand and my sister's hand, my hand and anyone's. But that's not it, not where. You are in back of my hand, behind my hand, always inside but outside my hand, over the shoulder of my hand, inside the skin of me. But not inside either. Me inside out, and outside in. You have no flesh, no body. You are not flesh, not body. Neither me nor not me. Neither my flesh nor not. Which of us ages? Which is lost? Which is dying here? You think we are not dying? Guess again.

Studies made in the Sellafield area during the mid-1980s

found plutonium 239, americium 241, ruthenium 106, and cesium 137 in ordinary household dust—all radioactive elements occurring naturally nowhere on earth.

I'm a balloon stretched to bursting, I have no more give—one more breath will break me. Even so, it isn't I who break, but you. I am unbreakable, eternally virgin. You're the one who dies each day. The one who grows fatigued. Hurts in the head. Aches in the shoulder, the neck, the kidney. Tears in the vagina, swells in the breast. It is you who give in, surrender. Not I. You who swallow speech, forget words, pretend to wordlessness. You who prefer sleep and insist on staying alive at any cost, even that cost: silence and sleep. Not I. You.

This is not the voice of action, not the voice of will and hope, or even of public despair. What is this daily death then? Daily life? Ordinariness? It will kill me—you—us. Like that woman next door. We become the walking dead. Former, nonexistent, passed over, unpreferred. Life? By itself is nothing. By its fruits you shall know it. Sing. Find a song. It is not possible that I should lose my grip, my will, my self. There is still too much to do, to be done.

The self discourses with itself. Who takes the blows? A child knocks at a house that stands empty forever.

Sometimes in my dreams, I return to that milk at the bottom of the sea. I search for my missing child. I hear her voice, singing like the voices of whales through the deep sunless water, but when I try to follow the singing, heavy white billows swirl into my path, encircle me, pull and drag and weigh me down to a motionless sleep, until I wake as if buried, confined as in a tube, a pressure on my chest and at my sides, my arms and legs rigid and strangely warm, as if enveloped still in pools of old forgotten death-laced milk.

The beach regions near Sellafield record a leukemia rate five times the national average, and in Seascale, to the south, the rate is higher than the average by a factor of ten.

Everyone knows how at Auschwitz the Nazis stole gold from the teeth of the dead. Not everyone knows that the prisoners who did the extractions were dental surgeons and stomatologists, professionals Mengele selected on arrival for their specialized skills.

Those who reason themselves free from the law must be challenged, accused, stopped. But from what law? Not the law of governments, nations—those who reason themselves free *are* the law of governments and nations. What law then do they seek to escape, what law have I tried in my life to embody? Higher law? Divine law? (If not the law, the apple?) Maybe law is the wrong concept. An ethic, perhaps, an ethos, a knowing, lucid in human action, an innocence, a will to innocence, an innocence that must be chosen, sustained, performed. (The warrior in search of the good war? Potential materialized in action? The old law after all? The law of jungles, the law of the fathers, the law of the Creons who bury us alive?)

In Hiroshima, a month after the bomb fell, my father, my stepfather, a young captain of medical engineers, saw the city overgrown with wild grass and weeds, weeds and wildflowers coming up everywhere out of the reddish-brown earth and the rubble of ashes and tiles and crumpled bicycles and buried bodies. He saw rats swarming and bodies stacked like logs for burning. In overcrowded hospitals and medical aid stations and in the streets he saw children covered with burns and sores, some quietly dying of diarrhea and fever, others running and laughing and shouting like kids anywhere. Everywhere he saw swollen, inflamed, and unhealed wounds. He saw people with hair falling out in their hands. It rained for weeks when he first arrived, and then came flood and typhoon. In the hospitals people suffered from blood disorders, bleeding gums, high white-cell counts, anemia, bodies gone to jelly. Burns, if they healed, left deep, rubbered scars. He was in the city for only two months, part of a team organizing delivery of plasma, penicillin, medical equipment, supplies. Before he left the city he toured the area said to have been the center of the bomb's explosion. The sight of the bomb's shadowprints— vague traces of human forms readable in concrete and granite— moved him to recall that on the day of Japanese surrender, still out in the Pacific, he had attended Mass for Mary's Assumption, and there at the bomb's heart he found himself imagining the Virgin Mother leaving a shadow that permanent as she rose to the light of God.

My father the Colonel was never a fighter. He was a desk man through and through. In the streets of Japan, though, even he felt the seduction of conquest. There you are in your government jeep, he told me, with your medicines and your candy bars and your power, just like that (snapping his fingers), to take everything away.

What a great miracle that into woman's body the king came. God did this and raised her humility above the world. And what great happiness in this body now, that evil, which flowed from woman, woman now drives away, and sweetens the air with virtue, and ornaments heaven, she that before rained confusion and shame down on the earth.

The dream never leaves me, Emma runs on the beach, missiles cross the sky. I sweep her into my arms, walk her into the water. We go under. We live in that blue water. And then the missiles come—from a long way off I see them pushing through, fish scattering, seaweed and flowers breaking into tiny bubbles,

Emma rising, black hair swirling to the surface and me beside her, in the sky the mushroom cloud. I wake and the darkness doesn't clear. The tunnel narrows before me. If I had a weapon I would kill something. Nobody knows me.

The nuclear shadows, the Sellafield flowers, the blood on Mengele's dissecting room floor.

Antonio Contini, so long ago in New York, the radiant red roses.

How many voices are there? The voice of her public self, the voice of her private self, the voice of her secret self. And me, then—what about me? I took the blows. I knocked on emptiness. In the gray night I swallowed tears. (For this?)

The means are the end, the only end. Peace will be brought about only by peace.

We planted saplings at Gorleben, where the bulldozers waited to plow up the earth. We helped our friends in the East.

Rosa Luxemburg: "The public always senses the mood of the combatants, and the joy of battle gives the polemic a clear sound and a moral superiority."

Catastrophe of a personality? *Folie à deux?*

I have fought this all my life. I have fought you.

The nuns hid the infamous Dr. Mengele in the convent where I went to school. I saw him there. Many years later I understood. I was sex. I was fear. I was reason. Years later I understood. I gave my body. I took with my body. I joined, with my body, my soul. I carry the men with me. Jim Wolf. Daniel García Guzmán. Antonio Contini. Patrick Curran. Hilmar Knapp (I never believed I could love a German). Then Lukas, and Sonam Pasang. So many older, so many with wives. Others of course, a few others. I know what they say about me, but it doesn't matter. I was fear. I was sex. None of it matters now. The nuns hid Mengele. Everything is over. The world has gone home. Darkness has fallen and the lights flicker out. I was reason. What more?

Missiles. Emma. Who takes the blows?

I am shot in my sleep, my face to the wall. Who fires the gun?

Perhaps, like Rosa Luxemburg, I have been greatly feared not by my enemies only, but also, in their hearts, by my friends.

We share a cup of tea. (Does it matter who?) My hands tremble. His are sure. I steady myself on the sight of them. The china is pale and thin. The tea is strong. A little bell is ringing, somewhere in the distance. Afternoon light falls through old lace, skips across the paper-laden table, comes to rest on the bare wood floor. His cat sleeps in the patch of sunlight, a black cat that will be hot to my touch. I meet his eyes. The world falls away. There is nothing but my desire for him and his for me, and the whole fallen-away world fills our desire. His wife is in the next room, coming in with the mail. The world re-forms its familiar shape. We are planning a demonstration as part of the struggle against the expansion at Windscale. I am a guest in this place, in his house, in his country, the voice of antinuclear Germany, come to make speeches and offer support. His wife walks into the room. We look up. She sees how it is. We all see. Nobody says anything.

The world is with us. We talk about the world. The cat wakens and stretches itself and crosses the floor to me. Its coat is hot under my hands. I am young still, young enough to burn for Patrick Curran, that day and for two years to come, and after that for his baby, six weeks in my womb, nuclear damaged. No one could tell me what to do. I wanted that baby. But I feared for it. X-rays, cancer treatments, nuclear plants. The doctors could give me no answers, no assurances. And Patrick Curran went back to his wife.

Members of my own party called me authoritarian, a Bonapartist, a prima donna. They said I encouraged a cult of personality, had a Lady Diana complex, stole the limelight, turned press attention to myself instead of our cause. The women censured me as not a true feminist. All factions demanded that I step down. But I did not step down. Our voters didn't want me to step down. And meanwhile the US ambassador became my respectful friend.

My friend Anna Albert: perhaps she is the woman I would most have liked to be. Not for her cigarettes and whiskey, not even her extraordinary vigor and physical health. Maybe for the paintings she locked away in her studio, a world to return to from the bitterness of politics. Her freedom to withdraw, to indulge her bitterness and live anyhow, smoking, drinking dark coffee, a shot of whiskey, preparing to paint. Even only preparing: the paintings wait there, and the space they inhabit, in her small apartment, in her mind and heart. For me there is no other home to go to. This room, this bed, the memory of Emma. Nothing in me permits me to opt out.

Ingeborg Bachmann: "Of course, massacres belong to the past. The assassins are still among us."

I raced with time. I knew I would die. This was taught to me by the nuns, by the nurses, the hospitals. By the pain in my little body that as a child I bravely forgot, until later it came to visit me, again and again. By the horror of anesthesia, the death repeated, time after time.

My allies were worse than my enemies.

At one time—for most of my life—I was able to construct a speech, marshal my arguments, in logical formation, one after another, like lines of disciplined soldiers. Suddenly this is no longer possible. Now everything comes in bits and pieces, from wild unpredictable directions—scattershot, sniper fire, ambush, guerrilla war.

My work began with my grandmother. Together we established a foundation in Emma's memory, devoted to a single purpose: to ease the suffering of children with cancer—a single purpose that like a tiny thread led me out along the webbed pathways of injustice in the world. The foundation devoted itself to planning and developing a holistic environment for the treatment of children's cancer, an environment not exclusively medical, cold and terrifying even to adults, but warm, playful, hopeful, creative, with teachers and a hospital school and guest apartments so that parents could stay with their children—a secure and loving world for the children themselves, a world with a future. This was our goal, and with it came another—to confront not only the illness, but its origins, to study and document the incidence of cancer in children, rising everywhere, to aid in the search for cancer's cause, to fight in advance of its hold on the body, to protect healthy children from becoming ill. How quickly this modest, domestic-looking goal led me back into politics and economics, not just the politics and economics of the nuclear and chemical industries in West Germany, or in the rest of Europe and the USA, but to politics and economics on the world imperial scale, to the grand, hidden, racist assumptions underlying the empires themselves.

Like Rosa I loved the campaign, the crowd. But I was forced to be afraid.

Who fires the gun? Let me suggest: former Stasi, hired, in the pay of nuclear power interests, material and financial, that is to say, bankers and brokers as well as nuclear producers and their intellectual enablers, the pronuclear forces in the scientific community, and other industrial and chemical interests as well. *Oh, come, you say? Surely that old Herr Professor and the young admirer taking notes at his feet have nothing to do with your death?* No no, of course not. No more than the old Herr Professor, years ago, or Lukas's father or Lukas himself had to do with the deaths of six million Jews. But Lukas knows. My Omi knows. My mother, in spite of herself, knows. Who killed one hundred thousand Japanese at Hiroshima? Not even the Nazis killed so many ordinary people in a single day. *Do I equate my death with these?* Don't be silly. I am one, Lukas two. We are singled out, chosen for death by name. The Hiroshima Japanese, the gassed Jews were selected for murder anonymously—one instant alive, the next *kaputt*. Despite this difference, we die at the hands of the same law, the same mentality. Skinheads beating foreigners in the street or nuclear state technocrats: don't ask which are the real new Nazis. It takes both.

How quickly one discovered that children everywhere are expendable, but especially the children of the so-called third world, and the children of indigenous and powerless peoples within the powerful states—and not only the children, of course, but their parents too.

This tiny thread, this enormous event, the death of my little sister, my freckle-faced, white-skinned, black-haired, green-eyed, little American sister: I followed this single thread and came up against the chain-link fence surrounding the Nevada Nuclear Test Site, leased without their consent from the Western Shoshone. I followed it to uranium mines leased by the US Bureau of Indian Affairs to Exxon, Continental Oil, Mobil, Grace, Anaconda, Pioneer Nuclear, Gulf Minerals, Kerr McGee, and so on, and found, for example, among Navajos working the mines the risk of lung cancer nearly doubled since uranium mining began. I followed this thread and in the high plains of Tibet found the occupied land of an ancient pacifist and spiritual people become home to Chinese uranium mines, and nuclear tests, nuclear missiles, nuclear waste. I followed this thread to French nuclear test sites in the South Pacific and found uprooted Polynesian peoples, abnormally high cancer rates, especially in the young, and a radical increase in ciguatera fish poisoning, a consequence of testing-related coral damage that kills or paralyzes or leaves survivors permanently unable to eat fish, even healthy fish, the region's main protein source, without suffering new attacks of vomiting, headache, fever, joint pain, dehydration, chills, and potential paralysis and death. This thread, this tiny thread of my sister's long slow dying, led me to other, more global consequences of South Pacific testing—raised ocean temperatures, which generate cyclone activity and in 1982 and '83 brought the return of El Niño, the warm Pacific current responsible for drought in Australia and Fiji, and for flooding rains and fatal mudslides in Peru.

Sleep came to terrify me.

Rosa Luxemburg writes of a night spent on a friend's couch in which she could not fall asleep from *the scream of her thoughts,* until finally *her heart grew lighter,* like that of a person who has found at last *a clear and simple answer to every question—even if it is the most painful, after endless riddles, complications, confusions, mixups.* I too have spent such nights—and one in particular, on Heike Bauer's couch, pregnant and afraid for the future.

At marches and demonstrations my grandmother, my Omi,

was my most constant companion: in Prague in 1968, in Wyhl in '74 and '75, in '76 in Brokdorf, in '77 in Grohnde and Kalkar, and again in '79 when in the wake of the accident at Three Mile Island in Pennsylvania 100,000 Germans massed in Hannover to protest the planned Gorleben nuclear storage and reprocessing complex. In 1968 I was an American college girl, Emma was sick but still alive, and the Soviet occupiers of Prague confined Omi and me to our hotel room. By the time of the Wyhl campaign six years later, I was working in Brussels for the European Economic Community and every weekend returning to Germany to join the fight against the reactors. I contributed cancer and radiation data to the local citizen action groups. I wrote articles and press releases and provided background to politicians and journalists. I helped organize and sustain local and national support for the nine-month-long occupation of the construction site. Thousands marched, Omi and I among them, and the following year we were at Brokdorf when three thousand of thirty thousand marchers attempted an occupation and the police barricaded the site and used batons and clubs and tear gas and chemicals and water cannon against them. From that day forward calls for violence increased within the movement, and in letters and speeches, small meetings and large, I pled for Gandhian practice, for *satyagraha*, truth force, for *ahimsa*, the way of no harm. By 1979, when we massed at Hannover, I was a federal committee member of the BBU, the national association of citizens action groups for the environment, and a candidate for the European Parliament, the featured speaker, seated on the platform with my Omi at my side.

Martin Luther King: "People cannot devote themselves to a great cause without finding someone who becomes the personi-fication of the cause. People cannot become devoted to Christianity until they find Christ, to democracy until they find Lincoln and Jefferson and Roosevelt, to Communism until they find Marx and Lenin and Stalin."

I read this quote in *Life* magazine when I was just a girl.

I believed these words.

Children need heroes.

Because of her lifelong opposition to sectarian divisiveness and factionalism within the party, Rosa Luxemburg never left the SPD. How it hurt me to leave the SPD, the party of Rosa Luxemburg.

Lukas knocks at my bedroom door—to rouse me, to take me to dinner, to sit with me, to bring me home. We have spent these twelve years together and every night now he is a stranger. I lean on him, he leans on me, his hand warm paper in my hand. In his pale eyes I see only the tears. I am too far away. His hair is white and thinning, his bones are long. I know his body, his pale flesh, the touch of his desire buried deep in my own. Sonam has taken this Lukas from me, erased him, and Lukas kisses me now with Sonam's lips, touches me with Sonam's hands—the strong and gentle phallus in search of my orgasm is Sonam's—Sonam's. But nothing happens. Every day is the same. Sonam no longer touches me. Like so many before him, he can love me only from a distance.

When Ismene, frightened, refuses to join Antigone in defying the king's law by keeping the law of the gods, Antigone dismisses her. Later when Ismene tries to atone, offering to die with her sister, for her transgression sentenced by Creon to die, Antigone, rejecting her offer, demands: *Who did the work?*

The child I didn't have. The baby that wasn't born. Because of radiation exposures I said, because of the exposures to so many X-rays in childhood, to Emma's cancer treatments, in protests at so many nuclear sites, because of my one kidney, because of concern for my health, and the baby's.

Lies.

Mine was a modeled life.
Like Hildegard, I . . .
Like Rosa Luxemburg . . .
Like Gandhi, like Kennedy, like King . . .

And who takes the blows?

Over and over, dirty hands. To live a moral politics had been my aim. But it was not possible. I was subverted from the start.

You wanted answers? I have no answers. I saw nothing, heard nothing. My face was turned to the wall.

By 1979 German courts had revoked construction licenses for nuclear facilities at Wyhl, Grohnde, Brokdorf, and Kalkar. Meanwhile NATO was preparing to upgrade its nuclear arsenal in Europe by deploying first-strike missiles in West Germany. In March, environment activists and defectors from the pronuclear SPD came together in Frankfurt to create an alternative political party to compete in the federal elections to the European Parliament. Over a hundred candidates were nominated. I led the party's list.

Anna Albert at this time was laying aside her paintbrushes, hammering shut her cans. Her daughter was ten years old. She had been painting her daughter, drawing her daughter, using her daughter's image, distorted and broken, in a series of critically dangerous prints. They lived in East Berlin (as they do now— despite reunification, still East). Quietly and without notice, Anna Albert went on strike.

In December 1979, when NATO adopted its double-track

strategy of negotiating with the Warsaw Pact in Geneva while preparing for deployment of Pershing II and cruise missiles, General Lukas Grimm resigned his commission in protest.

Throughout 1980 Hilmar Knapp and I and our friends in our new party labored to secure the party's commitment to ecology, peace, nonviolence, feminism, and universal human rights, both economic and civil. We pledged that we would continue taking democratic direct action, that we would be no mere parliamentarians, and everywhere the party absorbed local environmental parties and other small parties of the left, expanding its membership and extending our international ties. In March in Baden-Württemberg in the party's first electoral success our candidates passed the 5 percent threshold necessary for gaining office and sent six members to the state parliament. As arms negotiations proceeded in Geneva and NATO's preparations continued, we made local electoral gains, taking seats in Berlin, in Hamburg, in Lower Saxony, and Hessen. In the United States, Ronald Reagan became president, and the peace movements of Europe and America mounted mass demonstrations against NATO's first-strike weapons. I addressed crowds in the hundreds of thousands.

How the Polish people in 1981 demonstrated their resistance: at 7:30 every evening, the hour of the state-produced and only news broadcast, thousands left their homes to stroll in the centers of towns, while those living in the centers placed their television sets in open windows, screens empty, gray and silent, facing outward, toward the street.

Every day I was still working in Brussels for the EEC, and at night riding trains across Europe to rush from campaign event to office to rally to strategy meeting to action to office to speech and so on, until in November 1982 I collapsed in a Munich taxi and was hospitalized for a month.

Imagine a span of time, all the visible, audible actions. Expand the silences, the moments of stillness. Extend those silent seconds, make them hours. Speed up and compress the action, the speech. Expand the negative space relative to the objects that define it. Shrink the objects, human and otherwise. Go to the garden. Watch the bugs crawl. Wait for the light to rise. Feel the weight of this waiting. Feel the weight of the light.

At Nürnberg, in February 1983, we held a People's Tribunal against Nuclear Weapons of Mass Destruction in East and West. Basing our charges on the principles of international law established by the trials of Nazi war criminals in that city, we indicted the governments of West Germany, the United States, the Soviet Union, Great Britain, France, China, India, and any other states secretly developing or possessing nuclear weapons. We called for worldwide denunciation of the politicians, scientists, military strategists, and technicians whose work makes possible weapons of mass destruction and genocide. We put our case before an international jury of sympathetic scholars and churchmen. At the opening session, retired generals and colonels from NATO and Warsaw Pact states spoke one after another about the danger and folly of nuclear weapons—Lukas the most eloquent. For three days, with breaks for poetry and music, a thousand observers and participants heard antinuclear testimony and detailed questioning from the jury. At the end, the jury rendered its anticipated verdict: every aspect of atomic, biological, and chemical warfare was judged contrary to international law and criminal: planning, preparation, deployment, all criminal, along with military attack on nuclear power stations, proliferation of nuclear weapons technology, and squandering resources on arms at the expense of living human needs; the proliferation of the nuclear power industry was condemned as an intolerable risk (a judgment that hardly went far enough). Two weeks later, four years after our founding, with 5.6 percent of the national vote, we took twenty-seven of the 496 seats in the Bundestag; in the election of '87, with 8.3 percent, we would take forty-two.

In May, less than two months into our term of office, at the end of a conference in West Berlin, Lukas and I and Hilmar Knapp and three of our party colleagues crossed into East Berlin to demonstrate on the Alexanderplatz in support of East Germany's autonomous peace movement. We called on both German governments to oppose the nuclear build-up in both blocs. In response to this action our left attacked us for shifting the blame for the arms crisis away from NATO and the United States.

In June we demonstrated at Krefeld where US Vice President Bush was making a speech celebrating the migration of pacifist Quakers from that city to North America. An assault by demonstrators on the police—instigated, it turned out, by police *agents provocateurs*—intensified calls in the movement for acceptance of the legitimate role of violence. I rejected this call, I rejected the people who made it. To advocate violence was to betray our goals. *If any step toward the goal becomes corrupt*, I said, *everything becomes corrupt.* My enemies outside the party hounded and heckled me. Within the party I was closely watched.

In July Lukas and I led a party delegation to Washington and New York, where we met with legislators and government officials, defense analysts and American activists. We demonstrated outside the White House and issued a declaration with American peace groups reiterating the conclusions of our Nürnberg tribunal and calling for a campaign to delay the deployments another year so that negotiations could continue. I appeared on *Meet the Press*, and Lukas and I were invited to lunch with the publisher of *The Washington Post*. Not for the first time, my party colleagues demonstrated their personal envy and spitefulness, demanding their own invitations and during the lunch competing to draw attention to themselves, interrupting and jumping in to answer questions addressed to Lukas and me, until such chaos reigned that our hostess, Mrs. Graham, walked out.

On returning to Germany we held a press conference making public the briefing documents we had been given during our meeting with representatives of the US State Department. The documents made explicit what US journalists seemed to have overlooked: that NATO's plan to deploy first-strike nuclear weapons implied a willingness to be the first to use them, that the US government considered "limited nuclear war" in Europe a legitimate policy option. In such a scenario the two Germanys would be the battleground. This everyone in both Germanys understood.

In September the protests began with blockades at Mutlangen and Bitburg. In October, more than half a million Germans rallied in Bonn, half a million more in other cities, and from US Army headquarters in Stuttgart to an artillery unit at Neu-Ulm, nonviolent protesters made a sixty-mile-long human chain. A week later Lukas and I and five of our party colleagues went to Moscow to meet with various state-sponsored peace and environment citizens groups, very bureaucratic and dull; we met with students, whom we baffled; we met with Soviet officials, who repeated the same realpolitik nonsense we had heard in Washington. Before our departure, our hosts allowed us to make a little demonstration in Red Square. Our message surprised them. Our banners proclaimed in Russian: "Respect for human rights." My sweatshirt demanded: "Dissolve NATO and the Warsaw Pact!" Our party congress two weeks later urged the peace movement to go beyond mere opposition—to call instead for the political basis for peace: the dissolution of the power blocs. For ourselves, we determined to build a network of grassroots contacts, East and West.

In November, just before parliamentary discussion of deployment was to begin, the SPD officially changed sides and joined the opposition. At the same time a poll found 78 percent of West Germans were against the missiles. In the Bundestag, on a close vote after two days of debate, Helmut Kohl's Christian Democrats and NATO won. We continued our resistance. We challenged them to arrest us again and again.

Whenever Lukas and I got arrested, we were heavily fined and quickly released. A portion of our Bundestag salaries went into party funds to support the grassroots movement, and out of these funds the party paid our fines. In the East, when Anna Albert and her fellow dissidents got arrested, they lost their right to work and spent years at a time in jail.

I think of Anna Albert's kitchen, her friend the poet and musician who sold us all out: I remember his pretty blue eyes, his little freckles, his eyelashes like a movie star's, the vehemence of his speech, his adoration of Anna, his gentle way with Gertrude, Anna's daughter, his desire for me. It all escapes. It washes all down a hole. Who were these people? Was he any different from my own wretched political partners, from Rudi Schreiber or Monika Hertz or Heinrich Lamm?

In the garden—

No. Don't turn away, don't run.

From the beginning factionalism and personality clashes plagued the party and betrayed our cause. Some in the party and the movement wanted to campaign only against the Americans, against NATO, reserving their antimilitarism for the capitalists. Others craved traditional parliamentary power in alliance with the Social Democrats. When Lukas and Hilmar and I opposed Warsaw Pact missiles equally with NATO's and advocated working with the independent peace movements of Eastern Europe rather than their state-sponsored counterparts, for this principled position our Marxist faction accused us of being dupes of Ronald Reagan and the CIA. When I spoke for Gandhian direct action and against sitting in pubs getting drunk and horse-trading with the good old boys of the SPD, for this the ambitious young men in our party called me dreamer, idealist, puritan, naive. When I laughed with joy, and cried in pain or pity or frustration or rage, and made love with whom I chose and not with them, for these transgressions of their masculine code they called me neurotic, bitch, cunt, hypocrite, hysteric: woman. And as for the women: they had no understanding of leadership. I failed to consult them at every breath, refused to submit to their female circles for hand-wringing and groupthink and communal discipline, was too busy working to go all touchy feely for them and make myself available to their intimate adoration while pretending I was not a star: I was a star. I had become a star through relentless work and I used my stardom to say more about peace and nuclear and chemical danger and abuse of third world peoples than about abortion or day care—although I did not neglect these struggles either—but above all I had absolutely no interest in the bourgeois feminist demand for a larger piece of the western imperial pie. For all this, for the infinitely useful reality of my dedication and charisma and for my hard-won sexual freedom to make love with whom and when I chose, they condemned me as male-identified and not a true feminist.

Lukas made all that bearable. In Lukas I knew, for the first and only time, that I was not alone. In Lukas I saw my purpose realized. In his arms I emptied my spirit and let the strength of God make its way in. I no longer believed in God but I felt it just the same. I believed in something nameless, in life spirit, truth force, *satyagraha*, in doing without harm, in Buddhist compassion, Christian love. In Lukas I witnessed the radical choice to abandon catastrophic power. In his history I knew my own transformation. In his heart I encountered hope for the world.

Like me, Rosa Luxemburg was difficult and temperamental. (Did they think I did not know?) She had strong likes and dislikes that crossed all political lines. She was happier in a garden than at a party conference. She struggled to build a secure private realm. She was a tyrant. She was arrogant. She brooked no opposition. Study her carefully: she never loses touch with the masses; she appeals to the people over the heads of party leaders. As she said of the SPD when it voted for war credits in the Reichstag in 1914, so say I of Rudi Schreiber and Monika Hertz as I watch them push one another aside in their eagerness to be first to reverse the corrupted party's position on withdrawal from NATO, the more easily to get into bed with the descendants of Rosa's SPD: "Their bankruptcy is as complete as it is terrible." I would like to have spoken as harshly as Rosa did when she indicted the parliamentary cretinism within her party. I would like to tear the mask off the drunken envy and jealousy of Heinrich Lamm.

We sat in pouring rain at Hasselbach waiting for the arrival of the missiles. We sang, and talked with policemen who had been sent there to arrest us, until after a few minutes they carried us away. My party colleagues shuddered: *Jutta's got another big fine.*

Whenever I felt worn down by the cynicism and brute cruelty of so many of our colleagues, I went to my friends to say, "Let's do an action." Nothing could so refresh me, make me feel so clear and true, as placing my body side by side with others at the site of destructive power, whether military base or chancellor's office or defense ministry or our very own Bundestag. When I stood on the street with a sign, with ten other women, unknown women, and together we held a banner and one by one they told me their stories, told me and the curious passersby how they had come to stand there at that moment, what had moved them, what had awakened them, what hope, what loss, then—in the physical experience, the bodily presence, in that immediacy, I rediscovered the certainty at the core of resistance, the purity of heart, the clarity of motive, the desire of ordinary people (and my own desire) to live. Sometimes we were but two or three, some-times two or three hundred, two or three thousand. In action after action, Lukas stood at my side.

Weapons of mass destruction were not our only concern. In 1986, in April and May and into June, for forty-nine days we bore witness to the devastation that was Chernobyl and the winds it sent our way.

One feels—well, maybe nothing at all. Maybe animation flees and what is left is—naturally, vegetation, the plant life within the animal, the flora of the body, the vague stirring of roots and leaves, the hunger for light and water, the tiny tickling searchings in the earth, in the dirt, in the clay of the ground and the loam, the soil, for simple nutrients, nitrogen, potassium, phosphorus, elements, pure, undiluted, nameless now in this absence of locomotion, this fullness of passivity, the automation of this living mechanism that does its work despite one, despite everything, until one is oneself no longer, but only this, the vegetal machine.

Outside it rains. We go to Salzburg for the World Uranium Hearing. I feel Lukas's age, the wear in his body, the loss of heat. Something broke in him with his bones. Something broke in me. Yet the bond that holds us is stronger than ever. The more we break, the stronger it grows. Outside it rains. The garden floods. We pull each other down to the earth.

In reality Sonam is not so important. I remember his black liquid eyes. I remember his hair, so dark and thick and silken between my fingers, the desire of my fingers to touch it, the smile of his fruit-fleshy mouth, his eyebrows that danced in humor, the whispering depths of his voice, his purely accented German, his sparkling English, his music that laughed in my skin. But impor-tant? No, he is not. He left me and Lukas stayed.

Did I invite this? Did I say one time too many *I can't continue without him,* while watching Lukas fade? Do I lie here waiting? Have I forgotten something? Did I agree?

My face to the wall. Even I don't know.

What is past is not dead; it is not even past. William Faulkner wrote *never dead.* Not or never? Christa added her own gloss: *We cut ourselves off from it. We pretend to be strangers.* Each of them heir to monstrous guilt.

Lukas went light as paper. At first it was only his skin, gone hot and dry. Then it was as if all the liquid had burned out of him. He was paper and air. He blew with the wind. Objects became visible through him.

At the borderlands of my condition. Where nothing is familiar. Hildegard in this place knew humility before God. For me here there is only nothing. Shadows of a life. Abhorrence of all flesh, sensation, thought.

For Rosa, this state passes, or the terror of it does.

I dreamed of Lukas weeping. I looked for him in the dark. I stumbled, felt my way until I found him in the corner—naked, frightened, huddled in a chair. The screams, he said. The terrible screams. It was Leni screaming. It was all Leni. I woke alone, afraid in the dark, and slept and dreamed again. Emma and I were packing. They were coming to arrest us. It was hard to pack. I didn't know whether we were packing for prison or for escape.

Emma wanted her toys, her favorite clothes. I wanted to hurry, but I lingered over everything: over an apple with streaky red skin, over a worn-out teddy bear so old it must once have been my mother's, although I didn't remember its ever having been mine, its pale brown fur matted and in patches rubbed away so that only threads were left to protect its heart and soul, its reason for being, the music box in its belly that played Brahms' lullaby when squeezed, gone twangy and tinny like some old American banjo breaking its strings. I folded Emma's clothes, bright pink and yellow and green little daisy-covered sixties things, the exact clothes I remember her wearing when she was alive, folded them into the now old suitcase I had packed for myself when I first left Germany with my mother and the Colonel, before Emma was born. All this while they are coming for us. I can feel them coming. I know they are coming. I am afraid for Emma. I am worried about what we leave behind. It doesn't end. I wake in the worry, the packing, Emma's hand in mine.

People cannot devote themselves to a great cause without finding someone who becomes the personification of that cause.

I saw Mengele there in the convent, a furtive handsome man, sometimes visible in the shadows.

People cannot devote themselves—

Rosa: "I, too, am a land of boundless possibilities."

And then again maybe Lukas is killing me for reasons of his own.

Antonio Contini, so long ago in New York, the radiant red roses.

After Lukas I thought there could be no one, and then came Sonam Pasang.

With Rosa I have come to recognize the German principle: Woe to the victorious! She too is charged with putting her special concerns above the interests of the party. She too suffers a spectacular defeat and feels like a beaten dog. In her state of physical collapse, for three or four days work is out of the question. She too is unable to think, to sleep, or to eat. But listen to those words of hers—for three or four days! Only three or four days!

Kafka: "Let the bad remain bad. Otherwise it will grow worse."

I do not believe myself. Too much is missing.

Rosa identifies herself with Christ. I do not go so far. I share her militant optimism and her paralyzing depression—*incomprehensible and odious*. She complains that she goes around *like a mindless animal*. She fears that she might end up mentally ill. Everything comes to her *as if through absorbent cotton*. Anna Albert would make pictures for this feeling, for its lack. I too would like to paint, would like to find shapes and colors and textures that give form to this intimate waste. Words can't. Actions don't. I would not approve of the product. Everything falls away.

My solution to a spell of nightmares has always been to stay awake.

I believed I could never love a German. I believed I could never live in Germany again.

The assassins are still among us: I never for a moment imagined that these words applied to me.

That fat man. His face comes to mind before all others, before Mengele's, before Hitler's. I ask myself why. I try to remember my own father's face, the face in the photograph beside my mother's bed for years before the Colonel, and even briefly after him. I see the heavy brass frame, curlicued and artificially aged. I see the gray uniform, the cigarette in his hand, the gun at his hip. I see that he is smiling. But the smile itself I cannot see. I see that he is handsome, but not in what his handsomeness consists. I remember words he spoke to me, never his voice. The harder I work to see, to hear, the more vividly I encounter the fat man, the stubbly whiskers, the red-veined nose, the mottled skin, the wet and purplish lips, the scratchy voice that asks how things are going, what I'm doing, the heavy laughter that gurgles up from deep in his big old body and shakes out from under his leaden jello thighs.

Tibet, a high, snow-clad table, where Milarepa, the great yogi, was pierced by the sorrows of the world.

Whiteness, a list: snow, silence, cream, sky, paper, canvas, gallery walls, petals, peonies, sand, ice, lies, erasure, invisibility, light, stars, clouds, haloes, wings, satin, silk, cotton, linen, lace, lilies, mirrors, skin, hands, wax, teeth, death—("white" skin, "white" hands)—of the eyes, everyone's—heart, ghost, spirit, bones, daisies, empire, flag, ivory, invocation, candles, altar cloth and surplice, Mozart, blood and slavery, lash, chain, shackle, deceit, ignorance, water, waves, froth, shells, beads, pearls, the robes of Christ, the brides, the virgins, marble, plaster, masks, sheets, towels, hospital gowns, hospital blankets, tubes, medications, doctors, nuns, milk, frosting, coconut, sugar, Emma's coffin.

Sometimes the thought passes through me *I hate him*, but before it can find words my head begins to pound, my heart to swim.

A dazzling eyes-open blindness.

The body gone to jelly. Agnosia: failure of perception. Angor animi: fear for the soul. Paresthesia. Synaesthesia. Syncope.

Tibet: the roof of the world. Where for thirteen centuries spiritual masters practiced peace and the way of no harm. Where in this century Chinese invaders, believing themselves liberators, bringing industrial modernity and communism to a poor, oppressed, and feudal people, destroyed five thousand monasteries, killed millions of Tibetans, and drove hundreds of thousands from their home. Where today Chinese occupiers outnumber Tibetans. Where today Chinese nuclear weapons threaten nuclear India and hold within their range Burma, Cambodia, and Vietnam.

Sometimes lately I imagine myself at an earlier moment, making an alternate choice, a choice that leads me along an altogether other road. I imagine: she does not let herself go in the arms of Jimmy Wolf, therefore does not fall in love with Daniel García Guzmán, therefore is unprepared and unwilling to begin an affair with Antonio Contini and therefore not with Patrick Curran (or pregnant by him), or with Lukas Grimm, whose daughter Leni therefore lives. And again: she does not abandon herself in the arms of Jim Wolf, her prayers therefore remain pure and Emma survives, while she—this other you—neither abandons her vocation nor gives herself to any man, but saves her soul for its own work, identical to your work but untainted by worldly desire and ambition, by passions and crimes of the flesh. I despise this line of thought but cannot stop it. I have given up that Catholic egoism and sought Buddhist peace, Lukas and I together in our friendship with the Tibetan cause discovering a spirituality less destructive and self-hating than what we had known before. But this new knowing does me no good. The voice remains, imagining: she evades Jimmy Wolf, Emma lives, she takes American citizenship, does graduate study at Harvard, works for the McGovern campaign, then Carter, the State Department, the institutional nonprofit opposition of the eighties, hoping now to serve in the new government under Bill Clinton; or the alternative, does not run but stays with Jim Wolf, surrenders to the madness of the times, becomes a renegade and killer; or again, makes a baby before she has reason not to, gives birth, marries, lives on a farm, has two, three more children, feeds them at her breasts, reads to them, sings, becomes a real American, goes back to school, takes a profession in later life, painter or writer or journalist or nurse, mobilizes actions against the empire, marches in the streets shoulder to shoulder with her tribe of daughters.

Why Lukas has been everything to me: in profession both of my fathers (does anyone imagine I did not know this?), in generation my mother too, all three reborn in him—through me, through my vision and will. He is my creation. The human stuff that made me, the human I remade.

No. It is too simple. I know.

I imagine my daughter, the daughter unborn. She would be thirteen now, but never grows older than Emma. In her body I see how precious life is: for an instant I see it, a tenderness in her flesh, a smell of the outdoors, a dissolution of separation, barriers, my gestures in her hands, her voice in my own, a doubling, this painful doubling—and then it's gone, she's gone. No child now, no daughter: just Emma in her cancer hospital, wasted by radiation and anaplastic cells.

Meditate on death the Tibetan teacher says. To overcome the obstacle of attachment to worldly activities, meditate on death.

With Anna Albert, I recall Rosa Luxemburg the painter. Rosa, who once painted, loved to paint, found no time for painting. Would we wish she had struggled less, painted more? One must have painters. One must have revolutionaries. Anna Albert smokes and smokes. Anna Albert cannot bear to think of the paintings she has not made. She will begin again. She will not seek a place in the new Bundestag, she will no longer serve. She longs for a private life, a return to private life. An interior life, the inwardness of looking at the world in a single moment and rendering with pure desire that moment alone.

You will do nothing. The rain comes down. The grass grows. The stars burn and die. The sky rises, the sky falls. You are not important. You are not here. The heart pumps, the blood circulates, the lungs breathe. The day rises, the day falls. The earth is an organic creature adrift in a mineral sea. (Love your mother.) The earth is organic and mineral both, and so are you. You do nothing. You disintegrate.

The Tibetan teaches that the mind at the time of death must leave the body, this dead body, and find another, soon to live. The mind is not free to remain, nor has it choice of destination, but is blown by the winds of karma. If my karma is negative at the time of death I will be reborn in hell, or as a hungry spirit, or an animal. Now I recollect: so I am blown.

Antonio Contini, so long ago in New York, the radiant red roses. My first love after Daniel—so long after, I am virgin all over again, and there he stands, two dozen long-stemmed roses draped across his arms. Two dozen—my age, which he knows. My age, my birthday, everything about me. A man nearly as old as my Omi was then, and himself married to a woman not unlike her. A man powerful over me, my boss's boss's boss. Yes, of course I benefited from his attentions. Yes, he advanced my EEC career. But my career was not what mattered when he stood in that hotel corridor, with my room, my bed, behind me. He promised me nothing, offered me roses. He already knew me well, had chosen me to join his delegation and give testimony at the UN—*my* testimony, my work on cancer and radiation exposure. He knew this work of mine, had approved my research into environmental and industrial patterns of cancer incidence when I was no more than a name to him, not yet a face, or a body. And here suddenly he stands with an armful of roses at my open door. Grizzled, not yet gray. Heavy-jowled, with long drooping Germanic lips. His eyes, big and black and melancholy, perfect windows on the soul.

If we keep losing parts of ourselves it will take us both to make one whole girl.

I have been his spiritual teacher, his guide: an example to him in all things. Lukas tells me this over and over. It is observable in his eyes, in his gentle caring for me and humility. But he alone knows stillness. Only he can sit and go for refuge to Buddha, generate perfections for the benefit of all, contemplate, meditate, pray according to tradition for the happiness of sentient beings, for their freedom from misery and loss, for their equanimity and liberation from samsara, delusion, the wheel of rebirth. Myself, I am too restless, too active, unable to sit still. For every ten minutes of effort I think only of letters I should be writing, arguments I must make. I criticize myself for this inability but when I complained of it to the Dalai Lama, His Holiness smiled and said I should continue doing just what I did best, he would meditate for me.

Emma. The child I could not bury. In my house her picture stands as on an altar, like a saint's, a shrine. She stands at my side. A candle burns in her memory. I place fresh flowers on the mantle before her every day. I speak to her late at night. I promise her, again and again, that I will not retreat, will not allow this despair to take hold, this pain to defeat me, or lethargy, which I have fled all my life, to overcome.

At first, when we were together in Bonn, Lukas went back every weekend to Munich, to Therese. Or tried to go. I stopped him. Tried to stop him. Every Thursday night or Friday the struggle began. —*Don't leave me.* —*I must.* My terror at the solitude. My rage at these departures. My need of him, his absolute devotion. —*Don't leave,* until he stopped listening, turned away without a word, shaking as if in another moment he would strike me, strangle me, go for one of his guns. —*Don't leave. I need you. Without you I don't eat, I don't sleep, I can't get up from bed, can't read or write, good for nothing but talking on the phone, endlessly crying. The terror comes over me the instant you're gone. It's unbear-*

able. I've taken so much on my shoulders. How frail I am. Look at me, see me, my little bird bones. I'm your little bird, you always say so. Etc. —*Lukas!* Abject, begging, on my knees, wrapping my arms around his legs, gripping his ankles, as he stoops to lift me pounding his chest, his face, until he stands before me rigid, and in this rigid body I know his hatred of me, his contempt, and at last the terror, overwhelmed by despair and self-loathing, recedes. I cry, crumpled on the floor. I let him go. He goes. Hours later I crawl up from the floor. I wash my face, I look at myself in the mirror. I sigh. I breathe. I set myself to work.

Like me, Sonam Pasang is restless. Walls confine him. Even in the frozen moment of a photograph his endless mobility is visible. He does not believe in the old customs, the search for the reincarnated dead lamas among the children of the land. His meditations are empty of content, no buddhas or bodhisattvas, no streams of light and nectar, no rejection of self-cherishing, no prayer for samsara to cease. His meditations are moments of perfect stillness, moments of waiting, between one stroke of the brush and the next. Like Rosa, like Anna, he is a painter. Unlike them, he does not stop.

With his belt my father is beating my child, my daughter, who is four years old, who lived only for this.

I do not believe in reincarnation, any more than in heaven and hell. What I believe in is compassion. Without reward. For its own sake. This virtue exists in all religions, each naming it with its own name. I reject hell and heaven, punishing incarnations, afterlife and afterdeath torments, because I reject fear as the motive for love. The God, the Goddess, Buddha Krishna Christ, the law and the prophets, the wise the holy and the just, all teach the same lesson: peace, compassion, love, faith: Heaven is now, hell is now, karma is now. Beyond that nothing is knowable.

We helped our friends in the East in countless ways. Protected by our diplomatic status as members of the Bundestag, we smuggled in typewriters, fax machines, copiers. We took personal items to our friends as well, and visited them in their homes. We sat in their kitchens whispering with the radio volume set loud to defy the Stasi listeners.

Go for refuge, the teacher says, in the spiritual practice and awakening that protect you from delusion. (Delusion: samsara, attachment to impermanence, to absent fathers, lost lovers, unborn children, to daughters dead of cancer, anorexia, abortion, to enemies, fear, and melodrama, to your own helplessness and others' pity, to their obedience and constant attention, to self-righteousness and the moral authority of making the rules, to playing princess, queen, goddess, to your own martyrdom and sainthood, to playing God.) Go for refuge in Buddha, source of all refuge and awakening, and ask that your practice be blessed. (Blessed, like Jutta of Diessenberg, smiled upon by powers greater than herself.) Go for refuge in truth. Go for refuge to the spiritual friends who support your efforts toward liberation and release. (The Tibetan sangha and the personal masters and heroes and lovers of your soul: go to Emma, to Hildegard, Rosa, Gandhi, King, Robert Kennedy, and after them to the living, Omi, the Dalai Lama, the Berrigans, Cesar Chavez, Lukas, Sonam Pasang.) In so contemplating your faith, build your faith, and rededicate yourself to right action.

Buried in my bed. Without Lukas I would lie here and starve. I would never get up. Exhaustion passes through my body in waves, a nausea of the muscles. In the womb of my bed I dwell in the darkness, the humid airs of my body, curled into itself and hidden, coiled in anticipation of the light beyond, the cold, Lukas, the work. My skin against the sheets, against itself, dry and old, recalls his body as if it were beside me, his parchment skin. He is never in bed beside me. He rises when I sleep. We have almost lost each other. Over and over the words echo: he will grow old with

Therese, words he has spoken, in public and private, year after year. Against this threat I have grown old myself. My joints stiff, my neck stiff, my face in the mirror haggard. Perpetual sickness makes me the walking dead.

My friends have been my enemies, my enemies my friends. All strangers have been my mother, my mother a stranger. Out of this knowledge, says the teacher, comes compassion.

Only Lukas keeps me going. Without him I am nothing. When he goes, I will be gone. I cannot survive him. If I can't bear the thought of life without him, how should I bear the fact?

Patrick Curran. The only lover ever to make me want to marry. Against all my principles and hardest won beliefs. Because he was handsome? Because of the beautiful picture we made together, leading marches across the sand? Because he desired me absolutely and brought all other desires to bear inside my body? Because he believed in marriage himself, so much that forced by convention to choose, he chose his wife over me? Because for him the erotic was a penis opening into a vagina and he brought me to orgasm in coitus more than once in a night? Do I laugh at myself? From here, from now, yes, of course I do. But in those days, never. In real life, never. Possession was against my law, and even so, his flesh possessed me, and he my flesh.

Alone in Bonn, without Lukas, the terror always came back. It came without warning and without words. My heart would run erratic, my body glaze with sweat, dazzling light break up my vision, my head pound, my stomach cramp and go to nausea, my muscles weak and limp. I held the walls to make my way to bed, to lie in the darkness and wait for the terror to pass.

Mothers are said to be kind. In contemplation of this kindness, one develops gratitude. But what is the kindess of a mother? One hungers absolutely. One receives never enough. They choose the fathers over the daughters, as the fathers choose their wives. In the atmosphere of the mother I hunger, I starve.

I spoke in the press about sexual freedom: how the marriage contract kills the erotic, how erotic choice must always be open, unpossessed and unpossessive, equally free for women and for men. I was asked about my relations with married men, most of all with Lukas. I spoke of Therese, of my desire to befriend her, to make her part of our love. She was not evolved enough to participate in such a relation, I said. She would not allow me into her house. She would neither meet nor speak with me. She refused to receive my letters. This was a great sorrow to me. I began to go along with Lukas when he went home to Munich, to have his company throughout the hours of the journey, and during his family visit I waited alone at my hotel. Sometimes I went to Nürnberg, to Omi's, and Lukas accompanied me, then drove down to Munich and Therese, then back for me, to pick me up and travel with me home to Bonn.

When we called on our party to sponsor an international hearing on Tibet, the party's left opposed us, arguing that the Dalai Lama was an exploitative religious tyrant, the Chinese reality a liberation, and so on. But we prevailed. A month before the hearing, Chinese soldiers in Lhasa killed hundreds of Tibetans nonviolently demonstrating against the occupation. In April, in Bonn, we brought together scholars, human rights activists, and Tibetans living in exile for two days of information exchange and organizing for the right to self-determination and human rights for the Tibetan people. In June, in Beijing, Chinese troops put an end to months of mass protest against the government by killing thousands of Chinese demonstrators in Tiananmen Square.

*The means are the end, the only end. What is past is not dead.
We pretend to be strangers.*

The disciple of Buddha abandons self-cherishing. The disciple
of Buddha bears affectionate love for all living beings and values
their freedom and happiness. The disciple of Buddha remembers
the suffering of all human life, and the kindness, and in recollection of all human suffering and kindness surrenders self-cherishing
for the practice of cherishing love. These virtues I strove to attain.
I spoke of our need to remake ourselves if we would remake the
world. In a political climate both skeptical and wary, a political
climate that recalls that Nazis also made spiritual claims, I
asserted the need for spiritual values and became the living
symbol of the politically active, nondogmatic spirituality that
alone can lead the way out of the global crisis, the moral and
social catastrophe being enacted in our time.

At home I was a monster.

Triangulations. Hilmar Knapp and I are already lovers when
Lukas telephones his desire to meet with us. I had thought I could
never love a German and suddenly here were two. It began with
Hilmar. The abortion and the founding conference—my human
baby a clot of blood, vacuumed out. Seven months later in Frankfurt, our alternative political alliance was born. The color green.
In Ireland, Saint Patrick's day, and out beyond the conference hall,
the trees not yet in leaf. Hilmar Knapp at my side and the next
year my lover when General Lukas Grimm passes through our
freshly painted bright green office door. He does not bear himself
like a soldier, but stoops, from the shoulders—the posture of a
man taller than others, apologetic for his height. *Or perhaps for
his calling*, I thought, and saw in that moment that this apologetic
posture was new to him. I looked at his pale, clear eyes. Sky eyes.
The kind said, on first encounter, in distant memory, to have terrified brown-eyed peoples, as if they were holes through the head

that opened on heaven. (And they were, and everywhere they went the sky-eyes brought terror.) There was no smile in Lukas's eyes, and my second-language English suddenly recognized a truth in his family name. I imagined his uniform as he held out his hand. I heard the clicking of hard polished heels, saw birds and arrows, silver dazzling above his head, or brass, or gold. All that was in the air about him, and its absence made him insubstantial and its shadow weighed him down. I took his hand. In that first touch, that simple handshake, a certain destiny made itself present to me. We had met once before, in passing, knew each other's commitment to opposing NATO's new missiles, had spoken briefly on the phone. But nothing of that prepared me for what I saw.

Fed by many streams, I was subverted from the start.

I don't understand the marks Sonam makes. I see their intensity and beauty but am unable to stand still in the face of them. I have never known how to wait. I want them to make statements, want them to cry *Free my country!* as he himself sometimes will cry. But his paint does not speak this language. He does not paint buddhas or temples or landscapes of the high Tibetan plateau. He paints abstractions, modern, dense, scratched. I see colors. I see marks. I see runes, like language. If I stand quietly before them I imagine I will see the world as it looks from up there. But I can't stand that long or that quietly. Danger rises from the canvas, comes at me. I go to nausea. My head pounds. I turn to him and smile, big and broad. He sees right through me.

This is how it happens: you create, with a lover, between you, a relation. It starts in desire, admiration. It grows. The love, desire, admiration take form and become a life. Now together you have two things: a life together, and still, inside it, secret, hiding, sometimes frightened, the relation itself. Together you have an outside and an inside, a visible life and an invisible, the speakable life and the unspeakable. As the years pass it gets harder to keep that inner, intimate, secret life alive: there you begin to separate, carry your secrets away, your desires no longer perfectly matched, admiration encrusted with complaints and angers and fears. You dare not examine them, or bring them forward, lest the tiny fissures spread and grow, crack the solid foundation and bring down the facade of your complicatedly shared world. Most people stop here—don't they?—holding on to the life and chewing on its torments, until a new desire wells up to release them and the cycle begins again. Every man I've loved has come to me from this place, never from his solitude, and even Sonam Pasang went back to his wife.

Maintain a compassionate heart, says the teacher. Day and night.

Lukas's body, his pale skin, his compelling desire back at the beginning—all that, yes, but most of all his refusal to choose me absolutely. *I will grow old with Therese.* Repeated again and again. With his flesh filling my mouth, my throat, I heard these words. With his fingers deep in my body. With his tongue at my nipples, with his hands on my breasts. As he parts the lips of my body and claims all he finds there and all he does not find, these words echo in my heart, these words, this promise, this threat, that someday he will leave me, a day approaching faster in this year now when he so rarely touches his lips or tongue or fingers to the sweet erotic places where I know him still, or offers anymore his desire into my mouth, but touches me mostly gently, fatherly, motherly, through bedcovers and clothing, a day that comes nearer every hour now, brought close by electoral defeat and closer by accident, by the weakness and pathos of his torn shoulder and shattered knee, a day that waits always now somewhere near him, with him, just beyond sight.

Contemplate the suffering of all living beings. From hell beings and hungry spirits, through animals and humans, to demigods and gods—all are suffering, says the teacher. Take their suffering as a dissolving smoke into your heart. Allow the smoke of their suffering to destroy your self-cherishing mind. By visualizing their liberation and your own, generate joy. Make this joy the object of your meditation, hold it with single-pointed concentration. In subsequent practice relieve the suffering of others when you can, and patiently accept what misfortune comes to you.

Sonam Pasang was active everywhere during the Bonn conference, and in preparation for it, too, served as translator, host, guide, ambassador, from the Tibetans to the Germans and back again. He was not alone among German Tibetans in giving this service, but he was the closest to us, to Lukas and me, and the best, and he had become our friend. Sometimes I watched him, his eyes while he stood at the microphone, his body, the passion in his muscles while he listened and converted Tibetan speech to German, German to Tibetan, his white western shirt rolled up at the elbows, his collar undone and tie askew, his open black vest, his longish black hair falling down across his forehead, his black eyes big and bulging, heavy lidded, his dark face gleaming with sweat in the bright auditorium lights like the face of a rock-carved rained-on sun-bronzed Buddha embedded in a Tibetan cliffside. I had been watching my desire for him grow. I was making love with him in my dreams. I knew he dreamed of me also. I could hear it in his voice, even as he stood before a thousand people speaking my own words in a language I didn't know, felt his love and desire, his tongue, his throat, his deep breath caressing my body through the translated words, taking my body in, drinking it, swallowing, returning it to the world in words only half his own. I craved his touch, his skin, his eyes with mine and wordless, felt his body all over, around, inside me, his voice at my neck, at my ears, his tongue, his lips, kisses down the side of my face as I spoke, as he spoke, my words, his words, our voices racing out together into the dark hall, into the listening silence.

No one in samsara enjoys real happiness, says the teacher. Wish love for living beings, pure happiness for all. Imagine your body a wish-fulfilling jewel, radiating light. Take suffering, give joy. Inhale smoke, exhale light. Give goods, money, service, instruction and prayers—give courage. For hatred, offer love. For injury, pardon. Discord, harmony. Falsehood, truth. Saint Francis and the bodhisattva. *Inhale smoke, exhale light.*

I long for the daughter who wasn't born. I see her playing with Anna's Trudi. I watch them grow and become friends. I hear their giddy child voices but not their words as they sit in the springtime garden among the weeds and flowers, the sunlight making stars and rainbows in their hair. I see them come into girl-hood, naked and flushed at a mirror comparing beauties and flaws. I see them dreaming on their lives and sitting up late with Anna and me, their mothers, desiring everything from us and nothing and all our knowledge of the world.

Rosa complains that she has constantly had to look after the urgent business of humanity, to make the world a better place. They martyred her for it, assassinated.

The paradox of innocence and action:
Inwardness conflicts with the world.
Moral identity comes into existence only in action.
Action soils the hands.

But I do not believe this, have never believed it.

We traveled together, Lukas, Sonam Pasang, and I. We attended conferences. We spoke in Hiroshima. We represented the German nation in Stockholm when the Dalai Lama received the Nobel Prize for Peace. We accompanied His Holiness to Prague when he met with the new president of the new Czech Republic, our friend Vaclav Havel, the first and only head of state courageous enough to receive His Holiness officially. When Lukas traveled to Munich, he took me first to Sonam Pasang.

In punishment, Antigone is buried alive. To be buried alive is to descend to a living death. Like Orpheus. Like Jesus Christ. This is how we live now too. Not only Lukas and I (although we are entombed): but the figure for us all. Buried alive by a power that will not allow us to honor our dissident brothers. (Is the metaphor of the story too simple? Have we gone too far beyond the simple to understand? Those ordinary people, my neighbors, do they understand? The woman who writes to me that I am an inspiration, can she dedicate herself as I have? Is one letter to me the beginning of action? I used to believe it.)

And now, again, a resurrection based on ego-death. (And like a cat how many deaths the ego can endure.)

One works to liberate the self for the sake of liberating all living beings. One strives to become a buddha for the benefit of all.

The public always senses the mood of the combatants, and the joy of battle gives the polemic a clear sound and a moral superiority.

To release the mind from self-clinging we train it in tranquil abiding. We reflect on love and suffering until we have transformed the mind to compassion. We hold this compassion emptily, in single-pointed concentration. When compassion fades or the mind wanders we gently bring it back until again we hold compassion in the silence and absence of self. In this way we nourish the mind in tranquil abiding. Between meditations, we practice moral discipline and avoid distracting entanglements.

His Holiness will meditate for me.

Anna Albert is sick of ideas and sick of the struggle, sick of the treason, the traitors, the lies. She understands them—even loves them. But she is bitter. The betrayed also no longer move her. Smoke fills her rooms, and the smell of turpentine and oil. One sees nothing there, smells only. Her studio door remains closed. She makes tea, sighs, smokes, refuses. Refuses even me.

Time disappears, occupied, erased. Time is nothing. I destroy time. Life destroys it. (Time as the body of God?)

Incapable of stillness, I lie here immobile. If I move I become a distracting entanglement. Lukas is leaving me for Therese. He prays every day. He meditates. He returns to his wife. He cannot abandon me. He can't stay. I am killing him. He is killing me. My love for Sonam Pasang was not the answer Lukas hoped for. Losing our Bundestag seats was not the answer. Securing for me the Sakharov Prize will not be the answer.

The assassins are still among us. We pretend to be strangers.

It isn't true that Patrick Curran went back to his wife. For a while it was true. But in the end he left her. He wanted to hold me, to claim me. I was making love with Hilmar by then, and working with Lukas. I was ready for Lukas, waiting. I didn't care anymore about Patrick Curran and his wife. When I looked at him I saw the face of the child I hadn't dared to give birth to, radiated with history, public and private, nuclear damaged, conceived in argument and tears. Before my eyes my daughter became a son, accusing. I had demanded Patrick Curran all for myself and when I got him I let him go.

Fed by many streams, subverted from the start.

Lukas would like to achieve tranquil abiding. He would like to make a full retreat, withdraw from worldly activity, know the emptiness of the I and the emptiness of the body and in this way attain superior seeing. Milarepa pierced by the sorrows of the world. In the mornings when I sleep I hear him cleaning his guns.

Let the bad remain bad. Otherwise it will grow worse.

Antigone commits suicide to avoid death at the hands of the state. She is followed in suicide by her lover.

That fat man. I ask myself why.

This painful doubling.

Whiteness: heart, ghost, murder, bones.

And now again, another resurrection.

In Hannover with Sonam Pasang. We walk in the Herren-häusen Gärten, in the sun and the shade of the lime trees. He tells me I am neurotic. (This is not news.) Too neurotic for him. I destroy his serenity, his creative quietude, essential to his well-being and his work. It is not his passion for me that destroys him, not his desire, but I myself. He had known (should have known) this about me from the intimate distance of our political friendship, had failed to recognize or imagine how intensely in our sexuality I would change, even as I remained so profoundly the same. He loves me, of course: I am his beautiful painful saintly heroic iconic woman. But live with me, touch me? No more, he can't. We continue to walk. I talk across his words, ignore them. He must see things my way. If I talk long enough, hard enough, he will forget what he has said, as I myself am already forgetting.

We traveled together. We inhaled smoke, we exhaled light.

The dazzling open-eyed blindness. The body gone to jelly. Paresthesia. Agnosia. Angor animi.

Anaplastic cells. Perfect windows on the soul.

To render with pure desire: the lungs, the heart. I am blown.

Wish love.

Children, watch out for the baobabs!

And after this, the public record.

But not yet. I do not surrender. I do not pass away.

I have fallen into fragments that are seeking to realign themselves.

This is what happened: I woke up one morning transformed. I knew the fascist in myself. I lived with her intimately. I saw that I too was a Nazi, an imperialist, a superpower. She had been there all along.

At my window, what I see: trees, potted plants, birds nesting in the ivy along the neighbor's walls. Down below, the flowers— red, orange, yellow. A black cat sprawls in the sunshine. The trees haven't yet lost their leaves.

Like me, Rosa Luxemburg was difficult and temperamental. She was arrogant, a tyrant. She brooked no opposition.

Or was that I? Was that I or you (me?) who played with magazines and images, Kennedy and King shining at the crowds? I or you who set out to make me, to make myself, to *become*?

Maybe your sticky fingers, maybe your tears in the lonely Georgia summer. But the act of will: that was mine—all along, mine.

The light comes in like this, the time, the words—it is not a crisis of language, words aren't the problem. In Florida the Ku Klux Klan joins the environmental protection movement to argue that race mixing is a form of pollution. Is language at fault?

The lights come in, the tide, oil on the waters, on sand, in Alaska, in California, in Kuwait. Guns and oil kill the little birds. (Who kills me?)

Who is to understand without Lukas? How is to live?

I was the one who walked in the sultry night, Emma's hand in my hand, our parents and Peter at the fire ahead in the darkness, cold wet sand in my toes and the moon up above in an indigo sky—I, who with Emma watching, asking nothing, swore a fidelity I couldn't name.

Daughter unborn. Sister unlived. Mother never. Self?

Are you the price? All along, I thought it was Emma.

Have your Tibetan lover then. Lukas Grimm no longer wants you. Did he say these words? Exactly these?

I am supposed to be sleeping.

I hear my heart. Your heart. You. The sweet sick taste of you on my tongue, our tongue, us, the taste of myself, my body, the body that isn't my body, the self that isn't my self. Hello?

Doubt lines the interface, pain on one side, thought on the other.

The vegetal, the nonviolent—

Anna Albert: I hold on to her image, the smoke that surrounds her, the billowing clouds, her voice thickened, short on words, and her eyes—

I am too hard, too demanding. Sonam grew weary.

In Tibet, an ancient culture—

Come back to her. For God's sake, don't leave her. Sonam—! These words too.

I hate him and then the silence falls. Almost falls.

His hands.

Rosa: "Nowhere do I have my personal corner, nowhere can I exist and be myself."

Afternoon light through old lace—

Our allies worse than our enemies—

Without him—

Futureless. The planet. The fatherless girl. You. Not me. Destiny our own to make. Letters alone opened the doors, words like the keys to heaven. But Lukas is deaf. Becomes deaf. Leaves me. In my body I feel him. Sonam Pasang. The touch of him stark inside me. Strong. The pulse of his flesh into mine.

Like Rosa I loved the campaign, the crowd. But I was made to be afraid.

I walked a beach with Emma under a moon, white, blue. I became it: absent, image, untouchable—dreamer, sister—sterile sister.

Without him—

The letters never stopped coming. The phone calls, the threats. Lukas tried to conceal them. But I always knew.

At a hotel in Barcelona in 1984 my purse was stolen. We were there for the feminist book fair. My first book of letters and speeches had just come out in English. I was waiting for Lukas impatiently in front of the hotel when a man slammed into me. I had no breath, doubled over, gasped for air. By the time I could cry out the man was gone. As I staggered back into the lobby, babbling, crying for Lukas, women from the fair encircled me, American women and English women and French women, trying to comfort me, to calm me. I would not be calmed. In my purse had been all my medications, my many pills. For my heart, I told the women, the Americans and English women and French women. Where was Lukas? I demanded. Find Lukas. Only Lukas would understand that the man had come precisely for me, that this mugging was no random attack but part of a campaign of harassment that a certain small German party was already conducting against me. So long ago now.

Other strange losses that year. Leni starved herself to death. And Erika S.—who wrote my biography in German, and as soon as the book came out, in a bathtub with a razor blade and pills, took her own life—Erika S., who traveled with us persistently for months on end, obsessed with me, demanding time alone that I couldn't give. She had begun with my cooperation: a book about the glittering star of the meteoric new party, and so forth. But in the end I disliked the book, and said so publicly. I disavowed it, denied it, and her. And suddenly Erika S. was dead.

Fortification lights. A concentrated brightness. Hildegard saw God there, angels, heaven's gate. I am sick only with ghosts.

Hildegard the green saint. Visions migraine induced. Holy illness taming the powers that sought to constrain her. She won.

Downstairs, the typewriter, humming. Outside, the wind.

The whispering and laughing voices, hushed, the little girls, the nuns, the slap-slap of soleless slippers on stone floors, and somewhere in the shadows, that man—

I hear them whispering: What's wrong with Jutta? I hear them laughing: Ghosts, she's sick with ghosts.

I hear the music, Hildegard's songs, their voices in the distance singing. Somewhere they are singing still, singing vespers, singing compline, the nuns, the little girls.

I remember too much, too little. My mind has lost its anchor. I could do an interview, I could rattle off without stopping the facts of neo-Nazi violence, the reports of so-called ethnic cleansing from Bosnia-Herzegovina, the ongoing story of repression in Tibet. But of what has passed between us I know little. My mind quails, resists. The whole past goes blank and I remember only that he is here, downstairs, working, quietly, patiently, eternally, this work we share.

What is forgotten: you remember but uncertainly. *Did such and so really happen?* Did I weep—from incident or temperament?—and when he came to comfort me, to hold me in his lap like a child, did I feel his desire there under my cheek and for the first time unzip him and take him into my mouth, my tears disappearing, his arms around me, his hands on my neck, my hair, doing for him what Therese refused, oh foolish Catholic wife, and sending him off with the memory, of the forbidden, what he went to prostitutes for, what he had had affairs for with the wives of junior officers, fellatio and phallus worship and the feel of my young flesh? Was I bitter then, at first, before I became afraid? Was I angry? Did I feel my power to call him back, my freedom to turn from him to another, to Hilmar, to Patrick Curran? You almost remember, but do not quite. You recognize an image but tell yourself it could have come to you from a dream.

We flew to Turkey. We flew to South Africa. We flew to India. We gave our support to all victims of state repression and war. We articulated everywhere our vision for life, for hope, for a global future: a vision of nonviolence and antimilitarism, environmental stewardship and sustainable economies, social justice, feminism, and cultural plurality, spiritual compassion and human rights for all.

This was the world we lived in. This was our sadness. Nothing has changed. It cost us everything.

Joseph Goebbels, 1943: *Do you want total war? Do you want it, if necessary, more total and more radical than we can imagine today...?*

Does this explain my death, his death? My sadness, my paralysis? They had been with me for years. His bitterness, his anger? Not new. The gun had been in the house with us all along—that gun and others, and one in the car. I was constantly threatened. What—did I allow myself to be protected by a man with a gun? I, the too famous pacifist feminist? Yes. Yes, I did. I showed the guns to my friends. I laughed at the guns. As if they were a trifle, a small indulgence to my old general, who was learning from me the futility of weapons. But sometimes, alone, I felt their weight in my hands, caressed those guns against my cheeks, my breasts, breathed their cold, metallic, machine-oil smell—and held them, held them.

Walking in the Herrenhäusen Gärten, in the sun and shade of the lime trees, I wanted to be the Green Tara Buddha, the female buddha of compassion. It was not in my power. I shut my ears.

Lukas, my love, how can anyone understand us? Least of all our friends.

I am running out of time.

For my fears, they medicated me. For my racing heart, gave me pills. For my anxieties, pills. To sleep, to wake—pills, pills. Most of them placebos. They had no effect. The doctors wanted me out of their consulting rooms. When I collapsed from exhaustion they sent me as quickly as possible from hospital to rest clinic, where Lukas could attend me and in seclusion run our office complete with typewriter and fax. Medically enforced rest was always the cure, nothing organic ever wrong. The drama worked in my favor. I was martyred again and again. Lukas couldn't leave me. I felt safe, protected by doctors' orders, the need to cancel public engagements, the impossibility of travel. Lukas took the phone calls, spoke to friends and enemies, kept the world out. I lay in bed and watched and listened. I did not rest. I read, made notes, wrote speeches, followed the news and human rights reports, answered my mail, and raged my way through phone calls Lukas placed for me. In this fashion I was buffered. No one could find me. No one could touch me. Lukas brought my food, my clothes, the news-papers, my letters, served as my keeper.

What it was like for me—how few can know this: to know who you are, what you have to give, to tell, and how little time, and what you must take for yourself along the way. For the benefit of all. To be both great and small, to feel the power of your public figure, and inside a child, less than a child, an orphaned and abandoned child, a damaged and forgotten child, a child you can never acknowledge, even while you feel her there, know her, and her hunger, and her need.

The crisis is not of language. Language is not at fault.

Who lies? I do. Who is lazy? I am. Who tyrannizes? Not language. Me.

Although: the light steals words, darkness protects them. Silence is painful. Speaking is painful. Emma and Leni are friends on the other side.

I am running out of time. The narrator no longer knows who is telling this story. I am blown out of time. Drifting away from time. Gone from time. Fixed in time. Lost in time. Timeless. Consider this: it took only one bullet each, one for me, one for him. These bullets were well placed, perfectly placed, placed by an expert, or experts. Yes, he himself was such an expert, knew where to position a gun, when to fire. Did I pretend not to know this? But oh how swiftly the language of logic deceives. How little this question matters now. Now. Eat that word. Words are all I am now. Am. Eat. No appetite. No teeth, no time. But the words keep coming, the words in time, the last thread, the lost.

When Sonam left me I collapsed a collapse that had been coming for months: the election defeat; the party's refusal to give Lukas and me a stipend or a job or even an office in which to continue our work; the press neglect of our English-language book on Tibet; my television show, such a hoped-for opportunity, canceled after six weeks; my American biography abandoned by the writer at the moment we were set to begin; and suddenly the coup against Gorbachev, the systematic rape and racial atrocity in Bosnia-Herzegovina, and the desertion of Sonam Pasang. I took to my bed, refused to eat, cried from morning to night and then fell silent, for days lay in silence, turned my face to the wall when Lukas came to speak to me, to rouse me or feed me, then seized his hand when he rose in futility from the bed to leave, held his hand with the little strength of my whole body, held him, knowing nothing, only terror.

Have your Tibetan lover then. Lukas Grimm no longer wants you.

Alone, I felt Sonam in my body, guns in my belly, teeth in my flesh. I smelled him, turpentine and oil paint, the woodsmoke of the stove that heated his studio when we made love, and something sweeter, jasmine, honeysuckle, his wife's perfume, and the licorice of his son's favorite candy, the chocolate and cherries of his daughter. I wanted to know his children but I was forbidden. I tasted his sweat in my mouth, I bruised him between my teeth. With my little fists I pummeled him, I drew blood at his nipples, I climbed on top of him and shouted as if to a crowd of thousands so that he had to struggle me over and hold me down to stifle my voice. I taunted him, teased and evaded him and forced him to be rough with me, to take me standing, from behind, up the ass, with half his clothes on, his belt buckle pressed hard into my skin. I crawled on my knees for him, I sucked his fingers and his cock. I ate him, the meat of him, I cannibalized him, I tore his flesh from his bones. Nothing helped. Every hour I felt his hands on me, on my breasts, up my ribs, in the hollow of my diaphragm, down my tummy, down around and into my thighs, his tongue up my labia and vulva and clitoris, his fingers in the heart of me and down my legs to my ankles and up my chest to my head, my hair. His hands never left me, his eyes in my eyes, his sex in my sex. I was awake, in desire, in pain. Nothing changed.

Mind gone. Driven by sensation and image. Thought hurt worse.

After three months, Lukas wrote to him, begged him, on my behalf, for his friendship alone, described for him my condition, the impossibility it was to me to have lost him so completely. *I do not understand you*, Lukas wrote, again and again, as if Sonam's refusal were irrational. He pled for friendship on the basis of friendship, on the years of our common work, on compassion for my suffering.

Silence was the only reply.

In my dreams I saw Hildegard, eighty years old and white hair flowing, wearing the face and hands of my Omi, and naked in green starlight the figure of a little girl.

The shadows under my eyes grew deeper, darker.

Ashes. *Black milk of death—we drink you mornings, we drink you nights.* Literal ashes. Literal milk. Literal death. They are the words of a poem and they are alive. They are not words about poetry. They are not words about symbolic color, about Goethe, German culture, the white world of the white race. Death is not symbolized by the color black in this poem. Black in this poem is not a symbol. Black here is literal: smoke and ash. Literal smoke and literal ash that literally rose and literally fell and literally landed in literal milk, in buckets and pails, in pitchers and glasses, literal ashes from literal crematoria, literal remains of the literal dead. The crisis is not in language.

Until slowly I recovered. With Lukas's care, I recovered. First to the hospital, then to the clinic, as always before. He nurtured me, a baby, fed me with a spoon.

I went back to work. I wrote, I traveled, I spoke. I attended conferences, prepared papers and documents, edited my speeches and letters, translated everything for an American book, and the world closed more tightly around us. I felt this closure, this enclosure, without being able to name it. I called Heike Bauer in a panic almost every night. I was searching for something, the words—something new was happening but all I could see was the violence, the angry young Nazis returning. There was more, somewhere more. I felt it at night, in the silence, in the weight on my chest, in my heart, in words that couldn't be spoken, or even found, so forgotten, so emptied of meaning, so broken. At the same time I was watched, knew I was watched. From so many sides. I answered my mail and my heart would pound. I would hear maybe a cat cry, or Lukas snoring down the hall, and the silence grew thick around me, heavy, airless, dense. I would lose my breath. Lights would flash across my vision and all words become foreign until gradually the attack had passed, and in the first moments of recovery I would feel Emma beside me, or smell flowers out of season, or the salt-fish smell of the sea.

As if life would not let me leave it.

The telephone rings.

I count the rings. I lose count.

A dream I have, the handsome Dr. Mengele, furtive in the shadows, touches my hair, my lips, bends down and whispers in my ear. His fingers smell of lilacs, cologne. He kisses me, both gently and hard, a kiss full of power, a fairy tale kiss, a deliverance, a gift. I am a little girl. In the background I hear the singing of the nuns. I receive the gift. I carry it in secret, in my heart. I do not know this man, only his face, his hair, his eyes. Later I will know him—that is to say, will have learned who he is, was, his history, his story, his crimes beyond crime. But the little girl in my dream knows nothing of this, remembers it only when she awakens, the imprint of that kiss on her lips.

Finish. Finish. Come to an end.

I do not sleep when others sleep. This isn't life. I am a stranger in this body. Mengele remembered as friendly. The light so faint you don't see it. *I will die as I planned before.* The voice of the body.

Smashed up in Munich. Broken knee, torn shoulder. I wanted to take care of him. Heike had to take care of me. Did he do it on purpose? Or maybe the driver? Was he escaping me? Or the assassins, did they know us so well that killing him they could count on killing me? And failing that kill, came close enough— withdrew to watch and hide? Our old enemies, the LaRouchites? Paid ex-Stasi? Neo-Nazis? Chinese government avengers? Russian traffickers in black market plutonium? Imagine these assassins: I see two of them, dressed in black, silent as shadows. Like a bad tooth. I return to them, again and again—in dreams, in silence, waiting here for the bullet, for the death. I see the driver of the car: a middle management banker, a young man wearing a tie, his shirtsleeves rolled up at the end of the day, his windows raised, the heat set high inside the car. His credentials are flawless. It was a hit and run.

I wanted a child. The face of my father. Outside the child keeps knocking.

Mengele served at Auschwitz. On the selection ramp every day. At Windscale, routinely discharging plutonium waste into the Irish Sea.

We are locked together in our decline. We share a delicious pleasure, for each more delicious in our isolation one from the other. We pretend to dote on one another. In secret, we hate. We are polite and gentle. Alone, we murder.

My stepfather's bomb-damaged genes. I have fought this all my life.

Here in this waiting. These three dead weeks.

We made no secret of our problems. When Lukas spoke I listened. *Blameless, holy children of the universe.*

In the vicinity of Sellafield: this child for sale. What can it mean, to have been fond?

I performed a morality. There at Emma's bedside you were with me. This is not the voice of action.

If I can't bear the thought of life without him, how shall I bear the fact?

The beach regions near Sellafield record a leukemia rate—

In Hiroshima, my father, my stepfather—

What a great miracle—

There in your jeep, with your medicines and candy bars—

So long ago in New York—

I understood—

The physical being of words: Jim Wolf and Sonam had this in common: words became flesh, theirs, my own. I choked on words. I couldn't swallow. I couldn't speak or breathe.

I see myself, the photographs, the famous photographs, the photographs with the famous, and before. I see her, myself behind her eyes, can almost feel this body, my body inside her photographed skin. All her bodies, her histories, here in this last invisble silent body—now. I ask her, the child, the girl, the woman, who were they, those phantoms, those selves outside the self?

We shared a cup of tea. I raced with time.

The human body the best picture—

Who did the work?

This painful doubling.

Children everywhere expendable. My little freckle-faced, white-skinned, black-haired, green-eyed sister. Sleep terrified me.

Who fires the gun?

I pled for Gandhian practice, truth force, the way of no harm. I believed these words. Children need heroes.

You wanted answers? Anna Albert went on strike.

I addressed crowds in the hundreds of thousands. (Imagine a span of time, expand the silences, the moments of stillness.) We took twenty-seven seats in the Bundestag. We demonstrated at Krefeld. We exposed for American journalists what they seemed to have overlooked. In September the protests began. I think of Anna Albert's kitchen. From the beginning factionalism and personality clashes. The women had no understanding. I wanted to tear the mask off the drunken envy. I went to my friends to say, "Let's do an action."

Who did the work?

Outside it rains. In reality Sonam is not so important.

At the borderlands of my condition. The worry, the packing, Emma's hand. The vegetal, the nonviolent. My solution to a spell of nightmares. A furtive handsome man. Milarepa pierced by the sorrows of the world.

I imagine myself at an earlier moment. This new knowing does me no good. I imagine my daughter.

Meditate on death the teacher says. So I am blown. Lukas alone knows stillness.

The child I could not bury. *I am your little bird.* Fear as the motive for love. Go for refuge, the teacher says. Without Lukas I lie here and starve. The terror returns. In the atmosphere of the mother I hunger.

The disciple of Buddha abandons self-cherishing. I am a monster.

A certain destiny makes itself present. He sees right through me. Maintain a compassionate heart, says the teacher. Contemplate the suffering of all living beings. I watch my desire.

No one enjoys real happiness.

Lukas traveled to Munich. Antigone buried alive. Anna Albert sick of ideas. Time disappears.

He leaves me for Therese. He would like to achieve tranquil abiding. I talk across his words.

Anaplastic cells—

The public record—

I have fallen into fragments. The light comes in.

Have your Tibetan lover then.

I am supposed to be sleeping.

In my body I feel him. Other strange losses. Fortification lights. I hear the music, Hildegard's songs. You recognize an image. *Do you want total war?*

The light steals words. I am running out.

I smell him, turpentine, oil paint, woodsmoke. Thought hurts worse. *Black milk of death...*

Come to an end.

They medicated me. You. The split in the self, the body.

I went back. As if life would not let me leave it. I wanted to take care of him, a delicious pleasure. It rains. I hear music, foot-steps. Even the narrator doesn't know.

With the accident I saw each day more clearly the impos-sibility of my life. Saw Lukas dying. Saw myself killing him. Saw that without him I would not go on.

The telephone rings. How many times?

I counted the rings. I lost count.

The typewriter. No striking of keys.

No striking fingers, no active mind.

Rain. The silence when it stops.

Wind. Its absence.

Footsteps. That cease.

If we keep losing parts of ourselves—

Not even the narrator knows who is telling this story.

Who told it.

Blown. Here in this waiting.

These three dead weeks.

3. Still, there is that typewriter

It was murder.

—Ingeborg Bachmann

Still, there is that typewriter, downstairs, humming.

It speaks against planning, premeditation, suggests sudden interruption: one imagines: by the faintest sound of an assassin: at first one imagines that.

There are other possibilities.

This for instance:

Lukas, writing to his wife, then to his lawyer, until Jutta calls to him from above.

"Lukas!"

He rises from his letter as she comes down. He sees something fierce in her eye, some new determination, a look she reserves for enemies, others, rarely for him: The Wall, he calls it. Jutta's Wall.

"Lukas," she says, "we have to talk," which means he has to listen. "Lukas, I am no longer happy. We are no longer happy together."

But of course these aren't her words. She is incapable of speaking such words, so simple, direct, naive. These would be Therese's words, or Leni's words, or Lukas's own. But Jutta's? Three simple sentences followed by silence? Never.

What must she say to him then? Words of this kind, but not these words. Intricate, elaborate, elongated words, sentences woven and spun, circling the rooms of the house, the houses of the street, the neighborhood, the dull old city, the state, the nation, Europe, the earth, out to the moon and the stars and down again to the garden.

Tibet, the roof of the world.

He imagines himself in another life, feels that life, standing trapped here in the weight and web of sentences she spins, while she circles, retreats, returns, unable to find the courage for the simpler words she knows she needs, unable to stop talking.

How much longer is he supposed to endure it?

He asks himself, he closes his eyes, mentally places himself in lotus position, breathes deep of the high thin air.

But the words go on and on.

Or: she comes down the stairs, says again, for the tenth, the hundredth time, "I am Jutta! I must be free!" He has laughed in her face at these words.

But perhaps not today.

She calls from above. He stands in the bedroom doorway. She rolls over and smiles at him, her little waif smile. "I'm exhausted still," she says. "Salzburg, Berlin. Did me in."

Her little waif smile.

He has given up all other women for her, for this. Her aging gray-hollowed eyes, her rage and manipulations, her pathetic complaints.

And for this, this moment: her arms raised to him like a child's, a little girl child from her bed.

He kisses her cheeks, her mouth, her forehead, her fingers, the palms of her hands. She is unreal to him.

He remembers Therese. Therese has also become unreal.

Age has eaten him out. He desires her but the desire is hollow. Her mouth is kissing his mouth and his mouth is responding and everything is flat and woven in silk and cool and far away.

In the early afternoon they leave the hotel.

On the way out of Berlin they stop at Sachsenhausen, where four days earlier the memorial to the Sachsenhausen concentration camp victims was destroyed by fire.

On the road they stop for dinner. She picks at her food.

The silence between them thickens, even as they go on talking.

The silence is all his. He has built this silence in self-protection—he sees it clearly—against her endless flow of speech, and from behind his shield of silence he has watched her.

It used to be with love and appetite, but now his watching is nothing, her voice a knife-edge, a razor slipping across the downy surface of his skin, her image insubstantial, a play of light and color and shadow projected on a screen, animation without meaning, without connection, in her eyes the hard brightness of the person who doesn't listen to what other people say.

They have been on the road too long, first to Salzburg for a week of testimony from speakers from indigenous cultures who described the damage uranium mining and nuclear testing and storage have done to their health and lands and ways of life, then to Berlin for the Global Radiation Victims Conference and the Congress of the European Buddhist Union.

At the end they were done in, and stayed an extra two days, alone together, without meetings or agendas or work.

They relaxed, they read, they slept, they shopped. Jutta wrote postcards—in the first person plural, signed with both of their names.

He almost loved her again. Of course, he loved her.

In public he never stopped loving her.

She has been his hope for so many years. In public he can still see her in the light of that hope she has been.

In public she is still easy to love.

It is only alone, like this, the two of them, that she recedes farther and farther into shadows he can no longer reach, or has no will to reach, or no desire.

Or he recedes.

Alone with her, he remembers too well.

She is closer to him than to anyone. He knows more than he can bear.

The voice in his head grows louder, the voice that isn't hers, the voice that loathes and fears her, the voice that reminds him of humiliations, storms of passion, the voice that paints pictures as vivid as dreams: for the first time in a year they sat in the same room with Sonam Pasang.

They did not speak, they did not greet one another.

Lukas and Jutta on one side, Sonam on the other, across a room.

Sparks arced through the air, white, blue—Lukas almost saw them.

Nobody's eyes met.

After that, she was done in.

They changed hotels. They stayed in Berlin two extra days. No one knew where they were. They left Berlin going north to Sachsenhausen. On the road home they stopped for dinner. He recedes into the darkness. Her eyes flash their hard light. The darkness grows, the voice louder.

As if to silence it, without hope, he kisses her cheeks, her mouth, her forehead, her fingers, the palms of her hands.

In the night, he drives, the road fast and nearly empty, the darkness complete.

She dozes beside him.

It would be easy to smash up the car. But the results too unpredictable.

He has a gun in the glovebox. He could shoot her, then himself, let the car crash where it will.

These possibilities haven't occurred to him. He isn't thinking them now.

Or: he is and decides against them. First, he must write to Therese. An ordinary letter, but one she will know how to read.

Beside him, Jutta stirs, almost wakes. He drives faster.

A year and a half ago, she transferred 150,000DM to an account in his name, to be left to his family at his death. She insisted on making him this gift: all her work depended on him. They had collaborated for years. They shared life, labor, resources, but she was out of office then, as he had been already, since four years before, and on paper everything was hers: the bank accounts (savings, money market, mutual funds), the house (a 2000DM monthly mortgage), the television contract, the fame and probable future, even the copyrights on their joint work. His pension and investments already supported Therese. Only the car was his alone.

Maybe it was this that tempted him, no matter how briefly, to use the car as a weapon.

But he has read too many crime novels, his idle pleasure. Cars kill innocent bystanders and leave intended victims alive.

He doesn't mean this, of course. Don't take him seriously. He is telling himself a story, entertaining himself in a familiar fashion while he drives.

The attentive reader will have noticed that certain details begin to contradict, begin to shift and change. Jutta, for example, holds a mortgage, the house was never a rental. Lukas himself has been out of office since the election of '87, never having returned to the party and refusing to stand. Despite the couple's frequent financial complaints to relatives and friends, they accommodate themselves in luxury hotels and hold substantial cash reserves. Each claims the silence as his or her own. Other contradictions, confusions, will appear. The story is moving forward, and the tellings of the story, the public retellings of the story that run along in parallel to the telling unfolding here.

It is a game they play. He likes to think of it as a game.

It began with Sonam Pasang (he sees that now), but not out of jealousy, not really; it had been prepared for them before that, her affair with Sonam merely the trigger—a detonation device, not the true explosive, the chain reaction waiting to happen.

She is Jutta, she must be free.

That she must have this affair is distressing, yes, but also brings Lukas a little relief, frees him for Therese, delivers Sonam to him as a colleague in Jutta's maintenance.

After the first shock of adjustment he finds he is less alone. He submits, and understands how for so many years he has been submitting. First to his mother, then to his daughter, at the end only to Jutta.

For the first time Jutta, not Therese, looks to him like the end.

The clearer this fact becomes the more stubbornly he resists it.

He is baffled, full of confusion.

Sonam must help her in all things, as he has done, share the burden she is, not just the delight.

At the same time her new radiance excites him, reminds him of their first months, their first years. He takes her harder, his demands increase.

His violence excites her in turn.

They play games of the imagination, or he does: the games unspoken, safe, held in his secret mind.

For instance:

As a reader of crime novels, he works out the crime novel versions of their story. The jealousy plot is only one, and the most obvious. He prefers the espionage variation, the Stasi story, in which, living in deep cover, he takes orders for all his major decisions, except in this: that he really fell in love with the girl, more than fell in love, came to worship her, worships her still. In this version of the story, discovery is imminent: Stasi files are being opened, released, new revelations appearing every day; party leaders, and Jutta herself, anxious to read their Stasi dossiers, are preparing documents to expedite their review. He and Jutta have argued over this. His initial indifference was feigned. His later vehement objection—that the campaign to open the files is a waste of attention and resources they ought to concentrate on the neo-Nazi rise—has been no more than a pretext, in the end a failed diversion: the preparation of the documents proceeds.

He makes love to her in the fantasy of this plot, imagining his imminent degradation before her, his disgrace, the fear but also the triumph at having used and deceived her all their years.

Does he want her to know or doesn't he?

This is what he can't settle. In moods of anger he seems to want to punish her, to rub it in her face, to torment her with her folly, her idiocy in trusting him, her done-in innocence, her childish futile naiveté and will.

In moods of worship, though, this story changes, riddled with dread: he can't bear the thought of her knowing, neither the pain his betrayal will cause her, nor the contempt and refusal of forgiveness to come.

In both moods he holds out to the last, until the brink of disclosure, when he will enact their double death. He makes love to her in the fantasy that he is doing so for the last time, in the conviction that once it's over he will get his derringer and shoot her and then himself—or before it's over, will speak, reveal his secret, rape her with it, shoot her as he climaxes, or as she does.

The rage in these fantasies sometimes alarms him.

The more rageful these crime novel versions, the meeker in their daily life together he becomes.

Or the other way around.

It's true that the fantasies began with Sonam Pasang. The jealousy version of the story, all that. But Lukas didn't know then it was jealousy, maybe knows it only now, after seeing Sonam suddenly again across a crowded room.

Sonam had broken his heart, not only Jutta's.

That was the real humiliation.

Only Sonam knows to what lengths Lukas had gone on Jutta's behalf. Meeting with him secretly, pleading, writing to him after months of silence: begging him to take her back, if only as a friend, no more.

But Sonam's silence held.

The jealousy version, the Stasi version. Driving he thinks maybe they can be superimposed. *The worship is part of both stories, the humiliation, the rage.* He glances over at Jutta beside him. *And the will of this little girl.*

Something more is on his mind as he drives back to Bonn, something graver and less personal: his letter, his simple letter, on the rise of the new Nazis and the atmosphere of his childhood in pre-Hitler Germany.

It has troubled him since the first outbreaks after unification how the attacks on foreigners and homosexuals and synagogues and Jewish cemeteries and leftist cabarets have resembled so precisely the violence that preceded the Nazi catastrophe.

Not that he remembers so much directly—he was ten years old when Hitler came to power—but the atmosphere, the spirit, the tolerance, the unofficial encouragement, the privately voiced enthusiasm for the work the street thugs did.

Bolsheviks, his mother would say at dinner after hearing about some Nazi assault. *Good riddance!*

Lukas can see her ladling soup and his father down at the other end of the old mahogany table rolling his tragic eyes.

Jews, Bolsheviks, perverts, his mother would say—*what are they to us? Jews took your fortune, Hans, and the Bolsheviks would if it were left to take. And perverts, well*—with her eyes she would indicate Lukas and his brother, and then she would shrug. *Those fighters, such brave and angry young men, they are the true Germans, rough around the edges, so what? I don't have to invite them to dinner!*

Then she would turn to the children, this bitter, reduced daughter of counts, and say sweetly, *Heinrich, watch your bread-crumbs*, or *Lukas, darling, eat your soup*. Lotte, except when dressing her for church, she simply ignored.

Lukas's public letter, of course, isn't about his mother, not at all, but about the Nazi violence of those years, the failure of civil authority to stop it, the success of the Nazis' intimidation tactics, how widespread public silence and weakness—along with secret approval—had opened the way for the Nazis' democratic accession to the power of the state.

We want to think of ourselves as victims, we Germans, he had written, *victims of Hitler, victims just like the victims of the SS and the war machine. But we were not the victims. We were the Nazis. We were the war machine. Without us there was no Nazi party, no SS, no Wehrmacht, no Hitler Jugend, no Bund Deutscher Mädchen. Oh, not me, we say, not me. I'm too young. I'm of the amnesty generation. Yes, of course. What did we know? We were taught.*

And so on.

It was an angry letter, a gloomy, desperate letter. *It is happening again.*

But no one would print it—no magazine, no newspaper.

He no longer had a forum. Lukas Grimm? Nobody cared.

Not even Jutta Carroll could get his letter published for him.

They were in process of being forgotten, silenced through being ignored.

Was this an accident? Of course not. They were being cut off, systematically shunned.

It began in the party, where deals were struck.

Rudi Schreiber and Monika Hertz, or maybe Heinrich Lamm, taking secret campaign donations or guarantees for the future in exchange for further isolating Jutta from her public and party base: refuse her an office, deny her a stipend, deny her the support of the party infrastructure—well, if she insists, which she surely will, throw her a little bone, for the sake of the semblance of friendliness, let her fax a little, let her photocopy, but only after hours, make it inconvenient, discourage her, humiliate her, teach her her place—above all give her no forum, no Jutta-and-Lukas spectacles, no hearings, no speeches, no articles, no more impassioned appeals. She lost the election, after all. The party will be stronger without her. She's out of touch with the movement that made her famous. Look at the disaster that was her television show. All she's cared about for years is her own fame, remember—that and her special causes.

And so on.

It was easily done, even without donations or promises. Within the party leadership, who needed bribing?

Still, pushing Jutta to the sidelines was in somebody's larger interest than the usual ego interests of the usual party infighting. And the failure of her television show—that too. The way the producers had restricted her to reading a written text from a teleprompter, forced her to articulate slowly, unnaturally, all her power of speech and passion reined in. She was Samson without his hair. What did they expect? Of course the show failed, of course the station canceled even before the contract was fulfilled.

And in whose interest was that?

So now here they are, and here he is, chauffeur and *Kofferträger*—Lukas Grimm, former member of the Bundestag and general of the Bundeswehr (ret.), unable to get a simple letter printed anywhere in the press.

He is obsessed with this letter.

The longer he lives with it in its unpublished state the more toxic it becomes.

It is only a letter, after all, a mere maybe 1500 words—long for a letter, yes, but still, a letter. He has gathered enough information already to make a whole book. He hasn't asked for a book, he hasn't asked for money—only to be heard.

Everyone he spoke with in Salzburg, in Berlin, listened to these complaints and frustrations, from Jutta and even from him.

He has made himself ridiculous over this letter.

He has felt himself whining, cranky, become an old fusspot.

He imagined people laughing, gossiping when they saw him coming: *Has he carried on to you about this letter yet? Jutta's nearly killed herself trying to keep up his self-esteem.*

What *they* knew.

He grips the steering wheel more tightly. His shoulder aches, and his knee.

There is more to his fears than he admits in that letter, or to anyone.

Alone in the silence and darkness of the road he can almost see clearly what haunts him.

Leni, after all, was not really wrong.

Not that he had seen the camps, of course. Not that he knew. But the rest.

He was a soldier.

He had followed orders, given orders.

He had killed and ordered others to kill.

They were an army in full retreat. They lived off the land. They destroyed what they couldn't carry or use. They left no survivors.

He had returned to Munich by way of an American POW camp.

But his unit had first been taken in what would later be the Russian zone.

There were Red Army documents, records, later in the possession of and translated by the Stasi.

This was fact, not one of his crime novels. He was approached in 1979, in a Stasi attempt at blackmail and seduction.

He had been braver then. He had refused.

Not without first negotiating to read the records.

He hadn't recognized himself in what he read. He barely remembered. Remembered that he was a prisoner of the Russians when the news of Hitler's death came. Remembered flowering trees and that he cried. But before that? Days, weeks, months, years. The eastern front, the western front, the eastern front again, leaves at home in Munich, the love of Therese. He had been a good soldier, a leader, earned field promotions, the respect of his men. And everywhere women fell for him—prostitutes in the Wehrmacht brothels, nurses when he was wounded, wives and young girls in the occupied towns. But as he looked through his Red Army file he understood that his only actual memories of the eastern front were fragmentary and came from early in the war.

He sat in that hotel room with the Stasi agent and read the file—a photocopy of the file, of course, the agent reminded him as she handed it over, lest the General imagine he could escape disclosure by an attempt at false heroics.

"Of course," he had answered. He read the file.

He remembers answering, "Of course," and the flirtatiousness he indulged toward the woman without even thinking. He remembers her teal green suit, the white ersatz silk of her blouse, the trace of makeup showing around its collar, even remembers her sharp, slightly floral scent.

He remembers the smoke from her Marlboro cigarettes as he sat and read the file.

Remembers reading the file.

Remembers that what he read was foreign to him. Remembers the recognition that his only coherent memories of war and occupation were located in the West. Remembers his conviction that the file was authentic, the excitement and clarity of knowing that it lifted a veil, even though he had already known and still knows well enough the history of the Wehrmacht in retreat.

He no longer remembers the contents of the file.

Instead he remembers his own courage in the face of the agent: "There is nothing here that isn't in the record of every German soldier from that time, that place. We have been cleared of blame. Make it public however you like. This document can do me no harm."

But that was before he knew Jutta.

She wakes when they arrive at the house. She staggers in. He carries the bags. She reads faxes. He goes directly to bed. From a fog of sleep he hears her voice on the phone. He sleeps. He dreams.

She comes to bed. He holds her, weeping in her arms. She wakes him, strokes, comforts him—a whispered conversation.

To kill her would be too terrible. Unless he had her consent. He has killed before. It isn't the killing that stops him.

He has told himself this story again and again. He knows these sentences. He was twenty-two. He did what he had been trained to do. He, too, liked to think of himself as a victim.

Nothing is new in any of it.

Whatever was in that file is already known, has been known by everyone for years. The Stasi backed down. The file was no use to them. Maybe they even destroyed it.

The terror is the hollow in his memory, the hole.

He can tell himself the words, he can imagine—he's read other soldiers' accounts, and the accounts of survivors from the Russian side. But nowhere is any chord struck, no recognition comes, no image appears, no sound, no smell, no taste, no touch. Somebody else was there, not him.

He was wounded of course, twice in the chest, once in the head. In 1979, in that hotel room with the Stasi woman, when he became aware of his lack of memory, he attributed it to that head wound.

Now, since reunification, the images come in dreams.

He doesn't trust these images. They are too violent, repulsive. Clichés of propaganda and sadist pornography, images of infants smashed dead against walls, gang rapes, dismemberings and disembowelings, mutilations, mass executions into mass graves.

The butchery Leni always seemed to imagine.

As if Leni's visions were coming now to haunt him.

As if she had collected stories from all the dead on the other side.

As if she has been gathering witnesses against him these many years.

She wakes him, strokes and comforts him—a whispered conversation.

Jutta, Jutta, it is unbearable.

Again, so badly?

A woman, naked, cut, slit . . .

You must stop watching the television news.

I saw her face, I know this face.

Lukas, Lukas—

Flies. There were flies, buzzing in my ear and around my hands and around the bodies at my feet. I'm standing still. A chaos whirls all around me, my men ride a carousel. Orders come over the staticky radio. *Kill the horses.* We slit their throats with bayonets. The painted wooden horses bleed. At my feet I find the woman, her belly opened—

Stop.

It's worse, it gets worse.

Don't tell me.

I lie down beside her. I push into her wound with my hand. I crush my bloody hand to her face. She opens her eyes.

Phantoms, Lukas. Nightmares.

I kiss her, I fuck her, what's left of her.

Stop. Lukas, you were a boy, nothing more than a child—

Like this, Jutta. I kiss—

She's me.

She's you. I roll her over into the dirt—

Like this—

A whispered conversation. It starts in the dark, with tears, his tears. But he escapes them.

In the silence of the morning, alone before daylight, drinking his one cup of coffee, he easily finds more rational explanations than Leni's haunting or the hauntings of lost memory for the terrible, fading images of his dreams: the news from Bosnia, the dreadful testimony of the radiation victims, the sex murders in the crime novel he was reading in Berlin.

He goes out to his little garden while the sky is still black and showing stars. It has rained overnight and all around him the leaves are dripping. In the beam of his flashlight he finds only a few dead blooms to clip away, a handful of little weeds to uproot. The Kostners, former neighbors, have tended the garden well in his absence. The slugs are at work again, though, and he must set new traps for them before going in, a half dozen shallow food cans, which he saves for this purpose, dug into the ground and filled with beer. Even this little exertion, this stooping and standing, stooping and standing, this little troweling and hammering, tires his shoulder and knee. Between setting each can and the next, he stands and stretches and looks up at the fading stars, the rising sky. He savors this moment of rest and emptiness, listens into it, as if waiting, breathes awhile, whispers a Tibetan prayer, then squats on his haunches and sets another can. Before going in to his desk, he cuts sprays of blue and purple cosmos, yellow daisies, a dark red rose to replace the bouquet that will have dried and fallen by now on Jutta's altar to Emma. He salutes the morning's last star.

Many hours later Jutta rose and came down the stairs. He heard her coming. He finished the sentence he was writing in his letter to Therese. He switched off the typewriter. He got up from his chair.

"Good morning," he said. "Can I get you something?"

"Please," she said, and followed him into the kitchen. She sat down at the little table and watched while he boiled water and measured chamomile and peppermint leaves into the pot for her tea.

He told her about setting the slug traps and indicated the flowers he had cut for Emma's altar.

"Very pretty," she said.

"We've been gone so long," he said, "we're out of everything. No bread, no fruit. We should have stopped on the way for groceries."

"The tea will be enough," she said, and asked him to get the honey down from the cupboard.

He brought it and two empty cups and sat with her at the table.

They avoided each other's eyes.

"It was difficult to see Sonam," she said.

"Yes," Lukas agreed. "For me also."

"Perhaps you should write to him."

"Impossible."

"Perhaps after all this time, and seeing us and seeing that we left it to him and made no overture, no scene of any kind, which must be what he dreaded, seeing that and you and me together still and so serene, perhaps now he would allow us again—"

"Impossible," Lukas repeated.

The steam rose from the kettle and he left the table.

Behind him Jutta went on talking.

He stared at the stream of boiling water he was pouring into the teapot and the broken loose swirling leaves and the billowing steam.

"You're not listening to me," she said as he turned.

He shrugged and delivered the tea and sat down.

"You do what you will do, Jutta. But I won't write to him now. It is too humiliating. It is shaming to you. To both of us. I won't continue. I won't start again. I thought you had let him go."

"But yes of course," she said, and off she went again and Lukas stopped listening, his eyes glazing over, or so she accused him, until finally he said, "Do you really want this? Jutta, this isn't really what you want. Think. What you want is not Sonam Pasang or any other old lover or anybody new. What you want is a place for yourself again, an institutional role, leadership, a forum, a base. What does Sonam have to do with that? Nothing. You can't bully him into being what you want. You can't bully anyone anymore."

"Bully? You call me a bully? You dare to? You, the reconstructed general, drowning in nostalgia for the dignity of command, you dare?" And so on.

So it went.

It wasn't an unusual quarrel and ended in apologies and kissed fingers and tears.

"I'd better get to work then," Jutta said.

And Lukas had agreed to write another letter to Sonam.

They didn't come to agreement so quickly, of course. He is trying to remember now the turns their tempers took. Parts of the conversation were tender, gentle. They drank their tea. His agreement wasn't the end of it at all, not at all, just slipped into the negotiations somewhere and lost again until in the silence afterward he realized he had committed himself to writing the letter, a letter no longer so important anymore after everything was said, perhaps irrelevant altogether, unnecessary.

He isn't sure.

He goes over the conversation as best he can, unable to track the sequence, the fit of one moment into another.

Her anger had broken, as always, in tears. She couldn't bear it any longer, how was she to bear it? and so on, the same question he asks himself day after day.

His role then, once she cried, was to comfort her.

But today he refused.

He sat at the table and watched her as if from far away.

"I can't struggle like this anymore," she said, "we are too alone, and how will I carry on without you when without you I can bear nothing and you no longer have the strength to carry my burdens and my weakness, Lukas, what are we to do? Everything collapses around us. Evil and the will to violence are too great and we're abandoned here lost we've become no one with no base no means, you should go home to Therese now, I'm destroying your life, but I can't bear to live without you, when you die or when you leave me I won't be able to continue."

She has spoken like this before, off and on for years, but his own destroyed life and eventual death have come into her conversation only since the accident, when his age and weakness finally became visible to her.

Today, though, she went further, or he thinks she did.

"During the Gulf War we were hopeless," she said, "and I didn't listen to you, I carried on and all our protests did no good, during reunification we were hopeless, during the election hopeless, we carried on as if with hope but inside we were empty, we still are empty, empty shells of hope, we're dead anyway, already dead, the weight of the struggle is too great, the burden of testimony too heavy to carry, to live with," and he knew what she was asking, what she was trying to remind him of and refusing to say, and he sat there and watched her from his cool distance and waited to see whether she would allow herself the consciousness implicit in the words.

"Now again, still, we are hopeless," she said. "As our new unified German government signs agreements to deport Romanians to persecution and death. As new Nazis use the memory of the old Nazis to celebrate instead of to grieve. As war and systematic rape continue in Bosnia. As the backdoor market in Soviet plutonium opens. As the western nuclear powers maintain and increase and test their arsenals. As the western nuclear industry prepares to expand into the former East. Hopeless," she said. "Our efforts are only killing you, and without you," etc., but she wouldn't say it, couldn't, even though they both knew exactly what argument she was circling, exactly what proposal she was inviting him once more to make.

He had pled for it more than once. As early as the disaster at Chernobyl—to travel to the zone, to expose themselves, immerse themselves, to occupy, bearing witness for the world.

She was horrified. "To die?" she said, aghast. "Slowly? Terribly? Like Emma?" They bore witness from Bonn.

During the Gulf War, he had argued for going to Baghdad, to stand in the street in protest of US bombing, to risk being killed by a US bomb.

She had refused, even laughed at him. She was seeing the Tibetan then.

Now he isn't sure.

He has wanted to disentangle himself from her for so long and the more he has wanted to disentangle himself the more entangled he has become.

He has told himself he wanted to disentangle.

She is killing him. They both know it. They have told themselves. They have told each other.

But how can he leave her?

Over and over, the same questions, the same answer. Their shared death. Double suicide, as protest, as immolation.

"Never," she had said when he first proposed it. She was too young to die. Besides, no one would believe it. No one would believe that she could kill herself or agree to be killed. She was too brave, too life-affirming. Her will was too strong, even when her heart was hopeless. He alone would be blamed. They would say he was jealous of Sonam Pasang.

He had argued for a joint public statement, a letter, a video—proof of their shared intention.

"Never," she said. "You are not serious. Don't you see how suicide would taint and tarnish everything we stand for? Martyring ourselves would leave us powerless. Lukas, we would be dead." She laughed as if he had not considered this.

So this morning, as she circled the only solution he had to offer, he had looked at her without moving and finally interrupted her gently to ask, "Are you serious?"

She was silent then, as if she didn't know what the word, what the question, meant. "I suppose I should get to work," she said.

Just then, he thinks. It was then, when he asked her directly, that she withdrew.

In Berlin, at the congress of the Buddhist Union, they had heard remembrances of the monks of Vietnam who in the 1960s had immolated themselves publicly in protest of the war. In Sachsenhausen, at the fire-charred ruin of the concentration camp victims memorial, she had spoken of the camp dead as martyrs, the brief hope born in the aftermath and horror of their dreadful, unwilling immolations now destroyed.

"What must we do, Lukas?" she had asked him in the car. "If your letter is to be published, if we will not otherwise be heard or listened to, if our names and our work are to remain alive, what must we do?"

But as quickly as she spoke she leapt away from her words, directed his attention to something wholly other, a dark cloud across the moon, the speed of the wind, geese in flight, and broke into a story about Emma and an anecdote from the book of letters from Goethe to Charlotte von Stein that she had bought in Berlin and had been reading the last two nights in the hotel room while he slept.

Did she mean to live or didn't she?

He could never tell.

"Kill me then," she had lashed out at him at the little kitchen table. "Why don't you just kill me then? We're dying like this anyway. Make use of our misery, put an end to it, Lukas, we are so unhappy and there's no way out."

But minutes later she was demanding again, *Write the letter*, and he had agreed.

Or maybe minutes later. He isn't sure.

In the hotel room, their last night in Berlin, she had turned out her reading light and wakened him with her sobs. "Oh Lukas, Lukas," was all she had been able to say. He had held her, for hours it seemed, awake, in silence, except for her tears and his name.

He doesn't know where to go from here. The argument spirals in his memory. It had framed a patch of silence. That silence, maybe, was the key. What came before it? What came after? How long did it last? It's hard for him to know.

So many of the angers and accusations were old, familiar, so many times spoken they were well worn out.

Only the silence was new.

They sat in it.

He could feel the rage in his body.

Her tears came out of the silence.

Into the silence.

She lifted her wet eyes to him.

He looked at her without moving. With cold contempt, or so

he hoped. He willed every shaking muscle in his body, in his face, to be still.

Maintaining his body's stillness took all of his concentration.

That was the silence they sat in.

How long, he can't say.

After a while, though, maybe it changed.

Maybe it got gentler.

Maybe they came to agreement.

He isn't sure.

But the rage was gone from his body.

He saw how beautiful she was. He saw her as he loved her, worshipped, adored her. It was impossible that he could ever have wanted to hurt her.

She smiled and it was as if the sun came into the gloomy kitchen.

She reached out her hand to him. He kissed her fingers.

"I suppose I should get to work then," she said.

But that wasn't the end.

"What happened, Jutta?" he asked her. "What happened in Berlin?"

He was surprised by his own question. He had not been aware that he thought something had happened.

Yet when he heard his words, he knew they were true.

In Berlin her tears had been different from any tears she had cried with him: they were tears without words—without explication or provocation, drama, demands.

Since Berlin something inexpressible had made this new silence, this new grief.

It wasn't Sonam. Lukas had already lived through Sonam. They had lived through him together. Lukas knew the exact resonance of that grief, those tears.

This was something other.

But she denied him. "Happened? What could have happened?"

Indeed, what.

Except for the few hours that she spent alone with Anna Albert, they had been together every minute.

And late at night when she remained awake while he slept.

He had never mistrusted her. She had never lied to him.

It wasn't a man, a lover. She would have told him about a lover, would have no reason not to, would be wearing him to exhaustion with the many nuances of her heart.

Still, she resisted his question, refused it.

This was something new: unprecedented, unsayable.

He looked into her eyes and met the wall of her silence.

The rage came back, jealous for the truth.

Calmer now, he thinks he understands: she is leaving him, she is preparing herself to survive.

He should be grateful. He should feel released.

He returns to his typewriter, to his letter to Therese. He quickly reads over what he wrote earlier and begins a new paragraph in a deliberately cheerier tone, describes the journey, the stop at Sachsenhausen, the dinner he and Jutta ate on the road. He mentions the geese flying south, the rain overnight, the slugs in the garden. He writes that he expects to see her soon.

With that, the letter seems finished and as he signs and folds it and addresses the envelope, he becomes aware of a vaguely mounting dread.

It is true he has told Jutta he will write to Sonam.

He leaves the desk for the fax machine, where ribbons of messages have poured out in their absence. Jutta had gone through them quickly the night before.

"You haven't even called Hilmar, have you?" she demanded during their quarrel, and insisted at him that he keep up with things, Hilmar's fax was clearly marked urgent, Lukas had lost his sense of priorities, no doubt all he'd done the whole morning was tend his garden and write to Therese while she was up half the night preparing letters and faxes in the effort to get his letter published—and these faxes and letters were ready to be sent, by the way, or hadn't he noticed them here on the kitchen table where she always left her work for him, had they been gone so long that he had forgotten, and so on.

And then she had cried and apologized and said of course that she couldn't get along without him.

He locates the fax from Hilmar asking him to call at once on their return.

On the phone he apologizes for the delay. "I'm not so clear-headed lately," he says.

Hilmar tells him he must call the party staffer working on access to the Stasi files, something about a new letter to be submitted, their signatures, and gives him the name and number, apologizes himself, he's late for a meeting, has to run.

So much fuss over nothing.

He should write the letter to Sonam.

Something simple. *We were touched to see you at the Buddhist congress and saddened at the weakness we three shared, our inability to greet one another as friends after so much that was good and important has passed between us.* Something like that. Something delicate and brief. No pleas, no complaints.

But he postpones it.

First he must write to his lawyer concerning Heike Bauer's dispute with her landlord.

He sits at the humming typewriter a long while before he begins.

His mind is in a paradoxical state. He can recognize that. It wanders, for minutes at a time, but when he pulls himself up short he has no sense of where it's taken him, only that he's been away, trailed off.

As if into another reality. That's the feeling.

A whole world, a life, a set of problems, characters, concerns, all different from this life, these problems and concerns—co-existing and somehow in these missing moments slipped, leaked, the boundary broken.

It is not a better life, not a happier life. Just different.

He hardly knows himself anymore. He has always been a purely rational man.

Still, he remains himself, this unknown self, in both worlds. Or in all the worlds—his other world could be many, without continuity. He knows nothing about it, only the sensation of coming back and leaving a life behind, a life, a world, as complete and complex as the life and world he returns to.

There is a certain density about it.

As if it's really there.

He has spoken of this to no one, certainly not to Jutta, who already sees him as weakened, going vague on her, *losing his utility*, he thinks, after all these years.

The one he would most like to tell is the Dalai Lama. He has considered writing His Holiness about it but doubts his own capacity to describe his state of mind. In person His Holiness would understand, perhaps simply by looking at him, certainly by hearing his efforts, the stumblings of his voice, his inarticulate groping for right words.

It isn't true, what Jutta said, that all he's done this morning is tend the garden and write to Therese.

He's also sorted and screened the weeks of mail and newspapers the Kostners collected for them from the post office box.

And before all that he sat down to his meditation, or tried to.

Lately meditation has been difficult.

He seems to sleep. He seems to disappear.

He wonders whether it's true what he's imagined, that she is leaving him, that despite her protestations to the contrary she is ready finally to live alone.

What an irony it would be.

This woman, this demon—God in heaven, she has destroyed him, admits destroying him, says as much over and over, not only in private, not only to him, but to Hilmar and Heike and everybody in the party office and to friends over dinner and at the conferences in Berlin and Salzburg and even to mere acquaintances, perfect strangers, out it all pours, in front of his face—it's no wonder Sonam dumped her, he saw too clearly, even then, what has happened to me.

So now when at last he's ruined, useless—time to pack him off back to his wife?

Was this the same Jutta who was terrified of solitude?

The Jutta who couldn't be left alone in Bonn?—who had clung to his ankles, his knees?—who lay with him one morning on the cold bathroom floor weeping, threatening to kill herself (there was a morsel none of the jackals knew about!), begging him to help her, to stay, to keep her alive?

Of course, she didn't directly threaten—*don't go or else*—she's always been too subtle for that.

Her terror was itself the threat. Her unbearable terror.

I won't survive.

She had made it clear then, long ago, just as she makes it clear now. Without him she will not live.

At the beginning she was still seeing Hilmar, and even sometimes the Irishman Patrick Curran.

Lukas indulged her. He was fascinated. She was everything Therese and the many seduced wives of his junior officers were not.

Most of all she was free.

Is she under some illusion that she can get that freedom back now? Does she really imagine that she will leave him?

It isn't possible.

Not even with Sonam was she able to let him go.

And he had wanted to go. Had thought he wanted to.

And now?

He is past wanting.

It is into this moment perhaps that the interruption comes. He has begun his letter, the date, the address, the salutation, the setting out of Heike's conflict with her landlord. His mind has wandered, into its own paradoxical state. He is past wanting. But something else is going on.

When he finishes with this letter he will have to write to Sonam.

Then he will have to go out in the car and mail his letters and the letters Jutta wrote by hand the night before.

He will have to go to the post office and collect the few days' mail that will have arrived after the date of their expected return.

By the time he's doing these errands he will have written to Sonam.

But to do these errands won't be possible.
It will have been impossible for him to write such a letter.
It will be impossible for him to arrive at that place.

He comes back from a strange distance, remembers flowering branches, tears.
Absently, he reads over the sentences he has written so far and begins the next: *Wir müs—*
He breaks off. He can't do it. He drops his hands to his lap.
If he doesn't finish this word he can't finish the sentence.
If he doesn't finish this sentence he can't finish the letter.
If he doesn't finish this letter he won't have to write the next one.

He comes back from a strange distance. He ought to feel released. But he doesn't trust her.
There can be no letting go.
It's all too late.

He should take the car, go for groceries. Leave this letter unwritten. It's well past noon. He's hungry and the house offers nothing to eat. Even Jutta will be hungry eventually.
The thought of her upstairs working stops his thoughts.
He becomes aware of the silence.

Between one thought and the next there is a gap.
The gap is pure mind.
Extend the gap.

Usually when she's working he hears her from time to time, moving around the little study, pacing, gathering books or documents, her voice on the phone.
He has heard nothing for a long while.

He listens longer. Nothing. Thinks she must have gone back to bed.

It's unlike her to go back to bed at this hour, but consistent with the mood she's been in, the morbid wanderings, the lack of appetite, the old and foolish arguments provoked over virtually nothing, the instant regret, the tears, the silence, the tears.

A new wave of depression rolling in.

Unbearable.

How had he become responsible for this?

When they first met he had taken her for Penthesilea. A warrior woman.

He should have been warned by that first impression.

Much of the time now he feels like dead Achilles, cannibalized.

Then will come this wave, these waves.

When she can no longer demand or even beg. When he can refuse her nothing.

They are swept into it, drown in it.

He hates her for it. She hates it in herself.

All along it's been what's kept him.

He should have seen this coming, should have recognized the signs.

As always, they had both been looking for solutions in the world, working for publication, attention, funds.

His own attention had been traveling.

He tells himself the silence means she's gone back to bed, that maybe he should leave her there.

But he won't, can't. He never has.

His job is to wake her, to bring her back to life, to focus her again in the direction she has chosen for herself, to arouse her will.

The job gets harder.

From a distance, he comes back to the moment. He stands up from the desk, the unfinished letter still in the typewriter.

He stands, concerned for the silence, listening.

"Jutta?" he calls, and gets no answer.

Slowly he mounts the stairs.

At the end of the hall the bedroom door is open.

He was right. She's gone back to bed.

He stands in the doorway almost beside her. Their bed takes up most of the shadowed room, the black shades on the windows drawn down as always to preserve the darkness.

She is lying on her back in an attitude of surrender, or would be except that her head and shoulder and elbow seem flung, slightly askew, at odd, uncomfortable angles.

The night table beside her, between them, is piled high with books as always. He switches on the light.

She doesn't blink. Her face is strangely both pale and flushed.

He takes in the pile of books, on top the two she brought from Berlin, the Goethe and Alexandra Kollontai, beside them a stack of letters he recognizes as his own, and with his letters another, the old solitary letter from her father, in its ragged envelope.

Her rings are on the table, and the case for her contact lenses, and her reading glasses and a glass of water.

Everything is normal.

But the silence is unbearable. Too complete.

Between one thought and the next there is a gap.

Watch the breath. Become it.

Between the exhale and the inhale there is a gap. Become the gap.

She isn't breathing.

It is a sudden realization.

Her face strangely pale, strangely flushed.

She had filled a prescription in Berlin. He had paid no attention. She had prescriptions for everything.

Become the gap.

At her neck he feels for a pulse. Her flesh is almost warm.

He stumbles up from the bed, can't take his eyes off her. He forces himself to breathe. He waits.

He doesn't know for what.

Comprehension, maybe.

She hadn't trusted him to do it. She had done it herself. All alone.

He kneels beside her, feels for her pulse again, listens to her chest, for her heart, for breath.

He could call for help. He could try to bring back the dead.

He gets up. He feels around the bed, the body, looking for the prescription bottle.

Tricyclic antidepressants. Newly filled, a month's supply. Half the bottle gone.

This is a mistake he thinks. Somewhere in this death there is a mistake.

He is holding her, cradling her.

His child. She has always been his child.

Slowly he lays her body down, restores it to its sleeping position, attempts to improve its aspect of calm, to correct the crooked angle of the head and shoulder and elbow, to relax the stiffening fingers to a curl.

He covers her gently, as if tucking her in to sleep.

He stands and reaches over her to smooth out the covers and plump up the pillows on his side of the bed.

He switches off the light.

He doesn't know what he's thinking yet. He's simply restoring order.

He looks at her awhile, can't drag himself from the sight of her.

He would like to leave her like this, whole, sleeping, undisturbed, knows he can't. On the contrary, he has to act quickly or the deception will be evident.

Deception?

He becomes aware that he is forming a plan. It propels him out of the bedroom, and once away from the body he moves easily, with efficiency and speed.

He notices this sudden efficiency and speed. He notices a

strange exhilaration, a lightness. He notices everything as if from outside himself.

It is a feeling he remembers from the war, the facing of death, survival beyond a danger and the sudden understanding that he has survived it, the flooding gratitude for life, for sight and sound and breathing, and even when he was wounded, after the first shock, the astonished and happy awareness that despite the wound he was alive.

He was eighteen when he went to the war. In the face of danger, he felt the life in his body. In the face of dead and living bodies mangled and bleeding and torn, untouched himself, despite the fear, inside it, he felt untouchable. The illusion made him a hero. It was an illusion. Not even his wounds released him from it.

It was typically human, that was all, animal really.

Alive, he knows no death.

Meanwhile, his body, that part of himself which he is watching, has gone into action, first to the bathroom to place the half-used bottle of pills on the shelf with Jutta's many other bottles of pills, then to Emma's room, where the first thing he sees is the bouquet he cut in the morning, the blue and purple cosmos, the daisies, the rose, on the altar with the photos of Emma and the little candle flame that never goes out, not even during their absences, when it is one of the items on the Kostners' list, reminding them to see that it continues, to light a new candle from the flame when the old candle burns low.

In Emma's room, in the wardrobe, tucked away with winter sweaters and gloves and scarves, in the first upper drawer on the left, in its holster, is his derringer .38, a gun he added to his collection in the early 1960s under the influence of an American television show about a southern gentleman gambler living by his wits in the years before the Civil War. He and Dieter and Hans, his sons, used to watch the show together.

It is a gun that holds two bullets.

It isn't the only gun in the house, but the nearest, and the appropriate gun, the necessary gun.

He understands that he will be blamed.

He understands that it is his duty to take the blame, to make it possible for the blame to fall on him.

She was entirely right. No one will believe it, that she has killed herself. Even he does not believe it.

He feels her still in the room, almost hears her calling to him, telling him what he must do, hears her almost so clearly he becomes for a moment impatient, irritable, wants to quiet her, to say aloud *All right, all right, I understand, now let me get on and do what I must.*

But the exhilaration is greater than all that.

The exhilaration, the light that seems to fill his body, the room—the certainty, the freedom that has finally come.

The feeling is so pure, he finds it hard to go forward, to take the next step.

Still, he does go forward, back into the bedroom.

He places the gun to her head.

He lowers himself, one knee at a time, beside the bed.

He straightens her head, adjusts the placement of the gun, draws it back two inches from contact and fires.

He studies the mess on the pillows.

There is a splattering of bone and tissue, but to obscure the fact that she was already dead when the bullet hit her, her body, he thinks, must spill more blood.

She was close to alive. But not close enough.

A living body dying pumps blood with the force of the living heart, at least for a moment, one heartbeat, two. He has to try to simulate that heartbeat.

Has to try to pump the blood up out of her.

Has to press himself against her, has to bear down with all his weight on her dead chest.

As if desperate to bring her back to life.

In his favorite Stasi version of the story, he has been ordered to kill her. The Stasi, of course, is the Stasi no more—no more Ministerium für Staatssicherheit, no more Staat. Stasi networks exist nevertheless. It is a fact that he considered running for the Bundestag in the 1990 elections as a candidate of the PDS—the party of the former communists of the former East (and if he had, he might be in the Bundestag today, since in that election the PDS

took seventeen seats—and how would Jutta have lived with that!).
In this version of the story he has been in deep cover all along,
since the end of the war and his capture by the Russians: a spy in
the house of the right-wing party of his Bavarian political enemy,
Franz-Josef Strauss, a spy in the house of the new West German
army, a spy turned loose to join the anti-Euromissile campaign, a
spy commanded to influence the West German alternative through
his relationship with its well-known heroine and star.

How muddled this version gets, though—like everyone's Stasi
story, as time goes on—while his love for her grows, and her
dependency, as his sense of duty becomes a more private thing, as
the Wall falls and his Stasi obligations become ambiguous, and
finally nonexistent, his first priority to cover his tracks—more
than anything for her sake.

And after? Why do they want her dead?

He doesn't know. His masters are a jealous mother. Maybe it
is that simple. She is dangerous to them, or will be, but how?
Word is, they're doing business with the nuclear mafia, hire themselves out. Whose orders is he taking anymore?

So he resists, refuses, delays. Until they come for him, for
them.

Or worse: the Stasi chief is rumored to have destroyed the
records of all external agents, but his own record as an agent has
not been destroyed, has been held, precisely for this purpose, this
blackmail. They've threatened to make this file public. He has
ignored their threats. So they went to her. This was what happened
in Berlin. They had contacted her. He had left her with Anna
Albert and taken Trudi, Anna's daughter, to see a film. It was an
American film, full of violence and laughter. In Anna Albert's
studio they must have reached her. On the way back from Anna's
to the hotel she stopped at a pharmacy to fill a prescription. She
had already telephoned the doctor in Bonn. She explained nothing
else. Lukas didn't ask. He assumed it was for her headaches. As
much as he took pleasure in Trudi's company, he was tired from
spending so many hours with a teenager. His attention was vague.

He stands in the doorway holding the gun and staring at her

covered body and fractured head and the blood-splattered pillow beside her.

The bright lightness of certainty is still with him.

He can see that his attempt at deception has been a failure. Nevertheless, his duty is to protect her, and he has done what he could.

He steps out onto the landing and sets the gun down on the crowded bookshelf next to its leather holster.

He would like to wait awhile. He would like to live a little longer.

He sits down at the top of the stairs.

He would like another cup of tea.

Tea makes him think of his mother, when he was a child, reading his leaves.

She wore lavender and pearls. She smelled like powder, roses and lilac. Her red lips were painted on.

He was her favorite.

She always gave him good fortunes: long life, heroism, glamour, love, fame. In contrast, she punished Heinrich with his fortunes, and Lotte she ignored.

When Heinrich was killed in the war she wrote to Lukas about the necessity of duty.

When their father died she told him that now he must be the man of the family and didn't cry, at least not in front of him, or anyone else.

For thirty-five years she was cool to Therese.

She took little interest in his children, only in their obedience.

He thought she was indestructible. Until the day she died he thought she would live forever.

He was the only one who cried for her, the only one who really mourned.

Alive and waiting on the landing, he would like to live a little longer.

He would like to write that letter to Sonam.

He would like to know for certain who burned the memorial at Sachsenhausen. Would like to add this destruction of the memorial to his public letter. Would like to think this incident will be the one that makes his letter necessary in the eyes of the world. Would like to know what he's forgotten of his actions during the war.

He regrets now the interruption of attention that prevented his completing the letter to his lawyer on behalf of Heike Bauer.

He is relieved that more than a year ago he told Therese and Hans where to find the documents that will give them access to the 150,000DM.

He would like to feel again the weight of the gun.

He reaches for it from the shelf beside him and takes it into his hand.

He would like to hold the gun for hours longer. Would like to breathe in and breathe out. Would like to steady himself on the gap in his breathing. Would like to become his breath, and become the gap, and become his hands holding the gun.

It is impossible not to return to the bedroom.

To look again at her body, even so destroyed.

To look again at the walls, at the dark-shaded windows, at the room, at the bed they shared for twelve years.

To look again, and more closely, at the books and letters piled on the nightstand, at the last disarray touched by her life.

He would like to touch them himself, hold them, even read them, the marked pages of her books, his letters.

He would like to hold her in his arms.

He would like to hear once more the madness in her, the divinity.

In the presence of her body, the gun still in his hand, the artificial clarity of danger still heightening his senses and accelerating but unraveling thought, he wants to meet her again, wants to know the rage in her, wants her to tell him what she's done, why she's done it, why she's gone on without him, left him here alone, wants to hit her, really, to shut her up, to stop her, to keep her alive, to live himself.

In the presence of her body, in the artificial clarity, with heightened senses and unraveling thought, he is at peace.

First in rage, then at peace. Rage, peace. Tossed between them.

In rage or at peace, he returns to the landing. In rage or at peace, he raises the gun again, points it ceilingward, leans against the wall.

He has been in the habit of saying it was luck, only luck, that he had committed no war crimes: he received orders, he followed orders. A German soldier's duty was to listen, to obey, to kill. He had believed in the German cause, had believed it was necessary to protect the *Volk* from Bolsheviks and Jews. If he had been ordered to shoot a baby he would have shot the baby. If he had been ordered to order his men to massacre a town full of old women and children he would have given the order. He has not assumed for himself an innocence he knows he does not deserve.

But now he would like to remember.

He would like the weight of the gun in his hand to bring him to memory.

He would like the sight of the blood, Jutta's blood, in the bedroom to open the doors of time.

He would like to live awhile longer.

Would like to stand and watch the shadows shift across the wall.

Would like to stand watch over the body, both bodies, his own and hers.

It troubles him to know that he will be recorded as the liar, baffled, confused, she the open one—she as the victim, he the destroyer.

All along he has been the one who knew. Clear from the beginning.

It was he who saw the only direction this life and love of theirs could take them.

He had tried to resist. But her weakness was stronger.

He comes back from a strange distance, remembering flowering trees.

It occurs to him that his letter will be published now, once he's dead, discovered.

Their deaths will be a mystery, a scandal. Nothing will be forgotten. Everything will be exposed.

He would like to live a little longer.

He holds the gun with two hands, in the position of prayer. He lowers his head until his forehead meets the barrel. He lifts his head. He leans back against the wall, raises the gun, upside down, holds it high with two hands, aims it awkwardly, downward, presses the barrel tightly into his forehead, thumb at the trigger. He closes his eyes and squeezes.

It is possible, even likely, that most of this never happened—not her suicide or his attempt to cover it up, not the quarrel, not their shared pot of tea.

It is possible, even likely, that he killed her while she slept, shot her in the morning and lived a little longer, maybe hours, even days. Possible, maybe likely, that as soon as he saw her blood on the pillow, on the sheets, he fled the room, stumbled on the landing, knocked over the bookcase, raged at the books, the shelves, kicked, pitched, pounded, threw himself against the walls, his shoulders, his head, backed up against the wall in full sight of the horrible body and raised the gun to his forehead.

It is possible, if perhaps unlikely, that she swallowed a handful of pills before coming to bed, that he woke in the morning and found her dead, or that he shot her with her prior consent while she slept, and either way that everything he did afterward, including the interrupted letter, was designed to simulate the traces of the beginning of an otherwise ordinary day in which they were invaded, shot, taken by surprise and against their will.

It is possible, although the authorities insist improbable, that while she slept he started his morning, later than usual after the previous night's long drive, drank his coffee, sat down to write to his wife, reviewed the mail, called the party office, began the letter to his lawyer, when suddenly he heard the gunshot from the bedroom, rose, was grabbed, maybe even before he left the tiny study, struggled, was shot and framed for her death and his own. (Notice that suddenly, the typewriter is not downstairs—the study, the typewriter and its table on the same floor as the bedroom instead of below.)

Although the Bonn police eliminated this possibility almost at once, and its variations, the published accounts either withhold or differ over the reasons. According to one, it is the gunshot residue found on the General's hands that leads to their conclusion that there was no intruder, no third party. According to another, it is the mess, the pattern left on the walls and ceiling by the blood as it splattered from his head—a pattern, it is said, that would have been altered if another human being had been present and holding the weapon.

One has to wonder at this universal certainty when the chief investigator on the case told a reporter that "scientifically speaking" one couldn't entirely rule out the involvement of a third party, and when according to the same reporter police technicians were unable to get a single clear fingerprint from the gun.

Maybe the sequence of events could have been carefully planned to baffle and mislead authorities, or maybe things just happened any which way, swiftly, anomalously, in the course of a rapid, sudden struggle, the gunman leaping from the bedroom doorway, knocking over the crowded bookcase that occupied the landing and slamming the General into the wall, gun held high and hard to his head, and firing. (Maybe the gunman sprained his wrist with this move, or maybe he broke his wrist, or dislocated a shoulder or tore a rotator cuff. Anything is possible.) Or maybe the General was knocked unconscious at his typewriter, hit from behind, his back to the door, dragged out to the hallway, held up against the wall, head flopping, hanging down, when the gunman shot him as if from above.

But this would be another version of the story.

In Berlin with Anna Albert, Jutta sang the litany of her complaints. She was ready to be free, any day now would make a change, even these few hours alone with Anna gave her great room to breathe, it's the lack of breath that's killing her, she can feel it, drying her up, look at my hands, Anna, even my skin has gone leaflike and old, how have I brought this on myself? I'm reading the autobiography of Alexandra Kollontai and at every page I ask myself how I came to this, how from that powerful young person I was, laying hold of my freedom, liberated from the confines and conventions of my Catholic and officer's-family upbringing by the life and vision of that revolutionary woman, by what road I have come to find myself here, so immobilized, so dependent, so clinging, so hanging on, by what wrong turn. It isn't Lukas, it wasn't like this at the beginning, I wasn't like this, not for years, it only started later—

—When he tried to return to his wife.

—When the attacks and threats began, when I couldn't appear or travel anywhere without encountering physical harassment and threats, the letters and phone calls, it was a regular campaign of terror—

And so on. She talked about Lukas, her hateful dependence, her deepest concerns overshadowed, her behavior infantilized. Why, she wants to know, when she is so tenacious in all things, has she been unable to apply her will in this? She plans to consult a psychic again, needs direct counsel from Emma, is powerless without her, etc., until finally the afternoon comes to an end, Jutta crying and laughing and insisting one last time that Anna join her in entering the European Parliament campaign.

On the road out of Berlin this conversation is on her mind. She had not really heard Anna's occasional comments the day before, hears them only now, harsh words, humorous inflections, embedded in and emerging from her tenderness as she served Jutta tea and drank her own watered whiskey and made drawings at the table while Jutta talked. After a while and as if out of nowhere, Anna had called her an abstract idealist and kissed her for it, her fingers, just like Lukas, then her lips. "Russian style," she said. "I would kiss you everywhere, my darling, if I thought it would save you, but it won't." She must have been dying for a cigarette, from which she had been abstaining in deference to Jutta, because abruptly she crossed the room and flung open a window and stood there in the late afternoon air and street noise smoking three in a row, while Jutta never missed a beat and went on talking.

Now Jutta and Lukas are on the road to Sachsenhausen.

She is aware that she cried during the night, clung to Lukas crying. She had spent the day of her visit with Anna sure in the decision to campaign for the European Parliament, to use her international celebrity in the service of even the smallest acts of nonviolent resistance to nuclear interests, to will herself to the courage to work without Lukas if necessary in order to be free. All day she was hopeful and exhilarated, and long into the night, until in bed grief overtook her and the certainty of loss.

For today she has surrendered to the other extreme: not to run for office, to concentrate her energies on working with Lukas against the neo-Nazis, to make time in her harried life to nourish their neglected love. It has been a gentle day, full of little attentions, and toward the end of it they arrive at Sachsenhausen to add their own wreath of flowers to those placed by others in front of the burned-out concentration camp barracks and Holocaust memorial.

They stand in the charred ruins, the smell of fire still in the air. She remembers Anna Albert's advice: *You must learn humility in the face of the real.* Jutta had argued—such words coming from her, a dissident for more than ten years, jailed for her resistance, and so on, but Anna had only shrugged and responded, without explanation, *No, not that, that's politics.*

At the ruins, in the smell of smoke, Jutta almost understands, hope and hopelessness depart and instead a lightness passes through her body, as of something lifting, giving up. She knows with sudden clarity that it is over with Lukas at last. Anxiety and terror leave her. The sky has fallen to dusk and against its fading glow she watches a formation of geese open out and vanish into the darkness.

Of course nothing is so simple, how often has she known such moments? moments that give her a glimpse of a life not lived in oppo-sition, they come at strange times, during a television commercial in a hotel room in Hawaii, an ordinary American commercial, full of noise and color and light, and just for an instant she felt a sensation of innocence, of surrender, pure acceptance, life lived without resist-ance, and a moment later shame at that feeling and at her desire for it, a desire to give in to the world as it is, to give up, to move through it powerless like a fish through the sea, a goose through the air, commanding nothing but her own passage, coming into the light and vanishing, whole, there was something in this that she desired, and the desire made her ashamed, although less so on the day she looked out the open french doors at her garden, taking tea, a tiny break from her work, when the yellow of the lilies and the green of the summer leaves so harsh and loud in their beauty stole every thought from her and she felt it again, in her body, what life could be like without resist-ance, how everything became beautiful, not only the lilies and leaves, which were beautiful in themselves, but the cars parked there in their rows of garages, the concrete driveway, crumbling in places, the weeds breaking through, the voices of children shouting down the row, even the ugly traffic noise that reached her muted from the street, every minute of it precious, or could be, a living jewel, so present that her heart ached for it and she broke into tears, of longing and denial, forever outside, knowing for herself that she could never live in such moments, that in a world so unjust and endangered only opposition could ever be possible, and yet these glimpses when they come give her something to hold on to, not hope exactly, they are without hope, before or after hope, something more like faith, in the texture of existence maybe, in powers greater than herself, in the survival of things living, despite all human flaws and error and terror and evil, and this is what she tries to hold to, the clarity of the moment, the surety of herself, repeating over and over *this time it will be different* in the silence when they stop for dinner, in the silence of the long drive home.

Hours later, the house is cold and empty and surrounds a smell of strangeness, almost fear. It has been left alone too long, almost abandoned, untended. It has a presence of its own, its piles of books and papers and files and publications occupied, its pathways haunted. As if ghosts have passed here in their absence, not just the Kostners checking for urgent faxes and bringing the mail from the post office. Jutta goes through the motions, glancing over streams of faxes, the magazines and letters. There is work she means to do. She kisses Lukas goodnight before he makes his way up to bed. *Of course it's clear that she can't leave him, must make it possible for him to leave her, and maybe after all more than anything that's what her attachment to Sonam had been, no great love, just a means, and one that failed,* although she doesn't want to believe this, erases the thought as soon as it comes, but is reminded of passages she's marked in Kollontai's autobiography and opening the book to one of the marked pages, reads—

> The longing to be understood by a man down to the deepest, most secret recesses of one's soul, to be recognized by him as a striving human being, repeatedly decided matters. And repeatedly disappointment ensued all too swiftly, since the friend saw in me only the feminine element which he tried to mold into a willing sounding board to his own ego. So repeatedly the moment inevitably arrived in which I had to shake off the chains of community with an aching heart but with a sovereign, uninfluenced will. Then I was again alone. But the greater demands life made

upon me, the more the responsible work waiting to be tackled, the greater grew the longing to be enveloped by love, warmth, understanding. All the easier, consequently, began the old story of disappointment in love.

Reading these words in Berlin, with Lukas sleeping beside her, Jutta had felt a sense of sisterhood with Kollontai, compassion, *as if they had lived the same life, or two sides of the same life, Kollontai freeing herself again and again to repeat the same despair, Jutta no longer free, the despair itself confining her freedom, not Lukas but the weight of repetition within her, and a kind of comfort of experience, even a little wisdom, a peace*—but now, at home, in the cold empty house, *in the house that she will inhabit alone if she breaks with Lukas, or he with her, the house with its clammy musty air of an abandoned library, with so little sense of home about it, no comfortable chair that isn't piled with books, no table that hasn't become a desk, cluttered with files and papers, no cat or dog or bird or fish, no living plants, no food in the cupboard*—now these words suck out her courage and leave her afraid.

Kollontai, writing in the 1920s, had expressed such optimism for the future, such faith in the new young women coming up behind her, and twenty years ago Jutta had believed that she was herself such a new woman, freed from the conventions of female weakness, free to live and work and still to have that kind of love in her life that would share and support everything, *to love in work and to work in love and not to worry about her lover's wife and children, who lived, loved the man, in another domain altogether, she never meant for the men to to leave their wives, to leave their children, never meant for them to come to her as they had to their wives, to expect her to become a wife, because once they had given up the wife, that was exactly what they did expect, and then the battle ensued, as Kollontai says, so much energy lost, but with Lukas she had thought the battle was over, their work so perfectly knit, even when he left the Bundestag and she thought he would go back to Therese, when even he thought he would go back, he had not, for the sake of their work and their love, which lived in that work, and grew in it and became inseparable from it, they had made a life, a shared life, stronger than the life of families, wives and children and grandchildren, stronger than the life of passionate lovers, Sonam, who was Sonam? A piece of the work but not the whole, and too willful himself, just as Kollontai says, too insistent on making her over in his own image or to suit his own purpose, too locked into the world of love as possession, too fearful of losing his wife.*

But rereading Kollontai's words has made Jutta fearful herself, fearful for herself, *as if without Lukas, if she lets Lukas go, she will be thrown back into that whirlwind, tossed again every which way by her own emotions, passions, lost to herself, distracted, although she knows quite well that in her liaisons it wasn't she who was distracted from the trajectory of her life but her partner, the man, still for her there was distraction enough in it, gift and loss,* so she runs from Kollontai's words to Goethe's, the letters she has been reading, letters full of love and adoration for Charlotte von Stein, like the letters Lukas has written to her over the years, and she to Lukas, letters extravagant and worshipful, *they love each other soooooo endlessly,* and she opens the volume of Goethe's letters at random and reads "My love for you is no longer a passion, it's a sickness, a sickness that's dearer to me than the most perfect health, and of which I don't want to be cured," and her heart cries *yes, embrace that sentiment, love him, keep him, keep living in his love, breathe no other air, drink no other water, without him you gasp and choke, you die of thirst, revel in him, when he dies you die, you have no life except in him and he no life but you, so thoroughly bound in your work, your passion together to do everything that can be done to resist the horror, to confront the evil, as if you both know the weight of the guilt of life, of living, the guilt of survival that drives you to give every living minute to the prevention of pain and injustice and death, which can't be prevented but only rerouted, delayed, but for each of you an hour's reprieve, a day's, is enough, sufficient unto itself, an hour, a day, in which you have done all that was humanly possible and more, because winning isn't the point in a battle that can't be finally won but only continued, what matters is facing the enemy, raising resistance and courage in all who see you, love you, and you need each other to keep this courage to be these icons to do this work that many are doing but no one like you, not quite like you, and although you are neglected now your work goes on and with the right base of resources you will again establish your unique prominence, your special light, so that every speech, every appeal and letter will again carry your weight, will claim and receive the attention it's due, you need that or your efforts are wasted, and you must not succumb to this sense of waste, or worse, blame it on Lukas, his infirmity, his age, or on your love for him, which does not chain you but sets you free—* until this relentless appeal to herself brings her as if newly awake, ready at last to get to the work at hand, to the letters urging publication of Lukas's letter, even as something still nags at her about those words of Kollontai's, *the knowledge that she had read them twenty years before and understood in them something other than loneliness and defeat, instead a promise, doors opening onto a future freedom,* so turns back to an earlier marked passage in search of that hope, but finds no hope in it, only more of the same, *with its implication of love as failure, solitude as necessity, because when she was younger she had understood that she was one of these new women, able to balance love and work, harmoniously as Kollontai says, a new woman different from Kollontai herself, who admits she had succumbed each time to the belief that she had found the one and only in the man she loved, the person with whom she could blend her soul, until over and over things turned out differently and despite everything love became a fetter and she felt herself imprisoned and tried to loosen the love-bond—*and this frightens Jutta because she knows now, as she had not known at twenty-four, that in this she and Kollontai are the same.

She pushes the book aside, takes up her work, working passionately, writing by hand for hours, long letters and faxes, all the while in the back of her mind Kollontai's words echoing *the greater demands life made upon me, the more the responsible work waiting to be tackled, the greater grew the longing,* and she fears for herself and for Lukas and concentrates all the harder on the task in front of her until it's done.

She turns out the lights, closes the french doors, which she's opened earlier, *which she always opens, except in the coldest weather, to breathe in the silence of the night, without regard to the security system, which she can't be bothered to turn on or off, leaving it all to Lukas, although they had installed it for her sake, in anticipation of a time when she might be alone here, even then, nine months ago, before his accident, a time when she might be alone for an occasional week or weekend, or maybe, though they never said it, alone altogether, even then anticipating her solitude, her need for a sense of safety without his presence in the house.*

At the top of the stairs, Kollontai and Goethe in hand, Jutta hesitates on her way to Emma's room at the end of the hall, where her clothes are kept, and the meditation corner, their altar for the Buddha and for Emma, her little teacher, her spirit helper, reminded that she had told Anna that she planned to see a psychic again, although the intention hadn't come to her until the moment she spoke it, *the Englishwoman who lays on hands for spiritual healing and claimed to see Emma at Jutta's side, who described Emma touching her arm, holding her hand, kissing her cheek, gave her Emma's words of love and devotion, of encouragement and assurance that life continues after death, that all humans are spiritual beings passing through this material phase, that nothing real decays; the Englishwoman who saw calamity over Jutta's shoulder and said nothing, went hooded, withholding, unrevealing, looking for something better to report and saw conflicts, victories, love, fame, "great love," she said, "great fame"; the Englishwoman, so completely ordinary, attractive and charming, who carried a peace and a power about her which she said came from her Shoshone spirit guide; the Englishwoman who twenty years ago, when Emma's death was new and unbearable, assured Jutta that Emma would always be with her, she had only to ask and Emma would show herself in her heart. "She is holding your hand,"* the Englishwoman said, *"she will always hold your hand,"* and praying without intention fragments of Goethe's letters—*God help us out of this misery. Amen. Here I am now near my sister's grave*—Jutta goes into Emma's room and from her personal files takes out her collection of letters from Lukas, and on impulse *at Anna Albert's the old familiar psychobabble* the one letter she's received in all these years from her father *how longingly she had imagined him, his dark hair, his long thin arms, his fingers across the piano keys, his beautiful tenor voice and his laughter, but the letter whined, complained, played cat and mouse with her, and she had been angry after so many years, and hurt, but wanted to see him, yearned for him, wanted a great deal more from him than he in any way indicated wanting from her, and was ready to obey his little stip-*

ulations, "answer by newspaper ad exactly as I specify," all very secre-
tive and mysterious, to keep their meeting entirely private, out of the
eyes of the press (as if the press had been watching) and more realis-
tically she imagined, to keep it hidden from his family, the new family
of his new life, about which of course he told her nothing, but still she
wanted him, craved him (but why not just make a phone call?), and
the old excitement came back, the fear and exhilaration, the desire
and secret knowledge, and suddenly she loved this strange secrecy he
imposed on her, this placing of an advertisement, but on the day it
was to appear the specified newspaper had made a mistake, or maybe
she had, but it seemed impossible, the ad ran in the wrong section of
the classifieds and she never heard from him again, seven years ago,
and now she wonders whether the Englishwoman is still alive and
can help her contact the living, not only the dead, because she had
even sometimes thought of hiring a detective, until Omi advised her
against it, afraid for her greater pain—and out of nowhere her heart
breaks for Omi, so old and someday lost to her and then Jutta will
be an orphan, even though her mother and stepfather are still alive,
because it's Omi who has continued to live in her life and accepts
Lukas with gratitude, even love, understands all he does for her, his
necessity, when her mother and the Colonel have always seemed to
resent him in ways they never tell her and she fails to understand.

She looks at herself in the bathroom mirror, struck silent, her
face dripping water and tears. *Everything is repetition, nothing is
new, life was unbearable and always had been, painful or beautiful,
it always came back to this.* She wants to wake Lukas and cry
again, wants to go to the telephone and call someone, Heike or
Hilmar or Omi, more than anyone Sonam Pasang. She's in the
habit of calling Heike in the middle of the night overwhelmed
with energy and pain—she talks, Heike listens, she discharges her
suffering then gets back to work. But not tonight.

Washed and dressed for sleep, carrying her stack of letters and
her books, she enters the dark bedroom quietly, carefully slips
herself under the covers, books and letters still in hand. In the
utter darkness—door closed, window shades opaque and black—
she listens to Lukas sleeping, the half snore, the sharp rattling
intake of his breath. Carefully she feels for space on the night
table to set aside her books and papers, then pushes herself up

against her pillows. Beside her Lukas is twisting in the covers, making muffled exclamations, almost crying out, as if in pain. He is used to her reading light coming on, waking him, most nights lies here with her awhile and then gets up, but tonight they got back so late, and so tired from the drive, she expects he will sleep longer and despite his restless dreaming hesitates to wake him. One by one she pulls off her silver rings, gropes on the night table to find the little Spanish wooden box she stores them in. She sits in the darkness and listens and after a while pulls Lukas gently to her, offering her arm to his shoulder, her hand to his cheek, drawing his head slowly to her lap, until he has wrapped himself around her hip, clinging to her, to her hip, to her hand, and holds her tighter, sobbing without tears.

She shakes him, wakes him.

He clings to her and shakes and wakes himself more fully. "Mines," he finally says. "We laid mines. People died."

More and more he is like this, since the accident, overcome, baffled at the images that rise up from his sleeping mind, he's never dreamed like this before, he's never dreamed at all, never remembered, an absolutely logical man with no interest in dreams or the images that haunt the unconscious—it's this, his certainty of the power of reason, that has balanced her life these many years, and now this confusion and bafflement, disorientation, even terror—this role is supposed to be hers, she doesn't know what to make of it or how to help it or heal it, has no power to reason with it, only to help him hold on, and he hates her for it, she feels this hatred, receives it, and the longer it goes on the more he hates her, not for her failure to heal him, but because he can't bear to be seen in this weakness, this need.

He pulls away from her and sits up and takes her hand again. "We laid mines in ordinary places, in gardens, in houses, in kitchens, in nurseries, in toilets, in beds, anywhere, everywhere. Now I'm watching people die in those places, days, weeks, months after we left. Ordinary people, not soldiers. Women, children. I see their faces. I see their wounds. But that's not all."

She listens, but in the darkness her mind begins to wander, becomes impatient, she wants to be reading Goethe, Kollontai, Lukas's letters declaring his endless love, instead of aimlessly stroking his hand, *obsessed with Kollontai now, suddenly driven, as if the answer lies there, as if there is something she is seeing, not quite seeing, but would see if the room were not so dark, or on the contrary, if it were mystically impossibly darker, the missing connection, the missing loss, because really Lukas has not done what Kollontai says the man always does, has not tried to impose his ego on her or adapt her to his own purposes, or it doesn't look as though he has, but still somehow somewhere he seems to have done just that, that was it, the ungraspable thing, but it's elusive and slips away, the harder she chases it the more she sees only how he has changed himself for her and not the other way around yet still it's in her heart somewhere or out in the room, the knowledge that he has taken her, changed her, made her what he needed her to be, just as men do always, lovers do always, and suddenly the magnitude of her loss overwhelms her, and the passion to return to the heart of the party, to win back the party's love, its admiration, its confidence and respect, the party was hers after all, her own creation—without her vision and her work the party would never have come into being, let alone triumphed, the 1990 defeat was only a setback, not absolute, the party would return and Jutta Carroll with it,* and almost without realizing when it began she is saying all these things out loud, talking at Lukas now, her conviction again that she must stand for the European Parliament, although she knows he opposes it and even though she would rather take a seat in the Bundestag, where she would for example have power to prevent or at least to resist such a travesty as the government's new agreement to deport Romanians from Germany, 100,000 Romanians, more than half of them Romani— to deport them!—to the so-called new Romania, little better than the old, where Roma people have been beaten, burned, chased out of villages, arrested and beaten and otherwise brutalized by police, to say nothing of the offense of the German government itself, giving in to the pressures of xenophobia, paying—paying!— the government of Romania to take its people back, and despite all that, and it's only an example of course, there is so much more, the corporate interests, oil and coal, but still she knows that she must be practical, must compromise with the party, take what it offers, in ways she has always refused to compromise before.

Lukas resists her, accuses. He has neither the strength nor the will for a campaign, can't imagine her sustaining a campaign without him, says she will promise to manage alone and instead in practice will demand his constant uninterrupted attention and support.

But no, she will not be dissuaded. She has talked it over with Hilmar, with Anna, with many others. Anna will help her, campaign with her, she's sure of it, and in any case there are others, she will find others to help if Lukas isn't up to it, perhaps he should write to Sonam on her behalf, but of course that's out of the question Lukas says, but in any case even without him, without either of them, she will create a campaign team, a staff, the party will help her, she won't be alone, she needs the party, must return to the party's work, *it had broken her heart, more than once, many times, but she couldn't abandon it, it was a child to her, her child, damaged, bruised, and she too, but her child, and her enemies in the party too, her children in the world of the party, she was an unloved mother, a superseded goddess, and maybe after all, and she knows Lukas in particular rejects this possibility, but maybe really they were right, her isolation in the party was her own fault, or largely, she had lost leadership and relevance because she had failed to be a party player, and Lukas had assisted her in that failure, encouraged and supported her independence, and of course he was right, she and he were right, she doesn't mean to say that she should have compromised then or should compromise now on matters of principle, but perhaps if she had listened more thoughtfully to the other voices around her, the strategic voices, the tactical voices, then maybe now her own voice of principle would still be heard—he knows quite well it all goes back to 1985 and her refusal to rotate out of the Bundestag as required by the party's rules, even though she had always opposed that particular rule, although of course she had enemies long before that and it was true that she hadn't opposed the rule at first, had supported it originally, and on principle, until she saw the consequences in lost experience and committee seniority and collective party power and balked when she should have shared out her personal power, which no one seemed to understand she wanted not for herself but for the good of the movement, because it was that that had set so many against her, so long ago, when she should have given in to the will of the anarchists and egalitarians, the fundamen-*

talist faction, and as for that rule, should have changed it later, as in fact it has since been changed because it was a very naive, very stupid rule, but even so she should have obeyed it first, in the interest of her own long-term position and credibility, although of course she couldn't have foreseen that, or the ferocity of reaction to her stubborn disobedience, the permanent animosity she would build for herself, she had expected to be forgiven as all her life she had been forgiven, stamp your foot, raise your voice, shout, cry, do what you want to, and the next day turn up with a bouquet of flowers and a smile—well, okay, then, she's learned her lesson, it doesn't always work, but here's her chance to make amends, to reestablish her viability, to build a new base, and maybe in fact the party's judgment is correct that the European Parliament is the place for her, even though unlike the Bundestag it offers no access to real power, still she would be working in the international movement, which for a long time has been friendlier to her and her ideas than the party at home, and this too is like Kollontai, sent out of government in Moscow eventually to become ambassador to Norway, heart broken but loyal, she loved her party more than she loved any man, in her autobiography a single cryptic sentence covers this painful separation—"There were differences of opinion in the Party"—*and although Kollontai had hoped to write at some time in the future more fully about her conflicts with the party during that period, she never did, remained silent, or let herself be silenced, whereas she, Jutta, of course, will never allow herself to be used in this way, to be silenced in the name of her own party loyalty, still*—but Lukas, exhausted by this barrage *and anyhow half asleep again of course*, interrupts to say he thinks he'll sleep a little longer, squeezes her hand, kisses her goodnight again, lies down, rolls over, and she can feel the rage in him, the trembling in his hand, the hatred in his kiss, the cold stone rigidity of his back and body in the bed beside her, and snaps on her light.

She opens Kollontai. "I always went out alone, unarmed and without any kind of a bodyguard. In fact I never gave a thought to any kind of danger..." *It is unbearable*—clenching and unclenching her fist. *If only this sort of courage, this physical courage, had been possible to her, how free she might have been, but she has no endurance for physical pain, for violation, has had to make up for this failure of physical courage with courage of another kind, the courage to write intimate letters to the powerful, the courage to go where she was not wanted and address the powerful face to face, verbal courage and the will to courage, the courage of her convictions, the courage to make a spectacle of herself, to humiliate herself, to let herself be judged, the courage to begin each new day as though life were just beginning, full of hope and undeterred, unburdened by past failures and errors, unburdened by loss, even though the losses always mounted—but the simple physical courage to walk outside on the street alone? no, impossible, although in the past it wasn't always so, or not so debilitating, her fears had grown in proportion to Lukas's determination to protect her—*

Her heart is racing, her breath agitated. She sets Kollontai aside. *Where to go from here? How to quiet herself?* This is what Lukas's letters and little notes are for. She often brings them to bed. For reassurance, for understanding. *I love you sooooo endlessly.* But in Berlin reading Goethe's letters to Frau von Stein she became confused, the tone of them sometimes so familiar, so like Lukas's own, that the terror came over her (she didn't admit it, or that it was terror) that somehow all of his letters and repeated declarations of love were a lie. "I have no other wish but to please you, to make you as happy as I can, to be every day more worthy of your love." *Who wrote those lines, Lukas or Goethe?* "If only, my best beloved, I could seize and put down on this paper every good, true, sweet word of love, tell you and assure you that I am near you, very near, and that it is only because of you that I have joy in life." *Which one wrote that?* "I long for your dear eyes, which are more present to me than anything visible or invisible. Never have I loved you so and never have I been so close to being worthy of your love." *Which?* "I secretly long for you without admitting it to myself, my spirit grows petty and takes no joy in anything, worries sometimes gain the upper hand, sometimes ill humor, and an evil genius misuses my absence from you, depicting to me the most irritating aspects of my condition and advising me to take refuge in flight. But soon I feel that a glance, a word from you would disperse all these fogs." *And so on.*

Yet reading this book of letters she has also identified with Goethe, the young lover addressing the older beloved, has identified with his contradictory longings for the lover and for flight, with his adoration of Charlotte and his distance from her, with their *Seelenliebe*, their moral and spiritual and educative passion, and under that surface has felt also Goethe's other affinities until they break through in his love for another, younger woman, and to Charlotte he complains, "I cannot endure the way you have been treating me. When I felt like talking, you sealed my lips, when I was uncommunicative, you accused me of indifference, when I was active in the interest of my friends, of coldness and neglect. You have watched my every look, every gesture, you have criticized my way of being and continually put me ill at ease. How were trust and frankness to thrive when you deliberately repelled me?"—Charlotte here so exactly like Lukas in the early days of her own involvement with Sonam; but unlike Lukas, Charlotte remains unforgiving, never reconciles herself, abandons all intimacy with Goethe, repels him, just as he says, and in doing so sets him free, although of course he has already seized his freedom, fled to Italy, taken his young mistress, later wife, has been free all along, that was the point, as Jutta is free, but unable to free herself—

Her heart again, her breath. She can't sit still, *can't bear the silence, the steady inhalation and exhalation of Lukas's breath beside her, can't read more Goethe, more Kollontai, more letters, and can't sleep either, or continue thinking, isn't ready for the darkness to come, she was looking for hope here, in Kollontai, in Goethe, in Lukas's letters, even in the letter from her father, although she hasn't unfolded it yet, hasn't taken it out of its tattered, too-often-handled envelope, was looking for hope but found only grief and doubt, more doubt,* until she shivers into the covers, slides herself down, reaches over and shuts off the light, suddenly woozy with fatigue and wide awake. Her bones ache. *What more can happen? We've reached an impasse, the only way forward is out. Dream on the sun. Wish benefits on all sentient beings. The Buddhist prayer for good sleep and freedom from nightmares. Not a prayer really—words to clean, to clarify the mind. May all sentient beings be happy. May no harm come to them. May they always find success. May all sentient beings be free from enmity and anger. May all sentient beings be free from suffering and the causes of suffering. Whatever beings there are, may they abide in equanimity and perfect peace.*

So the mind is cleansed and quieted, the breath deepened,

the heart slowed, the clenched fist uncurled. In the darkness the fluttering eyelids rest, the restless spirit comes home, stops its wandering, the listening ear lets go its hold on space and night, falls back into its own silence, the tightened throat relaxes, the fearful chest, the hungry stomach.

She breathes. She sleeps.

Is there more?

Shot a few hours later. Dead. In this version, no, she doesn't wake again, is sleeping soundly when Lukas gets up—slowly, quietly, with infinite care not to disturb her, moving quietly out from the bedroom, into the morning, into the day. As he leaves he pulls the door to, but in order to keep the silence not closed enough to catch, to latch. He is wearing pajamas, bottoms and top, plans to wait to dress until she's awake. It's an ordinary morning, although later than usual thanks to their late arrival the night before. He needs a cup of coffee.

In this version he works downstairs awhile, sorts the mail, the faxes, drinks his coffee, tends his garden, telephones Hilmar Knapp, all quite routine but for the hour, so late to be downstairs unwashed, unshaven, still wearing pajamas, all in the interest of giving Jutta the rest she so badly needs after their long exhausting travels, just as he had needed it, until hours later he comes back up to work in the little study, to write to Therese and his lawyer, which he's doing when the interruption comes.

In this version we won't enter his thoughts, or even watch the action beyond this point, won't say whether the interruption comes from within his consciousness or body, or from without. We don't know. Remember that. Nobody knows. Everyone imagines. It's the best we can do. Maybe that Englishwoman, Jutta's psychic, could tell us more. Maybe the police record, if it were available to be read, which it isn't, although the families of the dead have been allowed access to it and no one among them has questioned its fundamental conclusion. The mystery for them is the motive, what the physical record can't reveal.

Or it can, but not in this version. In this version there is no police record, no murder, no suicide—nothing yet, only two people, a woman sleeping, a man downstairs in his pajamas drinking coffee and, hours later, at work in front of a typewriter, his back to the door in a narrow room.

Although perhaps in this version we can allow the woman another brief spell of consciousness, allow her to come awake in the darkened room, to walk to the window in the darkness, to raise the black shade and stand awhile looking out on a sunlit morning, on a blue sky, and down on a little garden in which an old man with white hair, wearing pale pajamas, moves slowly from plant to plant, cutting a flower now and then, blue and purple cosmos, yellow daisies, a dark red rose. We might let her have this moment, before she lowers the shade and goes back to bed, might let the sunlight fall on the garden, the man, might let hope come back to her one more time, faith in her power to love him, and his to love her, might let her believe again in the day and the work of the day and their work in the day together, might give her this victory, this triumph of the spirit, this leaping happiness, these tears of joy and forgiveness, for the man and for herself, this melting, this letting go, this life that will not end.

In the imagination everything is possible, in the imagination everything can be explained.

Let me imagine then let me imagine I am her father the father remember him who took her to the town square with a sign hung from her neck except of course it isn't true there was no sign no town square no child for sale nothing all made up lies imagined in her febrile mind and read in newspapers in magazines for years the more famous she got the worse the stories I used to beat her I never did I took her to the town square because she asked for a doll I hung a sign around her neck and left her alone there while I drank and this never happened I've been drinking this never happening all these never happenings all the years of her fame even after I wrote her a letter demanding she stop begging her to stop *I don't know if you want to see me or not but if you do place an ad in the* Frankfurter Rundschau *on such and such a day in such and such a place exactly as I tell you then we'll meet* and she didn't place the ad she prefers the lie of the father she made up to the reality of the father wounded by her fantasies and that was a lie too the whole thing is a lie I don't live in Frankfurt not even in the West old or new I came over from Berlin to mail that letter didn't even mail it myself passed it over to another to mail never left Berlin at all read the newspaper there on the appointed day the appointed hour and found nothing and even that wasn't me but another I'm their prisoner their tool they made me up found me erased me all they wanted from me was the letter the photograph some token to prove to her the identity they were creating for me they wanted to get to her through me you know who but it did no good she didn't want me didn't answer remembers only this steamy dream this sign on the neck these beatings that never were and God knows what else that she speaks to no one or I imagine to her old general she was a fey little child flirtatious and always the center of things a beauty and she loved her Papa loved to go walking with him into the town to sit with him with the men in smoky barrooms in the newspaper offices making pictures and letters with his heavy black pencils to sit on his lap and play with his telephone with his tie with his hair with his mustache and behind him on the couch with the buckles at the back of his vest to tickle him up his ribs and behind his ears to wrap her skinny little arms around him over his shoulders around his neck to kiss him a big messy little girl kiss it was unbearable it's no wonder I left said I was going to Hamburg but that was a lie I went to Berlin and in Berlin I went over to the other side not in a big way in small ways I did what I could I served now all this fuss about the Stasi files it's mine they ought to look at but then I am no longer myself no one knows me anymore my name or whether the I that I am is the I who was her father at all or only the I they created for the purpose of taking that part a part she rejected when she rejected my letter and left me here nowhere no one anymore a little Berlin bureaucrat is all I've ever been a bureaucrat with a Berlin gun and a bag of Berlin orders and even I no longer remember whether it's true or not that she was my daughter that I was married to her mother that I lived in that tiny house after the war in that tiny town with those women that beautiful grandmother young enough to desire more profoundly than before or since I've ever desired any woman why did they think I stayed away it was a hothouse the three of them wrapping themselves around me their flesh their breasts their eyes even Jutta had little flat-chested breasts little nipples that rose in the bathwater but it was Frieda who drove me insane so near and untouchable the smell of her like apricots the wisps of hair on the sweat of her neck in the kitchen while she cooked I can taste her even now so many years later when I've seen the photos of her old age beyond desiring but then oh then and still the Frieda-of-then Johanna was a foolish child beside her it was lust for Frieda that drove me to Johanna in the first place lust for Frieda that made Johanna pregnant that forced our marriage that brought that monster my daughter into the world fitting isn't it that she's been closer to Frieda her grandmother than to her mother all her life to Frieda her grandmother her true mother the mother of my longing I sat at her table and watched her move and imagined her hands on my naked skin imagined her mouth her lips her tongue imagined her long legs and her honey flesh and her hair in my hands her voice in my ear and while she read the newspapers aloud I changed her words to secrets I sat at that table and raged for her and they thought I was a dreamer I played the piano and all my music was for her I read poems to her and seduced only Johanna and later Jutta my child and even though today in Berlin I see those evenings remember in my body the rage of those nights the hours the minutes until more and more I drove myself out into the town where I could have any woman I was young handsome men were scarce instead of struggling there among the forbidden and the undesired even though I hold these moments like gold in my hands I don't know whether these stories are true whether this life is mine I've waited too long watching from this strange near distance I've seen her followed her my file is the one they should read and maybe if I read it I too would find out some truth that now eludes me something lost to me in the haze of memory and imagination that hard objective words in old dead unread filed bureaucratic language would reveal words I know words I've written *subjects register at such and such hotel attend such and such conference warmly welcomed no place on the program lunch with so and so dinner and so forth phone calls to ____ postcards to ____ books bought again and again* reports I had reason to file until the Wall fell and I was left to write reports for myself alone and discovered only a single subject interested me *her* my daughter if she was my daughter if I am her father at all *her* Jutta and her old general a man exactly my age a man of the army a man with a bag full of orders who threw it all away to take orders from Jutta who more and more had come to resemble the Frieda of those days when I knew her lived close to her one wall away made love to her through the wall made

Johanna against her will to discretion and silence cry with pleasure for Frieda alone in the night resembled the Frieda I carried with me the body I touched year after year lived with in Berlin alone the Frieda of my heart alive again in that child that girl that appalling political woman my daughter or maybe not who knows I remember nothing anymore October it was October but what was the year for example when I went to hear her speak and she didn't show collapsed they said gone into hospital but he was there the General on the platform delivering her words and I heard her voice in his and I watched his hands and I thought those hands knew her as no one had the right to know her no one but me and that weekend I went to the country and practiced shooting and pretended I'd been ordered to take him out imagined every target every bottle every bird as that arrogant general don't think I didn't know him I did I knew him too well knew them all those officers those military men it didn't matter what army they served whose orders they took they were all of them little Hitlers little Bismarcks little Kaisers little Friedrich the Greats they made me puke and her too a little *Führerin* who taught her to be like that it wasn't me and certainly not her mother it must have been the American her stepfather the Colonel and Frieda of course the tyrant the bitch the witch sometimes I imagine even now going to see her in Nürnberg my hat in my hand so to speak but I couldn't stand the humiliation she'd laugh in my face if she knew me and if she didn't what would she see but a worn out old dandy with blackened hair and a Spanish beret imagine but there I'd be I am we are Frieda and me two old people Johanna off in America and Jutta dead nobody left but us and maybe after all these years I'll sweep her off her feet do a little tango dance a jig or a polka or one of those Bavarian numbers the Nazis loved just for the hell of it just to see her face and then I'll tell her who I am and what I've done to my daughter if she was my daughter with the gun to her head his gun the General's gun I knew where to find it they'd been away for weeks I knew their schedule I kept track it was easy I knew my way around I practically lived in that house when they were hiding in the Black Forest waiting for her heart to cure although that was before the security system and easy but it wasn't long before I cracked that too could turn it off and on as smoothly as the General did Jutta never touched it just as she never drove and never typed and never cooked or vacuumed or ran copies or faxed except awake alone and urgent in the middle of the night she was helpless with machines no good with numbers or dates maybe that's how she screwed up maybe she tried to place the ad the way I told her maybe she got confused really wanted to see me who knows I just wanted to object to the bad press I was getting didn't want to start being her father at that late date didn't want to horn in on her action just thought it would be something to see her again after so many years and so famous I could have been anyone I could have got that photo I sent her the one she knew only I could possess could have got that from somebody else her real father or somebody who got it from her father the Stasi for example or lifted it from a file just out of curiosity or even obsession why not she was an appealing woman that waiflike face those big sunken eyes of a saint and the General was wasting her anybody could see it everybody knew she had a taste for older men maybe I just wanted to be next crazy as it sounds I knew I had nothing for her who was I a nobody a little bureaucrat in Berlin a clerk in an overcoat so to speak nobody at all why should she care to meet me so I tracked down her file I found the picture I sent her the picture maybe that's how it happened I don't know anymore was I following orders was I acting on my own whose orders I don't know and I didn't know then either when I waited in that house and to this day what I don't know is how I got away with it why I wasn't arrested made into a mad gunman like Lee Harvey Oswald or Sirhan Sirhan those guys and the one obsessed with the movie actress who tried to kill Ronald Reagan that was my cover delusional bureaucrat obsessed with Jutta Carroll believes he's her father writes her letters he doesn't mail drawers full of them back at his apartment in Berlin I've been writing them for years a diary full I imagined them coming out as a book my photo everywhere right beside hers under banner headlines like those pictures of Oswald and Sirhan I'd be the killer of the alternative darling out of favor now past her prime and with her almost an afterthought the old man her *Kofferträger* and lover who almost caught me but of course I had a plan was waiting hidden by the bookshelf at the top of the stairs jumped him from the front when he was only inches from me I'm old but so was he and still weak from that auto accident I got him by the shoulder and a knee to his knee and pushed him back the gun in his mouth the bookshelf crashing down books falling and his skull and hair and bits of brain hitting the wall and ceiling and as for the gunshot residue the police find on his hands as if he had shot Jutta and then himself well maybe he did I'm not saying but if I myself knew his hands were clean I'd have a hard time understanding how the police came to that conclusion but of course his hands weren't clean gunshot residue is easy to fake especially if you're prepared and when you know days will pass and if you're lucky weeks before the dead will be found although you can't help thinking as you're creating that chemical trace that it's a shame really that you do your job so well that no one will ever discover you've done it no headlines no photos no fame all the glory will go to him this old man and you'll have become invisible again vanished into the never was and no one will know you ever entered that little house in the darkness or that you hid for hours in the wardrobe staring through the keyhole at the candle flame on the altar with the General's gun in your hand even when he came in and sat on the floor and chanted will never know you waited for hours in that corner for him to leave the tiny study up the hall and go downstairs or that you fired that gun let alone be able to answer the more interesting questions whether you really were her father or believed you were or worked as a bureaucrat anywhere on earth let alone in Berlin whether you really were an Ossi at all and if not her father what your motives were and what your motives were if you were what you were running from hiding and if none of that then who sent you to do it who paid you if you had no motive of your own and after all whether you really are an old man as old as the General and the old man you would be if you were the father you say you are or old enough to believe you're him or to pretend you're him when in fact you might be someone altogether younger a bigger man taller even than the General and stronger a man who could easily have pushed the General up against the wall and held him there and fired at his head from above as some of the news accounts inex-

plicably will say you have done and this is a loss really you think
this invisibility that arises from the perfection of your craft and
you are tempted so tempted to leave a tiny clue behind a little
hint to catch someone's attention and you search all around and
can't think what until in the little study at the head of the stairs
you see the typewriter where earlier the General had been
working and you stand there reading the unfinished letter still in
the typewriter's carriage and you switch the typewriter on and
start a new sentence breaking off in the middle of the second
word *Wir müs*— "we mus..." not yet "we must" and leave the
typewriter there humming and go downstairs to the kitchen to
make the cup of coffee the General had begun to make for
himself and as you wait there for darkness more darkness the
lights to come on and then to go out in the neighboring houses
the sadness of it all comes over you again the anonymity of life
not your life alone but all these lives the loss it isn't the killing
that brings me down that's my job I'm trained not to think about
it it's this other thing and that's when I start thinking about Frieda
again and wondering would she remember me would she ever
admit she desired me too and I wonder what she's doing then
while I sit there waiting for dark telling myself stories about the
old days in that little town that little house full of women and
that little girl until finally it's dark enough and late enough that I
can leave without being seen and as I walk down the quiet streets
to the corner blocks away where the night before I parked my
rented car I begin to feel for the first time since the killings a
certain satisfaction in a job well done the care it took to slip into
the shelter of the open garage in the darkness in the rain to wait
there watching her through the sheer-curtained french doors at
work at the dining room table and that's when it started maybe
because the truth is you always fall a little bit in love or I do
anyhow take on the role make myself a player a man with a heart
a stake in the outcome a desire an anger a jealousy a lust any
motive that suits the case makes it human because the sorts of
people who hire me have the motives of machines and I may be
trained but I need my own reasons so I invent them standing out
there in the garage in the rain watching the woman work through
the night through the scrim of the curtains I've studied her read

her books of speeches and appeals her press the old biography
watched her on television followed her from town to town and
conference to conference and hotel to hotel on the arm of the
General but there's nothing in any of that that's shown me what
I'm seeing here such a concentration and intensity as she bends
for hours over her papers as if I'm seeing her power naked for the
first time and as pure and strong and undiluted as it ever was so
stark and self-sufficient it makes me want to take her fuck her
break her and for the first time I'm glad I'm going to kill her enter
into the spirit of it after these months of preparation and post-
ponement happy at last that the job is mine to do and wishing I
could do more than I know my plan has to call for wishing I could
see that face confront it instead of approaching her secretly while
she sleeps she'll never know she's going to die she never knew but
the General did and even as I got into my car and drove away out
of the suburb out of the city out onto the road back to Berlin if
Berlin is where I came from I couldn't help thinking about her
this woman this little girl so much power and so little in one tiny
person such concentrated energy and contradiction it was going
to make great press and I regretted again my skill and anonymity
and for the first time began to wonder who the machine brains
were that hired me and why but that's the kind of thinking that
gets you retired so I went back to my storytelling and her intensity
and concentration and what it was was it was like mine entirely
focused perfectly driven undistractable pure madness like poetry
and love she was mine my heart she was me and I wondered if
this was what everyone saw in her what made her their inspiration the pure driven madman in themselves the reason they loved
and hated her embraced and rejected her demanded and then
refused her destroyed her because she was destroyed already it
was perfectly clear or I had thought it was when I watched her
shuffle around with her old man looking nearly as old as he was
a woman still so capable of beauty I had seen the photos seen her
face change and until that night before I killed her while I
watched her through the window I thought she had just grown
prematurely old as if by osmosis from the old man or under the
strain of work and defeat the grief of isolation but while she
worked that night I saw her youth and beauty perfectly intact her

story was a fairy tale a princess under an ogre's spell released
when the ogre sleeps or something like that maybe the old man
was only baggage the frog or the beast the princess was compelled
to marry under the curse of a witch one of the wives of one of her
many lovers her mother her grandmother or some haunting
within herself the curse lifted at night by the grace of her little
sister the visitation of her sister's ghost Emma's spirit that kept
her going and maybe it's true maybe Emma's the little angel the
bodhisattva who keeps her alive who restores her power and
youth look at her there the radiance and fire she makes your heart
stop you have never shot a woman so intelligent and beautiful and
to have to do it in the head to destroy that face that mind but you
are a technician an engineer a technologist of death the poetry is
in the preparation the study of the subject or subjects the selection of a method and false narrative perfectly matched to their
conditions perfectly suited to the reading of the physical record
as you want it to be read and you know the details of this story
have it mastered but still are unprepared for this and see what you
have not seen before that no one who knows her will believe this
woman wanted to die or maybe it was in Berlin that you saw it
not through the dining room window because at night the heavy
drapes were tightly drawn but the day before through the
windows of her friend the painter where the two of them were
talking writing making notes laughing and you knew this woman
her friend would never believe she had chosen death and you
think about that afternoon and see it differently as you watch her
from the garage through the rain through the gauze of the curtain
through the windows because not long after the General left her
to go upstairs and closed the upstairs bedroom windows and put
out the lights she opened the drapes as you knew she would
because every night working alone that's what she's done opened
the drapes and opened the french doors to the garden to let the
air in and the night so try to make that fit with her dependency
and terror you can't it doesn't matter it's what you saw but you
never saw before what you saw that night and the difference
could only have been your knowing that that night was her last
on earth the difference that made you suddenly want her love her
hate her and want her dead your job the difference that made

your job come alive and your stories the difference that made you want perfection makes me want to reveal myself to say to the world I did it look how clever I am I fooled you all it's easy when you know your trade and when you study your subjects as thoroughly as I studied these and all my subjects and I still would like to do it would like to tip someone off to that flat in Berlin that stash of phony diaries that collection of clippings and photographs that manufactured obsession and identity that backup cover story in case the double-suicide or murder-suicide didn't hold would like to let someone know what art goes into this my specialty and this is what I always feel when the job is done I know but this time I'm impatient their deaths have been a scandal all over the tabloids and the serious news I've seen their faces everywhere and even leaving the country didn't help although it was a good thing I had another job lined up and waiting good to know what was coming next what was coming helped keep things in perspective and the dead at a distance where they belong

You wouldn't believe how these people lived. Regrets? None. What a sty. You'd think it was animals lived there but the mess was all books and papers. Not a chair to sit on, not a table that wasn't stacked, buried. The floor, covered in newspapers, magazines, everything filthy with fuzz balls and dust. The egoism! Her picture everywhere on the walls. Such a little old princess. Half the men in them her lovers. It's tragic to see a general so brought down. By such a dirty whore.

So in fact I do have one regret—that we haven't been permitted to lay claim to what we did. I would like to have the opportunity to say this to the world, why it was necessary, why we killed them, that we were the ones who had the courage and the will, that ours is the true alternative, not hers with its antiquated pacifism and universal compassion and postwar German guilt.

And where did she learn that pacifism, I ask you? From Hindus and Africans, Americans, degenerate races. Pacifism is not a German value.

Her father was a Pole, and dark-haired, a communist. That was the start of her trouble.

He looks how he sounds—blue-eyed, blond, tall, young, angry, lean. He is all muscle and wire. He chain smokes. He wears black leather, a row of silver earrings, black roots show at the base of blond bleach.

Maybe you don't believe we did it? What don't you believe, why or how? Why, maybe I can tell you. How, we have to keep to ourselves.
He drums his fingers on the table.

This is a film. He's lit hard, high, little haloes of white light radiating off his spiky white hair and gleaming leather—background black, thick as velvet, reflecting nothing, broken only by his animated form and swirls of smoke.
This is a film. There is no music. No scenario. Only this blond boy talking. Maybe twenty-five years old. You watch. You listen. You know him. You imagine you know him.

He drums his fingers on the table.
I am going to write a book. Even that whore wrote books. Hitler wrote a book. That's the thing. To put it down on paper, to sign it with your name. The right-wing scene looks disorganized, random, chaotic from the outside. But it isn't, not really. Chaos is only a ruse. Someday the public will be ready to be told. Then we will be here. We will be revealed.
Look—*he leans forward, intense, compelling*—we have arms, explosives, computer communications, links to the movements in Spain, Austria, Denmark, Sweden, the Netherlands, Russia, Finland, South Africa, the USA. We look separate, divided everywhere. In Germany we appear to be divided. To seem divided is the plan. Harder to infiltrate. Harder to ban. Secretly we are united. We share a vision.
Everybody knows it, everybody has it, they're just too scared, too weak and feminine to admit what they believe, would like to believe, would like to be freed to express, and that's what we do, each group in its own way, we free the others to join us, to regain their strength, to throw off their weak,

degenerate, feminine, leftist, foreign Jewish-Hindu-Turkish-African-Asian chains.

So that's why we did it, were ordered to do it, schooled. Just as we make war games in the Brandenburg forests, so the elect among us train to be assassins, learn security systems and means to falsify evidence, learn handguns and small explosives.

You want to know why these two. Who was she anymore, old and weak, no longer dangerous, half mad herself and her old general with her?

He shrugs, tilts this head, pouts his pretty lip.

Who am I to say? Just a soldier. Still, well, of course, like anyone else I may speculate.

For example, where do we get our money, the money with which we buy our radio equipment and computers, and arms from Soviet soldiers leaving the East and the propaganda materials we are forced by restrictive German laws to import from the USA? Who are we but a bunch of young punks and old crazies left over from the Nazi times? If that's who we are, where does the money come from? Figure it out.

So maybe it was a political strategy, to kill these two. Or maybe somebody just paid for it.

For politics, of course, it is well known that they were busy campaigning against us, against the violence and desecrations, but it is also well known that they no longer held power of any kind. Still, there is a certain logic in these days to taking out such an opponent while he is weak, before he can rebuild his base, his public image, and in the case of these two, who were so down-and-out, so overwhelmed and despairing, the timing obviously lends credibility to the verdict of suicide, with or without murder.

We ourselves are preparing for electoral victories. The alternative she created couldn't be further from us in principle or practice, yet it is true here as it has been shown to be true in the USA that on the whole the disaffected are not so clear about principles and practice, what they want is to see an expression of anger, outspokenness, revolution of any kind, they swing from left to right and back again without any consciousness, wanting just a channel for their anger, their disaffection, their otherwise mute

awareness of injustice. Whoever expresses that anger and awareness of injustice loudest, strongest, boldest, wins.

Well, it won't be her anymore. These days her party comes in
from the street, puts on suits and makes deals. We are not like
them. We enact the anger, we do not make pretty demonstrations
with flowers and banners and rainbow-colored flags, and secretly
or openly the people love us for the violence we do.

This is why it is such a shame to me that we have not been
permitted to announce our responsibility for these deaths.

*He is interrupted by a fit of coughing, doubled over, hand on his
chest, cigarette smoke still billowing. He takes a while to recover
himself. When he starts again, his heel, in heavy black boot, beats
rapidly against the floor. His knee jitters up and down. His fingers tap
the table.*

Believe me, despite my impatience, I understand the reasons.
The time isn't right for such an admission.

There is too much sympathy for the victims. We would
alienate the very people we hope to win to our cause. These two
were Germans. Not at all like your Namibians and Mozambicans
and Turks and Vietnamese and Albanians and Jews. It is one thing
to express communal hatred, to release communal passions, by
burning a Holocaust memorial or desecrating a cemetery or fire-
bombing a foreign workers' hostel—quite another to become the
cold assassin of blond and blue-eyed Germans.

But in fact, of course, these two were not true Germans. They
had surrendered their right to that claim by working against the
German state and the German people in the name of an inter-
nationalism that can only weaken the white European Christian
German race. The people have not yet been educated sufficiently
to understand this. The old ones know, if they haven't forgotten.
And the youth are finding out. When the time comes, the rest will
understand. Meanwhile we are under orders to maintain silence.

*He looks directly at the camera, down at his jiggling foot, back
up in the direction of the apparent interviewer, silent, off-screen.*

I suppose that means I shouldn't be talking to you.

A long silence follows. He fidgets, looks at his hands, toward the interviewer. The camera keeps running. His boot heel taps on the floor. Smoke billows. Finally he puts out the cigarette, lights another, begins again.

The important thing is to weaken the active layer, not only the visible leadership, but the leadership of the next ranks down, especially the local leadership, the opposition organizers, the candidates known in their communities who stand a chance to gain seats. It is their seats we are after, with voters from all parties. It is strategic, as I said. This is what Hitler did. This is what we do. It is very clear. We have been trained.

He sucks in his breath and pouts his lips.

As for the other thing, that our commanders were paid, hired to have it done, well that is possible too. These two had many enemies who cannot themselves directly do violence, and we have many secret donors, many prominent wealthy Germans and Aryan people of other nations sympathetic to our cause. It is easy to see who would have liked them taken out. We are moving into a new era, new expansions. These two obstructed progress. The nuclear industry for power and weapons has not been contained without resistance, without resentment. These are angry men. They have the potential to own the world, but of course they are too nice in their suits, too gentlemanly and international and businesslike to admit openly the depth and violence of their anger and ambition. So here we are. We work for them. They work for us. Who's to say who's in charge? Who financed Hitler, you know? Who won? Who survived?

He shrugs, stares at his hands.

I'm not saying I know, you understand. I don't know anything. I get my orders, I do what I'm told. I trust my commanders. They don't tell me the reasons or who pays. They tell me the tactic, the means, the target.

For myself, I had my own reasons. Not that I chose. I was ordered. Still, I was glad. These people advocated for mongrelization. They were degenerates. For two years she fucked a brown man while her General watched. It is disgusting. They deserved to die. They deserved their bodies to lie in that house rotting in the filth of time, days, weeks. It is fitting that he became food for maggots lying there in that hallway. It is fitting how fate left them there to stink.

I was afraid to stay in the house alone, they followed me to
Barcelona, they snatched my purse, they heckled my speeches,
they sent me filthy mail, the most violent pornography, I began
to suffer from nightmares and panic attacks, it was as if I were
under a spell, cursed by a demon, I didn't know then what these
attacks are called, a cold sweat, racing heart, I'm choking, I can't
get a breath, I'm suddenly overwhelmed with worries and go so
entirely weak in the body I nearly faint, and when it passes I
have a thought-numbing headache for hours, days. Now I know
the clinical name but never when it will start, how can I be
alone? Omi used to travel with me, but she got old, and the
weight of my dependence was more than she could carry, she's
carried so much already, and suddenly I needed him all the
time.

—So every problem and every solution originates outside
yourself?

—I've gone over it all so often, Anna, it leads nowhere, so
obvious and tedious, the little girl abandoned by her father and so
on, Sonam made me understand that intellectual understanding
would never be enough, I would have to go into therapy to unlock
it, to free myself from the hold of the past, if it is the past that
makes this terror in me, this hateful dependence, and I've been
unwilling, it's true, to spend that kind of time and money on

myself when there is so much in this world to do, and afraid also that I would weaken myself, that a therapist would take from me what's most precious and necessary, I ask myself would Alexandra Kollontai submit herself to a therapist? or Rosa Luxemburg? or Goethe? or Gandhi? and I think then Sonam was wrong, was not even really trying to help me, just trying to lighten his load, which he lightened soon enough in any case—did I tell you we saw him at the Buddhist Union? he was so beautiful but of course nobody talked, we didn't even look at each other, it was all surreptitious, I could feel him aching for me from across the room, and for that hour I wanted him back so absolutely and felt my freedom again so purely I almost forgot Lukas sitting at my side, and I was proud, and of course I didn't forget and to compensate for my desire and my freedom I became more visibly attentive to Lukas.

—It can be grotesque how easily you mistake your desires for reality.

—But what use would it be? When I hear the testimony of South Pacific islanders and the Navajo and Shoshone and Australian and Siberian indigenous peoples and everywhere the story is the same, how can it matter what happened in my life forty years ago to make me what I am? Is what happened forty years ago a cancer inside me just like the cancer inside the Navajo and the Polynesians? Is the loss of one little girl's father supposed to compare to the destruction of whole worlds? I know you will say I would let it compare if it were some other little girl, you will say I have compassion for every other child, none for myself, I've heard it all before, seeing Sonam brought it back, my heart overflows with tears for the world he used to say, and with tears to get my way in all things, but the one I wouldn't cry for was the one who needed my tears the most, and who was that according to him? my little child self of course, the little girl who lost her Papi, whose Papi left her and never came back, and all this from that? I won't believe it. If I had taken time to worry about that, would I have done what I've done in my life? I'd have gone to fat like some complacent *bourgeoise*, sat in my chair eating chocolates like Eliza Doolittle, become the second wife of Antonio Contini or Patrick Curran, maybe had children of my own, forgotten Emma, maybe if I'd been happier I wouldn't be such a fighter still, would have settled, given up, like so many others, and we mustn't give up, Anna, you mustn't, if you had heard the testimony at Salzburg, the important thing is knowing that the struggle goes on, it must go on as long as the production and deployment and testing of nuclear and chemical and biological weapons go on, too many people think because the cold war ended there is nothing more to fear, but there is everything to fear, you can't quit now.

—Don't start turning your will on me, Jutta, or I'll put you out on the street.

—Well yes exactly and isn't that exactly what some psychologist would try to take from me—*we must accommodate ourselves, dear lady, we must live with reality as it is.* But I say no, Anna, I won't attend to inwardness at that price. I'm so weighed down now, how is it possible that you can give up like this? They want me to run for the European Parliament, third spot on the party list. I wanted to run in Bavaria for the Bundestag again but it's clear I don't have such a campaign in me now. In Passau, northeast of Munich, 11 percent of the city voters just elected Republikaners, five SS party councilmen. This is where I want to fight, on local ground, but I no longer have the will. Hilmar says if I want the Bundestag race I will have to go to Bavaria and begin the campaign immediately. Everyone says the European Parliament is the correct place for me and a safer election and I try to listen to their advice, especially when I think about Lukas and what a campaign will do to him, and then once I'm settled in one place or another maybe he will be able to rest a little and spend more time with Therese.

—And that's what you want?

—I must have a place again, an office, this is madness now the way we live, we are buried in paper, we work constantly, we have no help, when I come to bed Lukas gets up, he's a ruin of his former self, I can't bear to watch him grow old like this, to see how he needs me when I am so useless to him and so in need myself, I don't know how I will continue without him.

—You are pure activity, Jutta. In your inner certainty nothing and no one can touch you.

—No no, not at all. I am guided, Anna, by Emma, without

this guidance I would be powerless, the world is much stronger than I am. My only power my whole will comes from her—
    And so on, to the end of the afternoon.

We harassed her we pursued her we destroyed her peace of mind.

Maybe that was enough. Maybe it wasn't. Maybe we did more. Maybe we didn't.

We were the best private intelligence operation in the world. We ran a global network of confidential sources. We maintained the largest private stockpile of political dossiers and files. We established long-term information-exchanging relationships with local police and military personnel throughout Europe, South Africa, Japan, and the US. We were specialists in dirty tricks.

Through defamation of our leader and seizure of his financial assets, the US Justice Department hoped to destroy this network. But nothing has ended. We are still here.

From the beginning we have had a strategic interest in everything nuclear and we maintain long-term international contacts throughout the pronuclear scientific community. We actively supported the development of fusion energy, particle-beam and laser weapons, and President Ronald Reagan's Strategic Defense Initiative, which he announced, not by coincidence, only four days before the election that brought Jutta Carroll into the Bundestag.

Jutta Carroll was our enemy.

We smeared her as a communist, a terrorist, a whore. We

cornered her on a train. We shoved her grandmother around. We drove Jutta Carroll into hiding, into dependency and fear.

Our leader is an American married to a German. He is the close personal friend of a former chief of counterintelligence in the West German armed forces. He has a strong following among retired West German military men and former Nazi scientists. He also has followers among the German police.

When unspecified personnel of the US embassy in Bonn advised certain Germans against involvement in business or political dealings with our leader, the State Department quickly chastised them.

Our leader teaches that what is really going on can be known only by inference, but is nevertheless a certainty.

No one has discovered to this day where he got the start-up capital that allowed him to build the empire he still commands.

He won't be in jail forever.

Here is the mistake: the belief that our movement can be destroyed by destroying one highly visible leader. Ours is not a cult of personality, nor do we rely upon the sacrifice of martyrdom. When one leader is taken, like the heads of Hydra new leaders will appear. The work carries on, in hundreds of groups, with hundreds, thousands of leaders. We are networked throughout the world with others who believe as we do, and work to prepare the way for the great unification to come. Together we have shared money, ideas, allies, and training in weapons for twenty years.

As for Jutta Carroll, she was isolated, vulnerable, weak, but potentially dangerous. She had fought us on nuclear weapons and nuclear power, and now she was becoming outspoken against our allies, the German neo-Nazis and youth gangs. She was out of office but not for long.

Did we kill her?

Maybe so, maybe not.

Maybe we killed her ten years earlier when we drove her deep into her own neurosis. Maybe we took advantage of her isolation and played a more active role. Maybe we hired out.

As our leader teaches, certainty comes only through inference. Knowledge is a vast spiderweb. We spin, we surround, we contain.

Catherine Gammon

Make of us what you will.
We don't go away.

But in reality, unless the Bonn police have simply lied about the evidence—which, as a policeman myself, I would not be inclined to suggest—your victims can't have died at the hand of any third party. If the determination that no one else was present is based not on gunshot residue found on the hands, but on the pattern of blood sprayed from the wound—well, that's a kind of evidence that can't be faked. We can read droplets of blood—for distance, direction, angle, and blood velocity. I can illustrate with rough drawings (I'm sorry, I'm no artist) the pure trigonometric precision of the reading of such traces. They leave an exact record of the position of the victim and the firing gun. When the gun is fired in hard contact with the head, blood and tissue burst outward back through the entrance wound—*blowback* it's called. A blank space in the blood pattern, the equivalent of a shadow, would indicate the presence of another party, a shooter. Apparently, no such shadow existed. Therefore, your man was alone.

I'm sorry if this disappoints you. I can readily understand the temptation to continue imagining exceptions, positions from which the shadow of a gunman might not fall. It's an interesting and puzzling case. But with this type of blood-pattern evidence, errors of interpretation just aren't even theoretically possible. Yes, as you say, many of the crime scene details are uncharacteristic of suicide: the obvious typewriter, of course, the unfinished letter, and other facts as well. The awkward shot to the forehead, for example. The front to back shot is rare for a suicide. He would have had to hold the gun upside down, pulling the trigger with his thumb. A shot to one or the other temple or upward through the mouth is more natural and therefore more common. Did he go to this trouble in an effort to make it look as if someone else had shot him? The standing position is also unusual—most suicides sit or lie down. Another thing: he had feelings for this woman. He seems to have taken protective care over her—she lies in bed, covered, unexposed—which leads me to wonder why in his protectiveness he didn't also take care that her body would be discovered promptly, why he didn't make a telephone call, alert someone before shooting himself, instead of leaving her there to decay. Was this strategic, a hope that delay in discovery would undermine the clarity of the evidence? Or simple arrogance, an assumption that they would be missed? Along the same lines: if this man was at all obsessive-compulsive, he would have taken more care with his own body too, would have positioned himself deliberately, in a chair, for example, rather than allowing himself to fall at random, knocking down bookshelves and landing any which way. He would avoid that loss of control.

But beyond all that, since only a general account of the physical evidence is available to us, well, even if I wanted to, I really don't have enough information to question the conclusions of the Bonn police.

As for his leaving her presence rather than lying down in the bed beside her, it's the one detail consistent with suicide. He loves this woman. He's just shot her. Her blood and possibly bone and brain tissue are sprayed all over the pillows. It's hard to see someone you love so violently dead.

This rage has no words, no language. It is unendurable and cannot speak. It cannot be attached to his character although it can be felt in the shaking of his hands, the pallor of his skin, the hard line of his back, the tension in his shoulders, neck, chin. This man, you know it but you do not know, this man can kill, will, has. This man has murder in his body and this murder comes from this place of no language, this place without words, this place where death has dwelled for half a century, hidden, unspoken, unknowable, without tongue, without shape, invisible, heavy, held in. Thought clamps down, like steel, all doors shut tight—no light, no sound, no word gets in. The body opens inside itself, stronger than it has ever been. Nerves, muscles, bones, nausea, exhilaration. Everything breaks around it: books, papers, walls, shelves, glass, flowers, photos, candles, coins, keepsakes, stones, shells, beads, feathers, holster. She's dead, already dead. And alive. The pulse in the throat of the body. The pounding in the belly, the chest. The animal inside him, ravening and venomous, ophidian jaw gaping in his viscera, eating its way out.

We can contain them. We know this. We are in control. In the meantime, we find them useful. They take actions we could never take, promote ideas we could never promote, contribute themselves to the spectacle. Such colorful characters, such fun to deploy. The scandal over these deaths, for example, it just keeps coming, article after article, book after book. What fine entertainment. Meanwhile the beneficiaries go ignored. As well they should. They hardly know what we've done for them, although I'm sure they feel the relief: a little guilt, of course, but mostly relief. They're weak. They're all weak. They put on their suits, they go before the people, they live and die for the vote, the deal. These people are her heirs, but like their establishment counterparts easier to buy.

Try to see them, see them like this: alone together, alone, in perfect harmony, cool, quiet, serene, in the darkness holding hands across the kitchen table, waiting for the day to come, in the slight but steamy dampness the sweet perfume of an orange herbal tea. Outside, the rain has stopped, the only sound the steady drip-drip-drip from power lines and leaves. Everything has been decided, everything agreed.

I wanted to write the angry version, the story where he kills her in a pure upsurge of rage. I couldn't find it, couldn't see it. In his own point of view, he always came out innocent.

They harassed her they pursued her they destroyed her peace of mind.

Sometimes I even think the murderer was me.

Wir müs—

Notes

Remember—truth always sounds incredible:
truth is the true fiction.

— Heinrich Böll

As the narrator says, this has been a work of fiction, invention orbiting fact. Although I have drawn Jutta and Lukas loosely from the lives and reported histories of Petra Kelly and Gert Bastian, nothing in this fictional world should be taken as revealing or reflecting, directly or indirectly, the living or the dead.

For such reflection and representation the interested reader must turn to the same nonfiction sources that have provided much of the "fact" this fiction orbits. ("Fact" in quotation marks because even in the world of nonfiction, facts are elusive, reports contradict.)

It should not be necessary to say so, but given this context of notation perhaps it is useful to state directly that although many of the secondary characters in the novel loosely parallel living persons in a general or functional way (for example, Jutta's Omi and other members of her family, and Lukas's wife and sons), they are here imagined entirely as fictional characters and are not based on the actual histories or actual members of the families of Petra Kelly or Gert Bastian. Others, such as Jutta's American friend Jim Wolf, her teacher Daniel García Guzmán, her friend Anna Albert, and Lukas's dead daughter Leni, are pure inventions from the start.

That said, and fiction's autonomy as work of the imagination fully claimed, *The Martyrs, The Lovers* remains a novel drawn in part from factual texts. The books and articles listed or discussed below prepared the way for my imagination of Jutta Carroll and her world.

First, as background reading, those written before Petra Kelly's death, some about the German Greens or the Green movement, others by or about Petra Kelly:

Rudolf Bahro, *Building the Green Movement*, translated by Mary Tyler (Philadelphia: New Society Publishers, 1986)

Rudolf Bahro, *From Red to Green: Interviews with the New Left Review* (London: Verso, 1984)

Murray Bookchin, *Remaking Society: Pathways to a Green Future* (Boston: South End Press, 1990)

Werner Hülsberg, *The German Greens: A Social and Political Profile*, translated by Gus Fagan (London: Verso, 1988)

Petra Kelly, *Fighting for Hope*, translated by Marianne Howarth (Boston: South End Press, 1984)

Petra K. Kelly, *Mit dem Herzen denken* (Munich: C. H. Beck Verlag, 1990)

Petra K. Kelly, Gert Bastian, and Pat Aiello, eds., *The Anguish of Tibet* (Berkeley: Parallax Press, 1991)

Jonathan Porritt, *Seeing Green*, foreword by Petra Kelly, (Oxford: Basil Blackwell, 1984)

Jonathan Porritt and David Winner, *The Coming of the Greens* (London: Fontana/Collins, 1988)

Monika Sperr, *Petra Karin Kelly: Politikerin aus Betroffenheit* (Munich: C. Bertelsmann Verlag, 1983)

Charlene Spretnak and Fritjof Capra, *Green Politics: The Global Promise*, in collaboration with Rüdiger Lutz (Santa Fe: Bear & Company, 1986)

In the first weeks following the discovery of the bodies of Petra Kelly and Gert Bastian, a variety of newspaper reports, obituaries, and brief remembrances appeared. Among them, I consulted *Die Zeit, The New York Times, The Times (London), The Washington Post, The Nation,* and *Z. Magazine.*

In the US, the more thorough journalistic examination of

Petra Kelly's life and death began with Mark Hertsgaard's "Who Killed Petra Kelly?" (*Vanity Fair*, January 1993). Hertsgaard's article, Petra Kelly's posthumous collection of essays, and three roughly contemporaneous accounts (listed below in the order of their publication), each illuminating in its own way and all rich with suggestive if sometimes contradictory detail, contributed throughout to this fiction and its variations:

Petra K. Kelly, *Thinking Green!: Essays on Environmentalism, Feminism and Nonviolence*, foreword by Peter Matthiessen; Berkeley: Parallax Press, 1994).

Alice Schwarzer, *Eine tödliche Liebe: Petra Kelly und Gert Bastian* (Köln: Verlag Kiepenheuer & Witsch, 1993)

Till Bastian, *Die Finsternis der Herzen: Nachdenken Über eine Gewalttat* (Köln: PapyRossa Verlag, 1994)

Sara Parkin, *The Life and Death of Petra Kelly* (London: Pandora/HarperCollins, 1994)

The novel's remaining sources follow, more or less in the sequence of their use:

For Jutta's infatuation with Hildegard of Bingen, and for my variations on fragments of Hildegard's songs, I have drawn from two authorities: Sabina Flanagan, *Hildegard of Bingen, 1098-1179: A Visionary Life* (London and New York: Routledge, 1989); and Saint Hildegard of Bingen, *Symphonia: A Critical Edition of the Symphonia armonie celestium revelationum*, introduction, translations and commentary by Barbara Newman (Ithaca: Cornell University Press, 1988).

The young Jutta's attempts to understand the Holocaust, as well as Omi's replies, rely on Raul Hilberg, *The Destruction of the European Jews* (New York and London: Holmes & Meier, 1985) and Arno J. Mayer, *Why Did the Heavens Not Darken?: The "Final Solution" in History* (New York, Pantheon: 1988). Omi's replies also draw on material included in Barbara Heimannsberg and Christoph J. Schmidt, editors, *The Collective Silence: German Identity and the Legacy of Shame*, translated by Cynthia Oudejans Harris and Gordon Wheeler (San Francisco: Jossey-Bass, 1993). All three books also provide background to the later fictional struggles of Lukas Grimm to come to terms with his forgotten past.

The photographs described from Jutta's collection appeared in *Life* magazine during the early 1960s.

Representations of neo-Nazi violence in Germany, although such violence has been widely reported, here are drawn from summary articles in *The New Republic* (Frank Thaler, "Bashers," December 9, 1991, and Jacob Heilbrun, "What German Crisis?" December 21, 1992) and a *World Press Review* reprint (August 1991) from *Der Spiegel*.

Jutta's narrative of the "For Sale" sign hung from her neck by her father was suggested by a short paragraph in a news story about Petra Kelly's death (James Barron, "Founder of Green Party Dies Mysteriously in Bonn," *The New York Times*, October 20, 1992). I give this passage in full to offer a small but complete example of the ways I have used reported "fact" to make this fiction:

> In her autobiography, she declared, "I made quite a story being the first child and not being a husky red baby boy." She also said that when she told her father she wanted a doll, he sent her to the town square with a sign that said, "This child is for sale."

It should be noted that no Petra Kelly autobiography exists. It is possible these remarks of hers come from an essay or interview, or perhaps Barron is referring to the Monika Sperr biography; unfortunately, the copy of Sperr I read in 1991 was a borrowed one, since returned, and I have been unable to locate another to compare Barron's anecdote to an original account.

The story of Gandhi's urgency in responding to his letters, as well as later passages quoted from Gandhi's writings, come from Mahatma Gandhi, *Selected Writings of Mahatma Gandhi*, selected and introduced by Ronald Duncan (London: Faber and Faber, undated).

Mary Edwards Wertsch, *Military Brats: Legacies of Childhood Inside the Fortress* (New York: Harmony Books/Crown, 1991), helped me to imagine the significance of Jutta's military upbringing.

"Storm troopers don't love back" is a line from "Is Love Obscene?," a story by John Kelsey that appeared in the *Canadian*

Free Press in May 1967, as quoted by Abe Peck, *Uncovering the Sixties: The Life & Times of the Underground Press* (New York: Pantheon, 1985). Peck's book was also useful to dramatizing Jutta's participation in the 1967 Pentagon demonstration, which draws from accounts of the demonstrations in *The New York Times* as well. Details of the Justice Department demonstration depend on Norman Mailer's *Armies of the Night*. Jutta's campus activities depend in part on accounts in *The New York Times* and *The Washington Post* of protests at American University during those years.

Because Petra Kelly wrote of her sister Grace's love for the Little Prince during the years of her illness, Jutta Carroll's Emma often speaks in the Prince's language: Antoine de Saint-Exupèry, *The Little Prince* (New York: Harcourt Brace Jovanovich, 1943).

It was Frank Bardacke who wrote that the counterculture movement was dissolving into radicals "playing with guns as a way to forget their own hopelessness" (quoted in Abe Peck, *Uncovering the Sixties*).

Jutta's readings of Rosa Luxemburg are quoted, here and later, from *The Letters of Rosa Luxemburg*, edited by Stephen Eric Bronner (Boulder: Westview Press, 1978).

Some of Jutta's reflections on the figure of Antigone were suggested by George Steiner, *Antigones: How the Antigone Legend Has Endured in Western Literature, Art and Thought* (New York: Oxford University Press, 1984).

The portrayal of Josef Mengele depends on Robert Jay Lifton, *The Nazi Doctors: Medical Killing and the Psychology of Genocide* (New York, Basic Books, 1986), and Dr. Miklos Nyiszli, *Auschwitz: An Eyewitness Account of Mengele's Infamous Death Camp*, foreword by Bruno Bettelheim (New York: Seaver Books, 1986; 1960).

The account of the accident at Windscale and its consequences depends on Dr. Rosalie Bertell, *No Immediate Danger: Prognosis for a Radioactive Earth* (London: The Women's Press, 1985), and J.A. Camilleri, *The State and Nuclear Power: Conflict and Control in the Western World* (Seattle, University of Washington Press, 1984). In preparation for this chapter and the treatment of these issues elsewhere I also consulted Mark Hertsgaard, *Nuclear Inc.: The Men and Money Behind Nuclear Energy* (New York: Pantheon, 1983). Jutta's activism during the 1970s is more West Germany–based than Petra Kelly's was, and the progress of German resistance to nuclear reactors throughout that period is drawn from Camilleri and Bertell. Bertell is the source of the story of the young *hibakusha* suicide, and the later description of the German Greens 1983 tribunal on nuclear weapons. Bertell and Camilleri both provide evidence of the global consequences of nuclear testing, and of South Pacific testing in particular (continued by France until 1996).

Descriptions of Hiroshima and the last days of the Pacific war draw detail from John Hersey, *Hiroshima* (New York: Knopf, 1946), and Studs Terkel, *The Good War: An Oral History of World War Two* (New York: Pantheon, 1984).

Descriptions of Jutta's efforts at meditation practice are drawn from a variety of sources, including Sogyal Rinpoche, *The Tibetan Book of Living and Dying*, edited by Patrick Gaffney and Andrew Harvey (San Francisco: HarperSanFrancisco, 1994).

It is Alice Schwarzer who tells us that Petra Kelly was reading Goethe's letters to Charlotte von Stein just before her death; Sara Parkin gives us Alexandra Kollontai as well, and Petra's letter from her father, while Till Bastian emphasizes the presence of his father's notes and letters to Petra on the nightstand. Thus, I have put both Kollontai *(The Autobiography of a Sexually Emancipated Communist Woman*, edited with an afterword by Iring Fetscher, translated by Salvator Attanasio; New York: Herder and Herder, 1971) and Goethe (*Selections from Goethe's Letters to Frau von Stein, 1776-1789*, edited and translated by Robert M. Browning; Columbia: Camden House, 1990) into Jutta's hands. Parkin provides the account of Petra's letter from her father on which Jutta's receipt of such a letter is based, while Schwarzer provides the text of a letter written by Gert Bastian to one of Petra's former lovers, the origin of the fiction of Lukas's letter to Sonam Pasang. In Schwarzer's account the gun is kept at the back of the bookshelf in the hallway, in Parkin's in a dresser drawer with sweaters and scarves. It is from Till Bastian's reminiscence of watching *Yancy Derringer* on television with his father that I borrow the account of Lukas's purchase of the gun.

For insight into the European Labor Party, the LaRouchite party that, according to Petra Kelly, harassed and tormented her, at least for a time, I consulted Dennis King, *Lyndon LaRouche and The New American Fascism* (New York: Doubleday, 1989).

Some last attributions—to a few isolated quotations and to the several epigraphs:

Christa Wolf, the opening sentences of *Patterns of Childhood*, as translated by Ursule Molinaro and Hedwig Rappolt (New York: Farrar, Straus and Giroux, 1980). Wolf's first sentence is itself a near quotation of William Faulkner's "The past is never dead. It's not even past," from *Requiem for a Nun*.

Martin Luther King, as quoted in *Life*, November 14, 1960.

Franz Kafka, from "Conversation Slips," in *Letters to Friends, Family, and Editors*, tr. Richard and Clare Wiston (New York: Schocken, 1978).

The Fire Next Time, James Baldwin (New York: Dial Press, 1963).

The Sayings of the Desert Fathers, translated by Benedicta Ward, S.L.G. (Kalamazoo, MI: Cistercian Publications, Inc., 1975), Epigraph: John the Dwarf, section no. 13, as quoted in Joan D. Chittister, OSB, *Wisdom Dististilled from the Daily: Living the Rule of St. Benedict Today* (San Francisco: HarperSanFrancisco, 1991).

Lines from *Antigone*: Sophocles, *The Three Theban Plays: Antigone, Oedipus the King, Oedipus at Colonus*, translated by Robert Fagles (New York: Viking, 1982).

Ingeborg Bachmann, the closing sentence of *Malina*, translated by Richard Boehm (New York: Holmes & Meier, 1990).

Heinrich Böll, from *Women in a River Landscape*, translated by David McLintock (New York: Knopf, 1988).

Acknowledgments

Some final words of thanks: for opportunities created, research assisted, and patience shown, to Barbara Moulton, Sallie Gouverneur, Carol Mahan Salazar, Ron Freeman, and Daniel Wild; to the Faculty of Arts and Sciences of the University of Pittsburgh, the Virginia Center for the Creative Arts, and Money for Women / The Barbara Deming Memorial Fund, whose generosity contributed to the completion of this novel; to my friend Deborah Morris and my daughter Heather von Rohr, for their unwavering loyalty and infinite support; to Geri Lipschultz for pointing my way to 55 Fathoms and Joe Ponepinto, without whose enthusiasm and commitment *The Martyrs, The Lovers* would not now be in your hands; and most of all to those who do the work.

About the Author

Catherine Gammon is author of the novels *China Blue, Isabel Out of the Rain*, and *Sorrow*. Her fiction has appeared in *Ploughshares, Kenyon Review, Iowa Review, New England Review, Cincinnati Review*, and *The Missouri Review*, among many others, as well as online at *The Blood Pudding, Vol. 1 Brooklyn*, and *Fractured Lit*. Her work has received support from the National Endowment for the Arts, the New York Foundation for the Arts, the American Antiquarian Society, the Fine Arts Work Center in Provincetown, Virginia Center for the Creative Arts, Yaddo, and Djerassi. From 1992 through 2000, Catherine taught in the MFA writing program of the University of Pittsburgh, before leaving for residential Zen training at San Francisco Zen Center, where she was ordained a priest in 2005. She lives again in Pittsburgh, with her garden and her cat. Twitter @nonabiding. Instagram @catherinegammonwriter. More at www.catherinegammon.com and www.littsburgh.com/qa-catherine-gammon-author-of-china-blue-and-sorrow/.